The Confederates' Physician

Novels written by Alison Blasdell:

Touch the Sky (Book One Touch the Sky Series)

Daughter of the Sky (Book Two Touch the Sky Series)

Power of the Sky (Book Three Touch the Sky Series)

The Confederates' Physician (Book One Confederates' Physician Series)

Diary or the Confederates' Physician: Samantha's Legacy (Book Confederates' Physician Series)

The Assassin's Protégé

The Ultimate Target: Code Name Agnel

THE CONFEDERATES' PHYSICIAN

Alison Blasdell

The Confederates' Physician Copyright © 2018 by Alison Blasdell. All Rights Reserved.

All rights reserved. No part of this book may be reproduced in any form or by any electronic or mechanical means including information storage and retrieval systems, without permission in writing from the author. The only exception is by a reviewer, who may quote short excerpts in a review.

Cover designed by Amanda Gardner

This book is a work of fiction. Names, characters, places, and incidents either are products of the author's imagination or are used fictitiously. Any resemblance to actual persons, living or dead, events, or locales is entirely coincidental.

Alison Blasdell

Printed in the United States of America

First Printing: April 2019

ISBN-9781796847185

THE CONFEDERATES' PHYSICIAN

This book is dedicated to:

*My daughters–
Ashley Coker and Raleigh Blasdell*

*My grandchildren–
Campbell Coker
Cooper Coker
Cash Coker
Cort Coker*

And to: Hubby

PROLOGUE

1865
The Northwestern Iowa Frontier

"That's enough! I won't hear another word," Samantha's father shouted. He was suddenly upon her. He grabbed her and slapped her across the face with a force that drove her backward, the sharp crack echoing off the sideboard that held her mother's china, reverberating off the walls of the house her father had built. Samantha would have fallen if her brother Troy hadn't caught her.

"Pa, no!" her brother shouted as he shoved himself between Samantha and her father, protecting her with his own body should his father's wrath be unassuaged.

Samantha reeled from the shock of her father's strike, her face burning where his tough, rancher-weathered hand seared her face. Her father had never struck her before. Never! Not when she was a child, not even last year when he'd summoned her home from Paris after discovering she had disobeyed him. He'd been so angry then but had forgiven her.

Samantha wiped a trembling hand across her lip, blood

smearing her sleeve. It was almost a year to the day that she had returned from Paris. One year. And during that year, she had gone from being an innocent, young woman, full of dreams, to being a traitor to her country, a murderer, and . . . a Confederate major's whore.

CHAPTER 1

March 1864
One Year Earlier

"Two years of deception and disobedience, Samantha!" Seth Carter roared.

Samantha winced at her father's reproach, but before she could respond, he turned his wrath on Lilly, Samantha's governess since childhood.

"And did you know about this, Lilly?" Seth demanded.

"Mr. Carter—"

"She didn't know, Papa. You can't blame her," Samantha said, coming to Lilly's defense.

Samantha looked at Lilly, exhausted, pale, and thin. She had not fared well on the long voyage across the Atlantic, plagued as she was by nausea and vomiting that was only marginally mediated by Samantha's herbal administrations. Then there had been the train from Boston to Chicago to Rock Island, crossing the Mississippi River on the first railroad bridge connecting the East and West, hailed as the longest swing span bridge in the world, five fixed, wooden arches totaling two hundred eighty-six feet. True, it was not as grand as Paris, but Samantha still marveled at the bridge as the train sped across it and on to Iowa City. The rest of the journey into the Northwest Iowa Frontier had been in a rough and dusty stagecoach.

Seth slammed his hand down on the table, causing Samantha to startle and return her attention back to her father.

"It was her job to know!" Seth retorted. "She's your governess!"

"Pa?" Samantha's brother Troy interrupted. "I'm sure Sam didn't mean to disobey you. Why don't you let her explain?" Troy turned to his twin sister, a mischievous grin on his face. "I, for one, would like to know how you managed to get into so much trouble without me."

"Do you think this is amusing?" Seth demanded.

"No, sir," Troy said hastily, averting his face as he struggled to hide his smile.

They were seated around the kitchen table: Seth, Troy, Samantha, and Lilly. Seth Carter was a widower with four children; Samantha and her twin brother, Troy, at fifteen years old, were the youngest. His daughter-in-law, Jeanie, had hastily retreated to her bedroom with her two young children, wisely avoiding the family conflict.

"All right, Samantha," Seth said, "I'm waiting for an explanation."

"I'm sorry, Papa," Samantha began. "I never meant to disobey you. I don't know what Aunt Beatrice said in her letter, but—"

"She said that she sent you and your cousin Francine to the finest finishing school in Paris, but you deceived her," Seth interrupted. "You didn't go to the school."

"That's true. I wanted to go to college and study medicine."

"Childish games! We discussed that before you left and I forbade it," Seth said. "You disobeyed me and tricked your aunt. Did you plan this before you left for Paris?"

"No, Papa," Samantha answered. "One night, Aunt Beatrice took us to the theater. There was a man playing the part of a woman, and the idea came to me. If a man could dress as a woman and fool everyone, why couldn't a woman dress as a man and do the same? I knew that the College de France only admitted men to study medicine. So, a few days later, when Aunt Beatrice thought I was at the Sorbonne, I went down to the theater district and bought some supplies from an actress: a wig, mustache, and men's clothing."

"You were walking around Paris alone? Do you know what could have happened to you?"

"I was fine, Papa. I had my knife with me, and I know how to fight," she reminded him and then continued. "The woman showed me how to apply a paste mixture to my face. When dry, it looked like fine facial hair. She also helped me forge admission papers for the College de France. The rest was easy. Each morning, Aunt Beatrice had a carriage take me to the Sorbonne. I went inside and changed into my disguise. Then I went to the medical college. No one at the college ever suspected that I was a woman. In the evening, I reversed the procedure."

"You got away with that for two years?" Troy asked. "Aunt Beatrice never suspected?"

"Aunt Beatrice may be Mama's sister, Troy, but she's a stupid woman."

"Samantha!"

"It's true, Papa. The only reason she found out was because nosy Cousin Francine followed me one day. She ruined everything. Damn her!" Samantha swore.

"Samantha! I will not have that kind of language in my house," Seth thundered from the end of the table. "Is that what you learned in Paris, profanity?"

"No, Papa. I learned that here, herding cattle and riding

THE CONFEDERATES' PHYSICIAN

fences with you, Charles, Robert, and Troy," Samantha replied.

"What are you smiling at?" Seth shouted at Troy.

Troy quickly hid his smile. "Nothing, Pa."

"As I was saying," Samantha continued calmly, "Cousin Francine told Aunt Beatrice what I had been doing. She went straight to the College de France, and they, of course, dismissed me immediately." Samantha shrugged her shoulders. "It was time to return home anyway. I'm needed here. There is a desperate need for surgeons in the Union Army."

"Sam," Troy cautioned. He silently shook his head, warning her.

Seth Carter was a kind and loving father, but he expected absolute obedience and cooperation from his children. Life on the frontier in the 1800s was harsh, and in order to survive and prosper, each family member, according to his age and ability, had to contribute to that goal. And there was one, and only one, head of the household with authority over the family. What Samantha had done—deceiving her father—was unthinkable to a young woman of the era.

Samantha read the warning on her brother's face and turned back to her father. She swallowed, steeling her resolve. "Papa, I want to volunteer my services to the Union Army," she said. "I want to go to Washington City."

Seth Carter's eyes widened. "Have you lost your mind? You will do no such thing. This isn't some fancy college in Paris where you can fool people into thinking you're a man. This is war!"

"I know that, Papa, and I can help."

"I forbid it, and I won't hear any more of this kind of talk. And don't you dare think of defying me again, Samantha," Seth threatened.

"Pa's right, Sam," Troy interjected. "It's bad. You know

that Charles and Robert joined the Union Army."

Samantha nodded her head, detecting something in her brother's voice that scared her. Her father had written her to say that her older brothers had joined the Iowa Volunteers.

"Charles was at Gettysburg," Troy said.

"Gettysburg! Why didn't you tell me?" she asked, turning to her father.

"It was eight months ago," her father said, the anger of a moment ago dissipated. "We didn't hear from him until a few months later. He lost the lower part of his arm but was staying with his regiment. He said there were still things he could do. But then, six weeks ago, we received a letter saying that he got a fever and the arm had to be amputated. He'll be coming home, but we don't know when."

"Oh, Pa, not Charles," she said as tears filled her eyes. "What about Robert?"

"He's been writing regularly, and the mail service has been surprisingly good. The last we heard, he had been promoted to captain, but that was in October, five months ago."

"I tried to follow the war as closely as I could in Paris," Samantha said. "Sometimes we would get conflicting reports. Do you know that we were stopped by Federal ships just outside Boston Harbor? They searched the ship."

"The Union is determined that France and England will not recognize The Confederacy as an independent nation. Most of the Southern ports are blocked, and all ships coming into Northern ports are searched."

"It's been real bad, Sam," Troy repeated. "Almost eighty thousand men have gone to fight from Iowa, and one fourth of them have already died or returned maimed. A lot of the townsfolk have lost kin."

Later that evening when she was preparing for bed, she heard a knock on her bedroom door. She looked up from where she sat on her bed, a pair of buckskin pants and shirt on her lap, to see her father walk in. At six feet, he was taller than most men, with a straight back from years spent in the saddle and strong arms from cattle ranching. His hair was still dark, no trace of gray, and he wore the stubble of a beard that would remain until Saturday night, when he would shave. He sat down beside her and reached for the buckskins.

"I remember when you first came home from the Lakota village wearing these," he said. "Your mother was horrified. She accused me of letting you become too wild." He smiled at the memory. "Before she died, she made me promise that I would send you to her sister in Paris. She wanted you to be a lady, Sam. You were just six years old when she died. I hired Lilly, hoping she could teach you the things that your mother would have," Seth said, his voice choking slightly.

He stood up abruptly and walked to the window, his tall frame and broad shoulders filling it. "It's not your fault," he said, his back to Samantha. "Living out here on the frontier, you must have realized that a lot of the things your mama was raised with in Boston just didn't make any sense here. Charles, Robert, and Troy needed to learn ranching, but you—you and Troy spent a lot of time with my brother and the Lakota Indians. You were a wild one, more Indian than white." Seth took a deep breath. "I love you, Samantha, and if I did wrong in raising you, I'm sorry."

"Papa?" Samantha said gently.

He didn't turn around immediately. Samantha could see him making an effort to control his emotions, standing a little taller, straightening his shoulders, and hastily wiping his hand across his eyes.

Samantha laid the buckskins down on the bed and stood.

"You did a good job of raising me, and I am a lady—sometimes," she said.

Seth turned and looked at his daughter. "Yes," he said, "I know you are. I had expected to see the wild girl of twelve return home. Instead, a beautiful, young woman has taken her place. You look so much like your mother."

Samantha ran to her father's arms. "I'm sorry, Papa. I'm sorry I deceived you."

"I'm just glad you're home," he said as he caught Samantha and pulled her tightly against him. "You're safe," he said, his voice trembling. "That's all that matters."

In the coming weeks, Samantha tried to settle into the routine of running the Carter household, but she grew more and more restless. At such times, she suddenly bolted from the house, wearing her buckskin shirt and pants, and raced across the prairie on her horse, Kota. She tried on several occasions to talk with her father about joining the Union Medical Corps, but he refused to discuss it. At the end of the third week home, she came to a decision.

It was the second week of April, and spring had arrived early in this part of the country; that was in Samantha's favor. She woke up shortly after midnight and gathered the supplies she'd carefully selected: the buckskin pants and shirt, along with the soft boots made of the same hides. The boots had been rubbed with additional oils to insure they would repel the snow or rain, and there was room in them to add fur to insulate in the coldest of temperatures.

She walked over to the mirror and removed her nightgown. Standing naked before the mirror, she withdrew a long gauze strip from the drawer. She had never expected to have to use this again. For a moment, she hesitated. She had been home almost a month, and she loved her father.

She did. Samantha shook her head to clear it and then began to methodically wind the cloth tightly around her breasts as she had done for the past two years, grimacing against the familiar tautness.

When that was finished, she donned the buckskin pants, shirt, and boots. At least they were more comfortable than the men's frock coats she had worn in Paris. As she tightened the rawhide strip around her waist, she smiled, her smile bittersweet. The pants of the Lakota braves were two leg pieces tied at the waist, leaving the groin and backside open for toileting. In the colder months, the shirt hung below the opening, offering protection. In the summer, when the braves were shirtless, two small panels hung from the waist to provide the same cover in the front and back.

Samantha remembered her mother's horror when she came home from the Lakota village wearing the buckskins. Her mother had immediately taken them from Samantha, forbidding her to wear them. Samantha had sulked through her chores for the next several days, until, one evening, she found the buckskins laying on her bed, the opening in the front and back sewn closed—a proper pair of pants to protect Samantha's modesty.

From the bottom of the drawer, Samantha removed a box containing the elements she had used for her disguise. She would need the mustache and paste mixture to conceal her face, but the wig? It had been easy to use in Paris because she removed it at the end of each day. That would be too risky now. She didn't know what her quarters would be like with the Union medical staff.

Reluctantly, she reached for the scissors in her sewing basket and loosened the braid that hung down her back. Her hair was long and thick with a natural curl. Even in the moonlight, the deep, rich, chestnut hues of her hair caught the light. Steeling her resolve, she gritted her teeth and began to cut. Most men in the towns wore their hair cut short around their ears, but those on the frontier, like her brother Troy, allowed their hair to reach the top of their shoulders. Samantha opted for that. When she finished, she brushed it back behind her ears. With the mustache and the stubby, fake facial hair, she would look like a young man. She took one last look at herself in the mirror and then walked soundlessly down the stairs and out the door.

Samantha went first into the barn. In a dark corner, she retrieved the pack she had hidden a few days earlier. It contained woolen, long underwear, food, water, money, and her surgical instruments. She removed a long, double-bladed knife from the pack and slipped it inside her right boot, where an extra piece of hide had been sewn to hold the knife in place. Lastly, she picked up the Henry rifle, patented just a few years earlier. It was lighter than the .58-caliber Springfield rifled musket used by the military and was astoundingly fast handling. The best a soldier could expect of his muzzle-loaded musket was to load and fire three shots in a minute. The Henry repeating rifle had lever action and held fifteen cartridges that could be shot in less than fifteen seconds. She checked the magazine in the dim light to see that it was loaded and then grabbed an extra box of cartridges. Everything was set.

She whistled softly to her horse, Kota, as she carried her supplies, a saddle, and bridle to the paddock. Kota had been a gift from her Lakota Indian cousin. Together, they had trained the horse, and had there been a practical way of taking Kota to Paris with her, Samantha would have done that. But it was not possible, and Samantha had worried that Kota would forget her while she was in Paris. But the Lakota do not train a horse as the white man does, the bond forged between woman and horse surviving two years and thousands of miles. She trusted Kota with her life, and she, in turn, would protect Kota with her life.

She placed a thick blanket on Kota's back as a saddle pad. On a cattle ranch, the blanket had several purposes: comfort for the horse carrying a rider for days on end, and warmth for the rider sleeping at night on the ground—both of which Samantha was familiar.

Kota stamped a hoof restlessly, as though he sensed Samantha's urgency. Once mounted, she had to calm herself so that Kota would walk quietly away from the house. She didn't want the sound of a galloping horse to alert anyone.

When she was out of the range of hearing, she stopped and looked back at the house. In the morning, her father would discover her absence, and it would not take him long to determine her intent. With luck, in a few weeks, she could send word to him so he wouldn't worry. She hadn't told her family everything about Paris. She hadn't told them how much she had missed them or how alone she had felt every day away from them. For two years, she was alone and pining for home. But for now, she knew what she had to do. She turned away from the house and urged Kota into a gallop across the prairie.

It was near dawn when Samantha finally stopped to rest. The land near her family's ranch was largely open prairie, the tall grasses brushing the bottom of her boots and stirrups as she rode at night. She had crossed the Missouri River some hours earlier, guided only by the moonlight and Kota's sure-footedness. Gradually, the flatland was replaced with gentle hills and trees, their first leaves of green emerging on barren limbs.

She was well into the Lakota Indian territories now. She found an area nestled between two small hills and dismounted to rest under the protection of a few trees near a stream. Samantha knew it was dangerous to rest in the open where she could be sighted from a distance, but this was the only stream for miles.

She removed food and water from her pack and leaned back against a tree, enjoying the smell of the spring grass, salted with white pasque flowers. An occasional patch of wild bergamot swayed with the morning breeze, the purple blossoms on tall, green stems staying upright as the grasses bent around them. She knew all the wildflowers in this area; more importantly, she knew of their medicinal properties. The pasque, which blooms in early spring after the winter snows have melted, is toxic if consumed; however, when dried, it can be ground and small amounts applied to a wound to combat putrefaction. Wild bergamot could be steeped and drunk to ease a fever, headache, and throat pain.

Samantha was deep in her own thoughts, watching a red-tailed hawk spread its wings and glide on the uplifting wind, when she became aware of the change in Kota's behavior. The horse had stopped grazing and lifted his head. His ears and eyes were focused over the top of the ridge, a soft, low whinny emitting through his throat—a warning. Samantha followed the horse's gaze and was just getting to her feet when she heard a cry. A horse and rider came thundering over the ridge and bore down on her. Adrenalin spiked through her veins as she reached for the rifle at her side, but it was too late. The Indian leapt from the back of his horse and hit Samantha in the chest, slamming her backward.

She hit the earth with a force that knocked the air from her lungs. Pain shot through the back of her head, causing shimmering lights to dance before her eyes. She didn't have a chance to reach for her rifle for he was upon her, his weight making it difficult to draw a desperately needed breath of air. He shifted his body slightly. As he did, she inhaled, her vision clearing, and she saw the blade of his knife as he pressed it against the skin of her face just underneath her eye. The Indian's face was but a few inches from hers, his body hot and gleaming, his skin dark, his hair and eyes black. She could feel his breath on her face and smell his musky scent as he stared at her. His chest was bare, the muscles of his arms taut as they pressed into her. She recognized him immediately and, against all instinct toward self-preservation, forced herself to cease fighting, to submit, to lie still underneath him, her heart pounding.

He maintained the pressure of the knife on her face with his right hand, and with his left hand, he grabbed her hair, threading its ends through his fingers. Then, with a perplexed look, he released it to shove his hand under her shirt and grope for her breasts. His confusion seemed to grow when his fingers touched the gauze wrapping, and he momentarily released the pressure of the knife.

With a swift movement, Samantha brought her knee up between his legs and slammed her fists into his ears. He cried out, giving her the seconds she needed to push out from under him. He recovered and scrambled to his feet with lightning speed, brandishing a knife in front of him. Samantha reached down and withdrew her own knife from her boot.

"Tonight, you will be a slave in my camp. I will make a present of you to my wife," the Indian said with a snarl.

"Tonight, your wife will be wailing at your fire, singing songs of mourning for you," Samantha replied in Lakota, one of the Siouan dialects.

The Indian began to circle around her. She waited for him to make the first move. When he did, she fought him as best she could. Several times, his knife sliced close to her skin, nicking her buckskin shirt. She tried to strike back, but he was too strong, too fast, too skilled. Suddenly, he swept her feet out from under her, and she hit the hard earth.

He was on top of her instantly, pressing the blade of his

knife against her neck, keeping just enough pressure to restrain her, but not breaking the skin. His feet pinned hers down so that she could not use the ploy she had earlier. She was helpless, the threat of a sliced carotid artery and imminent death forcing her to cease struggling and, once again, submit to his strength and power. His eyes were just inches away from hers when he spoke again.

"The two years in Paris have made you soft, Little Sister."

"And two years have made you strong, Brother," she replied, her chest heaving underneath his weight.

He reached for her hair and pulled it painfully. "You cut your hair and bound your breasts. What are you doing this time, Samantha?"

"If you will get off of me, I'll explain," she hissed.

The Indian released the pressure of the knife against Samantha's skin and broke into a deep laugh as he rolled off of her and stood. He reached down, grasped the front of her buckskin shirt, and jerked her to a standing position.

"You always did play too rough," she said, frowning as she slapped his hand away, gingerly feeling her neck where the tip of the knife had pressed in.

"I see you are still playing warrior's games instead of women's," he said ruefully.

"Huh!" Samantha said as she examined the marks the knife had made on her shirt.

Their exchange was interrupted by Kota. The horse approached the Indian, nuzzling him in the back. Many Horses reached to Kota and spoke affectionately to him as he stroked his neck. Then he turned his attention back to Samantha.

"I could have killed you, Samantha," he chastised. "You are lucky I recognized Kota from the ridge. Why did you not listen to him? He knew I was there, watching you."

"I know. I was foolish, but I won't let that happen again."

"What are you doing out here alone?" he asked. "It's dangerous."

"Sit with me and I'll explain. I need your help, Many Horses."

"Not here," he said with irritation as he mounted his horse, his face once again castigating her for her foolishness.

Samantha followed him in silence until they reached the top of a ridge and took shelter under the trees. She immediately understood their advantage, the trees shielding them while the height gave them a clear view of the surrounding area. She inwardly cursed herself for her recklessness. Once they dismounted, they sat while Samantha told Many Horses about her two years in Paris and her life since she had arrived home.

"So," she concluded, "you see how I need your help. I must get to Washington City, but by now, Papa has sent telegraphs and men to the nearby towns and the train. But if I could ride south through the Nebraska Territory and into Kansas, I could take a train from Kansas City. Or we could go north through the Minnesota lands."

"You are crazy, Little Sister!" Many Horses looked at her incredulously. "I will not help you do that. Even with the Union troops in Kansas and Missouri, there is still fighting. Confederate troops of William Quantrill have destroyed entire towns.

"To go north is dangerous for a white man. There are many of my people who are joining with Red Cloud, and many of the Sioux tribes have allied themselves with the Cheyenne. I will not take you north or south!"

"No? Then I'll do it myself," Samantha said with a huff and jumped up, but Many Horses' foot lashed out and knocked her down. This time, though, he caught her and eased her down next to him.

"You still have not learned restraint," he admonished.

She looked at him, seeing the interest in his eyes. "And you will help me."

"Why would I do that?"

"Because we're family; we share the same grandfather."

"And my father, your uncle, will insist that you are returned to your father."

"But Little Wolf needn't know that you have seen me."

Many Horses sighed. "Samantha, you are a woman now. You need a man who can give you children. Then you will forget this foolishness."

"It's not foolishness. Men are dying, and I can help."

Many Horses stared at his cousin. "You could be killed," he said.

"I do not fear death, Brother."

"No, there's no reason to fear death, but what of war? I have seen war; you have not. There is much to fear there."

"But—"

Many Horses raised his hand in an authoritative gesture that signaled silence. Samantha waited, respecting his ways. When at last he spoke, his words surprised her.

"I remember the first time I saw you, my white cousin. You were just a child. Your father had brought you and Troy to our camp to visit our white grandfather. I asked my father if I could have you for a wife."

"What!"

"My father took me to the holy man," Many Horses continued, "and told me to repeat my request to him."

"Charrah!" Samantha whispered.

"Charrah said that you were not to belong to a man of our tribe, for you had been chosen by The Spirits and a path had been set for you. And so it was that, when you were with us, you were allowed to run freely and not be confined with the women." He smiled. "You were not rebuked when you joined the warrior games."

"Not rebuked, but almost killed several times," Samantha said ruefully.

Many Horses nodded his head in understanding. "You were allowed to enter Charrah's tent when no one else was," he said.

"I remember the first time I went into his tent," Samantha said. "I'd heard him chanting over a wounded brave, and I walked in. Charrah didn't even acknowledge my presence. I sat next to the brave and watched. That was the first time. I must have been in there hundreds of times after that. After a while, I learned to anticipate what Charrah was going to do next, which herb he would use, which prayer he would say. I began to hand him the leaves or crush them myself and heat them over his fire. I silently mouthed the prayers with him." She paused. "He was very powerful."

"Yes," Many Horses said, "and he placed a powerful spirit within you, Little Sister. That was why he made you medicine woman among our people when you were just a child."

They both were silent, and then Samantha spoke. "Will you help me?"

Many Horses gazed at the sky and, at last, nodded his head. "Yes, I will help you. It is your path."

That same evening, hundreds of miles to the south, two others were talking late into the night.

"Be assured, Ethan," the general said, "only my immediate staff and most trusted generals know of your Northern connections and what it is that you do for me. As far as the South is concerned, your shipping lines continue to deliver supplies to us at considerable risk. But the other—

the vital information you bring to me—will remain our secret. I urge you to reconsider my offer of a commission in the Army of Northern Virginia. As a civilian, if you're caught spying, you could be hung. As a major in the Confederate Army, you'd be imprisoned and possibly exchanged. It's your choice whether or not you wear the Confederate uniform denoting your rank."

Ethan hesitated. For the past two years, he'd refused the general's offer. But it was becoming more dangerous each time he traveled north. "Very well, General Lee, I accept. Thank you," Ethan said and then focused on the map before them. "This is the latest report of troop movement from my contact in the War Department," he said.

General Robert E. Lee studied the map. "Grant's forces are far superior to ours. We shall force him to attack our fortified positions. Would he do that and risk the tremendous losses that would accompany such a maneuver?"

Ethan didn't answer for it was evident that Lee did not expect one.

"It'll be bloody," General Lee continued. "Let us pray that the people of the North will have had enough. I truly believe that if Abraham Lincoln loses reelection in November, the war will end and they will let us go."

CHAPTER 2

For the third time in the last hour, panic threatened to overtake Samantha. The sun had set two hours earlier, and Arlington was nowhere in sight. She was lost. She had considered turning around and retracing her path, but it was dark and she wasn't sure she could find it. Why had she ever thought she could do this alone?

Once again, she stopped Kota and gazed at the sky above her. "Damn!" she swore aloud.

She couldn't even locate a constellation to help her. The stars and moon were occluded by clouds, not that she would have fared better on a clear night. With some embarrassment, she remembered all the errors she'd made in trying to determine the directions that she and Many Horses were traveling. He'd chided her for her inability to read the stars or the path of the sun. Then he would once again explain it to her, only for her to repeat her mistakes. Finally, he'd thrown his hands up in exasperation. "Our children can determine direction. How is it that you cannot?"

He'd accompanied her to the forests surrounding Washington City. Then they'd separated—he to return to the Lakota territories, and she to go on to the Union Medical Corps in Arlington, Virginia. How she wished he were here with her now. She would even welcome his scolding.

It was no use. She was following a narrow road, its ruts deeply gorged by overladen wagons that led through open, grassy fields flanked by forested areas. There were no houses in sight. She would have to stop for the night. She guided Kota off the road, across the field, and into the woods. The forest was thick, mostly hickory and maple hardwoods with minimal undergrowth, but still difficult to penetrate in the dark. Samantha dismounted and selected an area on the edge of the forest that would provide some protection and cover, but close enough so that in the morning she could once again find the road.

She removed food and fresh water from her supplies and settled herself against a large tree trunk, propping her rifle next to her. When she finished eating, she tried to sleep. She was warm enough with the wool long underwear, buckskins, and blanket, but she was acutely aware that she was alone; this was the first time in her life she had ever spent a night without some family member with her. She listened to the sounds of the forest. Periodically, the moon broke through the cloud cover and cast surreal shadows on the forest's floor. At such times, she would grab her rifle and peer into the darkness. What kinds of predators roamed this part of the country? Cougars? Wolves? Kota whinnied softly to her, as though he could sense her fear and wanted to reassure her. She wrapped the blanket tighter around her body. By early morning, exhaustion finally overcame her and she fell asleep.

When she first heard a horse whinny, Samantha was dreaming. She and her brother Troy were racing across the open prairie with her cousin, Many Horses, and the young Lakota warriors. She was enjoying the childhood memory when again the horse whinnied. Samantha was confused, for there was no danger as they laughed and challenged each other in the race. Why would Kota. . . . Samantha bolted awake to see a man standing over her.

"Well now, what have we here?" a man said.

Confederates! Samantha automatically reached for her rifle.

"This what you're looking for?" the disheveled man asked as he held up the Henry rifle. The man grinned, showing gaps between his teeth, his scruffy beard unkempt. He was gaunt, wearing soiled, dark pants and a ragged Confederate Army jacket, half of its buttons missing, its tan color barely visible beneath the dirt. He wore a floppy, brown hat, a canteen at his belt, a mud-caked blanket roll twisted over one shoulder, and shoes that were so worn, Samantha could see his socks and two toes sticking out.

"This sure is a purty one, yes sirree. Where'd you get this, boy?" the man drawled as he examined the rifle.

Once again, Samantha heard Kota snort and stomp the ground. Her attention was diverted to where the horse stood. A Confederate soldier was trying to place a rope around Kota's neck, while another searched through Samantha's remaining supplies. Kota reared up each time the man approached him.

"Hey, can't you handle that horse, or are you Tennessee boys only used to mules?" the soldier facing Samantha called out to his friends.

Samantha glanced to the left and the right, seeking an answer to her predicament, a means of escape. She swallowed, trying to calm the pounding in her chest and the trembling in her limbs. "Leave the horse alone, monsieur. You can take what you want from my supplies," she said in English, lacing her words with a heavy French accent, hoping to dissuade any thoughts that she might be from the Northern states.

"I ain't never heard no one talk like that before. Where you from, boy?" the soldier asked as he viciously kicked with his foot, striking Samantha on the leg.

She cried out and was on her feet in an instant, responding to reflexes engrained in her as a child, sizing up her opponent, poised to fight; however, when she saw her Henry rifle pointed at her chest, she stepped back and raised her hands in the air in apparent surrender.

"I asked you where you from, boy," the Confederate repeated with a snarl.

Samantha glanced to the side to see that the other two soldiers had stopped what they were doing and started walking toward her.

"I am from Canada, monsieur," Samantha answered.

"Canada, huh? What are you doin' down here?"

Samantha hesitated. "I got lost," she finally answered as she lowered her hands to her side.

"Whoeee! I'd say you sure did," the soldier laughed.

His compatriots joined in the laughter, and then the two turned back to their task. One picked up her saddlebags, while the other, once again, tried to loop the rope around Kota's neck, the powerful horse shaking his head and rearing in the air, his hooves striking dangerously close to the man on the ground—a warning. The horse could easily end this confrontation should he feel it was necessary in order to protect Samantha.

The man near Samantha was distracted, watching his comrade fail repeatedly to capture the horse, and Samantha saw perhaps her only opportunity to escape. She lunged toward the man holding her rifle, knocking the rifle to her side. As she did so, the Confederate squeezed the trigger, causing the rifle to discharge harmlessly into the air. He still held it tightly, though, and swung it around toward her head.

Samantha ducked, and as she did, she pulled the knife from her boot. Before her attacker realized what was happening, Samantha was at his back, the knife pressed against the side of his neck. With her other hand, she twisted the man's arm behind him, painfully pulling his wrist upward, causing him to cry out and preventing him from moving.

At the sound of Samantha's rifle discharging, the other two soldiers grabbed their weapons and rushed forward.

"Let him go, boy," one of them said as he aimed his rifle at Samantha.

"Stay where you are," Samantha shouted. "You may shoot me, but not before I slit your friend's throat."

Samantha increased the pressure on the knife, slicing into the superficial layer of the skin. Immediately, a crimson line appeared on the man's neck, the blood running down to the collar of his filthy, frayed shirt.

"Do what he says," the man cried as he felt the blade of the knife pierce his skin.

Despite her fear, her hand was steady as she pressed the blade into the Confederate's neck. She kept eye contact with the approaching men, their muskets aimed at her. Within her peripheral gaze, she saw her Henry rifle laying just feet away. "I don't want any trouble. Put your weapons on the ground. You can take what you want from my supplies, but leave my horse alone," she said.

There was a rustle from the woods, and Samantha jerked her head to the side to see a dozen more soldiers emerge from the thicket, their rifles aimed at her. Then two more men appeared on horseback. One was wearing a long, double breasted, gray frock coat, with two gold horizontal embroidered bars on its collar and a light-blue cap. The other was dressed in civilian clothes.

"Lieutenant, I think you should order your men to do as the boy says," the man in civilian clothes said to his mounted companion.

"But, Major," the lieutenant began.

"Now, Lieutenant. Have your men stand down."

Samantha looked to the man who had spoken with authority. The lieutenant had addressed the man as "major," although he wore no evidence of a uniform or his rank. His hair was dark, and startling blue eyes stared back at her as though they had taken in the full measure of her.

"Yes, sir," the lieutenant said and turned to the men still pointing their rifles at Samantha. "You heard Major Winters-Hunt. You two men fall in back here. Lower your weapons," the lieutenant commanded.

The major dismounted and walked over to Samantha, stopping next to her. "I would suggest that you release that man, now. As you can see, you are outnumbered. You won't be harmed," he said in French.

Samantha swallowed. She released her grip on the soldier and lowered the knife to her side. The soldier stumbled away, pressing his hand to his neck to staunch the flow of blood.

"Le couteau," the major said to Samantha as he held out his hand.

Reluctantly, Samantha handed him the knife. He held it up as though examining it.

"Vous etes canadien?" he asked.

"Oui, monsieur."

"Qu'est-ce que vous faites ici?"

Samantha swallowed, trying to steady her voice. *"Je suis perdu."*

The major's eyebrows arched as though he'd just heard something amusing.

"Excuse me, Major," the lieutenant interrupted. "What's he saying?"

A look of annoyance flashed briefly across the major's face before he turned to the lieutenant. "He says that he's Canadian and that he's lost. You may question him yourself, though. He speaks English."

The lieutenant approached. "Lost? This is the Confederate State of Virginia. Boy, how can you have wandered so far south?"

"I'm going to New Orleans, sir. I have relatives there," Samantha answered.

"New Orleans is under Federal occupation," the lieutenant replied.

Samantha was encouraged. At least he hadn't said that he didn't believe her.

"I . . . I know that, sir. I have family there. If possible, I plan to bring them back to Canada until the war is over," she said.

"I see." The lieutenant seemed lost for a reply.

"Lieutenant, your men have marched through most of the night. Perhaps this is a good place to stop." The major glanced at Samantha. "I see no reason to detain the boy," he said.

The lieutenant nodded and then issued the order to his men.

"You are free to go," Major Winters-Hunt said to Samantha. "No one will bother you." He held the knife out for Samantha. As she took it, she looked again at his face. There was the hint of a smile in his eyes, although he kept his face impassive. He knew she was lying? And still he was letting her go?

She slipped the knife into her boot, conscious that he was watching her every move. She began to gather her supplies when Kota whinnied. Samantha walked over to the horse and spoke quietly to him, stroking his neck to calm him.

The rest of the soldiers had arrived and were wearily shrugging off their packs. They numbered about twenty in all. Samantha turned to watch, her attention caught by the sounds she'd heard from the last men to arrive. Two men were supporting a third between them. He cried out as they lowered him to the ground. Even from the distance that separated them, Samantha could see the bloody rags that'd been wound around the man's foot. He lay on the ground, moaning.

Samantha automatically stepped toward the injured soldier. As she drew nearer, she could see mangled flesh that had not been completely covered by the crude bandages. She also became aware of the major's eyes on her. She knew she must leave now; she couldn't risk her own safety, even if it was to help an injured man. She turned around and hastily walked back to Kota.

"It is not for the medicine woman to choose. It is for The Spirits."

Charrah! Samantha leaned her head against Kota's neck, the words echoing in her mind. Were these words from the past, or was this the spirit of Charrah speaking now? How many years had passed since she had heard the words of the old holy man? Charrah was powerful. His words were not to be taken lightly, no matter if spoken in the past by the embodiment of the holy man or in the present by his spirit.

She picked up her medical bag and walked to where the injured soldier lay. His boot had already been removed. As she reached out to examine the wound, the soldier's hand lashed out and caught her wrist.

"You're hurt. I can help you," she said.

Either the man was too weak to resist or, in his pain, he sensed her sincerity. He released her hand and lay back on the ground. As she removed the soiled linen from the man's foot, the wound started to bleed again. She could see where a projectile had torn through, shattering the outer metatarsal. The bone could not be repaired, but the mangled tissue and skin could be sutured.

"How long ago did this happen?" she asked.

"Yesterday," another soldier answered.

Samantha heard a commotion behind her.

"What are you doing, boy?" a voice demanded.

She glanced up to see the lieutenant looming over her.

"This man needs medical attention," Samantha answered.

"I'm aware of that," the lieutenant said. "We'll meet up with John Gordon's troops in a few days. He has surgeons."

Samantha stood to face the lieutenant. "I'm a doctor, a surgeon. If you wait a few more days, he'll either bleed to death or the wound will putrefy, in which case, the surgeons will have no choice but to remove his foot. Then, he still may die. He has a chance of living and keeping his foot if I treat it now."

"We'll take him to our surgeons. Be on your way, boy," the lieutenant said.

"Lieutenant, a moment of your time, please." Although politely phrased, it was clear that the major's words were not a request, but a command.

The lieutenant turned to his senior officer. "Sir?"

"Let the boy try to save the foot. If he fails, it will be no worse than what's waiting for your man at the surgeons' tent," Winters-Hunt said.

"But Major, we don't even know who this fella is."

The major didn't answer but looked directly at Samantha. His gaze was unsettling. It was as if he knew she'd been lying about trying to find New Orleans.

"Yes, sir," the lieutenant said, and then nodding at Samantha, walked away.

In all, it didn't take her more than a few minutes. She thoroughly cleaned the wound and then tied off the blood vessels that wouldn't stop bleeding. As carefully as possible, she realigned the metatarsal bone, even though she doubted it would ever be normal again. After stitching the wound closed, she splinted it with two pieces of wood and wrapped clean bandages around it. Samantha moved to the injured man's head. "It's finished. You need to rest now. When you arrive at your camp, have one of the doctors examine your foot."

"Will I keep it?" the man asked, his voice weak.

"I can't say for certain, but I believe you will if the wound is kept clean. Don't let dirt get on the bandages. Do you understand?"

The man nodded. Samantha stood. The men were all filthy. It'd be a miracle if the wound was kept clean. Charrah had taught her what the Indians had known for generations: that a warrior was more likely to recover from his battle wounds if they were bathed regularly. The water used had to be clear, running water, not water that had become stagnant and contained "bad spirits." At the College de France, the majority of surgeons ridiculed such attention to cleansing.

Samantha carried her bag back to Kota and was washing her hands and surgical needle when the major approached.

"You did a nice job on that man's foot. Where did you learn that?" he asked.

Samantha turned to face him. "I studied medicine at the College de France in Paris."

"You're very young to have studied medicine. What's your name?"

"Sam Car-Cartier," Samantha stuttered, using the French pronunciation of her last name.

"And Dr. Cartier, do you still plan on going on to New Orleans?"

"Yes. I'll leave as soon as my things are packed."

"Perhaps you should ride with us for a while."

Samantha tensed. "I can't. I must leave now."

"A few days won't matter. You'll be much safer with us," he said as he turned to leave.

"No!" Samantha ran up behind him. "I can't go with you, sir."

Winters-Hunt turned around. By now, the lieutenant and another man had approached.

"Perhaps I didn't make myself clear, Dr. Cartier," the

major said. "You have no choice. In a matter of days, one of the greatest Federal forces assembled will march through here. A Confederate force has dug in south of here. When the two armies meet, the losses are bound to be great. Your skills will be needed. The lieutenant and his men will see you to the surgeons' tent safely."

"Wait! You cannot expect me to work for the Confederacy," she blurted out, instantly regretting her impulsive words.

The major narrowed his eyes. "Why not? You're Canadian, and to my knowledge, the Canadian Frontier has not officially sided with the Union or the Confederacy, and you said you have family in New Orleans. Is that not so?"

Samantha hesitated. "Y . . . Yes."

"Then it's settled. The South is in desperate need of surgeons. You will accompany Lieutenant Quicken's men."

A soldier approached with the major's horse.

"Private, perhaps you should take the boy's rifle and knife," the major said as he mounted his horse. He looked at Samantha. "You'll have no need of them," he said and then turned his horse around and left.

The private stared at Samantha. "You really a doctor, boy?" he asked.

"Yes," she answered.

"You still look wet behind the ears to me," the private said. "Well, you heard the major. Hand them over."

Samantha's heart pounded beneath the tight gauze. She pulled her knife out of her boot and glanced to the side. Could she get away? Her rifle was in the scabbard on Kota, just a few feet away. But which way should she go? Back to the road? She glanced back at the man. She would have to injure, if not kill him.

"Don't try it, boy. Doc or not, the lieutenant will have you shot as a deserter," the private said, sensing her thoughts. He held out his hand. "Best give me the knife real easy like. It ain't worth tryin' to escape."

"But I'm not a deserter. I'm not even part of your army."

"You are now," the private said.

Samantha looked around her. Many Horses had chided her on her white man's impulsiveness. He said she needed to learn restraint. The major had said that these men would take her with them. She'd be mounted on Kota then. That would be her chance.

She nodded her head in acceptance and handed her knife to the private. "He won't let you get close to him," she said, pointing to Kota, who was already tossing his head in the air, his nostrils flaring, his large, black eyes locked on the private—the threat clear. "I'll get it," Samantha said as she reached out to the horse, stroking him assuredly as she withdrew the rifle and handed it to the private.

The private looked at her a moment and then back at his comrades. "Might as well come over and sit. Not likely we'll get much time to rest after tomorrow," he said as he started walking toward the group of men sitting around a small fire.

Samantha wrapped her arms around herself to quell her shaking and followed the private. There were three separate, small fires burning, with about a dozen men sitting or lying around each one. Hesitantly, she lowered herself to the ground next to where the private sat.

The first thing she noticed was the overwhelming stench emanating off the unwashed men. They were all thin, their clothes ragged and filthy, their shoes worn to the extent that she could see bare skin or socks underneath them. They were largely silent, their eyes vacant as they stared at the fire. They moved little, except to scratch at their clothing, no doubt in response to the vermin biting their skin.

She watched as a soldier pulled a hard biscuit out of his pocket. Breaking it in half, he dipped it into the dark liquid in his cup. Samantha stared in disgust as he withdrew the biscuit, leaving several worms wiggling around in the liquid. The man put the biscuit in his mouth and pulled the worms out of the cup with his fingers, casually tossing them to the side. He repeated the ritual with the remaining pieces of his biscuit.

"Boy?" one of the men said as he held a tin cup out to her.

"What is it?" she asked as she accepted the cup. She inhaled its aroma, unable to recognize the strange, pungent odor. When no one answered, she cautiously took a sip. The liquid was harsh and bitter. A few of the men laughed as she grimaced, forcing herself to swallow the small amount in her mouth.

"Don't got no coffee beans. That's made from chicory," the man said.

"You get used to it," another volunteered.

Samantha thanked him and returned the cup.

They'd been resting less than an hour, the conversation scant, a few of the men falling asleep on the ground next to the fire, when Major Ethan Winters-Hunt returned.

"Lieutenant, a small patrol of Federal soldiers is heading this way. My guess is they are an advance unit sent out to find how far ahead Lee's men are," Samantha overheard the major say.

"How many?" the lieutenant asked.

"Not more than a dozen."

The events that followed came so quickly, it wasn't until it was over that the horror of it registered for Samantha. The men extinguished their fires and crept closer to the road under the cover of the dense woods. They stayed there, lying on their bellies in the thick brush, waiting. Samantha thought they had all forgotten about her until the major grabbed her arm.

"This is no place for you, Doctor. Mount your horse and come with me," he said.

He pulled her to a standing position and then, keeping a grip on her arm, guided her over to where Kota was tied. He mounted his own horse and waited for her, keeping a sharp eye on her every movement. "Now is not the time to think of escaping, not unless you want to get yourself and that horse of yours," he said as he nodded to Kota, "caught in a crossfire. Follow me."

Samantha recognized the warning in his voice, and his reference to Kota being hurt was enough to make her mount her horse and follow him, winding through the trees, deeper into the woods. When he stopped, she could barely see the Confederates at the edge of the forest. The lieutenant was on his horse, behind his soldiers.

"If you value your life, Doctor, do not make a sound," the major said.

Samantha turned to look at him. His face was like stone except for his eyes—cold, piercing, menacing—threatening should she disobey his order. In the next minute, she heard the lieutenant shout, followed by a volley of musket fire. Men screaming. More gunfire. It was over in a matter of a minute. She still didn't understand. The Confederates were all standing now, running out of the brush, shouting with joy. She turned her face to the major.

"What is it? What happened?" she asked.

"Nothing you can do anything about," he said.

Samantha saw him squeeze his eyes shut and lower his head for a fraction of a moment. When he next looked at her, he had recovered, his face rigid again.

"We'll be moving on now," he said.

He gave no other explanation and urged his horse forward. Samantha followed him as they retraced their steps. As they emerged onto the road, she saw a dozen dead Union soldiers lying in various contorted positions on the road. Confederate soldiers were turning over the bodies, pulling off boots and searching through the dead men's clothing. One of the Union soldiers lying on the ground cried out. The Confederate grabbed his rifle and thrust the bayonet into the chest of the wounded man, silencing him.

"Stop it!" Samantha screamed.

For a moment, the Confederate soldiers raised their eyes to her. Samantha felt a vice-like grip on her arm that almost pulled her off of Kota.

"I told you to be quiet," the major said. "There's nothing that can be done."

The two horses were so close that their flanks were touching. Samantha tried to jerk her arm free, but the major only tightened his grip on her upper arm. She looked back at the soldiers, who had returned to their looting. Another wounded Union soldier tried to crawl away. In that instant, she forcefully tried to wrench her arm free, but she was too late. One of the Confederates also saw the man. In a matter of seconds, the injured man was silenced.

Samantha was trembling violently now, no longer aware of the major's arm still restraining her. He released his grip on her arm and took the reins of her horse with his own. Urging his horse forward, the two horses moved away from the bodies. Samantha twisted in the saddle, unable to take her eyes off of the grisly scene behind her. When they were a short distance down the road, he rode over to the trees and dismounted.

"Sam?"

She turned toward his voice.

"Get off of your horse, Sam," he said as he reached for her arm.

Samantha recoiled from his touch and whipped her head back around to the carnage behind her. *Oh, God.* She turned away from the grotesque scene, leaned over Kota's withers, and retched. She clung to the horse as her stomach repeatedly contracted violently.

Winters-Hunt swore and reached up, lifting Samantha off her horse. Samantha was oblivious as her stomach emptied its contents on his jacket. He set her down on the ground and supported her as her stomach gave its final heave. Then he sat down beside her and removed his foul-smelling jacket.

"Damn," he said with a sigh. "How old are you, Sam?"

Samantha didn't answer. She kept her face down, her eyes closed.

"Sam," he said gently. "Look at me."

Reluctantly, Samantha raised her face to him.

"How old are you?"

"I'm . . . I'm fifteen—almost," she stammered.

"You look much younger. As a matter of fact, it looks like you might be losing your mustache."

Samantha hastily reached up and felt the mustache, loosened during her vomiting. She pressed it back onto her skin, avoiding the major's gaze.

"Are you really a doctor?" he asked next.

Samantha swallowed again, and when she answered, her voice was faint. "Yes. I attended the College de France in Paris. That's the truth. I just recently finished my training."

"I see. I'm surprised they admitted a boy of your age. You look more like you're eleven or twelve," he said.

Samantha shrugged her shoulders. At least he still thought she was a boy. No matter what, she must maintain that identity. "I lied to them. The mustache helped," she said.

He smiled briefly and then sobered. "I would imagine that your training exposed you to all kinds of injuries and illnesses?"

Samantha nodded her head.

"But you've never seen a man killed before."

Samantha flinched.

"We're at war, Sam. Men are killed by the thousands some days."

"War?" Samantha jerked her head up. "That wasn't a battle. It was murder! Those Union soldiers were ambushed. And then your men murdered the wounded. They were wounded and unable to defend themselves." Despite her fear of the major, she glared at him as tears threatened.

"Sam, people who've never been in a war seem to think that there are rules, that there is a code of honor. They deceive themselves. War is killing. Both sides do it until one side has lost so many it can no longer fight. The other side is then declared the victor. In other words, the side that kills the most wins the war." He sighed and then continued.

"The Confederacy is not in the habit of murdering wounded Yankees," he said. "Lieutenant Quicken's men cannot take prisoners. They're a small patrol whose duty is to advance before the major Confederate units and determine the location of the Federal troops. Sometimes they're away from their unit for months at a time. Their supplies are always meager. They can hardly accumulate prisoners as they go along. The Federal armies have the same kind of patrols. It's no different."

Samantha stared at the man before her. "I will not help you," she said. "Let me go. I'll not treat your Confederate soldiers."

"You have no choice."

"You and your people are traitors to the Union and murderers," she accused. "You're tearing this country apart."

The major appeared to be studying her, and then he spoke. "You're not from Canada at all, Sam. You're a

Yankee."

Samantha swallowed, a new fear seeping into her blood. In her anger, she'd said too much, betraying herself.

"You needn't answer," he said, "but I would advise you to be more careful. Doctor or not, you're in enemy territory now. Your skill as a surgeon is the only thing that will keep you out of a prison camp or worse," he added. "Now, let's mount up. Lieutenant Quicken and his men are coming. And Sam, don't try to escape. You'd be dead within a few hours. By going with me to the Confederate encampment, you have a chance to survive."

The major mounted his horse. Samantha hesitated. Behind her, Lieutenant Quicken's men were approaching. She was trapped. Still trembling, she mounted Kota.

"Major Winters-Hunt?" Lieutenant Quicken said as he stopped beside them. "If you have no objection, I'd like to report to General Gordon as soon as possible. Those Yankees were probably an advance detail of Meade's men."

"Undoubtedly they were, Lieutenant. You should be able to meet General Gordon's forces by tomorrow. They'll be entrenched in the Wilderness by then."

They rode in silence the remainder of the day. That night, Lieutenant Quicken chose a place to camp. Samantha watched as the soldiers gathered together in small groups. These men were her enemies. Her own brothers were fighting with the Union. What if they had been among those so savagely killed today?

Samantha sat down to eat apart from the men. She started to remove pieces of dried beef from her supplies but stopped when she noticed some soldiers watching her. Uneasily, she reached inside her boot and realized that she didn't have her knife. Two of the soldiers approached.

"You got anything else in that bag of yours, boy?" one of

them asked.

Samantha didn't answer. She wasn't opposed to sharing her food, for she had seen the meager sustenance of these men, but she knew that they would likely take all that she had.

"Hey, you deaf?" the other asked. "Where you from? You sure don't dress like nobody from around these parts."

"He's wearing skins like the Indians do. I seen some once," his friend said.

"That so? How about if we look through them bags of yours?"

Samantha looked around wildly. Most of the other men were involved in their own conversations. No one seemed to be interested in her or the pair who were harassing her.

"Just leave me alone," Samantha answered. She knew she could protect herself against one of them, and possibly both, if they weren't armed.

"We're just being friendly." The taller of the two bent down on one knee in front of Samantha and reached for her bag.

"Are you looking for something in particular, Private?" a voice cut in.

Samantha felt the coldness of the voice and knew immediately who was speaking. She watched as the soldier stood, deferentially backing away from her.

"No. No, sir. Just being friendly with the boy."

"This boy," Winters-Hunt said in an icy tone, "is a doctor. I'll be taking him to join General Lee's Surgical Corps tomorrow. Should you have need to address him again, Private, it will be as doctor or sir. Is that clear?"

"Yes, sir. Y-Yes, Major."

"Do you have anything else to say to the doctor?"

"No, sir," the men replied.

The major turned to Samantha. "Dr. Cartier, would you

care to join me for coffee?" Samantha watched the men hastily retreat. She didn't speak as she walked beside the major over to a small fire. She sat down by it, grateful to have a more private place to sit. She took the cup the major offered and sipped the hot liquid. Although it was not as bad as the coffee she'd received from the soldiers earlier, it still was not very good. As if reading her thoughts, the major spoke. "It's hard to get coffee beans anymore. The soldiers brew a substitute from peanuts, potatoes, or chicory."

Samantha nodded and looked down at her cup. "Major," she said finally, "let me go."

The major sighed. "Believe me, Sam, I already regret forcing you to accompany us, but I don't have a choice. By this time tomorrow, this whole area will be a battlefield. You're caught between two large armies. You'd be killed on your own. It wouldn't matter which direction you rode. Some nervous picket would shoot you before you got a chance to identify yourself. The other truth is that the Confederacy is going to be in desperate need of your skills tomorrow."

"And if I refuse?" she asked as he sat down on the ground next to her.

"You won't," he said. "It's getting late. You're going to need all the rest you can get. God help us, but I fear it will be a long time before any of us sleep again. Fetch your supplies and come back here. You can tie your horse up with mine."

"I'll keep to myself, Major," Samantha said.

"That wasn't a request, Sam."

Although his voice was gentle, Samantha recognized it was an order she dared not disobey. She retrieved her supplies and tied Kota next to the major's horse. At least none of the men would bother her here, and she felt no threat from Major Winters-Hunt. But if what he said was true, what was she to do tomorrow?

She wrapped her blanket about her body and turned on her side, her back to the major. Lying there, Samantha was grateful he couldn't see her tears. Why had she been so reckless, so foolish? Suddenly, being a doctor wasn't so important anymore. Many Horses and Troy were right. Her father was right. She wanted to go home. Home.

She tried to will herself to stay awake in order to think of a means of escape. But despite her resolve, her body had been unprepared for the rigors of the journey east and the previous sleepless night. She fell asleep, only to be awoken suddenly. The major was bending over her in the darkness.

"Sam?" he said.

Samantha sat up. The fire had been extinguished, but she could see a flurry of activity around her.

"Be very quiet. We must leave immediately," the major said.

"Why? What's happening?"

"It will be dawn in a few hours. The Federal Army is already on the move. The advance units are only a few miles from us," he answered.

Samantha stood. The Union Army! This might be the chance she was waiting for. His eyes met hers.

"Don't try it, Sam. It's dark. The Federal troops will shoot anything that moves, including young Yankee surgeons."

He mounted his horse and waited for her to do the same.

"Let's go, but remember, be quiet," he said.

It was difficult to see in the forest in the dark, so Samantha followed closely behind the major's horse. They rode for half an hour before they came into a clearing. She turned around to see that no one was following them. She urged Kota up next to the major.

"Where are the others?" she asked.

"Lieutenant Quicken and his men are taking a different route. We'll go on alone. We have another hour before daylight. Let's go."

He urged his horse into a gallop. Samantha hesitated. Could she turn and race away in the other direction? To where? She had no idea where she was. That, and the chance of being shot in the darkness, was more frightening than staying with the major. She urged Kota forward to catch up with the major.

When the sun came up, they finally stopped to rest the horses. The major untied a leather bag from behind his saddle and offered Samantha food and water.

"Where are we?" she asked, sitting down on the grass to eat.

"Not too far west of Fredericksburg."

He removed a package from his bag. Samantha frowned as the major removed his shirt. When she realized what he was doing, she shifted her position, keeping her eyes focused on the ground as she ate. When he stepped in front of her, she looked up at him. He was standing before her in a gray coat that had a double row of gold buttons on the front. The collar had an intricate pattern of gold braid Austrian knots with one gold star in the middle. The gold braid was repeated on the sleeve, a patch of light blue culminating at the end of the sleeves. His uniform trousers were dark blue with a light-blue stipe on the outside seam. She knew the Confederates addressed him as major, but still, seeing him in uniform—being this close to a Confederate major—was unsettling.

"We're less likely to be shot by Confederate troops if the uniform is visible," he explained, "although as thick as this brush is, it will be difficult to identify anyone until we're face-to-face with the sentries."

He sat down across from her and leaned against a tree.

Out of the corner of her eye, Samantha could see that he was deep in thought. He was staring at her buckskin boots when he spoke.

"Sam, I'm going to ask you this just once. I expect the truth from you." He looked up, his eyes piercing. "Are you really a surgeon? I don't mean some frontier doctor trained by experience. Are you who you say you are?"

Samantha raised her chin defiantly. "Yes, I'm a surgeon, and I resent your reference to some frontier doctor. I was schooled in Paris, as I said."

"But you're Canadian," he said. "What did you do in Canada before going to school in Paris?"

Samantha hesitated. "I was a fur trapper."

The major raised his eyebrows. "It must have been a very lucrative business to provide you with the means to travel to Paris to study. Certainly your appearance would suggest the lifestyle of a fur trapper, but you speak far too well. You must have had some formal education before going to Paris."

"I had some," Samantha answered, trying to avoid his eyes.

"Well, I'll tell you, Sam, I think that you're no more from Canada than I am. I noticed that when you became frightened or angry, you lost your French accent. My guess is that you're from the North, Sam. So tell me, what is a young Yankee surgeon, dressed in buckskins, doing in the South?"

Samantha's heart pounded. Her palms ran with sweat. She swallowed several times, trying to think of a reasonable explanation.

"Are you a spy?" he asked.

"What? No! I'm not a spy."

He laughed shortly. "No, you don't lie well enough to be a spy. Where were you going when Lieutenant Quicken's men found you?"

"I told you."

"Yes, you said that you were going to New Orleans, but that was a lie."

Samantha was desperate. He sat there, calm and steady, his eyes still on her. She was saved from having to respond by the sudden crack of thunder in the distance. The major looked up sharply. Again a series of rumbles filled the air. Samantha felt an unfamiliar tremor of the ground beneath where she sat.

"Damn!" he swore and jumped up. "We're too late!"

"What do you mean?" Samantha stood as reverberations continued in the distance. "Is that a storm coming?"

"Look above you. There's not a cloud in the sky," he said as he gathered his supplies. "It's cannon fire, Sam, and volleys of gunfire."

As the noise grew louder, they could hear distant shouts.

"We've got to get out of here," the major said.

He swung up into his saddle and waited for Samantha to do the same.

"How well do you ride, Sam?" he asked when she was mounted on Kota.

Samantha saw the doubt in his eyes. "Better than you, Major," she challenged.

The major laughed. "This is no time to be modest, boy." Then his expression became serious. "Stay right behind me, and we just might make it out of here alive. Do you understand?"

Samantha mutely nodded as the major turned his horse to a narrow path in the woods. Within seconds, they were galloping at full speed. Because Samantha couldn't see the path ahead of them, she followed the major as closely as she could, the branches from the trees striking her in the face and on her pant legs as they raced through the woods. She lowered her chest down onto Kota's neck as she followed the major's lead, the horses jumping over fallen tree trunks.

Samantha didn't know how long they raced through the thick forest, but finally they emerged from the woods and found a road. The major kept their pace, urging his horse on. Without the impediment of the heavy brush, Kota stretched out and easily caught up with the major's horse on the open road. The two horses strained as they continued to run. Instead of the sounds of battle becoming fainter, they were becoming more intense.

As they rounded a curve in the road, the sight that greeted Samantha caused her to jerk in the saddle. A large Confederate force occupied the small open area of the plains. Officers on horseback shouted orders as they galloped back and forth behind a few strategically placed cannons. The sound of cannon fire was deafening, and Samantha involuntarily flinched with each explosion.

The major continued to skirt around the Confederate forces until they were behind the artillery. From this distance, Samantha could look back and see the forest they'd just come through. Now, those very trees were being cut down by cannonballs, their trunks crashing into the thicket. The entire hillside, woods, and field had erupted into a battlefield. With the exception of the opening where the Confederate cannons were positioned, they were surrounded by thick forests.

"Major!" Samantha shouted in alarm.

"Stay close," he commanded.

Samantha did as he directed, following him as they picked their way through the chaos, finally stopping as the major rode up to a Confederate officer.

"Ethan," the officer shouted in greeting, his voice all but drowned out by the sounds of battle. He gestured to the cannons. "Not much use. The Yankees are trapped, but we can't see anything."

"Who do we have?"

"Longstreet, Gordon, Gregg's Texans—sixty thousand total. If you're looking for him, Marse Robert is over there," the man said, motioning with his head.

For the next two hours, Samantha watched the surreal scene in front of her. It was difficult to see the fighting in the thick woods, but she could hear it—the screams, the steady musket fire. She could have sworn that the very trees pelted by lead balls screeched and moaned in devastation.

It was late afternoon when the major took her to a tent that had been erected behind the battle line. The major dismounted and indicated Samantha should do the same.

"In here," he said as he placed his hand on her back and guided her toward the tent.

They picked their way among the bodies of wounded soldiers lying on the ground. As she walked, Samantha felt her soft buckskin boots sink into the gory muck of earth and blood. She looked at the wounded. The clothing on the soldiers was so mangled that she couldn't separate bloody fabric from muscle and bone. She instinctively reached down to a soldier lying at her feet.

"Not here," the major said roughly as he grabbed her arm and propelled her forward.

His grip tightened as he maneuvered her through the bodies to the opening of the tent. They stepped inside and paused, letting their eyes adjust to the decreased light.

Samantha had practiced in the best and worst hospitals in France, but nothing in her training had prepared her for this. Two rough tables sat in the middle of the tent. A soldier lay on the nearest table. Three men held him down as he fought and screamed. Another man—the surgeon, Samantha presumed—reached for a crude wood saw. To her horror, he laid the blade against the mangled flesh of the conscious man and began quick, vicious thrusts into the skin of the man's leg just below his knee. A bloodcurdling scream pierced the air.

The surgeon continued his thrusts with the saw until Samantha heard the coarse sound of bone splitting. Blood sprayed everywhere, dripping off the table onto the ground inside of the tent, a steady stream pooling at the surgeon's feet. At last, the limb fell free. An attendant tossed it onto a pile of dismembered bloody arms, feet, and legs in the corner of the tent. The patient had fallen deathly silent, mercifully having lost consciousness as the surgeon bound up the stump of the leg and called for the next patient.

Samantha watched as the lifeless man was carried out and another protesting man was carried into the tent. No one bothered to clean the table. The attendants placed the injured soldier on the muddy, blood-soaked table and tore away his clothing to expose the wounded arm. No anesthetic was administered. The surgeon raised the same filthy saw and began hacking away again. He hadn't even tried to assess the circulation in an effort to save the soldier's arm. As Samantha watched the barbaric scene repeat itself, she felt bile rise up in her throat.

Suddenly, someone grabbed her arms and spun her around. She stood face-to-face with Major Winters-Hunt. A sharp pain registered in both of her arms as he shook her.

"Sam!" he hissed close to her face. "I didn't bring you here to have you retch all over the surgeon's table and then pass out on me. You said you're a doctor. Act like one!"

He released her, almost knocking her backward with his force.

"Ethan!" a man called from the other side of the tent. "What brings you to this circle of hell?"

"Clement," Ethan said, acknowledging the man. He

grabbed Samantha's arm and propelled her toward the other table where an older man with white hair and a beard had positioned himself.

Samantha watched as a wounded soldier was placed on this second table. The soldier was still conscious, begging the surgeon to spare him. The white-haired surgeon reached down and patted the soldier's arm.

"I'm sorry, son. You'll die if the leg doesn't come off. I'm sorry." The grief in the older surgeon's voice was apparent as he looked to the major.

"Clement, I've brought you another surgeon," the major stated, his hand still on Samantha's arm.

"What?" The older surgeon looked from Major Winters-Hunt to Samantha, still dressed in her buckskins.

"Sam," the major said, "may I present Dr. Clement Beauregard. He's in charge." The major turned back to Dr. Beauregard. "Clement, this is Sam Cartier, a surgeon," the major said.

"This boy?" Dr. Beauregard asked incredulously.

"Tell him," the major ordered Samantha.

Samantha swallowed. "I'm a doctor. I recently completed my studies at the College de France in Paris. I'm a qualified surgeon."

"What proof have you?"

Samantha hesitated. "I have no certificate with me, only my surgical instruments," she said as she held the black bag with her free hand.

"You're just a boy," Dr. Beauregard said, dismissing Samantha as he began the amputation.

Dr. Beauregard's patient screamed as three men restrained him. Although the major still gripped Samantha's arm, she jerked free of his grip.

"Stop it!" she shouted. "This man is conscious, for God's sake. Give him an anesthetic." She looked around the table beside her. "Where's the chloroform?"

Dr. Beauregard stopped and turned his eyes on Samantha. "We don't have any," he said.

Samantha looked around helplessly. "Ether?"

"None," Dr. Beauregard answered.

"Clement?" the major asked.

"Are you sure of this boy, Ethan?" the old surgeon asked.

"Give him a chance. What have you got to lose?" the major answered.

"Only a few more lives," Dr. Beauregard responded bitterly.

"Looks like there is a good chance you're going to lose them anyway," the major said.

"All right," Dr. Beauregard sighed. "Orderly! Set up another table and bring in another patient."

There was hardly room for a third table in the cluttered tent, but one was placed next to Dr. Beauregard's. Samantha frowned as she placed her bag on it and began to extract her instruments. She was about to ask for assistance when three attendants carried a wounded man in and placed him on the table in front of her. They ripped away what was left of his sleeve. Then the three men held the injured soldier down. Samantha looked at the soldier's face. He couldn't have been any older than she was, and he was crying, begging the men to release him. She reached out and touched his face gently.

"Let me die! Please, let me die! Don't cut on me!" the young soldier cried.

Samantha looked at his arm. She'd seen the effects of the .58 caliber Minie Ball before. The hollow base bullet, when fired from the rifled musket, was heavy and slow moving. When it hit its target, it tended to tumble with an explosive force, cutting a wide berth and destroying everything in its path. This boy's humerus bone was shattered well above the elbow, most of it completely blown away. There was nothing left to save.

"I'm sorry," she said to the young man. "It's the only chance you have of living."

A pool of blood had collected on the table as the wound oozed. "Give me a tourniquet," Samantha ordered.

"Sir?" one of the orderlies asked.

"A tourniquet."

The man looked blankly at her.

"A rope, a piece of twine—anything!"

The orderly looked around desperately and then returned with a piece of rope. Samantha twisted it around the soldier's upper arm until the bleeding stopped.

"Where can I wash my hands?"

The orderly looked at her blankly.

"Bring me water and soap. And this wound hasn't been properly cleansed."

Samantha was not aware that both surgeons had stopped their work and were watching her.

"Bring the doctor what he has asked for," Major Ethan Winters-Hunt said to the orderly.

"Yes, sir," the orderly said. He returned a few minutes later with a bowl and water. "Don't have no soap, sir."

"How have you been cleaning the wounds?"

The orderly frowned, not understanding her question.

"Find my bags and bring them to me," she said.

The orderly looked to Major Ethan Winters-Hunt, uncertain. The major nodded, and the man hurried out of the tent. When he returned, Samantha found the soap she was looking for and quickly scrubbed her hands, aware that she had lost precious time. She didn't immediately pick up her knife but spoke to the orderlies.

"Keep his head turned away from this arm and hold him still."

The man began to scream again.

"I'm sorry," Samantha said to the young man. "If there was any way for you to keep your arm and live, I would try to save it for you. There's no other way."

As she picked up her knife, her hand trembled slightly, and then froze.

"Sam!" Ethan growled as he gripped her elbow painfully.

Samantha jumped. She turned and glared at him until he released her. Then she looked at the wounded soldier struggling against the orderlies who were restraining him.

"Charrah, what am I to do?" she whispered in the Lakota language.

From somewhere inside of her, Samantha heard the old holy man's reply. *"Are you medicine woman?"*

"Yes," she replied.

"Then why do you ask?"

The change was immediate. Samantha's hand stopped trembling, and she focused on the mangled tissue before her. She shut out the cries of the wounded man beneath her, and with a firm, deft movement, sliced into the skin above the smashed arm. She didn't apply the crude saw to skin, muscle, nerve, and bone as she had seen the other surgeon do. Instead, she cut through the skin and reached for another instrument. She dissected the muscle apart and located the large subclavian artery. She tied that blood vessel with two separate ligatures, then located the smaller vessels and repeated the process.

She separated the muscle from the bone, cutting it with her knife at a point slightly below where she intended to saw the bone. She gently handled the major nerves, cutting them cleanly with her knife. All the while, her patient screamed and jerked convulsively beneath her.

Finally, she reached for her bone saw and made several smooth strokes, cutting the bone off. She had not yet released the tourniquet, so there was very little blood as she worked. No one reached to remove the severed arm from the table, so she pushed it away with her elbow. She withdrew a long file and filed the severed edge of bone until it was smooth. When she finished, she instructed the orderly to release the tourniquet.

The orderly hesitantly did as Samantha ordered as she watched to see that her ligatures would hold. Satisfied, she reached for her needle and fashioned the muscle and skin over the stump, cushioning the ends of the nerve within the muscle. She had observed in her studies that when the nerves were carefully handled and the ends protected this way, the patient had less phantom pain during the months following amputation. The entire process had not taken more than ten minutes when at last she stepped back.

"This needs to be wrapped in clean bandages, but I don't think there will be any more bleeding," Samantha said.

The orderly looked surprised at the neat, clean stump.

"Put something under it to keep it elevated. Do you have morphine?" Samantha asked.

"No, sir."

"What are you using for pain?"

"Ain't got nuthin', sir."

Samantha watched as the three men carried the man out of the tent, his screams now subsiding into sobbing. She turned to pick up her instruments when the orderlies entered with another wounded soldier. Before she could speak, they laid him down on the table. Thank God this man was unconscious.

Samantha looked down at her bloodstained instruments. "Do you have other surgical instruments?"

The orderly looked at her peculiarly. "Only those," he said, indicating a table next to her.

Samantha was appalled by what she saw. These were not

surgical instruments. It was an odd collection of kitchen knives, carpenter's pliers, and wood saws. And if that was not crude enough, they were filthy, covered in dirt and blood.

"These are what you've been using?" Samantha asked.

The orderly shrugged his shoulders. "Two cannonballs landed in the surgical tent a few months back. Caught fire. Killed two surgeons, four men, and destroyed their equipment. This is all that's left."

Samantha gasped and then recovered, aware of the orderly staring at her. "Bring me some water and a clean cloth so that I can wash my own."

"Sir? Beggin' your pardon, sir. Here's the next one," the orderly said, indicating the man lying before her.

"Is there a problem, orderly?" a man asked.

Samantha looked up at the other surgeon who had spoken. This was the doctor whose crude methods she had witnessed when she first entered the tent. He was tall, with blond hair and mustache and small, narrow eyes.

"No, sir," the orderly replied.

The surgeon left his table and walked over to Samantha. "What are you waiting for, Doctor? That's what you claim to be, isn't it?" he challenged.

"I'm waiting for water to wash my instruments," Samantha replied.

"Just because you have fancy instruments, that doesn't make you any better than us. I heard you over here. I've removed a leg and an arm in the time it took you to remove one arm."

The surgeon returned to his table. Samantha watched in horror as he picked up the dirty saw that he had used on his last patient and crudely applied it to the flesh above the ankle of the man writhing beneath him. The saw viciously cut into the skin, shredding it and the muscle below it as it made its way to the bone. Blood poured out of the ripped blood vessels.

"What are you doing?" Samantha shouted.

The surgeon looked up, his eyes blazing.

"You'll kill him!" Samantha accused.

The surgeon exploded, savagely tossing the mangled foot to the ground. "Who the hell do you think you are? How dare you!"

"Your instruments are filthy. So are your hands. That wound will probably putrefy," Samantha retorted.

"If you were any kind of a surgeon, you'd know that most of these wounds putrefy. There's nothing that can be done about it. You speak to me like that again and I'll have you horsewhipped," the surgeon threatened.

Samantha was so angry, she was shaking. She looked at the wounded soldier lying on the table before her. "Orderly, bring me a bowl with water," she said to her attendant.

The orderly reached behind him and placed a bowl of water on the table next to Samantha.

"No!" Samantha recoiled at the bowl before her. The water was almost black in color from the filthy, bloody bandages and instruments that had been dipped in it previously.

"Enough! Sergeant!" the other surgeon barked.

Samantha watched as a burly man in a tattered gray uniform entered, his eyes ignoring all the carnage before him.

"Remove this boy, immediately," the surgeon ordered.

The sergeant looked at Samantha, his face registering surprise at her attire.

"Now!" the surgeon shouted.

"No! I know what I am talking about," Samantha screamed as the sergeant grabbed her arm.

"Let the boy go." A cold voice cut through the mayhem

of the surgical tent. Major Winters-Hunt stepped forward.

"Major, I didn't know you were here. Yes, sir," the sergeant said as he released Samantha.

"Stay out of this, Major. This is none of your concern," the surgeon said.

Ethan turned an icy glare on the surgeon until he stepped back.

Dr. Beauregard moved toward the commotion and faced Samantha. "Dr. Cartier, we're operating under the worst of conditions," he said. "We have very few surgical instruments, so we make do with what we have. Dr. Schafley is correct: time is of the essence. We don't have time for your requests."

Samantha whirled around to Major Winters-Hunt. "Major, please. They'll die unless the instruments are cleaned. I know what I'm talking about. It's important!" She turned back to Dr. Beauregard. "Semmelweis demonstrated that twenty years ago."

"Semmelweis! Hah!" Dr. Schafley, the other surgeon, scoffed. "What do you think we are here? Backwoods doctors like you? Semmelweis studied childbirth. It has nothing to do with surgery."

"But it does! Major. Dr. Beauregard," Samantha said. "There is a surgeon in Germany who's been able to reduce post-surgical putrefaction by fifty percent just by proper cleaning of surgical instruments and insisting that all his students scrub their hands. I, myself, have seen a reduction of far greater than fifty percent when the wound, surgical instruments, and bandages are clean. Please," she pleaded.

Clearly, what Samantha was trying to tell them was beyond their experience. They, like most of their contemporaries, thought that infection following surgery was the result of bad elements in the air coming in contact with the wound. It had nothing to do with cleanliness or with microbes that were carried on the surgeon's hands and instruments.

Dr. Beauregard frowned. He appeared to be confused by what she said. She looked to Major Winters-Hunt. His eyes darkened as she caught his gaze. Then he nodded his head.

"Orderly, get Dr. Cartier what he's asked for—exactly what he's asked for," the major ordered.

"Clement!" Dr. Schafley protested.

"Are you sure about this, Ethan?" Clement Beauregard asked.

Major Winters-Hunt didn't answer, but the look he flashed Dr. Beauregard seemed to be sufficient.

"As you wish," Dr. Beauregard conceded. "We've wasted enough time. Everyone, back to work!"

That was not the only conflict Samantha had with Dr. Schafley. Most of the wounds were beyond saving—the bone, blood vessels, and surrounding muscle being completely blown away. It was impossible to save such a limb. But occasionally, the bone remained intact. If enough soft tissue and blood supply remained, Samantha elected to try to save the limb. Dr. Schafley was furious, insisting that she should amputate. The major had left the tent by then, and Samantha had to withstand Dr. Schafley's criticism by herself.

Samantha refused to compromise throughout the grueling day. On the battlefield, the fighting continued until after dark. As wounded men made their way back to the Confederate lines, they talked of soldiers getting lost in the thick underbrush of the woods. There were no clear-cut lines of battle. Entire units wandered off track and fired on their own comrades by accident.

Samantha was exhausted. Lanterns were hung in the tent so that the surgeons could continue their grisly work through the night. With dawn, more wounded were brought in, their bodies placed on the ground outside of the tent. She lost count of the number of limbs she'd amputated, her mind numb, her fingers, stiff and aching, moving with a will of their own, executing precise surgical techniques. After a while, the screams of the wounded blended into one another. It was a tent of pain and death.

Just when she thought she'd seen the worst that could happen, the second night of the battle brought a new horror. The cotton patches that were used in the muzzle-loading rifles ignited and fell onto the heavy thickets, causing brushfires to rage through the forest. Several hundred men, mostly wounded Union soldiers unable to escape the inferno, burned to death.

Samantha was spared the expression of grief by the steady stream of wounded soldiers placed before her. This continued for three days and nights until finally General Grant withdrew his troops. General Lee's Confederate Army, outnumbered two to one, had successfully held their ground. At the end of that third day, seventeen thousand Union soldiers lay dead in the scorched and bloody thicket called the Wilderness.

The last Confederate soldier had been treated, the wounded loaded onto wagons to transport to the nearest farm or house for quartering and care. The surgical tent was dismantled and loaded onto a wagon, along with supplies, to follow behind the infantry. General Lee, certain that General Grant would regroup his troops and march them toward Spotsylvania, hastily arranged for his Confederate forces to move south in hopes of arriving first.

After three days of explosions and the sounds of human agony, the deathly silence was eerie. Samantha sat on the ground and stared at the bodies strewn about as far as she could see. They had already begun to decay, their faces bloated and discolored, the stench filling the air and attracting hungry insects. A burial detail dug trenches, and she watched as they rolled the bodies into the trenches, burying them together. The blood of the dead, saturating the ground and seeping into her buckskin pants, was of no consequence. She was numb—she had to be. If she allowed herself to feel, she would lose her mind to grief. She didn't hear the major approach her from behind.

"Sam?" When she didn't respond, he placed his hand on her shoulder. "Sam!" he said roughly as he shook her shoulder.

She turned around to look at him. His face was blackened with gun powder, his eyes red and swollen with fatigue, his jaw clenched. Then his expression softened.

"Come with me," he said gently, assisting her to her feet. He guided her back to his tent and pointed to his cot. "You need to rest, Sam," he said.

She fell onto the canvas cot and turned on her side, curling up, her back to him. She closed her eyes but could still feel his presence standing beside her. She heard him swear softly as he stood behind her, watching her.

"I'm sorry, Sam," he whispered.

Samantha slept for hours, but it was not a restful sleep. So many faces, so many shattered limbs, so many broken bodies. She had pushed their cries of pain, their anguish, to the back of her mind. It was the only way she could function amid the slaughter. But now, she was defenseless in her sleep. She saw every face. She felt their desperation, their pain, their terror. Her cries brought the major to her side.

"Sam. Sam, wake up."

When she sat up, tears streamed down her face. It took a moment for the confusion of the dream to clear away. When she realized where she was, she turned her face away from the major.

"There's no shame in crying, Sam," he said gently.

Samantha blinked the tears from her eyes and shuddered as the memory of the dream returned to her.

"Are you all right?" he asked.

Samantha mutely nodded her head.

"There are a few more hours before daylight," he said. "Go back to sleep. I'll leave the lamp burning if you'd like."

She was afraid to close her eyes for fear the dream would return. Finally, exhaustion overtook her and she slept.

The following morning, the major entered the tent and placed a plate of food in front of her.

"I'm not hungry," she said as she pushed the food away.

"You haven't had anything to eat in three days," he replied. "You must eat."

"I can't," she said.

The major was insistent, and finally Samantha complied, only to vomit her food. He didn't relent. He brought her a cup of broth and dry biscuit crusts. She sipped and nibbled slowly until the vomiting finally stopped. Later that afternoon, he reappeared.

"The remaining troops are leaving. I've brought a change of clean clothes," he said as he placed them on the cot next to her. "Put those on and then we'll leave."

Samantha looked down at the clothes but made no move.

"Let's go," he said impatiently.

"I like my buckskins," she said.

"They attract too much attention," he said.

"I don't care, Rebel. I'm keeping them on," she replied defiantly.

"Rebel, is it? You haven't seen enough Confederate blood, Sam? You want to carry it around on you?" he said as he nodded at her shirt.

For the first time, Samantha glanced down at her shirt. The buckskin was covered with the bloody stains of her three days' work.

"I told you, the buckskins prompt too many questions. I'll get the horses. Either you change by the time I get back, Sam, or I'll do it for you," he said as he left the tent.

Samantha suspected the major didn't make idle threats. She hastily changed into the clothes he'd brought and folded her few belongings into her bag. She was waiting by the tent when he returned with Kota. She blinked, surprised that Kota allowed the major to touch him, and then to put his saddle and bridle on? Her horse seemed to be content in Winters-Hunt's presence. "Traitor," she whispered in mock reprimand to her horse as she mounted.

The major set a fast pace for the next several hours until finally he indicated they would slow down to rest the horses. Other than acknowledging her change in clothing, he hadn't spoken since they left the encampment. His face had assumed a permanent scowl as they rode.

At last, Samantha ventured a question. "Major, you didn't tell me where we're going."

"South."

"Why are we going south? And where, exactly?"

The major turned in his saddle, an exasperated expression on his face. "Your services are again needed. Where isn't important. My guess is that by the time we arrive, the battle will have begun."

"You're taking me to help Confederate troops again?"

"Isn't that obvious?" he asked.

She abruptly halted Kota. "I won't do it," she shouted.

"Yes," he said, "you will."

"You can't make me, Major!"

"Oh, but I can. Do you need to be reminded that you're in the Confederacy? Unless you wish to be handed over as a prisoner of war, you'll do as I tell you."

"You expect me to aid an army of slave owners and traitors who started this war in the first place?" Samantha's voice rose in anger.

The major laughed sarcastically. "Slave owners, indeed. And as to who started this war, may I again remind you that you are in Virginia? We did not invade the North, Dr. Cartier, the North invaded us. Now you either accompany me, or I shall arrest you on the spot."

Samantha's heart pounded beneath the gauze that bound her chest. She squeezed the reins in her hands to hide their trembling from the major's gaze. Instinctively, she glanced to the left then right.

"Don't try it, Sam. I'd have to shoot you as an escaped prisoner."

His eyes were cold as they bore into her, his right hand resting on his thigh next to his Colt six-shot revolver. "Will you come along peacefully?" he asked.

Samantha opened her mouth to respond, but her throat was dry. She turned away as she felt tears of fear and frustration threatening. She simply nodded her head.

"Stay next to me," he ordered. Again, she nodded her head in acquiescence.

Samantha didn't have to be told that they were approaching their destination that afternoon. By now, she recognized the sound of incessant gunfire and knew what misery followed. This time, the major didn't take her to the surgical tent but kept her with him as he rode over to the general's staff. The officers were mounted and watching the battle from behind the lines. One of the generals nodded to Major Ethan Winters-Hunt.

"Ethan," he said in greeting, "they came at us at dawn

this morning."

"Who's over there?" the major asked.

"General Hancock has about twenty thousand Yankees, or at least he had that many. The Yankees made it to our log breastworks, but Gordon's men pushed them back again."

The battle went on, surging back and forth all day as ground was gained and then lost again. Samantha was safely out of the range of the musket fire but close enough to see the horror played out in front of her. She watched as rank after rank of Union soldiers was riddled by shot, shell, and bayonet thrusts. Still, the Union soldiers advanced and were cut down, their mangled corpses falling on those who had gone before them. Hundreds of men fell in front of her, the sound of cannon fire deafening and the smell of powder burning her nostrils. All she could do was watch quietly. She sat there stone-faced, only her eyes betraying her grief.

By the next morning, surgical tents were set up a safe distance from the fighting, and the wounded began to be brought in. In that first day alone, both armies had lost twelve thousand men. When Samantha entered the tent, she did not hesitate, nor did she ask for ether, chloroform, or morphine for the pain, for she knew there was none.

Ethan made his way through the exhausted soldiers. There were thousands of them sitting around small fires, their eyes vacant, their clothes covered in dirt and gunpowder. A few had bloody bandages wrapped around their heads and arms—their wounds had not been severe enough to prevent them from fighting. After three days of battle, the Federal troops had withdrawn and a deathly silence had fallen over the area.

Ethan dismounted in front of the general's tent.

"Major," a staff member said as Ethan handed him his

reins. "He's expecting you."

Ethan nodded and pushed the tent flap aside.

"Ethan," General Lee said in greeting as he glanced up from a map he was examining.

"General," Ethan said.

"I need your help," the general said without preamble. "I need supplies. I don't have enough food for my men. I need decent food and ammunition."

"Our ports are all but cut off by the Federal ships, General. Fewer and fewer of my ships are able to get through," Ethan said.

"I've got to get supplies."

Ethan shook his head and then paused. "Not by sea, but there's another way."

Lee looked up quizzically.

"A few of the Georgia and South Carolina planters are able to send their cotton northward and receive goods and gold in return. They appear to be prospering."

"How?"

"Bribery. They send it overland, using contacts to bribe people on both sides of the line, North and South."

Lee's face darkened. "My men are eating worm-infested hardtack, marching in boots that even a slave would discard, and you're saying that some of our countrymen are profiting during this?"

"A few are, General."

"Find their connections, Ethan. Threaten to expose them if you must, but get me those supplies."

Ethan sighed. It would not be easy. He knew those men and despised them.

"I would go to see them myself if I were not needed here," Lee said.

"I know, General. I'll do what I can."

Samantha hadn't slept in days, her mind and body numbed by the grueling demand of almost two weeks of slaughter. Finally, under cover of darkness, Grant withdrew his troops, leaving behind thousands of dead. When she emerged from the surgical tent, the last soldier treated, the stench of rotting corpses penetrated her consciousness, bodies bloated, mangled, their humanness unrecognizable. She unconsciously pulled the collar of her shirt over her nose and stood there, feeling nothing. Once again, the major found her.

"This way, Sam," he said as he placed his hand on her shoulder. She didn't resist, but walked mutely beside him, guided by his hand, until they reached their horses.

As they were about to mount, Samantha turned back to the scene behind her. "Where are we, Major?" she asked, her voice barely above a whisper.

"A little town called Spotsylvania."

"No, I mean this place—here."

"They're calling it Bloody Angle now." His voice hardened. "Over twenty thousand men died here. They're still burying the dead. It could be thirty thousand."

Samantha turned in silence and mounted Kota.

"Sam, can you ride?" the major asked as he mounted his horse. "Can you make it through the afternoon? We'll stop for the night."

"I'll go with you, Major," she said softly. "I don't have the strength to escape, if that's what you're concerned about, and I prefer not to be among those buried in the trenches today. I'll treat your wounded, but you can't keep me a captive forever. Sooner or later, the opportunity will present itself, and I'll escape and make my way to the Union forces."

"I'll keep that in mind," he said. "But for now, I think you've done enough. We're not going with the others. We're going to Charleston. I have some business to attend to, and you need to rest."

Samantha came fully alert. "We're going to South Carolina?" she asked. The last thing she wanted was to be plunged deeper into the South. "Why?"

"One of our prominent widows is planning a social event for South Carolina's finest families—all to raise much-needed funds for the Confederacy. My presence is requested," he said with a hint of anger. "Let's go, and Sam, stay close to me," he ordered as they headed first west and then turned south to avoid the two great armies that were now racing to a crossroads called Cold Harbor.

CHAPTER 3

It took two weeks for Samantha and Major Ethan Winters-Hunt to reach Charleston. The first few days, Samantha had been exhausted and said very little. The major set an arduous pace, sleeping on the ground at night and riding from sunrise to sunset each day.

By the second week, although their pace had not slowed, Samantha was recovering from the physical and emotional ordeal of the battles. The deeper they penetrated into the South, however, the more uneasy she became. The major indicated they would refresh their supplies as they entered a small town. They dismounted and walked into a dry goods store.

"Keep quiet," the major warned.

Several men were discussing the latest act of the Confederate Congress. Their anger was obvious as they thrashed out the new Impressment Act, a law that empowered the army to take male slaves as laborers, paying a monthly fee to their masters. The man standing closest to Samantha and the major turned to them and spoke.

"You, sir, you don't look familiar," the man said. "You from around here?"

"No, sir," the major responded. "I'm from Charleston."

"So is South Carolina going to agree to this Impressment Act?" the man asked.

Before the major could answer, another man spoke. "The governor will refuse to sign this, just as he refused to sign

The Conscription Act. No congress or Jeff Davis can tell North Carolina what to do."

"I only have eight Negroes anyway," another said. "I can't spare them. Let the army take them from the big planters."

"What is South Carolina gonna do?" a man again asked the major.

"I don't know," Winters-Hunt answered, "but my guess is there will be resistance from the planters."

"Right!" another answered. "Let the congress buy their own niggers if they need them!"

"In God's name, you're talking about people—men, women, and children—not property!"

The room suddenly stilled as every eye turned toward Samantha. She had blurted out her thoughts without thinking or altering her natural Northern accent. A foolish mistake!

"Where you from, boy?" one of the men asked.

"He's not from around here," the major answered in a steady voice. "He's also young and hasn't learned to curb his tongue."

"Sounded like a Yankee boy to me," another said.

"You got something against us, boy?"

"He has nothing against you gentlemen," the major answered. "I think we'll leave before this young pup gets into trouble. You'll forgive him his outburst, I'm sure."

Smoothly, Major Ethan Winters-Hunt reached down to take Samantha's arm. Although the movement was fluid, his grip was like a vice. As he started toward the door, three of the men moved to block his way.

"Excuse me, gentlemen, we would like to pass," the major said. His voice was still calm as he maintained his grip on Samantha with his left hand and let his right hand fall naturally to his side.

"You can go," one of the men said, "but we'd like to talk to the boy."

"That's not possible. I'm expected in Charleston, and the boy comes with me."

One of the men blocking the door reached to withdraw his sidearm. Suddenly, a loud shot rang out, followed by a scream. A gun slid across the floor as its owner gripped his wounded hand. Samantha whipped her head around to see the major holding a pistol. He'd acted so quickly, she hadn't seen him draw his weapon.

"I could have just as easily shot you between the eyes," the major said. "And that's where the next bullet will go." He leveled his gaze on the two remaining men. "Now step aside, gentlemen, and there won't be any more trouble."

The men moved away from the door as the major, his weapon still in hand, pulled Samantha out into the street. By the time she looked back and saw the men emerge from the hotel, she and the major had ridden several blocks away.

Samantha was surprised when, instead of leaving town, the major turned onto another street and stopped in front of a wood-slat building. A sign hung down from the porch roof identifying it as the sheriff's office and jail. The major dismounted and grabbed Samantha roughly, lifting her out of the saddle. Despite her resolve, she began to tremble. She realized her mistake—she should have heeded his warning and kept quiet. Was he going to turn her over to the sheriff? Would the man arrest her? Without speaking, the major walked her up to the door, pushed it open, and entered.

"Are you the sheriff?" the major asked a man sitting behind a desk.

"Yes, sir, what can I do for you?"

"Sheriff, my name is Ethan Winters-Hunt. I'm traveling to Charleston. I'm also a major in the Confederate Army, reporting directly to General Lee." To Samantha's surprise, the major explained all that had just transpired in the hotel. "I have business to attend to on the general's behalf and do not wish to be bothered with watching my back the rest of the journey. I trust you can see that that will not occur?"

The sheriff eyed the major before he spoke. "You got any proof you are who you say you are?"

The major withdrew a sheet of paper from his pocket. The sheriff studied it and then handed it back.

"I'm sorry for the trouble, Major," he answered at last. "As you know, things have been rough around here and people are edgy. I'll go over to the hotel now and attend to the matter."

The major nodded to the sheriff and then guided Samantha back out the door and to her horse. This time, they did leave town. Samantha was nervous as she mounted Kota, but one look at Winters-Hunt discouraged her from speaking to him.

The major led the way out of town at a gallop. Samantha glanced behind her several times to be certain they weren't being followed; the major didn't look back once, but instead focused his eyes forward. Samantha wanted to say something to him, but his stony silence did not invite conversation.

They had ridden at a fast pace for almost an hour when the major indicated they were stopping on the side of the road. Dismounting, he again reached up and surprised Samantha by jerking her completely off of the saddle. In a swift movement, he went down on one knee and flung her over the other. When his hand first struck the back of her trousers, she was so shocked, she couldn't speak. The second time, the pain and indignity made her cry out. She struggled as his bare hand again slapped against her breeches. His other hand gripped her so tightly that she couldn't free herself. Again, she felt the sting and humiliation of his hand.

"Let go of me!" she screamed between sobs.

The major ignored her protests as she struggled and twisted to no avail. His grip didn't loosen as his hand came down again. When at last he stopped, he sat her roughly down on the ground. Her face was streaked with tears, more from anger and indignation than from any hurt his hand inflicted.

"If you insist on acting like a schoolboy, that's how you'll be treated," the major shouted. "You could have gotten us killed back there! Those men are full of hatred and prejudice. You can't reason with them. They'd feel fully justified in killing you *for the cause*. You do something so foolish again, and I just might turn you over to them. Now get on your horse and let's get out of here!"

He swung up into his saddle, his steely eyes still carrying a threat. Samantha seethed with hatred. Never in her life had she been handled in such a manner. It was only the look on the major's face that stopped her from saying what she wanted to. She jerked on Kota's bridle as she mounted, causing the horse to sidestep in protest. Involuntarily, she cried out as she sat down in the saddle, her backside still stinging.

For the next three days, Samantha refused to speak to the major. He seemed lost in thought, so the two barely communicated as they traveled. They stopped at two more towns before arriving in Charleston. Each time, he warned her about her behavior. The threat was clear, and Samantha was quiet while they ate and replenished their supplies. When at last they reached Charleston, she was relieved. Perhaps now she would not have to keep such close quarters with Major Winters-Hunt.

It was almost sunset, and Samantha saw late sunlight reflecting off the tall spires of the numerous churches. There was a distant thunder and a rumble, causing Samantha to involuntarily flinch in the saddle and turn anxiously to the major as he dismounted.

"Federal gunboats," he said in answer to her unexpressed question. "Federal ships block the harbor and have been pounding away at the city for some time."

"Federal gunboats?" Samantha asked with surprise.

"Don't get your hopes up, Sam," he said. The major's expression darkened. "Charleston is not ready to surrender to the Yankees yet."

Samantha dismounted and followed the major into a brick building. Inside, he walked across the lobby of the small hotel and approached a middle-aged woman standing behind the reception desk.

"Mr. Winters-Hunt! I wasn't informed that you were expected," the woman said. "We're pleased to have you join us again."

"Good evening, Mrs. Lynch. My plans were made in haste, and I had little time to make arrangements. I trust I can still find a room for a few days?" the major asked.

"But of course!" The woman looked at Samantha. "There will be two of you?"

"Yes," he answered.

"If you like, you can have your usual room," Mrs. Lynch offered.

"I would like my own room," Samantha interjected.

The major turned and frowned at her.

"I can pay for it myself," Samantha said.

Mrs. Lynch looked expectantly at Major Ethan Winters-Hunt.

"I think it would be best if you were to stay with me," he said to Samantha.

The warning in his tone did not escape Samantha. Still, she persisted. It was one thing to share a tent for a few days or to sleep on the ground next to him while traveling, but she was not about to share a hotel room and bed with this man.

The major turned to Mrs. Lynch. "My usual room will suffice," he said.

"Wait!" Samantha said as she placed her hand on his arm. She swallowed as he turned an icy look upon her. "Please," she said quietly as she removed her hand from his arm. "I will follow your orders, Major. You have my word on it. Just let me have my own room."

Major Winters-Hunt studied her face. "Your word?" he asked.

"Yes, sir," she said.

The major turned back to the woman behind the counter. "Mrs. Lynch, do you perhaps have two adjoining rooms?"

The woman smiled. "Several. Business has been terrible. I think I know just what you want."

She opened the ledger and handed it to the major while she secured the keys for the two rooms. He signed his name and then handed the pen to Samantha. She was so grateful at that moment that she smiled timidly and signed her name. When Mrs. Lynch returned, she placed both keys on the desk.

"Will you need help with your bags, Mr. Winters-Hunt?"

"No, thank you. We can manage. I'll see that the boy is settled, and then I'll be back down."

Samantha followed the major up the wide stairs to the second floor. He found the rooms easily. He unlocked the first door and stepped inside. Samantha followed him. He crossed to the door adjoining the two rooms and turned to Samantha.

"You may have your choice of rooms, Sam."

He stepped aside to allow Samantha to enter the next room. Both rooms looked comfortable. A brass bed, lace curtains at the windows, a wardrobe, and small writing desk furnished each room.

"This one is fine," Samantha said.

"I have some business to attend to," he said as he turned to leave. "I'll see that the horses are cared for and find some clothes for you. I'll probably be away a couple of hours. I'll have Mrs. Lynch bring a bath up to your room."

"Thank you," Samantha said quietly.

She heard him close the door of his room, and then the key turned in the lock. He left the door between their two rooms open. She cautiously stepped into his room and walked over to the door and turned the knob. Just as she suspected, that door was locked also.

"Bastard," she ground out between her teeth as she returned to the confines of her room. A few minutes later, there was a knock at her door.

"Mr. Cartier? It's Mrs. Lynch. May I bring the tub in now?"

"Yes, of course," Samantha answered from across the room.

Mrs. Lynch unlocked the door and ushered two young boys into the room. They were straining to carry the copper tub between them. Following her instructions, they placed the tub in the center of the room and then left. Mrs. Lynch smiled warmly at Samantha.

"Mr. Winters-Hunt said that you've been separated from your family and that he's looking out for you."

The woman seemed to be waiting for a response from Samantha. Samantha wasn't quite certain of what the major had told the woman, so she shrugged her shoulder. "I was lost and found myself in the middle of a battleground. The major helped me." Samantha had to admit that was the truth, even though she couldn't wait to get away from Major Ethan Winters-Hunt.

"He's a good and honorable man," Mrs. Lynch said. "I can't say that about a lot of the other wealthy planters in this area."

Mrs. Lynch stopped talking as the two boys returned, each carrying two large buckets of water. She watched as they poured the water into the tub and then left. A minute later, one of the boys returned, carrying an armful of clothes.

"Mr. Winters-Hunt's things go in the next room," she instructed the boy.

Samantha watched as the boy carried the clothing into the next room and carefully hung the items in the armoire.

"Mr. Winters-Hunt often has business in the city," Mrs. Lynch volunteered. "His plantation is several hours' ride from here, so he keeps a room and clothing here in the event that he must stay for several days. I had my son bring Mr. Winters-Hunt's shaving items as well. I'm sure he wouldn't mind if you used them. There are plenty of fresh linens and soap on the dressing table. Is there anything else that you need?"

"No, ma'am. This is fine. Thank you," Samantha answered.

"My boy will bring your supper up to you. You go ahead and climb into that tub while the water is nice and hot." She smiled warmly at Samantha and left the room.

Samantha noticed that Mrs. Lynch did not lock the door as she closed it. Was this the opportunity that Samantha was waiting for? But where would she go? How could she get past the lobby? And what about the major? Hadn't she given him her word that she would not try to escape?

She was thinking about this when there was a timid knock at the door. A boy entered and carried a tray over to the desk and set it down. He nodded to Samantha and then left. This time, when the door closed, Samantha heard the key turn, locking the door.

Her anger flared again when she thought of the major taking her across his knee. One thing was for certain: she could not make any more foolish mistakes. Once again, she had to admit that her father and Many Horses were right—she was impulsive. And Many Horses said she needed to learn restraint. In the meantime, she had at least an hour or more before she would be disturbed. She was so tired and hot. The bath was more than she could resist.

Samantha found everything she needed, just as Mrs. Lynch said. She removed her clothing and unwound the gauze. Her skin was irritated and reddened where the gauze had been in place for several weeks, and the past few days it had itched and burned as they rode. In this heat and humidity, she was going to have to find a way of removing the gauze periodically to prevent excoriation of her skin. She knew the soldiers used a talc powder in their underwear to prevent the same skin condition. She could ask Dr. Beauregard for the powder, but she didn't know when she would see him again. That left Major Winters-Hunt. She felt her face flush at the thought of asking him.

Just before she climbed into the large tub, Samantha looked around the room. It probably wouldn't stop him, but she took a chair and wedged the back of it under the knob of the door connecting the rooms. If the major returned early, he would have to go back out into the hall to enter her room, and that would give her the few minutes she would need to cover herself.

Finally, she stepped into the tub and eased herself down into the hot water. How long had it been since she had taken a real bath? She took her time washing her hair, inspecting it for lice, and scrubbing the paste off her face.

She winced involuntarily as she touched the irritation the paste had caused. She had managed to avoid getting the body lice that were the scourge of the unbathed soldiers. Satisfied that there were no vermin, she relaxed in the water, letting its warmth ease her tired muscles. When she thought that she could risk it no longer, she stepped out and dried herself. She didn't dress immediately but wrapped the large towel around herself and sat down to eat.

After she finished eating, she retrieved the gauze and washed it. If she could find a place for it to dry during the night, then she could put it on in the morning. Would the major come into her room when he returned? She longed to sleep without the paste on her face. Just then, there was a knock at her door.

"Mr. Cartier? It's Mrs. Lynch. May I remove the tub now?"

Samantha panicked. She was still wrapped in the towel and had not replaced her mustache or paste. She ran for the bed, slipped under the quilt, and pulled it up over her face.

"Mr. Cartier?"

Samantha heard the key in the lock and then the door opened.

"Mr. Cartier?"

Only the back of Samantha's head was uncovered as she lay still in the bed.

"Oh, dear, he's already asleep. Quietly, boys, take the tub into Mr. Winters-Hunt's room and heat some more water. Bring the tray out also," Mrs. Lynch instructed her sons. She crossed the room to where Samantha had placed the chair to secure the door between the two bedrooms. "Now what's this doing here?" she asked.

Samantha heard the woman move the chair and then a thump as she placed it with the desk. Then Samantha listened to the sound of the heavy copper tub being dragged into the next room. The door to Samantha's room closed, and she heard the key being turned in the lock. After waiting a few minutes, she cautiously peered out from under the blanket.

The room was dark. The only light was the moonlight filtering through the lace curtains and a soft, yellow glow coming from the major's room. Mrs. Lynch had extinguished the lamps in Samantha's room. It worked! Since she'd fooled Mrs. Lynch, perhaps she could fool the major, too. If she just kept herself covered up, he, too, would probably leave her alone. She longed to sleep one night without the paste and gauze.

She got up just once more to place her clothing and paste mixture on the floor under the bed. If she did need to dress quickly, she could. She also stretched the gauze out under the bed to dry. After weeks without bathing and wearing the same clothes, the clean sheets and soft bed felt wonderful against her naked body.

She was so tired. The strain of the last month had been almost more than she could bear. The last thing she did was to close the door between the rooms. She didn't place the chair against it. That would only serve to increase the major's curiosity.

Samantha had been more exhausted than she realized and quickly fell asleep. It was several hours later when the dream returned to her: men screamed in pain and begged her to stop as she amputated the leg or arm of one soldier after another. She looked down at her hands, and they were covered with blood—the blood of men and boys, suffering. She began to cry. Her cries brought the major to her side.

"Sam?"

The nightmare was broken, except for the visions that always persisted for some time afterward. Ever since that first night after the battle at the Wilderness, her sleep had been deeply troubled. Even when she and the major were traveling, the nightmare had come when they were camping. He had awakened her then, just as he was trying to do now.

Samantha suddenly remembered where she was. The major had returned! She pulled her blanket over her face.

"Sam? Are you all right?"

"Go away, Major," she said from under the blanket.

"Sam, you had the nightmare again, didn't you?"

"Just leave me alone."

Samantha's voice was muffled from her crying as well as trying to control her fear as she lay under the blanket. She could feel his presence by the bed. Then she heard his soft footsteps as he retraced his steps. She listened until, at last, she thought she heard the creak of his bed. Slowly, she lowered the blanket.

The room was empty. He had left. Samantha wiped her tears away and lay back against the pillow. She was still trembling as she waited for the visions of the soldiers' pain and anguish to fade from her mind. She raised her hands up and examined them in the pale moonlight, looking for traces of blood. That was when she noticed that the major had left the door connecting the rooms open. For some reason she couldn't explain, she took comfort in that.

Samantha awoke to unfamiliar noises. She sat up and gazed about the room. The sounds were coming from the next room. The major! He must already be awake. She'd planned on waking up early so that she could be dressed and have her disguise in place before he saw her. She noticed a pile of clothing on the chair. As quietly as she could, she wrapped the gauze around her breasts, dressed, reapplied the paste mixture on her face, and secured the mustache in place. When she pulled her hair back and tied it at the base of her neck with the rawhide strip, she once again looked like a boy. Samantha took a deep breath to steady herself and then walked hesitantly into the major's room. Major Ethan Winters-Hunt was standing before a mirror. He was dressed in his pants and boots but naked above the waist. As he dipped his razor in the water, he spoke.

"I see the clothes fit. Good. I wasn't certain. Very few of the tailors have received any dry goods for a long time. Most of what you see here is homespun."

He returned to shaving. Involuntarily, Samantha found herself watching him. His hair and mustache were dark, and his pants had obviously been cut to fit him. He was wearing black cavalry boots that glistened as though they were new. Samantha's eyes traveled back to his face reflected in the mirror and the startling clear blue of his eyes.

"You may use the razor if you'd like, Sam."

"No, thank you, Major, but I appreciate the clothes. I can pay you for them," Samantha offered.

"That's not necessary. I'm sorry they're not of better quality."

The major turned and walked over to the bed where his shirt and coat lay. As he finished dressing, he spoke again.

"Did you sleep well?"

"It was fine." Samantha hesitated. "I'm sorry I woke you during the night."

"No apology is necessary. Let's go," he said as he opened the door.

The first place that Major Winters-Hunt took Samantha was to a dining room in a larger hotel. After they finished eating, he indicated that they would walk. As they began to make their way toward the harbor, the first shell exploded, shaking the ground. Involuntarily, Samantha flinched. Cannon fire meant death and dismemberment.

"Relax, Sam," the major said. "They're firing on the forts

and the battery. They aren't in range for this part of the town."

Again, the thunder of the cannons rang in her ears.

"Who's firing?" she asked.

"The Federal Navy. It's been this way for almost two years. You'll see as we near the docks."

Samantha wanted to ask more, but there was anger in his voice. She was quiet as they walked, although she still flinched each time the cannons discharged. As they continued, she saw the effects of the two-year siege. Near the hotel, the buildings hosted graceful wrought-iron fences and balconies. Many of the houses were painted a sparkling white with verandahs that nestled among the trees. Cobblestone streets ran along houses with stone walls that enclosed gardens with arched entrances. Numerous church spires reached up to the clouds.

But as she approached the water, the scene began to change. Piles of bricks lay where buildings once stood. Large holes scarred the streets. The remains of chimneys stood stark and alone. As they drew closer to the battery, the shelling became louder and destruction was everywhere. Complete sections had been leveled by the Union cannons, and the major seemed intent on walking right into the cannon fire.

"Shouldn't we turn back?" Samantha asked.

"Not yet. I want to see what's left of the docks."

When they reached the harbor, the major stopped. His face was grim as he surveyed the devastation. The docks were completely destroyed, their planks floating in the harbor. Entire wharves were blown away.

Samantha was now close enough to see the Union gunboats just outside Charleston Harbor. She saw a fort on a small island at the entrance to the harbor. "What's that?" she asked, pointing to it.

He didn't answer immediately, but Samantha saw his jaw tense. He turned and leveled cold eyes on her. "That's Fort Sumter," he said.

Suddenly, Samantha understood. "This is where it all started! Charleston fired on the Federal forces here," she said as she turned back to look at the distant fort being pummeled by Union gunboats. "I'm sorry for the destruction I see here. I can tell that this was once a beautiful city, but Major," she said, looking directly at him, "what did you expect? You, South Carolina, started this war."

The look on the major's face caused Samantha to step back from him. When he spoke, it sent a chill through her. "If you wish to remain alive, I'd suggest you avoid making remarks like that while you are here."

He spun around and retraced his steps in a rapid stride. Samantha had to break into a run to keep up with him. When they returned to the hotel, she could tell that he was still angry as he maintained his pace across the lobby and up the steps to their rooms. He unlocked the door and stepped inside. Samantha followed.

"I still have matters to attend to. I think you should stay here the rest of the afternoon. I'll have Mrs. Lynch bring a meal to you and anything else that you may need. I shall return in plenty of time for us to leave this evening."

"Where are we going tonight?" she asked.

"There's a dinner party being given by Mrs. Cooper, a widow of one of our illustrious Confederate officers. I'm expected. I'll give you a choice, Sam. You may remain restricted to this room for the next week, or you will curb your tongue, conduct yourself as a gentleman, and accompany me. The choice is yours."

Samantha's afternoon passed slowly. There was nothing

to do in the room. Mrs. Lynch brought a meal to her. The rest of the time she spent pacing and looking out the window. She tried to lie down to rest but couldn't sleep. When at last she heard the major's door open, she resisted the impulse to knock on the adjoining door or call out to him. It was another thirty minutes before he opened the door and entered her room. He quickly appraised her appearance.

"So you've decided to come with me tonight," he said. "I expect you to remember that you are a guest in Mrs. Cooper's home and to behave accordingly."

"I know how to conduct myself in proper society, Rebel," Samantha said through clenched teeth.

The major seemed surprised at her response, and then he smiled. "Very well, Sam. I'll hold you to that."

"Are you going to tell me anything about this party we're going to?" she asked.

"What would you like to know?" he asked as they descended the steps.

"Where are we going? Who's going to be there? Why are we going?"

"Stop," he said, laughing. "You're going to make me think you're a spy after all."

They walked to the small stables at the back of the hotel where their horses were boarded. "Caroline Cooper is an old friend of mine," the major said. "We grew up together. She married a planter who was killed at the Battle of Second Manassas. He was older than she, but of course, I knew him also. She's been financially supportive of the Confederacy and is hosting a party for several of the large planters from South Carolina and Georgia. Actually, it's more than just a party. Because of the distance some have traveled, they will stay several days."

The major's voice lost its lightheartedness as he

continued. "Sam, these men are rich and powerful. They have more to do with the ultimate success of the Confederacy than does Jefferson Davis or the Confederate Congress. But they're a self-serving group of men who owe allegiance only to themselves and their way of life."

"It doesn't sound as though you think much of them," Samantha ventured.

"I don't, but I don't underestimate their power."

"Then why are you going if you don't like them?"

"Business," was all he said.

"So all of these men are going to be together discussing business," Samantha said as they rode next to each other, leaving Charleston behind them.

The major laughed. "No, Sam, not at all. It's a social occasion, at least on the surface. Food, drink, dancing. . . ."

"Oh, no," Samantha groaned.

"Cheer up, Sam. You'll undoubtedly be surrounded by pretty young women clamoring for your attention. A word of caution, though." Once again, his voice became firm. "In the South, there are certain unspoken rules. Young ladies are expected to remain chaste until they wed. Should you engage a young lady in conversation, a chaperone should always be present. I expect you to remember that. I don't want to find myself dueling with some belle's father because you've soiled his daughter."

Samantha was dumbfounded. At first, she hadn't understood his implication. When she did, she felt her face flush. "You need not worry, Major!"

Riding at a leisurely pace for an hour, they reached the Cooper plantation. They turned off the narrow road onto a lane that stretched a half mile, leading to the main house. Along the sides of the lane stood rows of oak trees that formed a canopy over the lane, blocking out the hot sun.

The symmetry was broken occasionally by sunshine where bare tree trunks stood, their branches broken over the years by strong winds.

"What do we do first?" Samantha asked as they neared the great house.

"There's still some sunlight left. They probably have tables assembled outside for dining. Later, when it's dark, everyone will move inside for dancing."

When they emerged from the lane, Samantha could see the house clearly. It was beautiful. It stood gracefully, surrounded by the green of the trees. It was white with massive white columns that spanned the front and sides of the house, extending from the ground to the top of the two-story structure. The windows and doors of the second floor opened out onto a balcony that was also supported by the columns. The porch stretched out the length and sides of the house on the lower level. In the middle of the front of the house, the porch extended outward in a semicircle, its shape defined by the columns that also supported the curve in the balcony above. It created an impressive entrance to the house.

When they stopped in front of the house, two Negroes came to take their horses. The major dismounted and handed the reins to one of the men. Samantha hesitated, feeling Kota's reluctance to be led by a stranger. The horse pranced nervously as she dismounted.

"Major, would it be possible for me to see that Kota is settled first?"

Winters-Hunt cocked his head, appraising her, and then glanced at Kota. "Of course, Sam. You take good care of your horse," he said kindly. "That's admirable." He turned to one of the livery men. "Would you see that Dr. Cartier finds his way back to me?"

"Yes'ur," the man answered.

Samantha followed as the Negro led the way around the house to the stables. Since some of the guests were staying the night, stable and pasture space had been provided for their horses. Samantha led Kota into the stall provided and removed his tack. A man appeared with a bucket of water and grain.

When Samantha was assured that Kota was settled, she returned to where she had left the major. Tables had been arranged under the shade of the trees, and people walked about the broad expanse of lawn. To the side of the house was a flower garden where couples strolled. The women wore dresses with wide hoopskirts; most of them carried matching parasols, creating a sea of soft pastel colors blending in with the idyllic setting.

Samantha searched among the faces for Major Ethan Winters-Hunt. Most of the men were dressed in the uniforms of Confederate officers. The remaining men were older and dressed in formal civilian clothes like the major wore: dark frock coat, waistcoat, and trousers, with elaborate cravats, a few wearing top hats. The contrast of the dark clothing of the men only enhanced the light, airy dress of the women.

It wasn't difficult to find the major. Samantha's attention was diverted, however, to a woman who had possessively taken his arm. A strange sensation came over Samantha as she watched. The woman must have just said something amusing, for the major tipped his head back and laughed. Then he smiled at her.

As they turned, Samantha was able to see the woman's face. She was wearing a wide-brimmed hat that shaded her skin from the sun but still revealed her creamy-white complexion and golden hair. The peach of her gown and matching hat accentuated the pale of her cheeks. The woman stretched up to whisper something in the major's ear. As she did, her wide hoopskirt raised up a little, revealing peach-colored slippers.

The image of the two of them together disturbed Samantha, and she was standing there with a scowl on her face when the major saw her. He motioned with his hand and guided the woman over to where Samantha was standing.

"Sam," he said as he approached, "I would like you to meet your hostess." Turning to the beautiful woman at his side, the major said, "This is the young man I was telling you about, Sam Cartier. Sam, this is Mrs. Cooper."

The woman turned to Samantha and offered her hand. There was an awkward moment as Samantha stood there until the major nudged her. Samantha tore her gaze away from the beautiful woman to look at him. His look of displeasure momentarily confused her. Then she realized her error. She was supposed to take the woman's hand in hers and bow over it. Samantha awkwardly reached for her hand.

Caroline Cooper smiled at Samantha. "Dr. Cartier, or may I call you 'Sam'? I'm pleased that you could join us today. Ethan has been telling me all about you. He says that you're a very skillful surgeon and doctor. That's quite an accomplishment in one so young. We're beholden to you."

Even her speech was perfect. Her soft, Southern accent was charming as she graciously welcomed Samantha.

"Sam?"

The warning note in the major's voice caught Samantha's attention. She frowned and looked to the major. It was clear he expected her to say something.

"Thank you," Samantha said reticently.

"We were just about to sit down to eat," Mrs. Cooper said smoothly, the smile still on her face. "Why don't you join us? I'm certain I can find some young lady close to your age who would enjoy meeting you."

Caroline Cooper still had her hand on the major's arm as she turned to gracefully take Samantha's in her other.

"Thank you, Mrs. Cooper, but that won't be necessary," Samantha said.

"No? Well, perhaps later when the dancing starts. This way," she said kindly as she indicated the tables that were beginning to fill with guests.

Samantha was quiet throughout the meal. The conversation revolved around the war, especially the Confederate victories. As the sun began to set, Mrs. Cooper indicated that the guests should move inside. Samantha was sullen as she walked beside the major, Mrs. Cooper having temporarily left the major's side to see that all was ready for the guests. A large room in the front of the house had been cleared of its furniture, with the exception of a few chairs that lined the walls. At the end of the room, musicians assembled and were beginning to play the soft strains of their music. Across the wide central hall, another room held a table with more food and drink for the guests to avail themselves of during the evening.

Samantha was watching the proceedings when an officer approached the major. "Good evening, Major Winters-Hunt," he greeted.

"Good evening, Major Clark," Winters-Hunt said. The two men shook hands and then Winters-Hunt turned to Samantha. "Sam, this is Major Clark. He commands a garrison in Charleston. Major Clark, may I present Dr. Sam Cartier?"

"Pleased to meet you, Major Clark," Samantha responded without altering her Northern accent.

Major Clark looked with surprise at Samantha. Then he extended his hand to her. "Dr. Cartier," he said as he nodded his head in greeting and then turned back to Winters-Hunt. "Major, forgive me for being blunt, but I understand that you're looking into other possible means of securing supplies," Major Clark said.

"Yes," Winters-Hunt replied.

"I was authorized to draw up a list indicating the items most needed and the disposition of the various armies." Major Clark withdrew a paper and handed it to Major Ethan Winters-Hunt. "Do you have any idea how long it might take?"

Winters-Hunt's face turned grim as he looked at the list. "The congress can't supply any of this?" he asked.

"The congress is broke. You know that, sir. That idiot, Treasury Secretary Memminger, is cranking out millions of Confederate dollars, and there's no gold to back up the script. Our Confederate dollars are worthless. I don't need to tell you, sir, how desperately we need arms and ammunition. Since we have no means to manufacture them in the South, they must come from elsewhere. We also need food and clothing." Major Clark cleared his throat to cover his embarrassment. "General Lee's aide prepared this list. I'm sorry, sir. The general didn't provide any means of paying you."

"Have you approached anyone else here?" Major Winters-Hunt asked pointedly.

"No," Major Clark replied. "I was directed to give this only to you."

Winters-Hunt sighed as he examined the list. "It will take time. How are these to be transported?"

"I'll make the arrangements. Contact me as soon as you have anything, and I'll see that the goods are routed to the appropriate armies. General Lee especially wants Richmond reinforced."

"And Atlanta?" Ethan Winters-Hunt asked.

"General Sherman's army left Chattanooga three weeks ago and is moving toward Atlanta. Joseph Johnston's army is between Sherman's and Atlanta. General Johnston is outnumbered two-to-one," Major Clark said grimly.

Major Winters-Hunt sighed. "I'll send word as soon as I've secured the supplies," he said.

"Thank you, sir."

Samantha watched Major Clark walk away to join his officers, and then she turned to Major Winters-Hunt, his face grim. Then he looked past her, and his expression changed from a troubled one to a relaxed smile as Caroline Cooper approached.

"Ethan, aren't you going to ask me to dance?" Mrs. Cooper smiled prettily at him.

"It would be my pleasure," he said as he escorted her to the center of the room.

Samantha watched as the major took Mrs. Cooper in his arms. She realized for the first time how strikingly handsome he was. He was tall and well-muscled, and yet he moved gracefully about the floor. His dark hair and mustache contrasted with Caroline Cooper's fair complexion. She found herself unable to tear her gaze away from him.

As Sam Cartier, she had seen Major Winters-Hunt as both her enemy and protector. She feared him but, strangely enough, also trusted him. Uncomfortable with her conflicting emotions, she walked out into the wide central hall. To the left was the main door, where she slipped out unnoticed.

It was dark already, and the sky was clear. Torches had been placed in the yard where the dinner had been served earlier. She made her away around the great house and past the kitchen building in the back until she came to the stable. It was dark inside, but she easily found Kota's stall. The horse nuzzled her as she petted his neck and murmured to him, drawing comfort from his nearness—he was home, he was family. Assured that he was all right, she left the stable and stood outside in the moonlight.

She heard voices beyond the stable and turned in that direction. Even in the dark, she could see rows of diminutive buildings with people walking between them. Small fires burned outside some of the cabins, illuminating the faces of the Negroes. Samantha approached the slave quarters. Several of the men and women turned to stare at her as she walked between the rows of cabins, but no one stopped her or questioned her.

She had almost reached the end of the row and was ready to turn back when she heard someone scream within one of the cabins. She could see light coming from the open door, and several men were standing outside. Again, there was a scream—the scream of a woman.

Samantha rapidly crossed over to the cabin. The men in the open doorway blocked her view. She could hear the muffled groaning of someone inside as she hesitantly stepped nearer to the men.

Again, a scream, and then other female voices drifted out the door.

"What's happening here?" Samantha demanded of the men.

They shifted uneasily. One of them finally spoke. "It's Chloe, Mas'sir. It's her time."

Samantha pushed the men aside and stepped into the dimly lit cabin. Three Negro women turned to face her.

"Mas'sir, you don't belong here now," the larger one said firmly.

A strangled cry pierced the still air in the cabin.

"The hell I don't!" Samantha swore and stepped around the women.

There, lying on a cot in the corner of the cabin, was a woman. Her clothing had been removed, her swollen belly glistening in the candlelight. Samantha's mind immediately took in the bloody clothes beneath the woman. She crossed the short distance to the corner of the cabin and knelt beside her. As she placed her hand on the woman's enlarged abdomen, she felt the muscles contract as the woman again cried out.

"How long has she been in labor?" Samantha asked.

No one answered.

"Give me that candle!" Samantha ordered.

The three women stared at her.

"Now!"

The large woman reluctantly handed the candle to Samantha. Samantha moved to the end of the cot, illuminating the writhing woman. She gasped when she saw the small foot of the unborn infant protruding from the birth canal.

"God Almighty! How long has she been like this?" Samantha turned sharply to the large Negro woman.

"Just a few minutes, Mas'sir. It's no use. She gonna die. You go on now. Please, Mas'sir. Leave her in peace."

Samantha didn't hear the Negro's last words. Her mind clicked with the precision she had developed the past two years. She knelt beside the struggling woman on the cot. The infant's leg still had good color. That meant that the cord had not become wrapped around its neck and that the birth process had not, as of yet, stimulated the infant to take a breath. If the placenta was still attached, they still had some time, provided the mother was not hemorrhaging.

She turned to the large Negro woman behind her. "Send someone to the stables where my horse is. You can't miss him. He's a large black horse. There's a bag with my saddle. It contains my medical instruments. I also need clean linen, a bowl with fresh water, and soap. Everything must be very clean, do you understand?"

The woman was standing there, a look of shock on her

face. Samantha started to raise her voice and then stopped.

"What's your name?" Samantha asked quietly.

"Bessie, Mas'sir."

"Bessie, I'm a doctor. There's a chance that this woman can live. Can you get the things I asked for? Quickly?"

Bessie hesitated a moment and then called out. "Job!"

A man stepped inside of the cabin.

Bessie repeated Samantha's instructions. "Take Dink with you. One of you go to the kitchen and the other to the stable."

"The linens, bowl, and water must be clean," Samantha again emphasized.

Bessie spoke to the men again and sent them on their way. Samantha went over to the woman who was continually moaning and crying out now.

"What's her name?" Samantha directed over her shoulder to Bessie.

"Chloe," Bessie answered.

"Chloe," Samantha said, stroking the woman's forehead. "I'm a doctor. I'm going to help you. When the pain comes again, don't push. Don't push. Here," she said, motioning for Bessie to come near, "when the pain comes, you hold on real tight to Bessie, but don't push. You hold her hands as hard as you can."

It was less than a minute when the woman screamed and Bessie grabbed her hands. Samantha moved to the end of the cot, resting her hand lightly on the woman's belly. The contractions came two more times before the men returned with Samantha's supplies, and still the infant remained lodged in the birth canal.

Samantha pulled a crude table over to the cot and placed one of the clean cloths on it. Then she removed her instruments from the bag, selecting those that she would need. The air in the small cabin was stifling hot, and perspiration was already dripping down her face. She removed her jacket, wiping it across her forehead, and rolled up her sleeves before scrubbing her hands and washing the woman's belly. When she finished, she turned to Bessie.

"I don't know if this will be successful. She and the baby will die if I don't try. I'm going to remove the baby through her belly by cutting here." Samantha indicated the area as Bessie's eyes widened in shock. "It's going to be very painful for her, but she must not move. You and the other women must hold her still. Do you understand?"

"Mas'sir, you can't. Please," the woman implored.

"She'll die otherwise. Do as I say."

When the women were in position, Samantha picked up her knife. She took a deep breath and calmly laid the blade against the woman's straining skin. With one swift and precise movement, she made a long incision, laying the skin open. She immediately brought the knife up again, cutting and separating the underlying muscle that glistened dark red before her. The tautly stretched muscle willingly split open. There it was! The enlarged womb presented itself.

Samantha had cut so quickly that Chloe was just now beginning to strain and twist against the women holding her. Samantha was dimly aware of the woman's horrible screams as she once again guided her blade. Under other circumstances, she would have taken the time to wipe away the blood at the incision site, but time was of the essence now. She wanted to cut into the womb before its muscles once again contracted.

She pushed her scalpel down and penetrated the womb, slicing it open. There was the infant, with the membrane still covering it. When that last barrier was removed, she put her knife down and gently reached in to take the baby. She was momentarily surprised at the resistance she felt as she tried to maneuver the infant. Slowly, she pulled him up, letting his leg come back through the birth canal, until at last she clasped the child in her hands. No sooner had she held him up than a lusty cry escaped the infant's mouth.

"Sweet Jesus!" Bessie exclaimed as Samantha wrapped a clean cloth around the infant and handed it to Bessie.

Amazingly, Chloe had not lost consciousness. Samantha now turned her attention to the surgical wound, which was bleeding profusely. She tied small vessels to stanch the flow of blood. Samantha's sigh was audible as the placenta separated naturally, leaving no unusual bleeding.

The heat intensified in the small, windowless cabin, and Samantha was beginning to feel dizzy. She had difficulty drawing her breath against the tight gauze. She looked down at her frock coat, waistcoat, and shirt, which were now soaked with Chloe's blood and her own sweat.

"Bessie, don't let anyone enter the cabin. Have the men stand at the door, and no one is to enter. No one!"

"Yes, Mas'sir."

"And stop calling me that."

Bessie went to the door to relay Samantha's orders. When she turned around, her eyes widened in surprise. Samantha removed her blood-soaked shirt and began to unwind the constricting gauze. Modesty was the farthest thing from Samantha's mind at the moment. She knew she still had a lot of work to do, and she needed to be able to breathe. She finished removing the gauze and knelt down again by Chloe. She ignored the shocked look on the women's faces as they stared at her exposed breasts.

"You will have to hold her again," Samantha said to Bessie as she picked up her needle and began the repair.

Chloe lay still as the needle was plunged in, again and again, as Samantha closed first the womb and then the abdominal muscles. She had blood all over her hands and her own chest as she worked, but at least she could breathe now.

Suddenly, there was a commotion outside the cabin, and Samantha looked up in alarm. Bessie ran to the door. A moment later, Samantha recognized the male voice outside.

"Don't let him in!" Samantha whispered fervently to Bessie.

"Sam! Are you in here?" Major Winters-Hunt demanded from outside the cabin.

"Bessie, tell him I'm in here, but there's a woman giving birth."

Bessie went outside and Samantha could hear her speaking.

"Sam! Is this true?" the major shouted into the cabin.

"Of course it's true, Rebel! What did you think I was doing in here?" Samantha yelled back.

Chloe reached out and touched Samantha's arm. "Take the baby to Job. Take him to his daddy," she whispered weakly.

Samantha looked at the woman. She had been so quiet, Samantha was afraid that she was going into shock. Now, Chloe smiled weakly. Samantha nodded as one of the other women took the infant.

"If you insist on staying around, Major, at least you can congratulate the new father," Samantha said as the woman took the baby outside. "I'll be finished soon. You can go back to the house. I know my way back."

There was silence, and then the major answered. "I'll wait for you."

Samantha sighed and returned to her work. She still had the skin to close. When at last she finished, she examined the incision for signs of bleeding. Satisfied that there were none, she felt for Chloe's pulse. It was rapid, but strong. Samantha wrapped a clean cloth around Chloe's abdomen and then stood. She stepped back and let herself slide down to the rough floor of the cabin, leaning her back against the wall. The sweat dripping from her face was burning her eyes, and cautious with the blood covering her hands, she wiped her face against her upper arm.

Bessie turned to her, a ladle in her hand. Samantha gratefully accepted the cool water, drinking deeply as she sat on the floor.

"I ain't never seen nothin' like this! Never!" Bessie exclaimed.

"Sam?" It was the major's voice.

Samantha jumped up. She quickly washed the blood from her hands and chest and picked up the gauze. She frowned as she wound the bloody cloth around her chest. When she had finished, she reached for her shirt.

"You gonna put that on again?" Bessie asked.

"I must. As you've no doubt seen, I'm not who these people think I am."

"You sure ain't!"

Samantha smiled as she put the bloody shirt on and reached for her coat. "I would appreciate it if you say nothing about my disguise."

"You're not from around here, are you, ma'am?"

"No, Bessie, I'm not. I'm from the North."

Bessie's eyes widened. "Why you dressed like this?" she asked, pointing to Samantha's clothing.

"It's a long story. It was the only way that I could study to be a doctor."

"A real doctor!"

"Bessie, Chloe must rest in bed at least two weeks. She needs lots of rest and plenty of good food. Her belly must be kept clean. Don't put anything on those stitches except for clean bandages. She should see a doctor in two weeks to have the stitches taken out."

"Ain't no doctor around."

"There must be someone. Who takes care of Mrs. Cooper?"

"A white doctor in town."

"Well, who takes care of you and the rest of you?" Samantha motioned to the other women in the cabin. "What about when you are sick?"

"We take care of ourselves. I do most of the doctoring."

"I see. I'll talk with Mrs. Cooper." Samantha took Bessie aside and spoke quietly. "Chloe still may not live. Some women develop the fever and die. You'll know in a few days."

"Chloe be dead by now if you hadn't come in. She and her baby, too. I ain't never seen nothin' like that."

Samantha turned to leave. "Remember what I said. Lots of rest and good food and keep her clean. I'm sorry I don't have any medicine to give her for the pain."

Samantha took one last look around the crude interior of the cabin. Then she stepped between the Negro men who were blocking the doorway. One of the men turned to her, holding the infant in his arms.

"Lord bless you, Mas'sir," the man said.

"My name is Sam, not Mas'sir."

"Sam? Sam. This is my son—Sam!" the man said as he held the infant up.

Even in the firelight, Samantha could see that the baby had good color as he slept. She smiled and turned to go. The major was waiting for her.

"You've had quite an evening, Dr. Cartier. Are they going to be all right?" the major asked as they walked toward the main house.

"The baby is fine. It will be a while before we can tell about the mother." Samantha was contrite as they walked. "I must speak to Mrs. Cooper. The woman, Chloe, is going to need to see a doctor, if she lives. Is it true that the town doctor does not usually care for the slaves here?" Samantha did not try to conceal the hostility in her voice.

"Caroline is a good woman. She will see that the woman is cared for."

"Oh, I can see what a good mistress she is," Samantha said bitterly. "What kind of people are you?"

She didn't wait for a reply but broke into a run toward the house. The major easily caught up with her and grabbed her arm.

"Sam, I know what you're thinking. This is not a simple matter." He sighed. "This is a complex issue that goes back a long time."

Samantha glared at him. "I'm tired, Major. I would like to speak to Mrs. Cooper and then return to the city."

They reached the steps leading up to the house. Most of the guests had left; those remaining were staying the night. Samantha started to reach for the door and stopped.

"I'd better not enter the house looking like this," she said.

The major looked at her. Samantha was wearing her coat, but it was cut away in the front, revealing her blood-soaked shirt.

"No, I think not," he replied. "Come around back." He led her around to the service entrance in the rear. "Wait here. I'll find Caroline."

The major returned a few minutes later with Caroline Cooper on his arm. Seeing her there, dressed in her beautiful silks, Samantha felt a rage boil up in her.

"One of your slaves, a woman named Chloe, has just given birth to a baby boy. It was breach, so I had to remove the baby surgically through her belly. Otherwise, they both would have died. The infant is fine, but it's too soon to tell about the woman. If she lives, she'll need to see a doctor in two weeks to have the stitches removed," Samantha concluded as she unconsciously wiped her hand across her face, smearing blood on it.

"Good Lord!" Mrs. Cooper exclaimed. She stared wide-eyed at Samantha's bloody shirt and reached for the major. He put his arm around her protectively, his gesture further infuriating Samantha.

"Don't tell me you're going to faint," Samantha lashed out. "Damn it, woman! There's a woman a few hundred feet from here who just had her belly cut wide open without anesthesia, and she didn't faint. But then, she's just a slave!"

"Sam! That's enough!" the major said sharply.

Samantha realized, too late, that she'd gone too far. The major's eyes darkened, and Samantha could see that he was barely controlling his fury.

"Apologize to Mrs. Cooper at once!" he commanded.

Samantha raised her chin up defiantly, although it trembled slightly as she stood her ground.

"That's not necessary, Ethan," Mrs. Cooper said softly. "I believe I'm in young Sam's debt. How awful for that woman. And you, you must be exhausted," she said, looking at Samantha.

Although Mrs. Cooper was still pale, she had recovered and was once again the gracious lady. "I shall, of course, see that she's cared for." She turned to the major. "You and Sam must stay the night; it's late and such a long ride back into town. We have plenty of room, and I'll have water and a clean shirt sent up for Sam."

"That's very thoughtful, Caroline, but not necessary," he replied.

"It would be my pleasure," Mrs. Cooper said softly.

Mrs. Cooper looked at the major, and for a moment, Samantha was confused. She seemed to have missed something in the conversation between the two. Then the major smiled at Mrs. Cooper.

"Perhaps it would be a good idea," he said.

Samantha was furious, but one look at the major stopped her from protesting.

"Please, come with me," Caroline said.

She turned, and the major grabbed Samantha's arm. He held it tightly as they followed Caroline up a back staircase to the second floor. She opened a door and stepped inside. The major and Samantha waited while she lit the lamp.

"I hope you don't mind sharing the room. We have several guests staying. I'll have everything brought up for you, Sam. Now, if you'll excuse me, I must say good night to my other guests."

"I'll go with you," the major ventured. "You change your shirt," he said to Samantha. "I'll be back." Again, the warning was there in his eyes.

After the door closed, Samantha stood there in shock. Now what? She was to stay here tonight? With him? In this woman's house? She started to pace the room when there was a knock at the door. A Negro entered carrying water, linens, and a clean shirt. He nodded quietly while he set everything down.

"Will there be anything else, sir?" the Negro asked.

Samantha shook her head, dismissing the man. The door had barely closed when Samantha picked up the clean shirt and, wadding it up, hurled it across the room. She reached for the pitcher of water on the small table and stopped herself. She could not risk allowing a foolish display of temper to expose her identity. She walked over to where the shirt had landed and brought it back to the table. She removed her frock coat, waistcoat, stripped off the bloody shirt and gauze, and bathed. It was not easy to remove the blood from the gauze, but finally satisfied, she wrapped the clean, damp gauze around her chest, donned the clean shirt and coat, and waited. The house had grown quiet, and still the major had not returned.

It was over an hour later when at last Samantha heard the doorknob turn and he entered. He walked over to a small table in the room and poured a drink for himself. Samantha watched as he tossed the amber liquid down his throat. He turned to Samantha, a questioning look upon his face.

"Brandy?" he asked.

Samantha frowned.

"Your outburst was inexcusable," he began. "Caroline Cooper is your hostess."

Samantha stiffened.

"Things are different here in South Carolina," he continued.

"Different? How about immoral? How can you—any of you—live like this? Look at this house." Samantha gestured wildly about the room. "It's beautiful, just like all of the people who were dressed in their expensive clothing tonight, dancing and eating. There was more food here tonight than most people eat in a month," she shouted.

"And the North does not have its share of wealthy people?"

"Yes, we have wealthy people, but the wealth was not derived from the work of slaves. I saw those Negroes, and I saw the cabins they live in," she said accusingly.

"And where do you think the wealthy businessmen of the North make their money? Have you been to any of the homes of the laborers? What about the dock workers and the factory workers? Have you seen the squalor they live in?"

"At least they are free men. No one owns them," she challenged.

The major sighed. "No, no one owns them." He looked directly at Samantha. "I envy your innocence, Sam. I wish it was that simple."

Something stopped Samantha from replying. He poured another drink from the decanter. With his back to Samantha, he continued. "Tomorrow, I shall expect you to remember your manners. I will not tolerate another outburst like that. We'll go back into town in the morning. For now, you will stay here. Caroline, Mrs. Cooper, that is, has found other accommodations for me. I'll see you in the morning."

Samantha watched as he put his glass down and walked to the door.

"Good night," he said as he opened the door and then paused. "Sam, I'm glad you were here to help that woman. Thank you," he said quietly and then left, closing the door behind him.

Samantha had been lying awake for an hour. The room was hot, and she couldn't sleep, bound in the damp gauze. She didn't dare remove it or her clothing, though. In frustration, she stood and walked to the door that opened out onto the balcony. She stepped out and breathed in the night air. The air was heavy and permeated with the sounds of crickets, an occasional frog, and owls. At least there was a breeze on the balcony. She leaned on the railing and looked out across the moonlit expanse of grass. It was all lovely in this light. The moonlight reflected off of the great white house, while the leaves on the trees swayed gently with the easy wind.

A sound caught Samantha's attention. She heard the low murmur of voices and then the soft laughter of a woman. Samantha turned to the left and took a cautious step in the direction of the sounds. Another door also opened onto the balcony, and the lace curtains at the door shifted gently in the breeze. This time, it was the man who laughed quietly. Something familiar registered in Samantha's mind. The moonlight crept into the room each time the curtains moved. Samantha knew she should turn around and go back to her room. Instead, she positioned herself in the shadows on the balcony and peered into the room.

It took a second for her eyes to adjust and another second before she saw the couple standing next to the bed. The woman was wearing a light-colored dressing gown, her golden hair cascading down her back. The man was stripped to the waist, his arms entwined around the woman as he kissed her.

Samantha felt heat rise in her cheeks and was about to back away when a gust of wind blew the lace completely aside. She could see clearly the face of the man and woman. At that moment, she felt as though she'd been struck in the stomach. Caroline Cooper moaned softly as the major maneuvered her back against the bed. Willing herself to break away, Samantha turned, and as quietly as possible ran back to her room.

Strange sensations washed over her when at last she reached her room. She sat down on the bed. She couldn't get the image of the major and Mrs. Cooper out of her mind. Other accommodations indeed—they were lovers! Her face burned as she thought of them now. She must leave. Immediately.

Samantha jumped up from the bed and crossed the room but stopped as she placed her hand on the doorknob. Where would she go? She couldn't find her way back home, not this far south, and it was unlikely she would find anyone to help her. Once again, she was helpless. She was dependent on the major to at least get her closer to Union lines. She hated Ethan Winters-Hunt. She hated Caroline Cooper, with all her beauty, charm, and soft silks.

Samantha glanced down at her own attire. Jealousy surged through her, although she never would have acknowledged such an emotion to anyone else. She threw herself across the bed and clutched the pillow as her tears came. Sometime later, the tears subsided, leaving her longing for her family and home, and she fell asleep.

It was the high-pitched cry that caused Samantha to pause midway as she desperately tried to pack the bleeding wound of the soldier placed on her surgical table. She forced herself to look at the soldier's face. "Oh, God, no," she screamed silently. The soldier was a boy, not more than ten years old. He still wore the tattered remains of a Confederate uniform. She looked back at his wound. His arm was missing, the shoulder socket blown away. She couldn't stop the bleeding! Suddenly, his chest bucked as he coughed, and blood poured from his mouth. His eyes widened in fear, and then Samantha saw his small body go limp, his fear frozen on his face as he died. "I'm sorry," Samantha cried. "I'm sorry I couldn't save you. I'm sorry. I'm sorry," she repeated as she sobbed. Then she felt strong hands on her shoulders, pulling her back from the bloodied boy on her table. She turned to the man who still held her shoulders. "I'm sorry," she cried desperately.

"Sam? Wake up, Sam. You're dreaming," the major said. He was sitting on the bed leaning over her, his hands on her shoulders.

Samantha stared at the face before her. Vaguely, she was aware of the major pulling her up into a sitting position. A glass was thrust into her hands and guided to her lips. Samantha swallowed the liquid and then coughed as the strong brandy burned its way down her throat.

"Sam? Are you all right now?" The major's voice was kind as he spoke. "You were dreaming again."

"He's trembling. The poor boy," a woman said.

The feminine voice startled Samantha. She jerked her

head to the side to see Caroline Cooper standing there. Her hair was still down, but she was wearing a robe over her nightgown. She took the glass from the major. Samantha turned back to him and took in his full appearance. His chest was bare, and he looked as though he had hastily pulled on his pants. He had brought his boots in with him, although he had not yet put them on. Samantha turned away from them both, trying to still the raw emotions that lingered after the dream.

"What are you doing here?" she asked quietly, her face averted from them both.

"We heard you cry out," he said.

"I'm sorry I disturbed you," Samantha said quietly. "I'll be all right now."

"Tell me about the dream," he said gently.

Samantha shook her head. "No, just leave, Major," she said. She could tell he was staring at her, and then she felt the bed move.

"Caroline," the major said as he stood up, "perhaps I should stay here."

Samantha heard him speaking quietly to Mrs. Cooper, and then she left the room. Samantha rolled over on her back and watched the major light a lamp. He then pulled a chair over to the side of the bed and sat down.

"Sam, I think it's time you told me about these dreams of yours."

"There's nothing to tell," Samantha replied as she sat up in the bed.

"That may be, but I can't sleep, and it's obvious that you can't sleep, so what else are we going to do?" he asked casually. He leaned back in the chair and put his feet up on the bed.

"Won't Mrs. Cooper be expecting you?" Samantha asked.

The major's eyebrows arched up in surprise at her

question. "Mrs. Cooper will be fine. You need not concern yourself. Now," he said, again shifting his weight, "what about these dreams?"

The silence stretched out in the room. Finally, Samantha leaned back against the headboard and started speaking hesitantly, uncomfortable in sharing her disturbed visions with the man seated beside the bed. As she spoke, however, she once again became caught up in her own nightmares, and the words tumbled out of her. When at last she finished, she was unaware that she had been crying again. The major sat quietly for a moment, giving her some time. Then he looked at her.

"You're not the only one to have nightmares about this war. We all do, sooner or later, and you're just a boy, Sam. For all your pretense at being a man, you're just a boy. You're lucky. You haven't done anything that would eat away at your conscience like the rest of us. Your actions have been noble. You must realize that there are men alive today who would not be, if it hadn't been for you.

"And there's one thing you had better accept right now: you can't stop this war. No one can. It's too late. The war must run its course, and it will." There was sadness in his voice. "Remember this when it's all over: because of you, a few more mothers will see their sons again; a few more wives will again have their husbands; and a few more children will see their fathers. That's what it all comes down to."

They sat quietly, Samantha thinking about what he'd said, the major lost in his own thoughts. After a while, he looked back at her. "It will be daylight in a few hours. Why don't you try to go back to sleep?"

Samantha mutely nodded. She started to say something about Caroline Cooper but thought better of it.

"I think I'll just sit here for a while," he said as he leaned his head back on the chair. "This is as good a place as any to catch a few hours of sleep."

Samantha watched as he closed his eyes. She slid down in the bed and turned on her side, away from him. She was glad he'd stayed. For a moment, a part of her consciousness rebelled at the warm feelings that gripped her, for he was the enemy, a Confederate officer. He had forced her to travel with him. He had taken her over his knee. He was Caroline Cooper's lover. But she was tired, and so she gave in to the feelings deep within her and let herself take comfort in his nearness.

CHAPTER 4

When Samantha awoke the next morning, the major indicated they would be returning to Charleston. Samantha ate quickly, went to check on Chloe and the baby, and returned to the stables to find the major waiting with their horses saddled.

"Are the woman and baby all right?" the major asked.

Samantha shrugged her shoulders as she took the reins from the major and mounted her horse. "The baby looks strong and healthy. The woman is fine so far. No fever. The incision is clean. But it's just like any other surgery—no matter what you do, some of them die anyway."

He nodded in understanding. "Did you learn that procedure in Paris?"

Samantha frowned.

"I've never heard of any of our doctors taking a baby surgically," he said when she failed to answer.

"Oh," Samantha said, comprehending his question. "It's an old obstetrical technique. It's the first time I've ever done it. I was scared, but there was no choice. The baby's foot was protruding from the birth canal and the baby was stuck. The woman couldn't deliver it, and I couldn't pull it out. They both were going to die."

The major shook his head and smiled. "You're an extraordinary young man, Sam," he said as he mounted his horse.

An hour later, they were nearing Charleston when the major turned to her. "I need to make a few stops before we return to the hotel. Then we'll see if we can find some clothes for you to wear tonight," he said.

"Tonight? Where are we going tonight?"

"Back to Mrs. Cooper's for a dinner party," he answered. "It's very important that I be there tonight."

"Why? To comfort the grieving Widow Cooper?"

The major's eyes narrowed. "Caroline Cooper is a beautiful and kind woman. And it's true, she's a widow. We're friends. You want to be a man, Sam? Then act like one. A gentleman doesn't discuss the personal relationship he has with a lady. Caroline Cooper is a lady."

"Are you going to marry her?"

"Marry her?" he said with surprise.

"Well, you two are"—Samantha hesitated, feeling the major's cold stare as they rode along—"friends," she finished lamely.

The major didn't answer. "The governor of South Carolina is going to be there tonight, as well as other influential men," he said. "You'll need to be dressed properly and be on your best behavior."

"Are you staying the night with her?"

The major suddenly turned his horse inward, stopping Kota in the process. "We are staying the night, Sam." He stared at Samantha but then his gaze faltered. "Never mind. Let's move on."

They both were silent as they rode the rest of the way into Charleston. Their first stop was at a brick building. A small sign in gold lettering on the outside identified the establishment as Winters-Hunt Enterprises. Samantha dismounted and followed the major into a simple, but tastefully decorated, reception area. A man immediately appeared as they closed the door behind them.

"Mr. Winters-Hunt! Father said we should expect you soon. He was surprised you didn't come yesterday," the young man added quietly, smiling as the two men shook hands.

"You two run this business so well, I wonder if I am even needed anymore," the major replied while the younger man beamed with pleasure. "Collin," the major said, "I would like you to meet Sam Cartier. Sam is a surgeon. He helped us at Fredericksburg and Spotsylvania. Sam, this is Collin Roland. He and his father somehow manage to keep me above water during these times."

"A task which is becoming more and more difficult, I don't mind saying," an older man said as he entered the room, smiling at the major. He turned to Sam, offering his hand. "I'm Stephen Roland, young man. It's a pleasure to meet you."

"Sir," Samantha said, shaking the hand offered to her.

"Collin, would you see that Sam is made comfortable in my office?" the major asked. "Your father and I have business to discuss."

The major already had his hand on the older man's back as they walked down a hall. Collin and Samantha followed the men into a richly furnished office that was adorned with paintings of tall sailing ships and the sea. The major and Stephen Roland went through a door into an adjoining office and closed the door behind them. Samantha turned to look at the young man beside her.

"They may be a while, Dr. Cartier. Make yourself comfortable. Would you care for anything?" Collin Roland asked.

"No, thank you."

"Very well, sir. My office is just down the hall should you need anything," he said.

After he left, Samantha glanced about the room. She was

about to sit down when she overheard the major talking. She hesitated a moment and then moved over to the door and placed her ear against it.

"Is Larson still getting through?" she heard the major ask.

"Yes. So far, the Yankees haven't been able to close Wilmington. Your ships are getting through there. Savannah is closed, as is New Orleans," Stephen Roland added.

"What about the others?" the major asked.

"Smith ran a blockade in Mobile. He sustained damage, though, and is still in port."

There was silence, and then Samantha heard the major again.

"There'll be new shipments in a few weeks—some arms, but mostly food and supplies. Here's the distribution plan. Supplies will need to be carried overland to these camps," the major said.

"Ethan," Stephen Roland began, "this will cost a small fortune. The government hasn't paid for the last four shipments. They offered Confederate script. I refused to take it."

"Take the script," the major said.

"What? You can't be serious."

"Take it, Stephen."

"It's worthless. You stand to lose a fortune. You can't afford it."

"Take the script, but continue to pay my crews in gold or Federal dollars."

"Ethan, you can't. You'll be broke in six weeks if you continue this. How did you pay for all these supplies: food, clothing, boots, medical supplies, guns? I'm telling you that you don't have enough money left in your accounts to continue to pay your ships to run the blockades and to purchase supplies like these. You must insist on payment in gold from the Confederate Congress."

"There's no gold, Stephen, you know that," the major said. "They have nothing but their script. If you saw the condition of the camps and the men, you'd understand."

"I do understand," Stephen said softly, "but I'm your attorney and friend. I can't do the impossible. I can't keep paying salaries once the money is gone. Unless you have a treasure chest buried somewhere that I don't know about, you're going to run out of funds in six weeks."

Samantha heard the rustling of paper and then the major spoke. "Contact Gerald Taper; he's a lawyer representing Rhodes and Hunt of Boston. Here's the address. You're authorized to withdraw whatever you need from the funds of Mr. Hunt."

"What do you mean I can withdraw whatever I want? Who is Mr. Hunt, and why would he allow me, a Southerner, to withdraw money from his funds? I don't understand."

"Calm down, Stephen," the major said. "I assure you it's all perfectly legal. When it comes to business and money, even politics don't interfere."

"What about the textiles and dry goods that we've been stocking in your warehouses here?"

"Sell them directly to the people and take—"

"I know," Stephen interrupted, "take script for it."

"From everyone except our wealthy planters. From them, you will accept only gold. See if some of the food can be shipped to the people of Richmond, too. It's been difficult to get any supplies in there."

"I'll see to it," Stephen replied. "Oh, and Ethan, Depardeu was in here last week. He knows that you have ships that are still running. He has some slaves that he wants to ship."

"No."

"That's what I thought," Stephen said. "I told him we don't ship slaves. He was quite angry when he left. You can expect trouble from that one and a few of his friends. I'd watch my back if I were you, Ethan."

Samantha couldn't hear the major's reply, but then Stephen Roland spoke.

"These supplies are coming overland from the North? Ethan, how are you going to get these through the lines?"

The major laughed. "Why, some of our illustrious planters have graciously agreed to share their private transport arrangements with us."

"They can get goods through?"

"With money, yes," the major answered.

"And who paid for these supplies? How were they procured in the North?"

Samantha couldn't hear the major's reply.

"Mr. Hunt? Ethan, why's he helping us?"

"He has his reasons," the major said. "I'll leave you to the details. I have other things to attend to. You can reach me at the hotel if you need to."

It sounded as though the major was taking his leave. Samantha ran to a chair and sat down.

"I've concluded my business, Sam," he said as he entered the room. "We can leave now."

Samantha stood, trying not to let him see her face. She was feeling slightly guilty about eavesdropping, but more than that, she was trying to digest what she'd heard. She was aware he was watching her, so she focused her attention on a portrait hanging on the wall.

"My mother," he said, nodding toward the painting.

Samantha was surprised. "She's very beautiful," she said.

"Yes, she was—in many ways. I think even a stubborn Yankee like you would have liked her, Sam."

"And you are the boy on her lap?" Samantha asked with

doubt.

"Yes. Don't act so surprised. I was a boy once." The major laughed. "Let's go. We don't want to be late for Mrs. Cooper's dinner."

"Major, I don't want to go tonight."

The major appeared to be studying her, and then he came to a decision. "All right, Sam. If you give me your word, as a Yankee gentleman, that you'll stay out of trouble and not try to run away, you can stay at the hotel tonight. I'll return in the morning. How does that suit you?"

"That suits me fine, Rebel," she said, extending her hand. "You have my word."

Samantha spent the afternoon grooming Kota and inspecting her tack. The two-week ride from Spotsylvania to Charleston had left her saddle caked with mud, which she had only hastily removed upon arriving. She thoroughly cleaned her tack and rubbed protective oil into the leather. Then she returned to the hotel.

"Good evening, young man," Mrs. Lynch said as Samantha entered. "Mr. Winters-Hunt asked that supper be brought up to you this evening. Is there anything else I can do for you?"

Samantha's skin was itching beneath the blood-stained gauze she still wore. She longed to wash it and bathe. "A bath before supper?" she asked.

"Of course," Mrs. Lynch said.

Samantha walked up the stairs to her room. It would be dark soon. She lit the lamp in her room and crossed into the major's room. She lit a lamp there and then returned to her room and sat on the bed. It seemed strangely quiet, and she was alone. She thought back to the only other time in her life when she had spent the night alone. That was the night she'd gotten lost outside of Arlington. The next morning, she'd been captured. How long ago was that? Her thoughts were interrupted by a knock at the door. Samantha assumed that Mrs. Lynch must have heated the water for her bath. She walked to the door and opened it.

"You must be Sam. Am I correct, young man?"

Standing at the door was one of the most unusual looking women Samantha had ever encountered. She was somewhere in her middle years, yet her hair was still coal black. Her eyes were also dark, and she had an exotic color to her skin. She was dressed in a low-cut red dress, showing off her full bosom. The dress, although very fancy, was unlike any Samantha had seen at Caroline Cooper's party. It was garish in appearance, and yet, the woman wore it with confidence and a certain style. Her lips and cheeks had been tinted red, reminding Samantha of women of the Paris theater district.

"Well, are you going to invite me in?" the woman asked.

"Uh . . . excuse me, ma'am." Samantha was still startled. "I think there's been some mistake. You have the wrong room."

The woman smiled, showing perfectly straight teeth. "No, young man, I don't make mistakes like that."

She laughed a deep, throaty laugh and walked past Samantha into the room. Samantha was still staring at her when the woman spoke again.

"It's been years since a young man has looked at me that way. It does my heart good. Now, are you going to close the door?"

"What? Oh, yes." Numbly, Samantha closed the door and turned again. "I'm sure you're in the wrong room, though. Who are you looking for?"

Again the woman smiled. "You are Sam Cartier, are you not? Temporary ward of Mr. Ethan Winters-Hunt?"

"Certainly not! I'm not anyone's ward. Why are you

here?"

The woman smiled. "Ethan, that is Mr. Winters-Hunt, thought you might like some company tonight."

"He sent you here?"

"No, dear, he did not send me here. He asked me if I would like to come here. There's a difference, young man. That's the first thing you need to learn about women."

"What? I don't understand."

"As Mr. Winters-Hunt was occupied this evening, he thought you might enjoy feminine companionship. There's no need to be embarrassed."

Samantha felt the color rise to her own face.

"Just relax. We can take this nice and slow," the woman said. "I understand that this is your first time. That's just fine. That's why I came personally, instead of sending one of my girls—that, and as a personal favor to Ethan."

Samantha was speechless. Was the woman saying that she was a. . . .

"Well, don't stand there with your mouth hanging open, young Sam. Aren't you going to offer me something to drink? If I know Ethan, there must be a bottle of good brandy around here somewhere."

"You must leave—now!" Samantha said, finding her voice at last.

"I told you. There's no reason to be nervous. For every man, there must be a first time. Now you just sit down and we'll talk. Hell, we can talk all night if you want to. Doesn't make any difference to me, but I think you might change your mind after a drink or two." Again, the woman smiled. "Come sit down beside me." She patted the bed next to her. "Tell me about being a doctor. You're very young to have had all that schooling. What's it like?"

Samantha clenched her fists. Her pulse pounded in her head from anger. Now she realized exactly what the major had done: he'd sent her a prostitute.

"That bastard!" Samantha ground out.

Samantha continued to swear as she angrily paced back and forth. When she at last turned around, the woman's smile was gone, replaced by caution and suspicion.

"What's going on here? Is this some kind of joke?" the woman demanded.

Suddenly, they were face-to-face. The woman's eyes were like daggers as she scrutinized Samantha's face. In the next instant, Samantha felt a hand shoved roughly between her legs, squeezing forcefully. Without thinking, Samantha reacted. With lightning speed, she stepped forward, pushed her shoulder into the woman, pivoted, and threw the woman to the floor. As she fell, Samantha twisted the woman's arm behind her, pinning her. The woman cried out in pain, and Samantha immediately released her.

"I'm sorry. I didn't mean to hurt you," Samantha said as she stepped back from the woman.

"Damn!" the woman swore angrily as she struggled to stand. Then she burst into a deep, throaty laugh. "Boy, honey, I could use a girl like you at my place," the woman said as she rubbed her arm and neck. She looked coyly at Samantha. "I think we do have some things to talk about, don't we, Miss. . . ."

Samantha blinked. The woman knew! She turned away and walked over to the window, her heart pounding. Her mind raced. Foolish! Another foolish mistake! What should she do?

Suddenly, Samantha jumped and spun around when she heard the howl of laughter coming from behind her. The woman was actually doubled over in laughter. What now? Was she crazy? Samantha stared in shock as the woman wiped the tears of laughter from her eyes. When she finally spoke, it was between short bursts of laughter as she gasped for her breath.

"He doesn't know," the woman exclaimed, "does he?"

Samantha was puzzled.

"Ethan doesn't know. He thinks you're a boy." Again, the woman burst out laughing. "I definitely need that drink now. Will you join me? What's your name, honey?"

The woman turned and looked about the room. Samantha walked through the connecting door into the major's room. She returned, carrying a decanter and a glass, and handed them to the woman.

"I prefer to be known as Sam," Samantha said with restraint as she sat on the chair next to the bed.

"All right, Sam. My name is Belle. Would you like to tell me what's going on here? Why are you passing yourself off as a boy? What has Ethan to do with this?"

Samantha was caught. There was nothing she could do. Belle would probably tell the major anyway. What else was there to hide?

"How much do you want to know?"

"All of it," Belle said. "I have a feeling this is going to be good."

Samantha studied Belle's face. Despite her earlier laughter, Samantha saw no malice in her eyes. There was actually the hint of kindness. Samantha took a deep breath and began to recount her story, starting with her masquerade in Paris.

The woman was quiet throughout, except for an occasional gesture. She nodded her head knowingly as Samantha described how the actress in Paris had helped her with her disguise. Her eyes widened in surprise when Samantha told of Many Horses's help in her journey and then of how she had been caught by Lieutenant Quicken and Major Ethan Winters-Hunt.

She gasped as Samantha described the carnage of war

and the conditions of the surgical care. She quickly covered her smile as Samantha became enraged, telling about how the major had laid his hand to her backside and threatened to do it again. She listened intently as Samantha told about the past two days at the Cooper plantation. And finally, Belle wisely hid her expression as Samantha raged against the major and Caroline Cooper.

When she finished, Samantha felt exhausted. Belle didn't speak but got up quietly and walked over to the table. She returned, carrying two glasses of brandy. "Here," she said, offering one to Samantha.

"No, thank you," Samantha said. "I don't drink spirits."

"I think you can make an exception this once, don't you? Think of it as medicinal, if you wish."

"Medicinal?" Samantha grinned for the first time in days as she accepted the glass. She took a sip of the warm liquid and coughed as it burned her throat. Cautiously, she took another sip.

"There aren't too many women that I'm proud to meet," Belle said. She was still standing over Samantha, a thoughtful expression on her face. "I guess it's an occupational hazard," she added ruefully. "But I'm proud to meet you, Sam, or whatever your name is."

"What are you going to do now that you know?" Samantha asked.

"Me? Why, not a thing. Your secret is safe with me. The question is what are you going to do?"

Just then there was a knock at the door. Samantha jumped up.

"Is it Ethan?" Belle whispered.

"No," Samantha answered. "He wouldn't knock. He'd just come in."

"Dr. Cartier? Your bath water is hot now," a voice said from the other side of the door.

"It's Mrs. Lynch," Samantha whispered.

"Go ahead and have her bring your bath in. I'll hide in the other room," Belle said.

Belle went into the major's room, and Samantha opened the door. Mrs. Lynch stood there with her two sons. Samantha motioned them inside and waited while they poured the hot water into the copper tub.

"Shall I bring your supper up now?" Mrs. Lynch asked.

"Yes, but just leave it outside the door. I would rather not be disturbed."

Mrs. Lynch frowned. "As you wish, young man."

"And Mrs. Lynch, I'm very hungry. Better send up enough for two."

Mrs. Lynch nodded and ushered her boys out of the room. Samantha then closed the door and leaned against it as Belle emerged from the other room, smiling.

"Would you care to stay for dinner?" Samantha asked.

Belle laughed, shaking her head from side to side. "People can be so stupid sometimes. Especially men! To think that you have fooled them all this time. And Ethan! He's by no means inexperienced, my dear. How can he fail to know? You're sure he doesn't suspect?"

"I'm sure, and as to why they don't suspect? It's the same here as it was in Paris. People don't suspect something that they believe to be impossible. It's never occurred to them that a woman could be in my position."

Belle seemed to consider this. "It's as you say." She smiled again. "You should get into that tub while the water is hot. We'll talk while you bathe."

Samantha hesitated.

"There's no need to be modest. We both have dealt with bodies in ways that are not conventional for most women. In my business, I see people undressed more than I see them dressed. I'll tell you about it sometime." Belle winked.

"Here, I'll help you get out of these clothes."

Samantha did not resist as the older woman proceeded with alacrity. Belle helped Samantha remove her clothes, but she frowned and stepped back when she saw the bloodstained gauze binding.

"It's not possible to wash it as often as I would like, and the stains won't come out," Samantha said as she reached to unwind the gauze.

Once Samantha was seated in the tub, Belle poured a bucket of water over her head and washed Samantha's hair. When that was finished, she pulled a chair over by the tub as Samantha washed the last trace of the paste off her face and let herself slide down into the warm water to relax.

"I haven't had someone pamper me so in a very long time," Samantha said dreamily, her eyes closed as the warm water erased the tension of the last days.

"I don't imagine so," Belle commented.

Belle stood and walked over to the door. She opened it and cautiously peered out into the hallway where she found two trays covered in linen. She brought them in and set the food and drink on the small table. Samantha opened her eyes.

"I have to be so careful on the battlefield and when traveling with the major. Even here, I never know when he's going to come in, so I can't remove my disguise. When he's away, there are still people around." She looked over at Belle. "I guess I had better get out. The water is getting cold anyway."

"Here," Belle said as she walked over and held up a large towel. Samantha stepped out of the tub and enfolded the towel about her. Belle was looking at her, a curious expression on her face.

"What's wrong?" Samantha asked.

Belle reached up and pulled Samantha's hair down, its

wet tendrils now resting on her shoulders. "You're a beautiful girl," she said, appraisingly. "Amazing. Even I couldn't tell how beautiful underneath that awful paste. And your figure. . . ." She pulled Samantha's towel open and boldly looked at her nakedness. "Slim, but nicely proportioned. You're still young."

Samantha was embarrassed and grabbed the edges of the towel to cover herself.

"Sorry, dear," Belle said. "It's my business, remember? You go ahead and get your nightgown on, and then we'll tuck you into bed and have a picnic on your bed—just us girls."

Samantha didn't move.

"What is it?" Belle asked.

Samantha shrugged her shoulders. "I don't have a nightgown. I've been sleeping in my clothes like the soldiers do. I haven't had a room to myself until now. I've had to share the major's tent or sleep out in the open with him."

Belle arched her eyebrows as she listened to Samantha. Samantha saw the gesture.

"He thinks I am a boy, remember? They all do," Samantha reminded her.

"So they do, my dear. Well, he won't be back tonight, so you can sleep in whatever you like. As tight as you have had yourself bound up, I wouldn't blame you if you slept in your natural state tonight." Belle laughed.

Samantha walked over to the wardrobe and removed one of the shirts the major had purchased for her. It was a little large for her and reached the middle of her thigh. She looked up at Belle.

"That's fine, honey. I told you, I've seen it all. And I've taken care of a lot of girls in my life. Now, you come over here and settle in."

Samantha did as instructed. Belle pulled a light quilt over

Samantha's legs and positioned pillows behind her back. Then she placed the food on the bed. When she finished, she sat down in a chair next to the bed.

"This is wonderful," Samantha said, smiling at the feast set out before her. It felt so good to be herself for once, to be free of the constricting gauze, to let her hair hang down, to let her guard down.

"Belle," Samantha said after they had been eating a while, "you know all about me. If it wouldn't be impertinent, I would like to know about you."

Belle shrugged. "What would you like to know?"

"Well, you're a . . . that is, you. . . ." Samantha blushed, searching for the correct word.

"I'm a madam, honey. It's all right. You can say it. I run a house of pleasures. I have a dozen girls who work for me. They're prostitutes, like I was once," Belle concluded.

Samantha stopped eating and looked at Belle. "I know nothing about that," she said in wonder. "I certainly have heard of women who do what you do, but I've never met anyone who does. I heard the men talk when I was a student in Paris." Samantha frowned. "Why would a woman do that? To . . . you know . . . with different men. And you're shunned by society—and the diseases. . . ."

"Honey," Belle said seriously, "no woman chooses prostitution on her own accord. Usually, it's a matter of prostitution or starving."

"But to do *that*?"

"What else can a girl do when she's alone? No food. No shelter. You don't know what can happen to a girl alone in the world. It's not pretty. These girls don't have families to care for them or protect them—no husbands, fathers, or brothers. Life dealt most of them a cruel blow, and they're getting by as best they can."

Samantha thought a moment. "What about you, Belle?"

Belle laughed sarcastically. "Me? My mother worked in a house of pleasures in New Orleans. You might say I was born into the profession."

"Is Belle your real name?"

"No, but it fits. It's really Isabella De Leon."

"How did you happen to come to Charleston?"

"As I said, I was born into the profession. I learned a lot as a young girl by observing what was happening around me. It can be a hard life for a girl. Some men mistreat the women. Then there are diseases, as you said. I decided that I wasn't going to work in someone else's house until my looks left me and I was forced out onto the street. I would have my own house someday. I was beautiful when I was young, so I watched and learned.

"A man came one day, a fancy man with lots of money. I made him a deal. He set me up in a small place of my own and visited me several times a week. He gave me pretty clothes and jewels and money, all of which I saved. I stayed with him for several years. Eventually, he tired of me, but he was a good man, and he let me keep the money and jewels. There were several more after that. I always chose carefully and saw to it that I got to keep everything.

"When I had enough money, I left New Orleans and came to Charleston. I started small. I still had my looks then, so I worked some myself. But my plan was to build my own establishment. And here I am now." Belle smiled and took a deep drink of her brandy.

"Remarkable," Samantha said seriously.

Belle almost choked on her drink as she burst out laughing. "Sam, or whoever you are, if you don't beat all. There aren't too many ladies of quality, like yourself, who would react the way you do. You're something."

"I'm not so sure about that," Samantha said ruefully. "I can think of a few people who would take issue."

"Oh, like who?"

"My father. And my brothers, except for Troy; he's my twin." Samantha smiled. "Troy and I are alike. We used to get into trouble when we were young. I have two older brothers, Charles and Robert. They're fighting with the Union. Troy is at home with Pa. My father is a rancher on the Iowa Frontier. Charles's wife and two children also live with us."

"You're very lucky, honey. I would have given anything to have had a family like that."

"I miss them," Samantha said quietly. "I missed them in Paris. I felt so alone there. And I was scared. I never told them that. I should have told them how much I love them, and I didn't."

"I'm sure they know, honey," Belle said kindly. "They know." She reached for the bottle of brandy. "Here," she said as she refilled both glasses. "Here's to family and Ethan's excellent brandy."

Samantha looked at Belle and smiled as they touched their glasses together. "Belle, tell me about Major Winters-Hunt."

Belle raised her eyebrows. "What would you like to know?"

"You and he are friends. Obviously, he knows you." Again Samantha stumbled over the words.

"Yes," Belle said slowly, "we know each other. He's helped me in the past. I knew his father, too." Belle smiled. "His father used to visit me on occasion. If he wasn't a randy one, that William. He was also kind and generous," Belle mused. "Of course, once he met Ethan's mother, he stopped coming to see me," Belle said. "He had eyes only for her."

"You said Major Winters-Hunt helped you in the past?"

"Yes, I did. He's been good to me and my girls when

others weren't. That's all I am going to say about it, though."

"Does he visit your girls?"

"No, Ethan has always found his own companions."

"Like Caroline Cooper."

"Yes," Belle said evenly. "I believe they're friends."

Samantha wanted to ask more about the major and Caroline Cooper, but didn't. Instead, she moved to another subject that had been puzzling her. "What about the war? How's he involved in the war?"

Belle eyed the young woman before her. "Why don't you ask Ethan these questions?"

Samantha shrugged. "The major can be very intimidating. I told you how he threatened me."

"Seems to me he's been protecting you," Belle said. "What I wouldn't give to see you two. Ethan thinking you're a boy."

"His taking his hand to my backside was not the least bit funny, I assure you. If I had had my knife with me, he wouldn't have gotten near," Samantha said angrily.

"And are you as handy with a knife as you were earlier with your hands?" Belle asked as she rubbed her arm where Samantha had twisted it.

Samantha smiled ruefully. "My cousin, Many Horses, said I had gotten soft the last two years in Paris. Undoubtedly, he was right. Our ranch extends into the Lakota Territory, and I have an uncle and cousin who are Lakota Indians." Samantha didn't say anymore, thinking that was explanation enough. She became serious again. "You didn't answer my question about the major."

Belle was quiet a moment and then spoke. "Ethan is a loyal Southerner. Anything else that you want to know, you'll have to ask him."

Something in Belle's expression closed, and Samantha

could see that she would get no more information from the older woman.

"Now, young Sam, I think I should go and let you get some sleep tonight. Do you know how long you'll be in Charleston?"

"No. The major indicated that he had business to attend to. Then I think he's taking me back to the battlefields. The Confederacy is sorely lacking surgeons."

"I'm sure you're a good surgeon, honey," Belle said.

When Samantha spoke, it was with a heavy sadness. "I'm a very good surgeon, but there's little I can do for most of them."

Belle patted Samantha's hand as she stood to leave. "I'll try to visit you again, provided Ethan allows it."

"What will you tell him about tonight?" Samantha asked.

"Nothing. I told you that your secret is safe with me."

"But won't he ask you about tonight? Won't he want to know if. . . ."

Samantha's awkwardness made Belle smile. "Honey, Ethan is a gentleman. He won't ask me what happened tonight. Now you sleep well," she said as she bent down and kissed Samantha on the forehead.

That night, the dream returned again. Samantha awoke, her face tear-streaked, the bloody images still clear in her mind. She trembled as she lay there alone, clinging to her pillow, wishing in the dark hours that the major was in the adjoining room.

CHAPTER 5

Ethan returned to the hotel the next morning to find Sam's room empty. With an explosive curse, he ran down the steps and found Mrs. Lynch.

"When did he leave?" he demanded.

"Sir?"

"Sam! When did he leave?"

Mrs. Lynch was flustered. "I don't know. I took breakfast up to him, and that's the last I saw him."

Again he swore as he ran out the back door, heading to the stables.

Samantha was shoveling hay into Kota's stall when the major entered the stable. "What do you think you're doing?" he demanded harshly.

"Major." Samantha smiled as she turned around. "You're back. I was just feeding Kota. You know how he is around strangers."

She stopped when she saw his angry face. He was standing there, his hair tousled and his shirt casually unbuttoned at the top, as though he only recently had gotten out of bed—Caroline Cooper's, no doubt.

"Just what did you think I was doing?" she demanded. When he didn't answer, she continued. "You thought I was running away, didn't you? I gave you my word. Don't you trust me? Obviously not. I am, after all, a Yankee. I'm not honorable like those Southern gentlemen I met at Caroline Cooper's," Samantha ground out sarcastically. "And what of the gracious Mrs. Cooper herself?"

Samantha saw the major's face darken.

"You leave Caroline out of this," he said steadily.

"Of course. We wouldn't want to sully the lady's name."

"Caroline Cooper is a lady," he said dangerously.

"Oh, yes. I'm learning a lot about Southern *ladies*, too."

He took a step toward her and gripped her arm, his face inches from hers. "Get your horse saddled up—now!"

Samantha wanted to defy him, but something warned her that she had pushed him as far as he would allow. He released her and turned to his own horse. She saddled Kota in silence and followed him out into the street.

They had ridden for twenty minutes when the major stopped on the side of the road. He dismounted without a word and removed a pack from his horse. Samantha watched as he pulled out the Confederate uniform. She averted her gaze as he changed clothing, and then they were riding again.

Soon the camp came into view. Samantha could see row after row of small white tents with different flags. She remembered the major explaining that there was no unifying Confederate flag. Instead, each state or unit had its own colors.

As they entered the camp, the guards saluted the major. Again, Samantha unconsciously tensed at being surrounded by hundreds of Confederate soldiers. The silent ride to the camp had not dampened the anger she felt back at the barn. Instead, it had intensified as she recalled the night at Caroline Cooper's plantation. She eased Kota closer to the major and spoke.

"Are you bringing me here to work? Am I expected to aid these men so they can keep fighting, perhaps even kill decent people, just so they can maintain their privileged lives on their plantations? So they can continue to enslave the Negro? Is that it?" she demanded.

His reaction was so swift that Samantha didn't see it coming. Kota, though, reared up. The major leapt from his saddle onto Samantha, knocking her to the ground. He was on her in an instant, pulling her to her feet. His grip was tight on the front of her coat as he pulled her to within inches of his face. She was paralyzed with fear as she stared into his eyes.

"School is in session, Sam. Starting now!" he hissed at her. "Private! Take care of these horses," he commanded.

The major grabbed her arm tightly and propelled her along with him, oblivious to the stares of the soldiers around him. They walked a short distance when he stopped among thirty men sitting on the ground.

"You, Private," the major said, addressing one of the men.

"Yes, sir," the private said as he stood up.

"How many slaves do you own?" the major asked.

"Sir?" the soldier replied.

"I asked you a question. How many slaves does your family own?"

"Aw, shit," the soldier began and then shifted uncomfortably. "Beggin' your pardon, sir. My family don't own slaves. We got us a small farm, that's all."

"How about you?" the major asked as he turned to another soldier. That soldier also stood up quickly.

"Don't have no slaves, sir. My pa, brothers, and me do the farmin', sir."

The major turned to another. "You. How many slaves does your family have?"

"We poor folk, Major, don't have no slaves."

They were looking at him peculiarly.

"Any of you boys here own slaves? Your families own any slaves?"

"We just enlisted men, Major. None of us have slaves. I think the captain over there might have some. He's from a fancy family."

The major repeated the scene with three more groups of men. Each time, the response was always the same. None of them owned slaves. They were mostly farmers who hadn't traveled more than twenty miles from the place where they had been born until the war started. Samantha was confused.

"I don't understand," she finally said quietly to the major.

"Don't you?" he said harshly. "Open your eyes, Sam. Wealthy planters aren't fighting this war. They buy their way out of it. Oh, there are a few decent men of means who, out of loyalty, have accepted positions as officers. But mostly, ordinary people are fighting it. Most of them own no more than a small piece of land that they farm with their own hands. They're lucky if they own a mule. They're farmers. They work hard and live close to the land."

"Then why are they fighting?"

His eyes were hard as he stared at her. "Ask them yourself."

He pulled her toward another group of men. The men immediately stood at attention. "At ease, men," the major said. "This is Dr. Cartier. He's a surgeon from the North. He would like to ask you a question."

Samantha could see the suspicion in their eyes as they waited in silence. She looked to the major, but his face was like granite.

"Why are you fighting in this war?" she asked hesitantly.

The soldiers stared at her as though they didn't understand her question. They looked back to the major, seeking an explanation.

"Answer the doctor's question," he ordered.

The hostility was immediately evident in the soldiers' eyes as they regarded Samantha.

"Why you asking us that?" one of them said as he stepped forward.

The man was filthy, his clothes ragged, his stench overpowering. Samantha unconsciously took a step backward.

"You came down here. We didn't march onto your farms. You came down here," he accused.

"I was out milking the cows one morning and looked up to see the hills full of blue coats," another volunteered.

"You all came marching down here onto our land, destroying everything you could. Everything!" an additional man said bitterly.

"We didn't start this war," a soldier added. "You did!"

"No one can tell us how to live."

"That's right!" several more answered.

"You high and mighty Yankees try to tell us what we can do and how we can live."

"How'd you like it if we made laws and came up to your land and told you what to do?" a different man threatened.

"Didn't have no choice," one man said. "The conscription got me. Had to go or be put in jail."

"You got no right to come onto another man's land and tell him what to do," an angry man shouted.

Several more soldiers joined in, echoing their comrades' last words.

"We got the same rights you do. I got family buried here who fought the British. You Yankees don't own all of this country. Get off our land!"

Samantha was shaken. These men were not the stereotyped enemy she had envisioned, and their answers were not the rhetoric she had expected. "Major, can we go now?" she asked.

"Not yet," he said, although less sternly this time.

He led her away from the soldiers. Samantha was troubled as they walked in silence, the words of the soldiers disturbing. She was so deep in thought that she was startled when the major suddenly grabbed her arm and stopped her.

"Watch your step," he warned.

Samantha looked down and was appalled to see open sewage on the ground. It jolted her into consciousness and she looked about her.

"Major, this place is a cesspool," she said softly.

"It gets worse," he said as they once again started walking.

Samantha could hear the productive coughs of men as she passed by. She noted their sallow appearance and those who, she was certain, were feverish.

"Major, some of these men are sick."

"Yes," he said.

"Why aren't they in a hospital?"

"There isn't one."

She looked around. "This is a breeding ground for dysentery, typhoid, and diphtheria."

"Yes," he said evenly.

"Why isn't anything being done? I'm sure some of those men have diphtheria."

"I know. We lose two men from disease for every one killed in battle. Entire camps have been wiped out."

"That's appalling. Why isn't your government doing anything?"

"What would you suggest?"

"Clean the camp. Isolate those who are sick. Get some decent food and see that it is cooked properly."

"Who's going to do all that?"

"Well, surely there are people who would come to your aid. Doesn't the state or the Confederacy have a citizen's sanitary commission?"

He sighed. "No, Sam, we don't. We don't have the vast wealth of the North. Most of our people are finding it hard to feed themselves. The men are off fighting, and the farms are laying fallow. We don't even have railways connecting our major cities so we can transport goods to the camps. I need to speak to Major Clark. It's not so bad over this way. The officers keep themselves separate from the men."

"But what of the citizens of Charleston?" she persisted. "Can't they do something?"

As they walked, Samantha covered her nose in an attempt to decrease the stench of sun-drenched human waste coming from buckets sitting out in the open. The buckets were covered with flies and other swarming insects that would eventually find their way from the human excrement to the food being prepared nearby.

"They don't have any money," the major said.

"Maybe not, but a lot could be done by simply organizing the camp better. Provide separate facilities for refuse and human waste. See that the food is stored properly. Just clean things. Any woman who manages a household would know how to do that."

The major was silent.

"Well? What about the ladies of Charleston? Couldn't they organize themselves and volunteer some time to do that?"

He stopped and turned to Samantha. "The women of Charleston and the entire South have suffered a great deal because of this war. Their husbands are gone, and they're trying to survive and feed their children. They do help. Wherever fighting has occurred, the women have taken in the wounded and nursed them. But," he paused, "you can't expect them to come into this camp."

Samantha didn't understand. "Why not?"

"Look at this place, Sam. Look at the men. You cannot expect a lady to come here. They sew clothing, knit socks, and send what food and bandages they can. They nurse the wounded in their homes when called upon to do so, but to suggest that they come into the camp? It wouldn't be viewed as proper."

Samantha sensed that even he found his last statement lame, but he didn't say anything more. It was for that very reason that she remained quiet, despite the urge to suggest that ladies, such as Caroline Cooper, should be dragged by their hair into the camp to see what life was like for the soldiers who were fighting and dying for the Confederacy.

Samantha walked beside the major until they reached another set of tents. Major Clark emerged from one just as they approached.

"Major Winters-Hunt! What can I do for you, sir?"

"I'd like to speak with you a moment, if you please," the major said.

"Of course, come in." Major Clark motioned for them to enter the tent.

"If you don't mind," Samantha said quietly to Ethan, "I'd like to wait outside."

He turned to her. The anger that had been in his eyes earlier was gone. "As you wish," he said.

A short while later, the major emerged from the tent and indicated that they would return to Charleston. They retrieved their horses, the major changed back into civilian clothes, and they left the camp. The major seemed deep in thought, and Samantha was reluctant to voice what had been on her mind since the major forced her to confront the soldiers. Finally, when they approached the outskirts of Charleston, Samantha ventured to speak.

"No one mentioned the Union. It must be preserved. Can't you see that?" She turned in the saddle, a look of desperation on her face. "Doesn't anyone here care about that?"

"Oh, they care. The Constitution was ratified right here in Charleston in 1787, remember? They know that. But what is the Union? Individual territories elect to join it. It's the state's choice. Where, in the Constitution, does it say that a state can't also elect to no longer be a part of it? By what legal justification can Abraham Lincoln force a state to remain? What gives him the right to invade another state with armies if it refuses to be a part of the Union?"

Samantha had no reply. Everything that she had believed in had been challenged. What she had seen today was not the South that she was fighting against, and she didn't know the answer to the major's last question. There was still the moral issue of slavery, even if it was only the aristocratic few who continued the practice. As if reading her mind, Ethan spoke.

"The system wouldn't have survived. There were enough Southern people of conscience who were beginning to speak out against it. If you had let us, we would have eventually ended slavery ourselves."

They unsaddled their horses in silence. It was midday, and Mrs. Lynch had a meal waiting for them when they entered. Despite the delicious aroma of the food, Samantha had little appetite.

"You should eat, Sam," the major said. He waited until she had taken a few bites of the food and then spoke. "I'm going to leave for a few days," he began. "I may be gone as long as a week."

"I'm not going with you?" Samantha asked.

"I can't take you with me this time. You'll have to remain in Charleston. I've asked Caroline if you can stay with her while I'm away. She said she would be delighted to have your company. Most of her guests are leaving today, so it will be much quieter there."

"No." Samantha pushed her chair back. "I won't stay on that plantation."

His voice hardened. "I understand your objections, but there's no other choice. You cannot stay here alone."

"Why not?"

"Who would look out for you?"

"I don't need anyone to look out for me," Samantha replied through clenched teeth. "I can take care of myself."

"All right, you can take care of yourself, but what will you do? You can't just sit around a hotel room all day long. You don't know anyone in town."

"Yes, I do. I know Belle. I can visit her if I get lonely."

The major's eyebrows arched up in surprise. "Sam, you can't just visit Belle whenever you want," he said quietly.

"She said I could. And I'll report in daily to your attorney, Mr. Roland, if you like." Samantha became very serious. "I give you my word. I'll be here when you return."

He stared at her. It unnerved her, especially in such close proximity. She had determined that the major was no fool, and too often he had deduced what she was thinking before she voiced her thoughts.

"What is it, Major?" she asked uncomfortably.

"There's something about you that just doesn't ring true, Sam." He paused, still staring at her. "But, all right. I'll take your word on it. God knows there's been enough destroyed between our people. Surely that still remains between honorable men."

He extended his hand to Samantha across the table. Cautiously, she shook it.

"Do you remember how to get to my offices?" he asked.

"Certainly," Samantha replied.

"I'll explain to Stephen Roland. I'll ask him to look in on you once in a while. Should you need anything—money or whatever—he'll take care of it. Mrs. Lynch will see that meals are provided for you. I'm also certain that you would be welcome at the Cooper Plantation any time. Does that sound fair enough?"

"Yes," Samantha said. "Very fair."

"Good."

"When are you leaving?" she asked.

"In a few hours."

"So soon?" Samantha said with surprise.

"It can't wait. There are some matters of urgency." He stood. "I need to pack a few things before I leave. Want to come upstairs with me?"

"Yes."

She followed him upstairs and sat quietly while he gathered supplies he would need. When he was ready to leave, he turned to Sam.

"I'll speak with Mrs. Lynch and stop by my offices to discuss this with Stephen as I leave town."

"I'll walk out with you," she offered.

They had reached a truce again. Samantha was surprised when he rested his hand on her shoulder as they walked out to the stable together. She took comfort in the gesture and realized that she was going to miss him over the next few days. On impulse, she turned. "Is there any danger in what you're going to do?"

"This is a war, Sam, there's always danger," he said seriously. Then he flashed a smile. "Don't worry, Sam. You're not going to get rid of me that easily. I'll be back."

Samantha waited while he saddled his horse. He mounted and then looked down at her.

"I left some money on the bed for you and something else," he said. "Now stay out of trouble, you hear? I don't want to have to take you over my knee again when I get back."

He waved goodbye and then rode out into the street. Despite his last sentence, Samantha felt terribly alone as she watched him leave. She walked slowly back to her room and then remembered what he had said about the money. She crossed into his room and over to his bed. There was a small leather pouch that clinked when she picked it up. She inhaled sharply. It was not the gold pieces inside the pouch that caught her attention. There, laying on the bed, were her Henry rifle and her knife.

As he promised, Ethan stopped to speak with his friend and attorney, Stephen Roland, before leaving Charleston.

"How bad is it?" Stephen asked when they were alone in his office.

"General Sherman's army left Chattanooga last month. They're ninety-eight thousand strong. They've reached Georgia."

Stephen visibly paled at hearing this new. "Can General Lee send reinforcements?"

"No," Ethan said. "General Grant is on the move again. General Lee is trying to shore up defenses in Richmond."

Stephen nodded his head, his face grim. "What has General Lee asked you to do, Ethan?"

Ethan sighed deeply. "It's changing. I remember during the first two years of the war, battles were occasional with long periods in-between. We could shift troops and supplies, set up defenses. Now, hardly a day passes when our forces aren't battling the Yankees on Southern soil." He paused. "Sherman has destroyed our rail line beyond repair. General Lee needs alternative routes for supplies and intelligence information on Federal troop movement."

"Is there anything I can do, Ethan?"

"Actually, there is. That's why I'm here. I'll be away at

least a week. I've left Sam, Dr. Cartier, at the Lynch Hotel. I'd appreciate it if you would look in on him. I told him he could come to you if he needed money or anything while I'm away."

"Of course, Ethan. If you don't mind my asking, what is this boy to you?"

"I'm responsible for him," Ethan said.

Ethan recounted the event of Sam's capture. He didn't miss Stephen's look of disapproval when he told him how he had forced Sam to work in the Confederate surgical tents.

"I don't know why I did it," Ethan said. "I should have let him go when we first found him. Then it became too dangerous. He wouldn't have survived. And we needed surgeons."

Stephen Roland frowned. "He's very young."

"Clement Beauregard said Sam is the finest surgeon he's ever seen," Ethan countered. "But something about Sam just doesn't ring true. I felt it the first time we came across him trying to defend his horse. It's a feeling I get."

"Still you trust him to care for our wounded?"

"Yes, without question."

Stephen thought a moment and then smiled. "You not only feel responsible, but you care about this boy, don't you?"

For the first time since they started talking, Ethan smiled. "Sam's stubborn, willful, argumentative, and disobedient. Keeping him out of trouble is no easy task. But he's also displayed courage and honor rarely seen in men twice his age."

Stephen nodded his head in understanding. "Don't worry about the boy. I'll take care of him. He can even stay with me while you're away."

Ethan stood and reached across the desk to shake his friend's hand. "Thank you for the offer, Stephen, but Sam's not too fond of us Southerners. I dare say your wife would never forgive me. Best to let Sam remain at the hotel."

Samantha spent the afternoon alternating between lying on her bed and pacing back and forth between the major's room and hers. The words of the soldiers kept echoing in her mind. "You came here. You started this war." Those men were not fighting over the slavery issue. Most of them were defending their land. Would she or her brothers have done any differently? Weren't the Lakota Indians trying to defend their lands and maintain their way of life?

And what about the right of secession? Should individual states have that right? Samantha recalled reading Lincoln's "House Divided" speech. She had been inspired by those words. The Union must be preserved, but did the Northern states have the right to force the Southern states to remain a part of the Union? Or, as the major said, was it constitutional?

If so, then on what legal basis was this country formed in the first place when it broke away from England's rule? England was trying to force its laws upon the colonies just as the Northern states were trying to do to the Southern states. And didn't the Constitution establish the rights of individual states? Territories were not required to apply for statehood and to join the Union. Once they did, should they be compelled to remain? Should the colonies have been forced to remain?

Still, the slavery issue always loomed in the back. Ethan had explained to her that the wealthy planters had more votes than the rest of the people, for they received a fraction of a vote for each Negro they owned. That was how they had been able to control the legislature in their states. But he also said that some Southern people had begun to speak out against slavery. Would the South have eventually abolished slavery? Did this war just hasten the inevitable? She thought of her cousin, Many Horses. The Cherokee, Comanche, Lakota—they enslaved the women and young of their defeated enemy. She wished she could talk to Many Horses about this.

Samantha's thoughts were interrupted by a knock on the door.

"Dr. Cartier? Ma would like to know if you would like your supper brought up here or if you will be coming downstairs?"

Supper? Was it that late already? Samantha sat up on the bed. "Please bring it up here and just leave it outside in the hall," she said through the closed door. After the major had left, she had washed the paste off her face to relieve some of the irritation developing on her skin; she didn't want to have to put the paste back on her face. When she heard the young man return with her supper, she waited until she was sure he had gone back downstairs before she retrieved the meal.

As the evening progressed, Samantha's thoughts began to solidify. There was nothing she could do about the politics that had initiated this war, and she couldn't stop it. But there was one thing that she did know, and that was medicine. She couldn't sit by idly while men suffered diseases rampant in the camp. Slowly, a plan began to formulate in her mind. At first, she rejected the idea as preposterous, but by the time she finally fell asleep that night, she knew exactly what she was going to do.

Samantha woke early the next morning. She reapplied the paste and mustache to her face and dressed in a pair of pants, shirt, waistcoat, and sack coat that the major had secured for her. She had one stop to make before she left for the morning. She considered asking Mrs. Lynch, but thought better of it. Instead, she waited until Mrs. Lynch's eldest son was alone. He was surprised when she asked for directions, and then a grin spread across his face as he surreptitiously whispered to Samantha.

Samantha found the house easily. It had a walled garden area that provided privacy from the street. She tied Kota under a tree in the garden and approached the door. Before she could knock, the door was opened by a Negro woman.

"What you doin' here, boy? Customers go 'round to the back entrance, and Miz Belle's girls don't see nobody lest you clear it with Miz Belle first. Now, go on. Get out of here," the woman said.

"I'm here to see Belle. Please tell her that Sam is here."

"Pretty uppity, aren't you? Don't matter to Miz Belle whose boy you are. She sees only who she wants. Now get yourself out of here."

The door started to close in Samantha's face, but she pushed it open and surprised the woman by stepping in. "I'll wait inside. Please tell Belle that Sam needs to talk with her. She'll understand."

"She'll wup your backside, more than likely," the woman said in a huff and then left.

A short while later, Belle appeared, dressed in a nightgown and bed jacket. "Sam! Do you know what time it is? It's not a decent time for a lady to be up." Belle looked at her suspiciously. "Does Ethan know you are here?"

"No. He's away."

"Well, come on in. Jesse! Bring some coffee into the parlor." Belle led Samantha into a comfortable sitting room.

"This is a lovely house, Belle."

"It's said that in the early days, it was headquarters for pirates. It has some very interesting hidden rooms, stairways, and tunnels. I haven't had to use them yet, but you never know."

"Did I come in the wrong door?" Samantha asked.

Belle grinned. "This part of the house is where I live. In the back, there are separate stables and a discreet garden and entrance into my business establishment."

"I didn't want to leave my horse out in the street, so I tied him under a tree out there." Samantha pointed toward the entrance.

"What! You tied your horse in my garden?" Belle stood and walked to one of the lace-draped windows.

"No one will bother him there, will they?" Samantha asked.

Belle frowned. "No, no one will bother your horse. Must be some horse," she said grumpily as she sat down. "So what brings you here at such an awful hour in the morning?"

"Belle, how much do your girls charge? Say, by the hour or day?"

"What?"

"How much would it cost to hire one of your girls for a day?"

"Who wants to know?"

"I do."

"Are you crazy?"

"How much, Belle?"

Belle shrugged. "If a gentleman wishes to stay the whole night. . . ."

Samantha whistled as Belle quoted a sum.

"This is not just a whorehouse, young Sam. My girls are clean and schooled in the art of entertaining gentlemen. I'm very particular about who may visit my establishment. Gentlemen come from all over the South to see my girls."

"I see," Samantha said, although she didn't really understand. "Are they still coming?"

Belle snorted. "No. This war will break me. And then

what will happen to my girls? Where will they go? They're not street whores."

"I have a proposition for you. I would like to hire six of your girls for several weeks' work, eight to ten hours a day. I can pay you the first two weeks in advance."

"Has that binding you're wearing cut off your senses? What are you talking about?"

Samantha took the next several minutes outlining her plan. When she finished, Belle was staring, wide-eyed.

"Well, do you accept my proposition?" Samantha asked.

"Have you discussed this with Major Clark?" Belle asked.

"Not yet."

Belle laughed. "Do you really think he'll agree to let me and my girls march over to his camp and give orders about cleaning the place up? That's not what he'll want my girls for."

"No!" Samantha's voice was firm as she continued. "There'll be no fraternizing with the men. You're being hired to show the men how to dispose of refuse, clean the camp, quarantine the sick, and properly store and cook food. I'll show you what needs to be done. The men will do all the physical labor. Your girls will organize them and see that everything is done correctly. That's all. Understand that now, Belle, or this deal is off."

Belle thought a moment and then finally nodded her head in agreement. "I understand, and my girls do what I say, but do you really think you can convince Major Clark of this harebrained scheme of yours?"

"Why don't we ask him?" Samantha said sweetly. "Get dressed. I'll wait."

"Now?"

"Belle, in the short time that we've been sitting here, I'll wager that two or three men have come down with any number of diseases in that camp."

"What about my girls?"

"There's no guarantee that they won't become sick, but if you do as I tell you, it's less likely."

A half hour later, Samantha was driving Belle's carriage, with Belle seated beside her, into the camp. They were stopped at the entrance. The soldier looked at Belle, obviously recognizing her.

"Uh . . . sorry, ma'am, are you expected?" he asked, looking unsure of what to do.

"Private, I'm Dr. Cartier. I was here yesterday with Major Winters-Hunt. I would like to see Major Clark."

The private looked confused.

"I'm here conducting business for Major Winters-Hunt," Samantha said.

"Oh, yes, sir. It's the tent—"

"I know where it is, Private. Thank you."

Samantha urged the horse forward without waiting for a reply. She was aware of the stares of the men as they passed but kept her eyes ahead until she came to the cluster of tents occupied by the officers. A young lieutenant looked up in surprise as Samantha disembarked.

"Uhrmm." Belle cleared her throat, looking at Samantha expectantly. Samantha frowned. Belle extended her hand.

"Oh!" Samantha whispered as she reached up to help Belle down.

"Mind your manners, boy," Belle whispered slyly.

"What the . . . ," the lieutenant began.

"I'm here to see Major Clark. Please tell him that Dr. Cartier, Major Winters-Hunt's friend, is here to see him."

The lieutenant stared at Samantha and then at Belle. "What about her?"

"Lieutenant, I suggest you deliver the message as I gave it to you," Samantha said.

The lieutenant took one last look at Belle and then turned

and walked over to one of the tents. A moment later, Major Clark emerged.

"Dr. Cartier? Ma'am," Major Clark said as he nodded in Belle's direction. Then he returned his gaze to Samantha. "I understand you want to see me?"

"Yes, Major. Could we talk in your tent?"

"What's this about, young man?"

"I'll explain in your tent," Samantha said.

Without waiting for a response, Samantha offered her arm to Belle and escorted her to Major Clark's tent. The major was beside them and held the flap open. He was frowning as he offered Belle a chair and then indicated a place for Samantha to sit.

"Major Clark, are you aware that I'm a doctor serving with the Confederate Surgical Corps?"

"I believe that Major Winters-Hunt mentioned it when we met at Mrs. Cooper's party."

"I'm prepared to offer assistance that may decrease the number of deaths you are having in your camp."

Samantha outlined her plan, explaining what needed to be done and the role that Belle's girls would play. When she finished, she sat back and waited for the major's response.

"You cannot be serious. We can't let these women into the camp," Major Clark exclaimed.

"You cannot let conditions continue as they are."

"Look, Doctor Cartier, I know things are bad. We do the best we can, and everything you said should probably be done, but not by these women. The men wouldn't stand for it. They're not going to take orders from whores." He stopped, his face red. "My apologies, ma'am," he said to Belle. "But surely you must see that it won't work. Your girls wouldn't be safe. The men have been away from home a long time."

"Are you saying that your men don't know how to treat a

woman with respect, Major?" Samantha interrupted.

"Now hold on here. I didn't say anything of the kind," Major Clark said.

"Are you unable to control your men, Major? Do they not follow your orders?"

Major Clark's face darkened.

"Or is it that your men aren't that important to you?" Samantha challenged.

Major Clark's jaw tensed. "Does Major Winters-Hunt know of this plan of yours?"

"It seems to me that the decision is yours," Samantha continued. "You're the commanding officer. I've offered you the chance to improve the conditions in your camp, decreasing your death rate, with the help of these women. It's up to you to see that the women are given the proper respect that they deserve. Miss Belle has assured me that the women will, in no way, invite familiarity, but the men must follow their instructions. That's the condition of my assistance."

Major Clark didn't respond immediately. He walked to the open tent flap and stood there, staring out at the camp. Samantha realized that, once again, she may have spoken without restraint. Her boldness may have insulted the major, and if he refused her offer, just how would that help the men in the camp? She was about to apologize when he turned to face her.

"Very well, Doctor, you will have my cooperation," he said.

Samantha inwardly breathed a sigh of relief. "Good. I need to make some notes. With your permission, Miss Belle and I will tour the camp before we leave, and the women will arrive tomorrow."

Major Clark assigned a lieutenant to accompany them as they toured the camp. Samantha made notes as they walked, explaining to Belle all that was to be done. It was midday when they left the camp.

Belle was quiet as they rode back into town. As they neared her house, she turned to Samantha. "I had no idea it was that bad," she said. "Those poor boys."

"Can you do it, Belle? Can your girls handle this?"

Belle smiled slightly as she patted Samantha's knee. "They're good girls, Sam. We can do it."

They put the horse and carriage away, and Samantha followed Belle back into the house.

"I've made a list of the supplies you will need immediately," Samantha said.

Belle surveyed the list. "Sam, supplies are scarce in Charleston."

"I believe that a lot of what you need is available in one of Major Winters-Hunt's warehouses. Go see Stephen Roland, the major's attorney. Here," she said as she reached into her pocket, "this is all the money I have with me. There's enough for the first two weeks' salary for you and the girls, as I promised, and money for supplies. Buy what you can, and I'll try to get more money for you."

"These are Federal bills!" Belle exclaimed.

"Yes, won't they take them here?" Samantha asked, suddenly concerned.

"Take them? They're like gold. I can get two or three times the amount of goods if I have Federal dollars."

Samantha stood to leave.

"Where are you going?" Belle asked.

"I have things to do before tomorrow. We'll need medicines."

"There's no medicine in Charleston," Belle said.

Samantha smiled secretly. "The Spirits have placed medicine everywhere. I just have to find it, and then tomorrow, I'll show you how to prepare it."

"Spirits? What are you talking about?"

"I'm a Lakota medicine woman, Belle," Samantha answered, as though that should be an adequate explanation. "I have to go. I'll pick you and the girls up at seven in the morning."

"Seven!"

"Yes, seven. And Belle, don't tell Major Winters-Hunt or Mr. Roland about the payment for the girls or where you got the money for the supplies."

Samantha spent the afternoon searching through the wooded areas and fields outside of Charleston. The vegetation here was different from that on the frontier where she grew up. She had to be certain of what she was gathering. Choosing the wrong root or plant could have deadly consequences.

Most of the disease at the camp was due to poor sanitation and lack of adequate food. Those diseases would have to run their courses. But there were things that she could do to help increase the chance of survival from those diseases. The bark of a willow tree could reduce fever. Agrimony, echinacea, and the pods of carob, when ground up and boiled, would stop diarrhea and the deadly dehydration associated with it. Barberry was especially helpful in dysentery and cholera. Eucalyptus leaves, when steamed, helped to open up the lungs and enable a soldier to cough out the thick fluids that brought on pneumonia and death from consumption.

Most of this knowledge she had not learned during her two years of training in Paris. It was Charrah who taught her to recognize the medicinal trees, plants, and herbs as they grew and how to prepare them to the correct concentration—blackberry, dogwood, slippery elm, cattail, sumac, yarrow, sassafras, sweet gum, white oak, and so many more—all of them placed here by the Creator. It was the wisdom of that old Lakota holy man that she now depended on.

When she returned early that evening, her saddlebags were full of leaves, bark, and roots. She found Mrs. Lynch in the kitchen, preparing the evening meal.

"Mrs. Lynch, I would like the use of your kitchen tonight."

Samantha explained what she needed, including jars to store her medications. After dinner that night, Samantha sorted her leaves and roots. Then she began the task of boiling the leaves and skimming the elixir off of the top of the fluid. She ground up roots and bark into fine powders. She placed them all in the bottles and jars that Mrs. Lynch had provided, carefully labeling them. She only made enough for immediate use. The rest she packed away to be hung up and dried. Later, she would instruct Belle in making the medications. Samantha didn't know how long she would be in Charleston. It was best that Belle, or someone else, learned how to prepare them.

It was well past midnight when she finally finished. Mrs. Lynch found her, head resting on her arms on the table, sound asleep. All around her, placed on the table, were neatly labeled jars and bottles.

Samantha jumped when she felt a hand on her shoulder.

"I'm sorry, young man, I didn't mean to startle you," Mrs. Lynch said. "Why don't you go on up to bed now?"

Samantha sat up, clearing her vision. "I've left a mess," she said as she stood. "It won't take me long to clean it up."

"You go on, now. I'll clean up here. In the morning, you can pack up your medicines."

Samantha hesitated.

"Go on, now, they'll be fine here, and it won't take me

long to wash these pans." She ushered Samantha out of the kitchen and up to her room.

Samantha washed the paste off of her face and removed her clothing. That night, however, her nightmare returned. It was during the early morning hours when Samantha awoke. There was no use in trying to go back to sleep. The sun would be up in another hour. She dressed and went downstairs. By the time Mrs. Lynch came into the kitchen, Samantha had her medications packed and ready to take with her.

Belle did not disappoint. Samantha arrived to find the madam and eight young women waiting.

"I told them it was strictly volunteer. Two more wanted to come, so there are eight of them. You don't need to worry about the money. You gave me enough for all of them," she added. "Girls, this is Sam Cartier. He's the doctor I told you about."

The women smiled and greeted Samantha. They were all dressed in sober clothing, dark dresses, their bodices buttoned up to the neck, their hair tied up in nets. They looked very much like a church ladies auxiliary.

"I've gone over your instructions with the girls. We divided up the tasks," Belle said as she proceeded to explain how everything would be coordinated.

The next five days passed in a flurry of activity at the camp. Major Clark was true to his word. Except for those men who were sick or building fortifications around Charleston, all were put to work. The major assigned an officer to each of the five work details that Belle arranged. She had two of her girls working in pairs, coordinating each task. Samantha soon learned that Belle was a superb manager, and the girls worked hard. They were bright and willing and didn't shrink back from the more unpleasant tasks before them.

The men dug new latrines and burned refuse and garbage in a separate area of the camp. Infested bedding and clothing were burned and fresh supplies delivered. Although Belle had brought a few needed items the first day, more arrived. Samantha had a feeling that these were the supplies she had heard Ethan instructing Stephen Roland to deliver.

The women sorted through the food stores, discarding rotten items. Then they instructed the men on proper storage of food and saw that the cooking areas were moved away from the latrine. They taught the soldiers how to cook and correctly preserve food and organized laundry and bathing facilities.

Belle and Samantha then set up a hospital tent. Samantha explained the use of the medications and showed Belle how to clean the open sores on the soldiers. All of the soldiers had rashes and bites from the plethora of insects and vermin. Dysentery, typhoid, diphtheria, and pneumonia accounted for most of the deaths in the camp. Samantha arranged for immediate removal of the bodies. Because of the heat and constant presence of flying insects, bodies decayed quickly.

Belle and the girls usually left around suppertime, while Samantha stayed, working in the evening, treating those she could and isolating those she couldn't. It was always late by the time she saddled Kota and left. After the second night, Major Clark offered to send an escort with her to see that she got safely back into town. Samantha refused but, on his advice, did begin carrying her rifle with her.

When his duties permitted, Major Clark usually stopped by the hospital tent before he retired for the night. The first night, he appeared with a bottle of bourbon and two glasses and invited Sam to join him.

"You dressed me down pretty hard when you first showed up with Miss Belle, young man," he said.

"I was rude and disrespectful," Samantha admitted.

"Yes, you were, but I'm grateful," Major Clark said. "What you've done here is miraculous."

"Not me, Major. It's Belle and the women."

"Here's to Miss Belle and her ladies!" Major Clark raised his glass in a toast. Samantha found his use of the term "ladies" interesting, for he appeared to be sincere. She clinked her glass against his and drank to Belle and her ladies.

She usually returned to her work after Major Clark left the tent. She now had soldiers serving as orderlies in the hospital tent, but there was still a lot to be done before she finally left late at night.

It was the end of the second week, and Samantha experienced a particularly rough day. Several more men had died despite her efforts. She had been too busy to visit with Major Clark and share a glass of bourbon, as had become their habit. Exhausted, she fell asleep, her head resting on the table that served as desk and pharmacy.

Ethan returned to the hotel at night to find Sam gone. He went to Mrs. Lynch first and heard a surprising tale of how Sam was working at the camp with Miss Belle and her girls. He was certain that Mrs. Lynch misunderstood and went straight to Belle's. Belle admitted him and told him of all that had transpired in his absence. Ethan was incredulous. He could hardly believe what he was hearing. He left Belle's and rode to the camp. He woke Major Clark and listened to the events of the past two weeks.

"Sam usually works in the hospital tent until late," Major Clark explained. "If his horse is still here, you can find him there. I'll walk over with you. Major Winters-Hunt," Major Clark continued, "the death rate in the camp has dropped fifty percent this week. It's all because of that brash Yankee boy, Sam—Dr. Cartier."

The two men crossed the camp to where the large tent had been erected. There were a few lamps burning in the tent, one of them at the table where Sam slept.

"There he is," Major Clark said. "He comes at sunup and stays late each night."

"Thank you, Major," Ethan said. "I'll take him back to the hotel."

Ethan bent over Sam's sleeping form. Who would have thought this slip of a boy could accomplish so much? Ethan grinned, remembering the day he and Lieutenant Quicken came upon Sam, outnumbered three-to-one, his knife pressed against the neck of one of the lieutenant's men. And then to have found out that the boy was a surgeon. Ethan couldn't believe his luck. A lot of men wounded at the Wilderness and Spotsylvania owed their lives to Sam.

Ethan gently shook the boy's shoulder. "Sam? Wake up, Sam."

"What is it, orderly?" Sam said as he struggled to stand.

Ethan grabbed the boy's arm. "Come on, Sam. It's time to go back to the hotel."

"Major? You're back!"

Ethan laughed as he picked up Sam's hat and put it on his head. Sam could hardly hold his eyes open.

"Come on, Yankee," he said. "Lean on me, and I'll get you to your bed."

Ethan managed to help Sam mount Kota, and they rode back into town. A few times, he was certain Sam was going to fall off his horse as he slumped over on Kota's neck.

Somehow, the boy managed to stay on, and soon Ethan was unlocking the door to the room.

"You go to bed. I'll take care of the horses and get your bag."

When Ethan returned, he found Sam sound asleep, face down on top of the bed covers, boots and clothing still on. He thought about undressing the boy and putting him under the blanket, but Sam seemed so exhausted that Ethan decided to just remove his boots and extinguish the lamp. He then went back into his room to sleep.

Ethan was awakened during the night by muffled cries coming from the other room. He walked into Sam's room. The room was dark, except for what little light filtered in the window. He could see the tears escaping the boy's tightly closed eyes.

"Sam, it's all right. You're dreaming again," Ethan said gently. He reached out and took Sam's hand. He was surprised at how strongly the boy gripped his hand and held on to it. Finally, the boy's breathing eased and his grip on Ethan's hand lessened. Apparently, Sam's torment had passed. Ethan released his hand and returned to his own room, leaving the door open between the two rooms.

Samantha awoke the next morning as if coming out of a deep fog. She sat up in bed, clearing her head. The major! He was back. She looked down at her rumpled clothes. She could hear sounds coming from the next room. Quickly, she walked to the mirror. The paste mixture was still on her face, although it had rubbed off in some places. She reapplied the mixture, and when she was comfortable with her appearance, she walked to the open door and knocked.

"Come in," the major called.

Samantha walked into his room. He was sitting at a small

table, eating.

"Sit down, Sam. Your breakfast is waiting." He motioned to the chair across from him.

Shyly, Samantha walked over to the table and sat down. The major finished eating and pushed his chair back.

"I spoke with Major Clark last night," he said.

Samantha looked down at the table. She was afraid to look up, expecting that she would see that angry glint in his eyes.

"He said what you accomplished is miraculous. You saved a lot of lives, Sam. He's grateful." Ethan paused. "I am, too."

Samantha looked at Ethan and nodded her head. She was embarrassed by the sentiment, but then he sat back in his chair, a puzzled grin on his face.

"Did you really arrive at the camp with a wagonload of prostitutes? Damn, Sam, that was crazy." Ethan burst out laughing.

Samantha groaned. "You sound like Troy."

"Who?"

"My brother Troy. He says I do crazy things."

"How many brothers do you have?" he asked.

"Three."

"Any sisters?"

"No."

"So you're the youngest of four boys?"

"Troy is my twin. He just thinks he's older."

The major grinned. "Tell me about your brothers."

Samantha shrugged. "Charles is the oldest. He's married and has two young children. They live with us. Robert is two years older than me. Troy is my twin. He helps my father on our. . . ." Samantha stopped, aware she had to be careful what she said.

"Troy helps your father. What about the other two?"

Samantha hesitated. "Charles and Robert are captains in the Union Army," Samantha said evenly.

"I see," he said. "And your father sent you to Paris to study medicine?"

Samantha hesitated. "Not exactly."

The major cocked his eyebrow in question.

"I did study medicine at the College de France, as I told you."

He seemed to be studying her, and Samantha found it disquieting.

"I'm proud of you, Sam. I know I'm just a disloyal Rebel to you, but I would be honored to have you as a brother." He stood up from the table. "I need to talk with Major Clark today, and I assume you plan on going to the camp again. I'll go saddle the horses while you finish eating."

Samantha was still sitting there after the major left the room. She felt a rush of confusing emotions. Why should what he thought of her matter in the least? It shouldn't, given the nature of their relationship. But it did. For some reason, his approval was important to her.

A few minutes later, Samantha bounded down the steps, just in time to see two men standing in the lobby talking to Mrs. Lynch. "I'm sorry, Mr. Depardue, I think Mr. Winters-Hunt just left," Mrs. Lynch said. "But he might still be in the stable out back."

"You go check his room, and I'll go to the stable," Depardeu said to the other man.

Depardue. Samantha recognized that name. She recalled hearing the major's attorney say Depardue was angry because Ethan refused to ship slaves for him. Samantha hurried out the door and ran to the stable. The major was there, waiting with both horses.

"Major!" she said excitedly. "There's a man, Depardeu, and another man looking for you. They're coming out here."

Samantha saw the major's face tense. "It's all right, Sam. I'll deal with them."

Depardeu entered the stable and walked over to where Samantha and the major were standing with their horses.

"Mr. Winters-Hunt, I thought perhaps you might reconsider my business proposition," Depardeu said. "I'm prepared to offer you other incentives to ship my cargo."

"I'm not interested in anything you have to offer. I won't ship your slaves for you. Good day."

The major turned to mount his horse. Samantha did the same. In that moment, another man entered the stable. The major stopped and turned. Samantha was very near the major, and she saw his eyes narrow and jaw tense as he recognized the second man. She frowned and turned to see a fat, balding man, richly dressed.

"I believe you're acquainted with my new business partner?" Depardeu said, an expectant look upon his face.

"Ethan, it's been a few years, hasn't it?" the fat man said. "I couldn't believe it when my friend here said that you refused to consider shipping his goods. I told him I was sure that you'd reconsider if we increased the offer. We're prepared to pay you double your usual price."

"As I told Mr. Depardeu, I don't ship slaves. Sorry you had to travel this far to find that out." The major's voice was like ice. He turned to mount his horse.

The man took a few angry steps forward and grabbed the major's arm. "Now see here! Men are selling their Negroes for rock-bottom prices, and I've already made private arrangements to buy. I stand to lose a fortune if I can't ship them."

"Take your hand off of me," the major warned.

The look in the major's eyes was one of pure contempt for the man in front of him. The man hesitated, and the major reached with his other hand and grabbed the man's fat hand. In a slow gesture, he pried the man's hand off and twisted it backward until the fat man cried out in pain. The major released his arm and pulled him forward until the man fell down onto his knees.

"The answer is no and will always be no. We have nothing more to discuss."

The major turned and mounted his horse. Samantha did the same and urged Kota up next to him.

"You'll regret this, Ethan. No one treats me like this. No one!" the fat man screamed as he stood.

The major ignored him and rode out of the stable. Samantha twisted around in her saddle and shivered when she saw the fat man glaring at the major's back, a look of hatred in his eyes. She waited until they were at the edge of town and then spoke. "Who was that man with Depardeu?"

"His name is Montgomery, Franklin Montgomery. He owns a cotton plantation near Savannah."

"He looked as though he would have liked to kill you," she said with concern.

"Undoubtedly. But he hasn't the courage to do it, at least not himself. He's a coward at heart who uses others to get what he wants."

"Is he dangerous?"

"Yes."

Samantha started to ask another question, but the major changed the subject.

"We'll be leaving tomorrow," he said.

"Where are we going?"

"To Atlanta. The Confederate forces are dug in about twenty miles northwest of Atlanta. Sherman has been flanking around the Confederate troops, forcing them back. He'll either attack now or flank again. Either way, they'll engage in battle. I fear the losses will be great."

Samantha pondered this as they arrived at the camp.

Belle and her girls were already at work. The major had matters to attend to and left Samantha alone. She found Belle in the hospital tent.

"I was wondering where you were, Sam," Belle said in greeting.

"I slept later than I'd intended this morning."

"Well, good. You've been working too hard." Belle patted Samantha on the back.

"No harder than you or your girls," Samantha said.

"The camp looks good, doesn't it?" Belle asked.

"You've done a wonderful job, Belle. You all have." Samantha guided Belle away from the orderlies. "There's something we need to discuss. I'll be leaving tomorrow. Would you and your girls consider continuing? Someone will need to oversee the running of the camp in terms of the sanitary measures we've established. It shouldn't take much time now. The rest of the girls could work in the hospital tent. Major Clark said that now that there's a hospital established, more sick soldiers may be transported here."

Belle considered this. "But we won't have a doctor. What can we do?"

"Just keep doing what you've been doing. I'll continue to compensate you. We can make the arrangements before I leave."

"Is it dangerous where you're going?" Belle asked with concern.

Samantha hesitated. "The major is taking me back to the battlefield."

"No! Oh, honey," Belle said as she pulled Samantha into her arms.

Samantha hadn't seen Major Ethan Winters-Hunt all day, so when evening came, she was surprised to see him enter the hospital tent. Belle and her girls had left hours earlier.

"That's all for today, Sam. Let's head back into town."

"But I still have things to do."

"Enough. We'll be leaving early in the morning, and I don't want you falling asleep in the saddle like you did last night."

The sky was clear and the moon was bright as they rode out of the camp. Even in the darkness, they could see the road ahead of them. Samantha relaxed as they rode along, talking of inconsequential matters. The major teased her about her Yankee stubbornness, and she retorted with aspersions of her own regarding his Southern heritage. Their relationship was back to normal, if such a thing existed. They had been riding for about twenty minutes when there was a pause in the conversation. Samantha broached the subject directly.

"Major, I'd like to borrow some money from you."

The major raised his eyebrows. "What do you need money for?"

"It's personal." Samantha was not comfortable telling the major of her compensating the prostitutes for their work. This was something she must do because she was a doctor and medicine woman—not because she was his captive or forced into the service of the Confederacy. She did some rapid calculations in her head and then named a sum.

"That's a lot of money," he said. "Before I would loan that amount of money, I would usually need to know the nature of the man's business."

"I can't tell you that. If you don't have the money, I understand," Samantha said.

"Oh, I didn't say that I don't have the money. So do you have any references, anyone to cosign the loan with you?" he asked.

"You know I don't," she said quietly.

"How about collateral? Your horse, maybe?"

"Kota is worth a hundred times that," she retorted. "And I would never put him up as collateral. Never!"

"Well, then...."

"How about my skill?" she said seriously. "You want me to accompany you to Atlanta? Then give me a fee for my services to the Confederacy."

"A fee for services rendered. That's a thought, although I really don't have to pay for those. I've been providing room and board for you, and as we both know, you would do it anyway. You're a doctor. Why should I pay for something that your own conscience would dictate that you do?"

Samantha pulled Kota up into an abrupt halt and eyed the major severely.

"How about because of that damn Confederate honor I keep hearing about?" she retorted. "It would be the honorable thing to do, Reb."

The major broke into a deep laughter. "So it would, Yankee, so it would."

In that instant, a shot rang out from the woods on the side of the road. A second followed closely behind.

"Get out of here, Sam!" the major shouted as he slapped Kota on his rear haunches.

Kota bolted. The major withdrew his revolver just as two men on horseback emerged from the dark woods. He fired. The first man fell to the ground as the second rode straight toward him, shooting. The major spun his horse around and aimed again, hitting the second man. Then he heard another shot, this one coming from behind him.

Samantha galloped ahead and then turned Kota around just in time to see the major shoot the second man. In the moonlight, she saw two more men emerge from the other side of the road. Another was coming out from the side where the two lay on the ground. The major was outnumbered and caught in a cross fire between the remaining three men. She saw him suddenly lurch forward onto the neck of his horse and then raise himself up, taking aim again.

Without thinking, Samantha applied pressure to Kota's sides. The horse responded in a burst of speed back toward the shooting. Samantha reached for her rifle. She was a child again, playing at the war games taught to the young Lakota warriors. She was once again galloping at breakneck speed with Troy, Many Horses, and the other Indian boys, learning how to direct the horse with her lower legs, freeing her hands, letting her spine absorb the rhythm of the horse's movements so that her arms could remain steady as she aimed.

She leveled the sight of her rifle on the man behind the major. She automatically exhaled as she squeezed the trigger, all the time guiding her speeding horse with the subtle pressure of her legs. The man fell backward off his horse as Samantha's bullet found its mark. She gracefully swung the rifle as she cocked the lever, took aim again, and fired, the bullet striking the second man in his chest. The fifth man turned his horse around and disappeared into the woods.

Samantha pulled Kota to an abrupt halt, slid off, and expertly dropped to one knee. She still held her rifle aimed as she searched the shadows of the surrounding trees. The major did the same. Satisfied that no one else lurked beyond the woods, he turned to Samantha.

"I told you to get out of here. You could have been shot!" he exclaimed.

"And leave you to defend yourself against five men?" she retorted as she stood.

He exhaled, running his hand through his hair. "I guess I should be thanking you instead of scolding you. Where the hell did you learn to shoot like that? That was some of the finest shooting I've ever seen."

Samantha's attention was drawn to the two men lying sprawled on the ground where they'd fallen. She walked over to the first man she'd shot and knelt down beside him. Her bullet had indeed found its mark. A large, dark-red patch appeared on the chest of the man. She looked over at the second man and began to tremble as she surveyed the results of her instinctive reaction. This hadn't been a game. She'd killed two men. The bile rose up in her throat and she leaned to the side, her stomach contracting violently.

The major was checking the other two bodies when he heard Samantha. He walked over to where she stood and handed her a cloth when her retching subsided. She wiped her mouth and then hugged her arms to herself.

"I've never killed anyone before," she said with a tremor in her voice.

"It's never a good thing, Sam, but in this case, I'm glad you did, for I think it would have been me lying here otherwise."

Samantha nodded in understanding.

"As it is, Sam," he continued, "I think I'll have to start collecting on your services sooner than I had planned. One of them hit me in the arm," he said.

"What?" Samantha frowned as she took in the major's appearance, and then she noticed the blood on his coat.

"Major!"

"It's not bad. The bullet just grazed the skin," he said.

"Let me see."

Samantha helped him remove his coat and shirt. "You're right. It's a superficial wound. It looks clean, but the skin should still be sutured. Sit down. I'll be right back."

She ran over to Kota and retrieved her bag. When she returned, she sat beside him on the ground. "Hold still. This will be quick," she instructed.

He sat on the ground while she stitched and bandaged his arm. When she finished, she helped him put his shirt on.

"What did these men want?" Samantha asked at last.

"My guess is they wanted me, or more precisely, they wanted me dead."

"But why? Who are they?"

"I can't prove it, but they were probably hired by Franklin Montgomery and Gerald Depardeu."

"What are you going to do?"

"Nothing. I can't prove anything—at least, not yet." He stood. "Let's get back to the hotel." He moved over to his horse.

"But what about these bodies?"

"Leave them."

"We can't just leave them here."

"Yes, we can. Montgomery will send someone out looking for them. The man who got away will report back to him. Montgomery will want the bodies searched to make certain there's no link to him."

Samantha walked over to Kota and mounted. As they rode away, she looked back at the four bodies lying on the side of the road.

When they reached Charleston, they went straight to the hotel. That night, they ate in the hotel room. The major suggested she get to sleep early since they had a full day's riding ahead of them tomorrow. Just before she retired to her room, he surprised her by giving her the money she asked for.

"Southern honor, remember? Good night, Sam."

They left early the next morning. Samantha convinced him to let her stop by Belle's so that she might discuss the running of the hospital tent. While there, she furtively passed the money to Belle.

They arrived in Atlanta June 26, 1864. Samantha had

never seen anything like it. Surrounding the entire city were trenches dug into the earth with rings of large, wooden spikes fashioned into the shape of an "X". The spikes were all attached to each other, forming a wall. They stretched out in rows, two and three deep, completely surrounding the city. The sharp spikes projected up into the air, making a direct assault upon the city almost impossible. The sight that greeted her further convinced her of what she had already learned from the major: Atlanta was the second most important city in the South. Its defense was paramount to the survival of the Confederacy.

Samantha and the major rode beyond the city to the northwest, where Confederate forces were dug in across the face of Kennesaw Mountain. For almost two weeks, Union forces had fired round upon round up onto the mountain. Although casualties were high, Sherman's forces had not been able to push the Confederates back. Atlanta was still safe, for the time being, and Samantha once again found herself plunged back into her nightmare.

CHAPTER 6

The noise was deafening as cannons and rifles fired repeatedly. Samantha found the surgical tent set up behind Confederate lines. How well she recalled this scene. The wounded lay on the ground, candidates for surgery closest to the tent. Soldiers with chest or abdominal wounds were placed farther away or left on the battlefield, for there was no treatment for so severe a wound.

She knew from her previous experience that the fighting went on continuously, with little chance for a litter to pick up the wounded. Unless a wounded soldier was able to crawl back on his own, he was left where he fell until a ceasefire was called by one of the sides, it grew too dark to fight, or one side withdrew from the battle.

"If you aren't a pleasing sight, young man!" Dr. Beauregard said when Samantha entered the surgical tent.

Dr. Beauregard was at one surgical table and Dr. Schafley was at the other. Dr. Schafley looked up from his surgery to see Samantha standing there. He returned to his work without saying a word.

"Orderly! Set up another table for Dr. Cartier," Dr. Beauregard said and then turned back to Samantha. "I'll assign a couple of orderlies to work with you. You can explain to them what you need."

Samantha and her orderlies quickly settled into a routine. The orderlies restrained the patients as Samantha went about her grisly job of amputation. She cut through skin, tied off blood vessels, watched as muscle shrank back when it was severed from the wounded limb, sawed off bone, cushioned nerves to reduce the incidence of "phantom limb" pain, and fashioned stumps that were clean and did not bleed. As hard as she concentrated, she could not, however, shut out the screams and crying of the men around her and under her knife. The few periods of relief she felt came when she was able to remove a lead ball, repair the mangled tissue, and leave the limb attached.

Late that night, there was a break. No more wounded were brought in, and the shooting stopped because there was no moon to see by. All day, it had been hot and suffocating inside the tent. Dr. Beauregard and Dr. Schafley had stripped to their bare chests as an escape from the stifling heat, and also because their shirts had become soaked with the blood of the wounded. Samantha had removed her coat and rolled up her sleeves. Still, the heat had been unrelenting.

As she stepped out of the tent and into the night air, she used her sleeve to carelessly wipe the blood and sweat from her face. Her skin itched and burned under the tight gauze. Her blood-drenched shirt clung to the gauze. No one seemed to notice her macabre appearance as she walked among the exhausted Confederate soldiers who sat on the ground, staring vacantly at their campfires.

Samantha stopped and looked down the slope of the mountain. A short distance separated the two armies. She was staring at the campfires of the Federal soldiers below when she heard a familiar voice.

"Sam, I've been looking for you. Have you eaten anything today?"

She turned to see Major Ethan Winters-Hunt. In the dim light of the campfires, she could see dark powder smudges on his face.

"Let's find a place to sit," he said as he put his arm around her shoulder, heedless of the blood rubbing off onto his coat. "I brought food."

They found a small ledge on the face of the mountain. The major built a fire, explaining that the smoke would help to deter the mosquitoes. At first, Samantha was too tired to talk. She ate in silence. Then, from below the mountain, came the plaintive sound of a bugle from the Union camp below. The bugler played favorite songs from the North, and Samantha could hear the Union soldiers cheer after each song. Surprisingly, the Confederate soldiers also began to clap their hands, signaling their enjoyment of the music.

As Samantha and the major sat together and listened, a strange thing happened. The bugler finished a lively folk tune, and both sides clapped and cheered. The Confederate soldiers on the mountain shouted friendly words to the Union soldiers camped below. Suddenly, the bugler began to play "Dixie" loudly and clearly. He played the Southern anthem with gusto, and when he finished, there was a loud roar from the side of the mountain as the Confederate soldiers showed their appreciation. From below, Samantha could hear the cheers of the Northern troops, too. The bugler followed this with three more Southern melodies as both sides took delight in the music.

From the bugler's notes, clarity came to Samantha, bringing with it a quieted conscience. She looked directly at the major.

"This war should have never happened," she said softly. "These men aren't enemies. How did it ever get this far?" she whispered.

They talked well into the night. Samantha felt a fresh openness as she listened to the major. He told her about his parents and growing up in South Carolina. At one point, he started to talk about his involvement in the war, and then he stopped. Samantha, sensing something, probed.

"Major, you told me about your ships, and I know about the supplies you bring in. What I don't understand is what it is that you do in the army. You're a major, and yet you don't command any troops. I've watched you meet with various generals, and I gather you even meet with General Lee. You rarely wear your uniform. You say that you are attending to business, and then you leave for days. When you return, you go right to those Confederate generals again. What is it that you do?"

He sighed. "I'm sorry, Sam. I'm not free to discuss that. It's not that I don't trust you, but there are others involved, and I'm honor bound. I hope you understand." He paused and then continued. "What I do, in the long run, will probably have very little effect on the outcome of this war. I don't see that the South can ever force the North off of Southern soil. In the end, I believe the superior numbers of the North will defeat the South. What I believe will result from my actions—and I must believe it—is that when the South is finally defeated, there will be some Southerners who survive to return to their barren farms and burned cities. No matter what moral wrong was done by my people, they don't deserve to be destroyed completely."

Samantha's question wasn't answered, but she did gain another insight into this man who had become, at first, her captor, and then her constant companion. And now? Her friend? Was that possible?

"There's one more thing, Sam. When this battle is finished, Atlanta will either be saved, for the moment, or under siege. Regardless of the outcome, I'll be going to Washington City. I don't know exactly when, but I can take you with me. Once there, you are free to go as you wish."

"You'll let me go, Major?"

"Don't look so surprised," he said, laughing. "And Sam, I think it's time you start calling me by my given name. It's Ethan."

They talked for a while longer until he suggested that Samantha sleep. She leaned back against the rocky ledge behind her and instantly fell asleep.

Ethan didn't sleep immediately. He stood and added more wood to the small fire and then sat down next to Sam. As he did, the boy moaned and moved his head to rest on Ethan's shoulder. Ethan couldn't see Sam well, but a strange feeling came over him. Sam was a puzzle, and a piece of the puzzle was missing. This wasn't the first time that analogy had come to mind. Why did he always return to the idea of a child's puzzle and a missing piece?

When he finally fell asleep, he had a bizarre dream about searching for a puzzle piece. He looked everywhere. For some reason, he knew that he had to find this piece quickly. Time was running out. He was on his horse, riding as fast as he could, but he discovered he'd been riding in circles. He was desperate, when suddenly an old man appeared, strangely dressed in buckskins, standing in the road ahead of him. The man's skin was dark red, his hair jet black and adorned with feathers. It was his face, though, that caught Ethan's attention. It was deeply etched with lines, out of which his eyes shone brightly. The old Indian extended his arm, and there, in the palm of his hand, was the missing puzzle piece.

Ethan awoke with a start, disturbed by the dream. He shook his head to clear it. There was activity all about him. He gently nudged Sam's foot with his own. "Sam, you'd better get back to the tents. It looks like the Federal forces are forming up down there."

Samantha awoke to see the movement of the men in blue below. There was a flurry of activity on the mountainside, too, as the Confederate troops positioned themselves across the mountain. Samantha and Ethan moved back behind the lines, but she didn't return to the tents. Her services wouldn't be required just yet. Instead, she ended up watching one of the worst massacres of the war.

The Union had used cannons to blast away at the mountain for days. Now, Samantha watched as line after line of Union soldiers started marching up to the mountain. The Union soldiers were completely defenseless in the open as they charged up the mountain while Confederate firepower rained down on them. Line after line of them fell, like toy soldiers, thirteen thousand in all that day. The battle continued to rage, with few of the injured ever making it back to their lines. Above the mountain was a cloud of gun smoke that hovered, announcing the ominous occasion.

When Samantha could watch the slaughter no more, she returned to the tents. She hadn't seen Ethan since they had awoken that morning. Slowly, a few Confederate soldiers who had been shot made their way back to the tents, and the surgeons once again began their bloody work. The battle continued for three days and nights until the fourth day, when suddenly everything grew quiet. Dr. Beauregard called Samantha and Dr. Schafley to his side.

"An armistice has been granted for the day. Trenches will be dug, and the dead buried. God willing, there may be a few still alive out there."

The stench of rotting bodies in the Georgia heat was unbearable. As Samantha learned, that was the main reason for halting the fighting. Neither side could function any longer amid the bloated, infested corpses. The odor alone was enough to make a hardened veteran of the war retch. It was a strange site as both Confederate and Union soldiers walked among each other, sorting out the dead. Long trenches were dug and the bodies—thousands of them—rolled into common graves.

After that, the Union forces did not again attempt a direct assault on the mountain. General Sherman realized his mistake and had his artillerymen return to their cannon fire. This was cause for rejoicing among the Confederate troops, but it was short lived. In a matter of days, Sherman's plan became evident. He moved the bulk of his forces around the side of the mountain, forcing Johnston's Confederate forces to abandon their positions on the mountain and race ahead to block Sherman's path to Atlanta. There were multiple clashes as they moved. Frequently, the line drawn between the two sides was less than a hundred feet before they would again pull away from each other. It was a skirmish such as this that Samantha was caught in, and her world was once again forever changed.

Samantha hadn't seen Ethan since the night they had spent talking on the ledge of the mountain. She heard that he left to attend to a mission directed by the general's staff. The surgical tents had been dismantled, and the surgeons and their staff were on the move with the Confederate soldiers. Although the surgical staff usually traveled behind the troops, frequent skirmishes between the two sides happened directly in front of Samantha, and she would find herself seeking shelter as rifle and musket fire exploded before her.

They were traveling south when Union forces attacked the Confederate unit directly preceding the medical unit. Samantha heard a captain shout for all to take cover. She ducked as she heard a lead ball go flying past her and pressed Kota into a grove of trees for protection. Several

Confederate soldiers fell before her eyes with the surprise attack. Samantha saw Dr. Beauregard and Dr. Schafley race ahead of the shooting.

A bloodcurdling howl erupted as the road suddenly filled with men in gray. Another unit of Confederate soldiers came hurling down upon the Union soldiers, shouting that peculiar Rebel yell that always sent chills down Samantha's spine. The dead, blue and gray, lay everywhere in the road and surrounding area. Union soldiers retreated into the woods where Samantha had taken refuge. She could hear lead balls strike the trees around her as the men came closer and closer to where she was crouched down behind a tree.

Samantha rose up and mounted Kota. Just then, a Union soldier broke through the trees not five feet from her. Samantha froze, but the soldier didn't aim his gun at her. In that instant, there was a loud shot, and she saw the Union soldier before her fall to the ground. He screamed as he clutched his leg, the blood already soaking his pants.

"Help me!" the Union soldier cried. He raised himself up on his hands and tried to crawl to Samantha. Kota pranced nervously as the musket fire exploded around him. Samantha gave a short command to the horse, and he stood still as she slid off him and ran to the wounded Union soldier.

"Grab my shoulder," she said as she struggled to help the man stand. Just then, there was a loud explosion, and her body was pushed into the soldier. The next thing she felt was an excruciating pain—a searing heat that spread over the right side of her chest, burning her. It was difficult to breathe. The Union soldier yelled once more and fell to the ground, a dark patch of blood appearing on his back. Samantha reached for the burning on her right side and was amazed when she pulled her hand back to see it covered with blood.

In that instant, there was an eruption inside of her head, bursting. Light flashed in her eyes, the explosive pain blinding her. She heard Kota's frightened whinny as he reared up. She was vaguely aware of the ground coming up to meet her. She could smell the rich scent of the Georgia soil amid the pain. Once again, she heard Kota, although this time, it seemed as though he was far away. She struggled to rise up on one hand, her breath ragged, her skull feeling like it was breaking open. Something warm and wet was flowing over her left eye, occluding her vision. She squeezed it shut, trying to focus through the pain with her right eye. She saw Kota.

Kota! Not Kota! Nothing must happen to him. In a final effort, she supported herself on her left arm and struggled to draw a deep breath. "Kota! Go! Go!" she commanded.

The last thing she saw was the great black horse rearing up amid the lead balls. Then he whirled around, his powerful hooves gripping the earth in speed, sending dirt, leaves, and debris scattered behind him as he shot forward and disappeared among the trees.

Slowly, she sank down into the darkness.

There was nothing—just blackness. It was neither hot nor cold. There was no temperature. There was no sensation or feeling at all. She was alone, but she was not frightened. She rested in this void. Time did not exist.

She sensed rather than felt it; a presence was with her now. It seemed familiar and she drew comfort from its nearness. Slowly, a light began to form in the blackness. It grew stronger and was amazingly warm and restoring. A face began to take shape in the presence with her, the light guiding its formation—a dark-red face with deep, timeless furrows etched in it, and eyes that shone brightly with the wisdom of eternity. Suddenly, he was there before her, dressed as she remembered him in fringed buckskins and feathers in his hair. He reached out and took her hand. She stepped toward him.

"Charrah! How is it that you are here?" she asked.

"How is it that you ask such a question?" he countered.

She watched as he knelt beside the body. He motioned for her to kneel beside him as she had so many times as a young girl.

"There is much blood," he said as he examined the body.

Samantha looked down upon her own unconscious form lying on the ground. "Yes," she answered.

"The heart is beating too fast. You must slow it," he said.

She looked at him, confused by his words. He took her hand and placed it upon the chest of her own body lying on the ground.

"It is beating too wildly. Slow it," he said as he held his hand over hers.

She looked at the old fingers. Such power they had held! He removed his hand, leaving hers there.

"Slow it," he again commanded.

"Yes," she answered.

Her heartbeat slowed down until it was barely perceptible.

"Now, the air rushes in too quickly. Calm it," he said.

"Yes," she answered.

Her breathing quieted and became slow and shallow.

He moved her hand and placed it upon a leg.

"There is too much warmth here," he said, "and here," he said, moving her hand to the other leg, "and here," he said, placing her hand upon each arm.

"I understand," Samantha answered.

The blood vessels in her arms and legs constricted, decreasing the flow of blood to her extremities and shunting it to the vital organs of her heart and brain.

"It is good," the holy man said. "You must return now."

Samantha was surprised. She hesitated, looking at the still form on the ground.

"It is not for you to choose," he stated.

Samantha nodded. Again she looked down at her body on the

ground.

"There is great pain in this body," she said, a moment of memory and fear coming back to her.

"Yes," he replied, "but many have pain. You are medicine woman."

"I understand."

The light began to fade, and with it Charrah's form. Samantha felt herself move into the body on the ground. A shock went through her as the pain assailed her senses. In that instant, just before she completely joined her body there, she felt her spirit reach out. She connected with the dead lying there on the battlefield around her. The grief and anguish of hundreds shook her very soul.

"Charrah! Don't leave me! I can't do this alone. I don't have the strength for this," she cried out.

"No," she heard him say, "but there is one who does. That is why he was sent to you."

"Where?" she asked, struggling. "I am alone! I see no one!"

"Foolish child! A medicine woman does not see with her eyes alone."

Then he was gone. She was alone. She was lying on the ground. She tried to move, and her head again exploded in pain. Was her skull still intact? Was part of it blown away? Her chest was burning. Were her clothes on fire? She tried to open her eyes, but her left eye was still occluded with blood. She could barely see the sky above her, obstructed by the leaves of the trees. Slowly, everything began to fade away. Even the pain started to grow paler, and everything grew dark. In the darkness, she kept her heart beating faintly and her lungs barely breathing.

Ethan sat with a few of General Johnston's officers. Sherman was definitely pressing to Atlanta. General Lee was trying to shore up forces around Petersburg in preparation for Grant's inevitable attack; there were no other Confederate forces to mobilize to Atlanta to help. They were quietly going over their plans when they heard a commotion in the camp.

"Excuse me, gentlemen. I'll see what's happening," Ethan said as he stood. He exited the tent and walked to where he heard men shouting.

"Catch him!" a soldier shouted.

"Over here. Drive him this way. Get him!"

There was a shrill cry of protest as the great black horse reared up, his hooves coming dangerously close to the man's head.

"This horse is crazy!" the soldier shouted as he jumped back.

"Looks like he's been hit," another said. "See the blood on his neck?"

A half dozen men were trying to circle the horse but were driven back by the powerful hooves lashing out. Ethan recognized the horse instantly.

"Kota!" he shouted and ran over to the men.

As Ethan drew near, he slowed his pace and calmly approached the horse that was still rearing in the air, the horse's ferocity sending the Confederate men scattering.

"Kota," Ethan said softly.

There was a wild look in Kota's eyes, but he stopped rearing and stood, nervously pawing the ground, but allowing Ethan to approach.

"It looks like you're hurt. Easy boy. Let's look at that neck of yours."

The horse whinnied softly as Ethan placed his hand over its nostrils. Kota sniffed and inhaled Ethan's scent.

"Where's Sam?" Ethan asked of the crowd around him. "Where's the young man who owns this horse? Where's Dr. Cartier?"

None of the soldiers seemed to know. Ethan turned to the man closest to him.

"Go find Dr. Cartier. He should be with the surgeons."

Ethan turned back to Kota. The horse had grown restless again, prancing nervously. When Ethan reached out to grab his reins, Kota pulled away and turned. The horse started to trot a few feet and then turned back to Ethan. Once again, he reared up in the air. When Ethan approached him again, he stepped away, throwing his great head up in the air and shaking his powerful neck.

Something was wrong; Ethan could feel it. Sam would never leave Kota alone like this, and the horse would not likely leave Sam. On several occasions, Ethan had seen Sam loosely throw Kota's reins over a tree branch or hitching post and murmur to the horse. The horse could have easily gotten loose if it had wanted to. Even the temptation of fresh grass a few feet away or the threat of snarling dogs or gunfire had not caused the horse to move from where Sam had left it. A feeling of apprehension came over Ethan.

"Ethan, what's wrong?" Clement Beauregard called as he ran to where Ethan was standing. The older surgeon had a look of concern on his face. "A man just came over to our tent and said you were looking for Sam. He's not here."

"Not here? Where is he?" Ethan asked with alarm.

"I don't know. I assumed he was with you. I haven't seen him since we made camp."

"When did you last see him?" Ethan asked.

The white-haired surgeon thought for a moment. "This morning, when the end of our column was attacked."

Kota reared up again and began to prance nervously. He bolted away a few feet and then turned, pawing the ground. Ethan eyed the horse closely.

"That's the last time you saw him?"

"Yes! We hightailed it out of there. I assumed he was behind us."

"Where was this?"

"Three or four miles back on the road. Our boys caught up with us. They brought a few wounded men with them. They said everyone left behind was dead." A deathly pallor came upon Dr. Beauregard's face. "Sam couldn't have been killed. Someone would have recognized him and told us."

Ethan walked slowly toward Kota. "Easy boy," he said softly. "You know where Sam is, don't you?"

The horse snorted as Ethan reached for the reins. Cautiously, Ethan took the left stirrup in his hand and placed his left foot in it. As gently as he could, he swung himself up into the saddle. The horse sidestepped and twisted under the unfamiliar rider. Ethan started to apply his boot to the horse's sides, but before he got the chance, the horse shot forward. Ethan settled into the saddle and allowed Kota's powerful strides to carry him forward at lightning speed.

Even before the horse slowed down, Ethan could see the mass of bodies on the road ahead of him. He started to rein in the horse, but Kota slowed down on his own. Dead soldiers lay everywhere. Ethan tried to halt Kota, but the horse jerked its head, pulling on the reins. Kota walked through the bodies, sickening Ethan once when the powerful hooves came down on a dead man. The horse headed directly for the woods on the side of the road. There were more bodies here as they entered the shelter of the trees. Then he saw it—the last thing he ever wanted to see in this hell on earth—Sam's body. The horse let out a powerful whinny that echoed through the now-silent woods.

"Sam!" Ethan jumped off the horse and knelt beside Sam's body. "Sam!" he cried in anguish. "Oh, God, no, not this boy!"

The left side of Sam's head and face were covered in blood. As Ethan reached out to him, Sam's coat fell away. The right side of his shirt was drenched in blood.

"Not Sam. Please, God, please, not Sam," he prayed as his eyes filled with tears. He searched the silent heavens above in desperation. "Please, I'm begging you," he cried in a strangled voice.

He cradled Sam against him and wept openly for the boy whom he was responsible for, the one he'd begun to think of as a brother and friend.

He didn't know how long he knelt there, clutching Sam's lifeless body to him, when he was suddenly aware of Kota. The great horse reared up, its hooves coming down to land within inches of him.

"What the hell!" Ethan cried.

He twisted on the ground, away from the horse as it once again reared up in the air. As he did, something caught his attention. He was still holding Sam in his arms. He looked at the boy. A glimmer of hope shot through him as he lowered his face down to Sam's. He felt it! The very soft exhaling of air on his cheek. He placed his fingers on the boy's neck. It was faint, but it was there. A heartbeat! Sam was still alive—just barely, but still alive.

Amazingly, Kota stood still as Ethan struggled to mount the horse while clutching Sam to him. He was settling into the saddle and about to reach for the reins when the horse turned on its own and headed back out to the road.

"I'll be damned!" Ethan laughed in relief. "You know where to go, don't you? All right, Kota, let's go."

The horse leaped forward, carrying Ethan and Sam back to the camp.

"Clement! Clement!" Ethan yelled as he galloped into the camp. "Sam's hurt!"

Clement Beauregard ran over to Ethan, and Ethan lowered Sam into his arms. Dr. Beauregard shouted to his orderlies as he carried Sam into the surgical tent. He laid the boy down on one of the tables as Dr. Schafley came running in behind them. Dr. Beauregard looked at the quiet form before him. His face was grave as he felt for the pulse. Dr. Schafley also felt Sam's wrist and then opened the one eye that was visible. The pupil was widely dilated. He looked up at the older surgeon, a stony expression on his face.

Dr. Beauregard sighed, the sorrow in his voice great. "I'm sorry, Ethan. It's too late. There's nothing we can do."

"What do you mean?" Ethan answered angrily. "He's not dead. He's still breathing."

"For not much longer, Ethan. His heart has almost stopped. He's not in any pain," the older man said as he placed his hand on Ethan's shoulder, his own grief evident. "He'll just slip away now."

"No!" Ethan said. "Sam!"

Dr. Beauregard motioned to Dr. Schafley and the others to leave. When the tent was empty, he turned back to Ethan.

"I'm sorry, Ethan," he began.

Ethan grabbed Dr. Beauregard's arm. "Do something, Clement!"

"I would if I could, Ethan. You know that," the old man said.

"It is time," she heard the holy man say. *"The heart must beat strongly now, and more air must flow into this body, as must the pain. Do you understand?"*

"Yes, I understand," she answered.

She came out from the darkness and felt the warmth return to her limbs. Her chest expanded. A great tide of air rushed in, and with it, the explosion of pain engulfing her body.

Ethan turned, startled by the gasp of breathing. He saw the rapid rise and fall of Sam's chest. Blood began to flow down from Sam's matted hair and pooled beneath his head. "Sam!" Ethan shouted.

"Good Lord!" Clement exclaimed. He reached for a stack of bandages and pressed them to Sam's head.

"Shall I call the others?" Ethan asked.

"There's no time," Clement answered. "Grab that bowl over there and fill it with water. There's clean water in the bucket and soap next to it."

Ethan flashed a queer look in Clement's direction.

"So the young pup taught me a thing or two," Clement said.

Clement washed the matted blood from Sam's scalp. "There's one wound to the head. Let's check his face," he said. As he wiped the blood off Sam's face and eye, he frowned. "What's this?" he asked, looking at the gritty substance on the cloth.

"I suspected Sam's beard wasn't real," Ethan said. "Neither is the mustache. He was trying to make himself look older."

"Foolish boy," Clement said as he cleaned the wound. "The lead ball didn't enter the skull, but it made a hell of a groove in it. Looks like a small skull fracture, too. He probably has a concussion; that's why his breathing was so shallow. I can stitch this to stop the bleeding, but I can't be certain the concussion hasn't damaged his brain."

"Clement," Ethan said, noticing the fresh pool of blood on the side of the table. Ethan pulled Sam's coat aside to reveal his blood-drenched shirt.

"Hold this," Clement said grimly as he handed Ethan a bandage to press against Sam's head. With one quick motion, Clement ripped Sam's shirt open. "What's this?" he asked, pointing to the gauze tightly bound around Sam's chest.

A strange feeling came over Ethan as he gazed at the peculiar gauze wrapping. He suddenly felt disoriented as he stared at Sam's chest. Clement reached for a pair of scissors and began to cut through the layers of gauze. Ethan inhaled sharply as, with the last cut, the gauze fell away, revealing Sam's breasts and the wound on the right side of the chest. "What the hell!" Ethan exclaimed.

"What's going on here?" Clement Beauregard demanded. "Did you know about this?" The old surgeon unceremoniously unbuttoned Samantha's pants and thrust his hand into them. He withdrew his hand, an ashen color on his face.

"Good Lord!" Dr. Beauregard exclaimed.

Ethan gaped at Sam, too stunned to speak.

"By the look on your face, I gather you didn't know anything about this," Clement said. "Our surgeon here is a young woman, my friend, and if we don't get busy, we still might lose her."

Clement pressed a clean cloth against the chest wound. "That damned gauze probably saved the boy's . . . err . . . the woman's life. Her chest was so tightly bound, the lead grazed past and didn't enter the chest cavity, thank God. Look. It tore through the skin here and back out. Looks like it broke three ribs, though," he continued as he inspected the wound, "and tore some major blood vessels. She's lost a lot of blood. I've got to close this wound."

Dr. Beauregard spent the next few minutes suturing Sam's head and chest wounds. Then, satisfied that all the bleeding had stopped, he wrapped a bandage around her head. "Ethan, help me lift her up so I can wrap another bandage around her chest to support the ribs."

Together, Ethan and Clement wrapped clean gauze around Sam's chest, covering the dressing Clement had applied to the sutured wound. Just then, one of Dr. Beauregard's orderlies entered the tent. "Do you need anything, Doctor?" he asked.

Clement hastily covered Sam's chest and stepped in front

of her, obstructing the orderly's view. "No, Private. I wish not to be disturbed."

"Yes, sir." The orderly nodded and left.

"I doubt that young man has ever seen a woman's breasts, but I'm sure he would know what they are," Clement muttered to himself. "Ethan, we're going to need a shirt for her, and then we must talk. Would you mind getting one? I'll stay with her."

Ethan nodded, his mind still reeling from what he'd just seen. When he returned, he stopped suddenly, staring at the site before him.

"I thought I might as well clean the rest of the blood off her face," Clement said. He had washed all of the paste from Samantha's face and removed the mustache. In the process of inspecting the rest of her head to make certain that he hadn't missed any other wounds, he then loosened her hair. "How did she do it?" Clement asked softly. "How could she have fooled us all?" There was the hint of admiration in his voice as he looked down at her quiet form.

Ethan swallowed. He was dreading the answer to his next question. "Is she going to live, Clement?"

"I don't know. You never know with a blow to the head; the skull is fractured. I cleaned and stitched the wounds, but they could still putrefy. She lost a lot of blood, too. I'd say the chances are not good, Ethan." He paused and wiped his eyes. "You know how people we care about are ripped away from us in this godforsaken war. It makes a man not want to feel anymore, but, damn if I wasn't fond of this boy—starting to think of him as a son. . . ."

Ethan looked down at the woman before him. She was beautiful. Her complexion was clear, her eyelashes long and dark. He could see the delicate angle of her jaw and neck. Her eyes were closed, but he recalled the vivid shade of green and the spark that came to them when she argued with him. He looked at her hands. He remembered Sam clutching his hand during one of his nightmares. How could he have thought those were the hands of a boy? How had she managed to conceal her form from him? She was a young woman, slim, but still in the bloom of womanhood. "I took her over my knee once. Thrashed her hind end," he said softly.

Clement Beauregard looked aghast. "You what?"

"I thought she was a boy, and she almost got us killed with her incessant arguing against slavery and secession and any other issue that came up between us." Ethan swore. "I've eaten with her, spent hours talking with her, even slept with her."

"Ethan!"

"It's true. Hell, she was Sam, a boy, remember? She shared my tent. We traveled to Charleston together and slept on the ground next to each other." He smiled grudgingly. "In Charleston, she was adamant about having her own room, though. I thought it was just because he—she—hated me. I forced Sam to come with me the first time I brought her to you."

"What do you mean *forced* her?"

"Sam was lost. I was with Lieutenant Quicken's patrol. A few of Quicken's men found her. They were trying to take her horse when she pulled a knife on one of them. She bested him, had the blade against his neck. I was going to let her go until I found out that she was a surgeon. I didn't give her a choice." Ethan saw the surprised expression on the older surgeon's face. "She wouldn't have survived on her own. We needed doctors. She was our captive, so I made her come with me. And I felt responsible for her. Of course, I thought she was a boy."

Clement looked down at Samantha's quiet face as he felt for her pulse. "Her heartbeat is strong now. No more bleeding," he said as he inspected the bandages. "She's an exceptional surgeon, Ethan, by far the finest I've ever seen in peacetime and war. Do you think she was telling the truth about training in Paris?"

Ethan thought back. The missing piece was finally in place. It all made sense now, and what a fool he had been not to have seen the truth. "Yes," he answered. "I think she told the truth about everything except who she is, something we still don't know."

"You never picked up any hints all the time you were in Charleston together?"

"No, she disliked me and distrusted me." Ethan's throat tightened as he stared at Samantha's pale form. "How long will she be like this?" he asked.

"I don't know," Clement answered. "A few hours, a few days. The lead didn't penetrate her skull, but there still could be swelling in her brain. She shouldn't be moved. I'm sorry, Ethan." Clement's shoulders sagged, his own grief evident. "It's doubtful she will survive these wounds. Then again, she's got a strong spirit. That counts for something."

Ethan came to a decision. "Put another cot in my tent. She can stay with me until she recovers."

"What? No!" Clement said.

"Why not? Where else are you going to put her? We want to keep this quiet, don't we?"

"It's not proper, Ethan. We must think of that now."

"To hell with what's proper. Sam is my responsibility. I'll take care of her."

Clement frowned but finally agreed. A few minutes later, Ethan carried the unconscious Samantha to his tent and gently placed her on the cot next to his.

It was a long night for Ethan. Samantha alternated between lying deathly still and periods of restlessness. She moaned and tossed her head from side to side. At one point, he sent for Dr. Beauregard.

"She's feverish, Clement. It just started an hour ago."

Clement felt Samantha's forehead. She began to mumble. "What's she saying?" he asked.

"I don't know," Ethan answered. "She speaks that language when she gets restless. It's the same language she uses with her horse."

"Help me remove these bandages," Clement said. Ethan helped the older man unwrap the bandages on Samantha's wounds. "No putrefaction," Clement said as he inspected Samantha's injuries. "I don't know what's causing the fever, unless it's the concussion. You never know what's going to happen with blows to the head. One thing's certain: we must get this fever down. I'll send for some water and cloths. We can sponge her down."

A few minutes later, an orderly appeared at the entrance of Ethan's tent with the supplies. Ethan reached for the bucket of water and dismissed the orderly. "I'll do it, Clement," he said as he approached Samantha's cot.

Clement grabbed Ethan's arm. "Her clothes should be removed and her body sponged off until the fever breaks. She's not a common woman, Ethan. Her education, speech, and manners testify to that. Look at that horse she rides; it's worth a fortune. My guess is that she's grown up privileged, and until I learn otherwise, she'll be treated like a lady."

"And you don't think I'll do that?" Ethan asked angrily as he shook off Clement's hand. "Sam is here because of me. She was shot because of me. She's my responsibility, and I'll do whatever is necessary to keep her alive."

"You feel guilty," Clement said with a sigh. "Very well. Send for me if there's any change."

For the rest of the night, Ethan bathed Samantha in cool water. It was daylight when Clement returned to the tent.

"Her fever broke an hour ago," Ethan said as the older

man entered. "She's been resting quietly since then."

Clement felt Samantha's forehead and nodded in satisfaction. "I've got to go to work soon. There's been more fighting."

"I heard the guns earlier," Ethan said.

"If you need anything, send word."

Ethan nodded.

For the next two days and nights, Ethan never left Sam's side. Several times, the fever returned, and each time, he bathed her in cool water as she thrashed about, unconscious. Between the feverish episodes, she was deathly quiet.

Ethan hadn't slept for three days. On the third night, he was sitting beside Sam, his eyes closed as he rested, when he startled. He looked over at Sam.

"Where am I?" she whispered softly.

"Sam?" Ethan leaned over her. "You're back at the camp." He saw her wrinkle her brow.

"Camp?" She squeezed her eyes shut and then opened them. "I don't . . . how did I get here?"

"You were caught in a skirmish leaving Kennesaw Mountain," Ethan said gently. "You were shot. Kota came back to the camp."

At the sound of the horse's name, Samantha jerked her head in an attempt to sit up. "Kota!" Then she screamed in pain and reached for her head.

"Lie still," Ethan said as he gently pushed her back onto the cot. "Kota is fine. He was grazed on the neck, but that's all."

He watched as she labored to breathe, and beads of sweat broke out on her forehead.

"It hurts," she whispered. "It feels like my head is being squeezed in a press."

Ethan watched as one and then a second tear escaped from under her closed lashes and she began to tremble. He reached out and took her hand in his. "You have a concussion, Sam, but you're going to be all right. Your wounds are healing." She was holding his hand tightly, and then he felt her grip loosen as she slipped back into unconsciousness.

For the next twenty-four hours, Ethan remained by her side. His feelings alternated between guilt and anger. He was furious with Sam for lying. She had deceived him—not once, but all the time they'd been together. Had he known she was a woman, he never would have forced her into service. He would have arranged for her travel to Washington City. She would be safe now instead of lying on his cot with two gunshot wounds, clinging to life. He'd put her in harm's way. "Damn it, Sam," he swore to himself.

"Ethan?"

Ethan jerked his head to the side. Samantha was looking at him, her eyes clear.

"How long have I been here?" she asked.

"Five days," he answered.

"Five days," she repeated. "Kota?"

"He's fine. Do you remember what happened?"

Samantha frowned. "The mountain. We were following the Confederate forces. We were attacked. I directed Kota into the woods. There was a wounded Union soldier. I . . . I tried to help him. I don't remember much after that—just this loud explosion in my head."

Ethan watched as she felt the bandage wrapped around her head and grimaced.

"It hurts to breathe. How badly am I hurt?" she asked.

"Clement cleaned and stitched your head wound. Fortunately, the lead didn't penetrate your skull, but you have a skull fracture. You were shot in the chest, also. Three ribs are broken. He stitched that wound, too." Ethan sighed, five sleepless days and nights filled with guilt, worry, and fear taking their toll on him. "You were unconscious when I found you. You lost a lot of blood, Sam. Clement didn't think you'd live." Ethan stood and walked to the entrance of the tent. "I'll be right back. I'll send someone to find Clement and let him know you're conscious."

Samantha watched Ethan leave and then turned her head to look around the tent. This was Ethan's tent. She didn't remember being brought here; she didn't remember much at all. She reached under the blanket to feel the bandage wrapped around her chest. She was naked.

Just then, Ethan pulled the tent flap aside and entered. He walked over to his desk and poured a glass of bourbon. Without saying a word, he sat down next to her, the drink in his hand. He was just inches from her as he leaned his head back and stretched his legs out in front of him.

Samantha swallowed nervously. "Where are my clothes?" she asked timidly.

Ethan drained the last liquid from his glass. "We had to remove them," he said as he stood and walked over to the desk where he poured another glass of bourbon.

"We?" Samantha asked.

"Clement and I," Ethan said, his back to her. He swallowed the bourbon in one gulp and then slammed the glass down on the table. Samantha jumped, and a wave of pain shot through her head. Just then, the tent flap was thrown back and Clement Beauregard entered.

"So you've decided to rejoin the living." The gray-haired man smiled and walked over to Samantha. He bent down and felt her forehead. Then he lifted the edges of the bandage on her head and inspected the wound. "Does it still hurt?" he asked.

"Yes," she said, grimacing.

"When you were unconscious for so long, I was afraid of

too much pressure building up inside your skull."

"Thanks for not making burr holes," Samantha said.

"I thought about it. Dr. Schafley advised it, but every time I've seen those holes drilled into a patient's skull, the patient dies of brain putrefaction."

"Dr. Schafley was here?" she asked with surprise.

"No, but he asked how you were doing. When Ethan brought you back, I dismissed everyone. He and I tended to your wounds. You were very lucky; I guess you know that."

Samantha didn't say anything.

"Let's check your chest wound," the old surgeon said.

As discreetly as possible, Dr. Beauregard moved the sheet to the side and lifted the bandage to peer at the wound underneath. "It looks good. No putrefaction. I was worried when you developed the fever."

"I had a fever?"

"All through the first night. I didn't have any medicine to give you to reduce it, and you were burning up."

"What did you do?"

"I didn't do anything. Ethan washed you and changed the linen throughout the night until the fever broke the next morning. Then the fever returned two more times. He bathed you in cool water again. He hasn't left your side in five days."

Samantha blushed. That explained why she was naked. She turned her head away.

Clement took her hand in his. "You know how dangerous a fever can be with a head wound. We had to bring your temperature down, and your modesty couldn't be a consideration," he said gently.

Samantha nodded her head in understanding, although it bothered her that it had been Ethan who had bathed her instead of Clement.

"Do you feel like talking?" Clement asked.

Samantha didn't answer.

"Perhaps it can wait until you have more strength," Clement said.

"How much strength does it take to be honest?" Ethan countered.

Samantha looked at Ethan and felt unnerved by his eyes. "What do you want to know?" she asked quietly.

Clement Beauregard positioned the chair so that it was facing the bed and sat down. "You can imagine our surprise when we ... uh ... began to inspect your wounds. Perhaps you should start at the beginning. What's your name, and why are you disguising yourself as a boy?" When Samantha didn't answer, Clement continued. "Come, my dear, your name can't be Sam."

"It's Samantha, although my brothers, especially Troy, have called me Sam ever since I can remember."

"Very good," Ethan said sarcastically. "If you are going to lie, keep an element of the truth in it. It's easier."

"Ethan!" Clement admonished. Frowning, he turned back to Samantha. "Why the disguise?"

Samantha reluctantly told them of her disobedience while in Paris, her return home, and then her effort to reach the Union Medical Corps. Clement shook his head in disapproval.

"You shouldn't have deceived your father. And then to disobey him and run away?" He shook his finger at her. "I've a mind to take you over my knee myself."

Samantha looked at this kind man. "You're right. I shouldn't have disobeyed my father. I never meant to be disrespectful. I love my family and I miss them terribly, but I had no choice. I had to help. I was trying to reach General Lee's home in Arlington. I was told that it had been converted to a Union medical headquarters. But I got lost. I was so afraid. It was the first night I had ever spent without my governess or father or brothers present. Kota was with me, though. If I had just listened to his warning, I would have gotten away before those Confederate soldiers caught me."

Ethan had been quiet while Samantha recanted her story. Now he stepped forward. "Does your family know where you are? Do they know you're alive?"

"No," Samantha said quietly.

"Shit," Ethan swore softly. "I'll take you north as soon as you're able to travel," he said as he turned to leave.

"No, you can't," Samantha said, shuddering as she tried to take a deep breath.

Ethan turned around. "I can. I can cross the lines easily."

"No," Samantha repeated.

Ethan eyed Samantha closely. "Why not? That's what you've wanted, isn't it?"

"Yes, I did." Samantha's head was pounding and she was growing weary. "But now I want to stay," she said softly. "You need me here."

"You can't possibly stay," Clement interjected.

"Why not?" Samantha asked.

"Sam," Clement began, "you're an excellent surgeon, but you're a woman. You presented yourself as a man. That's against the law. You could be arrested and imprisoned for that."

"You need me. I'm staying." Talking had taken its toll on her. She was losing strength. Each time she took a breath, it felt as though her chest was being crushed. She didn't want Clement or Ethan to see how much pain she was in, so she closed her eyes and clenched her teeth together.

"We're not going to argue about this, Sam. I'll take you north as soon as you're able to travel," Ethan said firmly.

Samantha heard the rustle of the tent flap as Ethan left.

"Ethan's right," Clement said. "You should be at home

with your family. He'll return you to the North."

"Why? Why should he care what I do?" Samantha whispered as the pain started to overwhelm her.

"He feels responsible for you. He hasn't left your side since he found you. We had a lot of casualties, and I couldn't be here. Ethan took care of you. He has your welfare at heart." Clement stood and patted her shoulder. "You rest. I'll be back later."

Samantha remained on her cot the rest of the day. She slept some, but the continuous pain in her head and the burning in her chest made it difficult to sleep. Ethan returned to the tent several times during the day. He looked worried, but when Samantha asked him about the cannon fire she could hear in the distance, he assured her she was safe and told her to rest.

When evening came, Samantha became concerned. She was starting to cough, which made the pain from her broken ribs excruciating. But more than that, her chest felt heavy. She must walk, no matter how painful. It was dangerous to lie so long after a chest wound. She rolled onto her side to push herself up into a sitting position. Pain shot through her ribs, and she cried out. She clenched her teeth through the pain as she struggled to sit. Just then, Ethan entered the tent.

"Sam!" he said as he rushed to her side.

"I'm all right," she said as she steadied herself. She clutched the blanket to her neck and waited for the pain to subside.

"What are you doing?" he asked.

She breathed slowly, letting her fractured ribs expand as far as she could tolerate. "Ethan," she said after several breaths, "I want to go outside. I must walk."

Ethan frowned. "I don't think you should do that. It's too soon. It's been five days since you were shot. You should remain in bed."

"No," she said, shaking her head. She spoke softly, her speech measured in response to the pain. "Please. I've no intention of making myself worse. A wounded Lakota warrior walks as soon as he's able to stand. It decreases the likelihood of his lungs filling with fluid and the warrior dying of consumption."

"Lakota warrior? What are you talking about?" he asked. He reached for her forehead.

"The fever hasn't returned. I'm in my right mind. I want to see Kota."

"Your horse? Is that why you want to go outside?"

"Kota is special. He shares his spirit with me." It was becoming more difficult to breathe, but she continued. "I'm a wounded warrior. I must walk." She could see his skepticism. "Ethan, it's important. I know what I'm talking about. I need to walk, and I would like to see Kota. Will you help me?" He appeared to be studying her. "What is it?" she asked.

"Your words are peculiar, Sam. Spirits? Warriors? But then, I did capture a boy dressed in buckskins and wielding a knife. Very well, I'll help you." He paused, and Samantha saw a twinkle in his eyes. "Does the warrior you're talking about walk naked? You're going to need clothes."

Despite her pain and difficulty breathing, Samantha felt herself blush. Ethan turned to where Samantha's bag was laying. He sorted through her supplies, finally finding a shirt and pants.

"Just put them on the cot," Samantha said, clutching the sheet to her neck. "Wait for me outside. I can manage."

"I doubt that," Ethan answered. "I'll help you."

"No!" Samantha said, holding the sheet tighter. "You can't!"

"Of course I can," Ethan answered matter-of-factly.

"You can't possibly expect me to dress while you're in

here."

"Why not, *Sam*?" he asked. "You and I have shared lodgings for two months now." He picked up the shirt. "This first, I think."

"Leave."

"Must you always argue?" he said as he unfolded the shirt.

"I'm not going to let you dress me. If you have any decency, you'll wait outside."

"Decency isn't the issue. You can't manage on your own."

"I'm not helpless, and I'm not a child." Samantha snatched the shirt out of Ethan's hand, and as she did, she cried out. It felt as though her ribs were being torn from her chest. She dropped the shirt and clutched her side. Ethan was beside her in an instant. Samantha held her breath as she waited for the pain to subside. "I was foolish," she said when she could breathe again. "I need to move slowly, and I do need your help," she admitted.

Ethan's face was grim as he knelt beside her. He helped her put her arms through the sleeves. Then he pulled the front of the shirt together to cover her as she let the blanket fall to her waist. Samantha's hands trembled as she tried, unsuccessfully, to button the first button.

"I'll do it," Ethan said, his voice deep and soft.

Although Samantha was aware he was careful not to touch her as he buttoned her shirt, she still held her breath. When he finished with her shirt, he motioned to the long underwear. Samantha mutely shook her head, refusing, although she had come to understand why the Confederates wore the additional garment under their uniform pants even in the extreme Southern heat. The coarse fabric of their homespun trousers chaffed mercilessly; the long underwear was softer and was one more barrier against biting mosquitos and lice. Ethan picked up her pants and held them low to the ground so that she could slip her legs into them. His hands brushed her calves as she lifted one foot up and then the other. "I think I can finish," she said quietly.

Ethan looked at her, his eyes intense. "Very well," he said and stood. "You can lean on me." He turned his back to her, giving her privacy.

Samantha stood to pull the pants on. She was unsteady and reached for Ethan's shoulder. As she struggled with the pants, she gritted her teeth against the pounding in her head. She managed to pull the pants to her waist, when her arms began to tremble. Ethan turned around, and without a word, fastened the buttons on her pants and then knelt down to put her socks and boots on her while she held on to his shoulder. When he finished, he stood up. "Are you certain you want to do this?" he asked.

"I must," she answered.

He nodded his head and handed her a hat. Then he helped her into her coat and they stepped outside.

Samantha's steps were slow and unsteady as she clutched her broken ribs to splint them and tried to ignore the pounding in her head. She had underestimated the degree of pain she would experience. They had only walked fifty feet when she stumbled. Ethan caught her. Her legs were trembling so badly, she couldn't will them to step forward. She clung to Ethan in the darkness.

"I'm taking you back to the tent," he said.

"No," she whispered.

"You think that because it's dark I can't see your tears?" he demanded. "I'll carry you back."

"No, please, Ethan. I must do this. My lungs are taking on fluid." She struggled to breathe. "I'll die if I don't walk."

His arms were still around her, and he pulled her closer to him so that her chest was pressed against his. She was fleetingly aware of the intimacy of their bodies—his heart beating against hers, his breath upon her neck—but the searing pain in her chest and head were dominating her senses.

"It's killing me to see you hurt like this," he whispered, "but one thing I've learned to trust is your medical judgment. We'll walk. Are you ready?"

She mutely nodded her head. Ethan released her but kept one arm around her waist as they walked. She heard Kota before she saw him. Kota sensed her approach in the dark and responded with a powerful whinny. Then she saw him. He was twisting and pulling against the rope tie. "Ethan, release him so he can come to me," she said.

"Sam, are you sure you can stand alone?" he asked with doubt.

"Yes."

Ethan held on to her until she was steady, then he walked to where Kota was tied. As he reached for the rope, Kota reared up.

"Kota! Stand!" Samantha commanded in the Lakota language. Her voice was weak, but the horse immediately quieted as Ethan untied him. "Ethan, stay where you are," Samantha said, and then, with great effort, she whistled.

Kota spun toward Samantha and closed the distance between them in four powerful strides. He stopped in front of her and reared up, his hooves slashing the air above her head.

"Sam!" Ethan ran to where she stood and reached protectively for her.

"It's all right, Ethan. Kota would never harm me. He's angry that I'm wounded," she said as the horse once again reared up, tossing his head about. Then Samantha spoke soothingly in the Lakota language. The horse stopped rearing and reached his nose to Samantha, gently nuzzling her. Samantha stepped forward, closed her eyes, and rested her head on his neck, drawing strength from the great horse.

When at last Ethan and Samantha returned to the tent, they found Clement Beauregard waiting. "Sam, what are you doing out of bed?" he exclaimed. "Ethan! She should remain in her cot," the old surgeon admonished.

Samantha was leaning heavily on Ethan, her steps slow and uneven. She was rapidly approaching the limit of her endurance, but she was not going to let Clement or Ethan know that. "No, I shouldn't," she countered, her voice weak. "Clement, why do you think I instruct the orderlies to walk my patients the day after surgery? And if they can't walk because I've removed a leg, they are to hold on to an orderly and move as best they can."

Clement frowned. "Dr. Schafley says you're a fool for doing so. You risk the patient hemorrhaging."

"Highly unlikely, unless I was as inept a surgeon as Dr. Schafley," Samantha said pointedly. "I have one-tenth the post-operative consumption of either of you because I don't allow fluids to pool in the lungs."

Clement appeared to be considering what she said. "Did you learn that in Paris?"

"No, the Lakota Indians taught me that," she said simply.

"Ethan, get her back into bed," Clement said.

It was a painful process, but once she was settled on the cot, Clement reached for her wrist to feel her pulse. He frowned.

"I told you the lead didn't penetrate your skull," he said, "but it cut a groove in it where it hit, and you have a skull fracture. Now you're trembling and drenched in sweat. Your heart is working too hard."

"It's the pain," she said weakly. "I fear it's more than I can bear, but bear it I must. I'll do what's necessary to stay alive," she finished, her breath coming in ragged gasps, her skull feeling like it would explode. She didn't want to cry in front of the men, but she could contain her tears no longer. She squeezed her eyes shut, the tears running down her face, and gave into the pain. It washed over her, tearing her apart. *"Charrah, give me the strength to endure this."*

She wasn't sure how long she lay there, trembling. Then she felt a cool, damp cloth against her face. She recognized Ethan's touch as he gently wiped the sweat off her brow and the tears from her cheeks. Then she felt his strong hand grasp hers.

After a while, her body relaxed as the hot coals she imagined pressed into her flesh were mercifully removed to be replaced by a continuous, but acceptable, ache in her side. The explosive pressure in her head had likewise diminished to a dull ache. She opened her eyes to see Ethan watching her. She was still clutching his hand.

"Better?" he asked.

"Yes."

"Drink this," Ethan said as he pressed a glass of water to her lips.

Clement was standing behind Ethan. "I wanted to make certain you were all right before I left," Clement said. "There's a break in the fighting, but I don't think it will last long."

"What's happening?" Samantha asked.

"Sherman's troops forced Johnston's army back toward Atlanta. They're both trying to gain ground," Ethan answered.

"In a few days, I should be able to help you," Samantha offered.

Clement frowned. "I don't think you realize how seriously you were wounded. Quite frankly, you shouldn't be alive. I don't understand how you survived, but you did. You need to rest." He looked toward Ethan. "So what are we going to do about her?"

"There's no reason I can't continue as I have been. You two are the only people who know, correct?" Samantha asked, her voice weak.

"What are you suggesting?" Clement asked.

"As soon as I'm able, I'll resume my disguise as the boy surgeon, Sam Cartier."

"No," Ethan said firmly.

Samantha started to protest when Clement intervened. "We have a more immediate problem. We need to consider the arrangements for your quarters. You cannot continue to share Ethan's tent." Clement turned to Ethan. "I'll have another cot put in my tent, Ethan. You can bunk with me."

Ethan nodded his agreement. "I still have some work to do tonight," he said as he turned to Samantha. "Do you object to my working here for a while?"

Samantha felt her strength leaving her, but she persisted. "Of course I don't object, but won't your moving into Clement's tent raise questions? You're both officers. Officers of your rank don't share tents. Giving me your tent, even though I'm wounded, would be highly unusual. The medical staff, the soldiers, they know I'm your prisoner. That's why you've kept me with you."

Ethan sighed and turned to Clement. "She's right. We need to keep her identity a secret. Everyone knows Sam's a Yankee, and if it's discovered she's a woman, she'll be imprisoned."

"She can't remain with you!" Clement said.

"She's been with me for two months. Protecting her identity is more important than protecting her modesty. I captured a Yankee boy, and that's what she'll remain until I can arrange to return her to her home."

Clement continued to object but finally agreed that it was the safest arrangement they could make for the time being.

He said good night to Samantha and left.

Ethan's tent was crowded with the two cots separated by just a few feet. A small desk and chair were squeezed between the cots. Samantha closed her eyes, but she could hear Ethan sitting down in the chair next to her. The sound of Ethan shuffling maps less than a foot from her was oddly comforting, and despite her pain, she slipped into a deep sleep.

Ethan was having difficulty concentrating. General Lee depended on him to use his political and business contacts in the North to obtain and validate intelligence reports. Ethan was scrutinizing a recent report of Northern troops' positions and strengths when Samantha moaned.

He turned in his chair to see her tossing on the cot. Soon, her moans turned into the familiar cries that he had heard Sam make the many nights they had been together. It was not surprising that the horror of war was having this effect on her. She was a young woman who'd been captured and transformed into a battle-hardened surgeon in just two months.

As she began to cry softly, he moved to her cot. He sat down on the side of it and took her hand in his. He thought about her dreams. As she had described them, it wasn't the revolting sights of the wounds that caused her such distress, but rather her inability to stop the carnage. He remembered thinking at the time how young and naive Sam was to assume any responsibility for this war.

"Sam?" he said softly. "Wake up, Sam."

She turned her tear-streaked face toward him. He watched as her eyes focused and she left her nightmare behind.

"The same dream?" he asked as he gently wiped a tear

from her face.

"Yes," she whispered.

"Sit up," he said as he carefully helped her into a sitting position. "Listen to me," he said gently. "You can't stop this war, you can't stop the killing, and you can't save every soldier who is wounded. Why do you feel that you must? They will keep on coming, with their shattered limbs, until one side is declared the victor. Many will live because of you." He paused. "You can be no more than you are. Do you understand, Sam? You can do no less—and no more—than you are to do. You must accept that."

She stared at him.

"What is it?" Ethan asked.

"You remind me of a man I once knew."

"Oh, do I?" Ethan smiled.

"A holy man," she said softly. "That's something he would say."

"Who was he?"

"A medicine man among the Lakota Indians—a very old, very wise man."

"So now you see me as an old man?" Ethan gently teased.

Samantha smiled and then looked down. She was still holding his hand tightly. She blushed and withdrew her hand. Ethan found that amusing but said nothing.

"Can you go back to sleep now?" he asked.

"Yes," Samantha answered. "Thank you."

Ethan returned to his chair.

"Ethan?" she said hesitantly. "Can you get a letter through to the North?"

He put his pen down and turned in his chair to face her. "Where's it to go?" he asked.

"To my father. It doesn't have to go all the way to the Iowa Frontier. If it can be delivered to Boston, my father's business acquaintances can see that it is sent on."

"You can deliver it yourself when I take you north," Ethan said.

"How is it that you can travel so easily there?" she asked.

"I have business acquaintances in the North that were formed long before the war started."

"Is that where you go when you leave?"

"Sometimes."

"Will you take a letter with you the next time you go?"

Ethan was silent. He stared down at the papers before him and then turned back to Samantha. "That will be tomorrow morning."

"So soon?" Samantha was surprised.

"Yes. I'll be gone several weeks. I'd take you back tomorrow, but I don't think you could make the trip. I'll take you north as soon as you're able to travel."

"No," Samantha replied.

"Damn it, Sam. Why must you always argue? You have to return home. I shouldn't have brought you here in the first place, and had I known you were a woman, I most certainly wouldn't have."

"Major . . . Ethan, please listen to me. I can't return home, not yet. I know this is difficult for my family. I never meant to hurt my father. I love him, and I want him to know that I'm all right. But I can't go home, not yet." Samantha paused. "I've been trying to tell you," she said softly, "I don't have a choice, not anymore. I made that choice when, as a young girl, I first walked into his tent."

"Tent? Whose tent?" Ethan was confused.

"Charrah's."

Ethan's interest heightened. That was the name she kept calling for in her delirium. "Who's Charrah?"

"The Lakota holy man I told you about. When I was young, my brothers and I spent time in his village. We practically lived there. One day, a wounded warrior was brought into the village and taken into Charrah's teepee. I knew it was forbidden to enter the holy man's teepee— and women never were allowed in—but I walked toward it anyway. Several of the old women called to me, and one of them grabbed my arm to stop me. Then suddenly, they backed away from me. They were afraid of me.

"I walked into his teepee and sat down by the fire. Charrah didn't even acknowledge my presence, but I think he'd been waiting for me. That was the beginning. He taught me the art of healing. He had abilities that were beyond mortal men. In all those years, he never spoke to me, and yet I could hear his words. They were just there in my head. You probably think I am delusional now."

Ethan smiled. "No, but I can't say that I understand."

"It's difficult to explain to a white man," she continued. "I learned that in Paris. I tried to tell my professors about the Lakota methods, but they scorned anything I had to offer. After a while, I, too, forgot the Lakota ways and became immersed in the white man's medicine. Charrah's spirit seemed to depart from me until that day you took me into that first surgical tent. I was so frightened and appalled by what I saw. Then he was there—in my head. He guided my hands," she said as she stared at them. "He guided me.

"There are many things I'm trying to reconcile, but I know this." Samantha looked at Ethan. "I'm a doctor, and if The Spirits are still with me, a Lakota medicine woman," she whispered. "I must follow the path set for me, and the path has brought me here."

Ethan was moved by her story. He studied her for a long time. Who was Sam, really? What other secrets did she carry with her? He stood and paced the small confines of the tent. There was something in her story that disturbed him. He recalled a dream he'd had not long ago—his desperate search for something and the appearance of an old Indian holding a puzzle piece in his hand.

He picked up a paper, pen, and ink and handed them to Samantha. "Write your letter, and I'll take it with me tomorrow. But Sam, nothing has changed. When I return, I'll take you north at the first opportunity."

Samantha wrote to her father, and when she was finished, gave the letter to Ethan. "I assured my father I was safe, but didn't tell him anything about the past two months. Can this letter be delivered without him knowing exactly where I am?"

"Yes," Ethan said as he read the address. "Seth Carter. So you are Samantha Carter, not Samantha Cartier?"

"My grandfather was a French Canadian fur trapper. I used the old spelling of our name. I thought it would make it more difficult to trace."

"Where is this to be delivered?"

"To the First Bank of Boston."

Ethan had not expected Samantha's answer and tried to conceal his surprise.

"My father has some business interests that are handled by the bank," Samantha explained. "The bank will see that the letter reaches him. Give it to a man named Brown, Silas Brown."

"And this man, Brown, will know your father?"

"Yes. I told you, he handles investments for my father."

"May I ask you what your father does?"

"He's a rancher on the Iowa Frontier near the Lakota Indian Territory."

"A frontier rancher with business interests handled by a Boston bank?"

"Yes, but be careful. Have someone else deliver the letter to Mr. Brown. If Mr. Brown knows of my disappearance, he may try to detain you."

"He might do that?" Ethan tried to hide his amusement. She was so serious.

"Yes!"

"Are there others in Boston who are acquainted with your father and may know of your running away?" he asked.

Samantha shrugged. "My mother was from Boston. Since she died, my father doesn't travel there anymore. I'm unaware of who my father may have contacted in Boston, but you aren't likely to know them anyway."

"Doubtful," Ethan said, again trying to hide his smile.

Samantha seemed satisfied that Ethan would deliver her letter, and she fell asleep while Ethan examined his papers. Once Ethan was certain that she was sleeping, he picked up the letter again. What had he gotten himself into when he captured young Sam and forced "the boy" to accompany him south? So Silas handled the investments of Sam's father. And what about Seth Carter? Who was this rancher who had the means to have his investments handled by a prestigious bank in the East? How would he feel about his daughter's abduction? She was obviously a disobedient and rebellious daughter. Still, he probably wouldn't take kindly to a Southern officer forcing his daughter to travel south and treat Confederate soldiers.

Ethan looked at Sam sleeping on the cot. He'd almost let his surprise show when she mentioned the First Bank of Boston. He laughed to himself. Well, if this Seth Carter tried to retaliate against Ethan for the part he played in Sam's disobedience, Ethan would handle that. After all, together with Nathaniel Rhodes, Ethan and Nathaniel owned fifty-two percent of the First Bank of Boston. Ethan didn't know the particulars. Nathaniel Rhodes had acquired it for him and managed it. That was how Ethan knew of Silas Brown.

CHAPTER 7

For the next week while Ethan was away, Samantha gradually recovered her strength. She returned to wearing her disguise and could be seen walking outside of Ethan's tent several times a day. She struggled. By now, most in the camp knew young Yankee Doc Sam had been wounded and almost died. Like many of them, Sam had a bloody bandage around her head, a common mark of battle. Her steps were slow and painful as she moved silently past them, clutching her ribs. Sometimes, it was difficult to remain upright, the pressure and pain in her head almost unbearable; there were other times when she stumbled and fell. She would remain there on the ground, eyes closed, trembling in agony. When the pain eased and she opened her eyes, there was always a soldier silently waiting with an outstretched hand to help her up.

Some soldiers, seeing her struggle to walk, approached her and offered water from their canteens. Some offered their own meager food supply to her. Others caught her eye and silently nodded as she passed by them.

Dr. Beauregard came daily to monitor her progress. He still didn't approve of Samantha walking so soon after being wounded, but he realized he couldn't stop her. And at the end of the first week, he acknowledged that she was recovering much quicker than expected. The following week, she convinced him to allow her to work. The constant clashing of the two sides as they moved south left many casualties.

At first, Dr. Beauregard watched her closely. She had to take frequent rest periods when dizziness threatened. At other times, when performing difficult amputations, the pain in her ribs became unendurable. That's when Dr. Beauregard appeared at her side to help. Dr. Schafley, while still disapproving, was not as critical as he had been before she'd been shot.

In time, Samantha settled into the routine of the surgical tent. The days were long. The fighting started at dawn and continued until dusk. Then the litter bearers went onto the battlefield to collect the wounded before dark. Samantha always tried to leave the surgical tent for a few minutes at that time to search among the dead corpses of Union soldiers. A fear gripped her as she looked at each face, praying that she would not see either of her brothers, Charles or Robert.

The heat was intense during the days, and Samantha had to remind herself to drink water. She became accustomed to the sparse supply of food, although she and the officers had slightly better rations than the enlisted men. She recalled her revulsion at the sight of worms in the biscuits of Lieutenant Quicken's men the day she was captured. Now, the infested hardtack no longer affected her.

Samantha and the medical corps moved with the troops as they advanced toward Atlanta. She recalled Ethan's words the night before he left: it was only a matter of time. Atlanta was attacked from the north by Union General Sherman. A few days later, another division of Union soldiers attacked Atlanta from the east. The Battle of Atlanta began, and the surgeons again set up their bloody tents to receive the wounded.

Samantha was surprised when, the following week,

Clement Beauregard came into the tent late at night. He had a young officer with him. "Dr. Cartier," Clement said, "this is Lieutenant Avery Scott. For the past two years, he's been assigned as special assistant to Major Winters-Hunt. He's just arrived with orders from the major. I'll let him explain."

Samantha glanced at Clement. Obviously, the lieutenant didn't know of her disguise.

"Dr. Cartier, I've recently left Major Winters-Hunt. I've been instructed to escort you to Charleston immediately," Lieutenant Scott said.

"Charleston! I can't leave now," Samantha said.

"Those are my orders, sir."

"I can't go. You'll have to inform Major Winters-Hunt that I can't leave Atlanta. Not now. There are too many wounded. We don't have enough surgeons."

"Sam," Clement Beauregard interrupted, "you must do as the lieutenant says. Ethan's instructions were that if I felt you were recovered enough to travel, you were to leave. The lieutenant is under orders to arrest you if you refuse to go."

"Beggin' your pardon, Dr. Cartier, but the major said you might resist. The arrest procedures are standard in such a case," the lieutenant added apologetically.

"It's for the best, Sam," Clement said. "Who knows how long we'll be dug in here, or how long our lines will hold against the Yankees. It's not safe. If you were wounded again or captured...."

Samantha was frustrated. She was needed here, but she understood Clement's unspoken warning. She turned to Lieutenant Scott. "When are we to leave, lieutenant?"

"First thing in the morning, sir."

"Do you know why I'm to be taken to Charleston?"

"No, sir, but the major will meet us there."

"Very well. As it appears I have no choice, I'll be ready in the morning," Samantha said.

After the lieutenant left, Clement remained. "Are you up to traveling, Sam? You haven't had any more headaches, have you?"

"No, and my wounds are healed, except for my ribs. As long as I keep them wrapped securely, I can ride. In another week, they'll be completely healed. Clement, why am I to go to Charleston?"

"I don't know. I'm going to miss you, child," the older man said. "May I?" He held his arms out. As Samantha stepped forward, he kissed her lightly on the cheek and hugged her to him. "Thanks for letting an old man feel like a father again," he said as he gave her a last squeeze before setting her apart from him.

"Clement, do you have a family?" Samantha asked as she looked at the kind face before her.

"I did," he said softly. "My wife died several years ago. We had four children. One daughter died of a fever when she was young, the other died in childbirth. Both of my sons were killed at Antietam."

Antietam! Before Ethan had brought her south—before she'd seen what war really was—that had been a word that had given her pride. No matter that Union General McClellan had lost over twelve thousand men that day. He had stopped General Lee's advance into Maryland and into the North. Lee, himself, had lost over ten thousand men, all in a day's fighting. Close to twenty-three thousand Americans died that day. The North still considered it a victory. That was almost two years ago. Samantha no longer rejoiced in victories for either side, for victories meant pain, mutilation, and death.

"Oh, Clement." Samantha cried and threw herself into the old man's arms again. She felt his silent pain move into her own heart as they held each other. When at last they separated, he hastily wiped his reddened eyes.

"You do what Ethan says," Clement said. "He'll protect you." When Samantha started to object, he stopped her. "Don't argue about this. He knows what he's doing. You promise me you'll cooperate with Lieutenant Scott? If you don't, it will be that young lieutenant's hide."

"I'll go to Charleston," Samantha said.

Samantha departed the next morning with Lieutenant Avery Scott. "I'm aware, Doctor, that you were recently wounded," he said. "I believe we can avoid both armies with the route I've chosen, but it will still be dangerous. The fighting has become unpredictable. We'll need to cover as much distance as possible in the daylight."

"I'm sufficiently recovered, Lieutenant. I won't slow you down," Samantha said.

"Very well, Doctor."

Despite Samantha's frustration with being forced to leave, she found the lieutenant to be a pleasant young man who took his responsibility of safely escorting the young Yankee doctor to Charleston seriously. He set an arduous pace, traveling from dawn to dusk. He was ever alert to the sounds of cannon fire and musketry surrounding them.

Most nights, he deemed it safe to build a small campfire. They would share a meal at that time and talk quietly. The lieutenant was friendly and willing to talk about everything, except his work with Ethan. He became evasive whenever Samantha asked a direct question about that. Instead, he told her of his family and his love of Virginia. He was from Arlington, and his family knew General Lee's family. The general, himself, personally assigned him as an aide to Ethan, something the young lieutenant was very proud of. When he spoke of Ethan, it was with respect and admiration.

After two weeks, they reached the outskirts of Charleston. Samantha was surprised when Lieutenant Scott turned onto a road leading away from the town. She stopped Kota. "I thought you said we were going to Charleston. Where are we going?" she asked.

Lieutenant Scott reined in next to Samantha. "I was instructed to take you to the Cooper Plantation. Major Winters-Hunt will meet us there."

"What? I'm not going to that place. I refuse."

"Those are my orders, Doctor Cartier."

"I'll stay at a hotel in Charleston, but not on that plantation."

Lieutenant Scott seemed momentarily surprised, then he recovered. "I'm sorry, Doctor," he said. "I either deliver you to the Cooper Plantation on your own volition, or I'll arrest you and take you there bound. Those are my orders."

Samantha knew Kota could easily outrun the lieutenant's horse, and Lieutenant Scott was not likely to shoot her as she escaped. But what would be the point? He'd only follow her into Charleston and arrest her as he'd said.

"Very well, Lieutenant, the Cooper Plantation it is."

She no sooner finished speaking than Kota bolted forward on the road toward the plantation, leaving the lieutenant far behind. When Lieutenant Scott finally reached her, Samantha had already dismounted and was leaning against one of the tall, white pillars of the house. Caroline Cooper emerged from the house at the same time Lieutenant Scott arrived. The lieutenant looked briefly at Samantha and then hurried up the steps to greet Caroline Cooper.

"Mrs. Cooper?"

"Yes." Caroline smiled pleasantly.

"Allow me to introduce myself. I'm Lieutenant Avery Scott, aide to Major Winters-Hunt. The major instructed me to bring Doctor Cartier here and asked that your hospitality be extended to the doctor until the major arrives. That will probably be tomorrow."

"It's a pleasure to meet you, Lieutenant Scott. Of course Sam is welcome." Caroline then turned to Samantha. "Sam, it's so nice to have you visiting us again. And Lieutenant, you're welcome to stay also."

"Thank you, ma'am. I was ordered to stay with the doctor until the major returns," he said sheepishly.

"You are most welcome, Lieutenant. Please come inside out of the heat. Tester," she said, turning to one of the Negro slaves, "take the gentlemen's horses to the stables."

"This way, please," Caroline said as she turned to lead the way into the house.

"I'll take Kota myself," Samantha said.

Lieutenant Scott seemed surprised by Samantha's abrupt speech. Caroline simply smiled pleasantly. "As you wish, Sam. I'll have refreshments waiting," she said.

Samantha tried to calm herself as she led Kota to the familiar stables. A few of the Negroes exchanged glances in the stables as she untacked her horse and rubbed him down. Once she was satisfied that he had ample food and water, she reluctantly headed back to the large house. She thought about going to the slave quarters to check on Chloe and her baby but decided that had better wait. She saw the look Lieutenant Scott had given her. He would probably come looking for her if she delayed any longer.

Samantha returned to the house to find them both waiting. Caroline served them on the large side porch shaded by trees. Samantha listened in silence as Caroline and Lieutenant Scott conversed. In her mind, she began to mimic their slow Southern drawls as they exchanged pleasantries. She was doing that when their conversation suddenly caught her attention.

"You must join us tomorrow night, Lieutenant. These days, it isn't often that we socialize. I try to plan dinner parties for the neighboring planters. At these socials, we manage to raise considerable funds for The Cause."

"Mrs. Cooper, may I say what you're doing for the Confederacy is admirable. It would be my pleasure to join you, providing, of course, that I don't have other orders."

"Did you say that you expected Major Winters-Hunt to arrive tomorrow?"

"Yes, ma'am, assuming he's not been delayed. It could, however, be several days before he arrives."

"I do hope he's able to join us also. But if not, you're welcome to remain as long as you're able." Caroline turned to Samantha. "Sam, I'm delighted you'll be joining us again. And you'll be pleased to know that Chloe and her baby are doing fine. I shall always be grateful for your assistance."

Samantha looked at Caroline and felt a twinge of guilt. Caroline was sincere and obviously trying very hard to make the obstinate Sam feel welcome.

"I'm glad I was here to help," Samantha said honestly.

A short while later, Caroline showed Samantha and Lieutenant Scott to their rooms. Samantha wasn't given the room she and Ethan shared the last time she was here. Instead, she occupied a room directly across from it, separated by the long central hall that ran the length of the house. Lieutenant Scott's room was farther down the hall.

Samantha closed the door to her room. She found a pitcher with water, a wash bowl, clean linens, and a cake of soap on a small table. A mirror hung above the table. She looked at her reflection and was shocked at seeing the face staring back at her. Dark circles were visible under her eyes. She appeared dirty, thin, and haggard from the two-week ride. She removed her coat, waistcoat, and shirt. The gauze binding her breasts was soiled; she longed to remove it, but dare not. Without looking, she knew her skin was reddened and raw underneath the gauze. She would remove it tonight when she retired for the evening.

Samantha took her time scrubbing the dirt from her arms and neck. The paste disguise on her face was still intact, although dirt clung to the stubble. She cleaned her face as best she could without removing the paste. When she finished, she retrieved a clean shirt from her saddlebag. She dressed and then used the soap and water to wash her soiled shirt. She placed the shirt to dry on the back of a chair and looked about the room. She didn't want to be here. This was the home of Ethan's lover. Images of the night several months ago—the night she saw Ethan and Caroline together in her bedroom—filled her mind.

She flopped down on the side of the bed and pressed her fingertips to her temples. Her head was hurting. It was probably just the heat. Besides, why should she care if Ethan and Caroline were lovers? Undoubtedly, that's why he had Lieutenant Scott bring her here instead of taking her into Charleston. Ethan wanted to see his lover. And just because Ethan had cared for Samantha after she was wounded, it didn't mean that he had feelings for her other than those of responsibility and guilt.

And what were her feelings? She was confused. When he first captured her, she had feared him, and she wasn't the only one. She had noted the caution and deference others afforded Major Ethan Winters-Hunt. He was not a man to cross. He could be ruthless and unflinching when confronting danger. But he was also selfless, compassionate, and a man of principle. Even before she'd been wounded, she and Ethan had established a companionship, within the context of her being his prisoner, of course. The Yankee boy, Sam, and Major Ethan Winters-Hunt had developed an unusual friendship. And friendship was what she felt for

Ethan, and nothing more—at least nothing that she was willing to admit, even to herself.

That evening at dinner, Samantha remained silent as Caroline and Avery politely conversed. Caroline graciously tried to include Samantha, but to no avail. Samantha was trying to think of an excuse to go to her room when the houseboy interrupted, announcing to Caroline that she had a visitor. Just then, Samantha heard a familiar voice in the hallway outside.

"I can show myself in, thank you," Ethan said as he entered the dining room.

"Ethan," Caroline said, "how wonderful to see you. We weren't expecting you until tomorrow."

Ethan walked over to Caroline and took her hand in his. As he kissed it lightly, he smiled at her. "I hope you don't mind my imposing on you," he said, still holding her hand in his.

"It's no imposition. You and your friends are always welcome, Ethan. You know that."

Avery Scott had stood when Ethan entered and was still standing when Ethan turned to him. "Avery," Ethan said, "I see you've arrived with Dr. Cartier. Thank you."

"Sir," Avery responded.

"Please sit. There's no need for formality here," Ethan said.

Throughout dinner, Samantha resented having to be at Caroline's plantation, but she knew that she must control her emotions in order to maintain her disguise. When, however, she watched Ethan warmly greet Caroline, anger inexplicably flooded her mind. She knew she was being irrational. She looked down at the table and concentrated on the uneaten food on her plate.

"Sam?" Ethan said.

Samantha took a deep breath and raised her eyes to him.

"Sam? Are you feeling well?" he asked. "I was afraid that the trip to Charleston might still be too much for you."

Samantha was confused. There was concern in Ethan's eyes as he looked at her. "I had no difficulty, Major. I'm fully recovered."

Caroline called to one of the Negro servers and had a place set for Ethan. As he sat down, he looked across the table at Samantha.

"Your letter was delivered," he said. "I hope you don't mind, but I gave permission for it to be opened and its contents sent by telegraph. I have a reply for you."

Samantha was surprised. "How did you do that?"

"That's not important," he said as he reached inside his coat and removed a piece of paper. "Here's the reply. I also brought some Northern newspapers. They're in my saddlebag. I thought you might like to see them."

"Thank you," Samantha said quietly.

"I had your bag taken upstairs for you," Caroline interjected. "You have the room you occupied with Sam previously. We have no other guests, so Sam has his own room across the hall from you."

"Thank you, Caroline," Ethan said and turned to Samantha. "You can get the papers after dinner."

"Sam," Caroline said gently, "Ethan told me how you've cared for our soldiers. Comin' from the North, I'm sure it hasn't been easy for you. We're beholden to you."

Samantha was about to declare a truce and apologize to Caroline, when Ethan turned to Caroline. Caroline smiled and touched Ethan's arm. It was a simple gesture, but she conveyed an intimacy that Samantha could not help but see.

"If you will excuse me," Samantha said suddenly, "I would like to go to my room and read this."

"Of course, dear," Caroline said.

Ethan frowned but remained quiet. Samantha hastily said good night and retreated to her room upstairs. She couldn't stay here. Tomorrow, she would convince Ethan to allow her to return to the battlefield. And if he refused? She wasn't foolish enough to think she could find her way back to Clement's medical unit on her own. And she knew firsthand the terror of being caught in a battle. She was contemplating alternatives when she remembered the paper she still clutched in her hands. She opened the telegraph and smiled as she read her father's words:

SAMANTHA WHERE IN THE HELL ARE YOU STOP WHAT KIND OF FOOLISHNESS ARE YOU UP TO STOP PLEASE COME HOME STOP I LOVE YOU STOP PAPA

No doubt her father had to bribe the telegraph operator to send the message just as he dictated it. She could see the old man who worked in the telegraph office resenting Seth's use of profanity.

Samantha lay down on the bed. How had Ethan managed to get this? She knew she should be grateful to him. Unconsciously, she reached for her newly healed ribs. Ethan had taken care of her when she was wounded. She remembered his gentle touch when he wiped the tears from her eyes, the feel of his body pressed against hers when she stumbled. He had held her tightly against him. She felt her body grow warm with the memory and her pulse quicken.

Samantha jumped up, confused by the rush of emotion. "Damn!" she swore. She walked to her door, opened it, and peered out into the hallway. The house seemed quiet. Perhaps she could get the newspapers Ethan spoke of. That would give her something to do.

She crossed the hall and tapped lightly on the door.

There was no answer. Just as she thought—he had probably already joined Caroline Cooper in her room. Cautiously, she opened the door and stepped inside. Immediately, she heard someone inhale sharply and then a female voice.

"Ethan!" Caroline exclaimed.

Ethan whirled around to see Samantha standing inside the door. He groaned. "Sam! What are you doing here?" he demanded angrily. "Don't you knock?"

Samantha was so surprised, it took a moment for her to comprehend what she was seeing. The room was dark, the only light coming from the doors that were open to the balcony. Ethan was fully clothed, but Caroline Cooper stood behind him dressed in a thin nightgown, the top of which had been lowered to her waist. She hastily pulled it up over her shoulders, covering her naked breasts.

Samantha turned around, fumbling for the door. Whether it was from the darkened room or the tears that had formed in her own eyes, she couldn't find the doorknob. She was grappling for it when Ethan reached her. He seized her arm with one hand while he opened the door with the other. In one swift movement, he propelled Samantha across the hall to her room. Once inside, he held on to her as he slammed the door shut. When he released her, she stumbled backward. Instinctively, she reached inside her boot. All the self-control and reasoning she had mastered the past two years departed from her, replaced with irrational jealousy and anger. She withdrew her knife.

Ethan exploded. "You dare threaten me with a knife? What the hell are you doing, Sam? Give me that!" He took a step forward, and she sliced out with the knife, just barely missing him. Ethan jumped back. "I ought to take you over my knee for that," he shouted.

"Try it, Rebel, and I'll cut you to pieces," Samantha shouted back.

"We'll see about that!"

Ethan lunged. Samantha artfully dodged him and, using his own weight against him, swept his feet out from under him, sending him falling back against the wall. A wicked grin spread across her face as she crouched down a little, holding the knife toward him. "The next time, I won't be so gentle," she said, the menacing knife flashing before her.

"There won't be a next time," Ethan ground out.

She saw the change in his eyes as they narrowed. He circled cautiously now, but each time he started to lunge, she was able to force him back with the knife. Then she changed tactics. The major needed to be put in his place. Once again, she drove him back with the knife, but this time, she left her arm extended for a second. Ethan seized her wrist above the knife, just as she knew he would. With his other hand, he gripped her around her waist to subdue her. As he did, she skillfully spun around and threw him to the floor. She then released him with a taunting smile and stepped back. "I told you I wouldn't be so gentle the next time, Rebel."

Ethan growled as he scrambled up and lunged for her. She crouched down just a split-second before their bodies met. She deflected the crushing blow of his weight by twisting and using the momentum to rise as she sent his body flying into the air. He landed with a loud thud on the floor. "That's twice I could have killed you, Reb" she said. "I could have easily driven my knife into you."

Her victory was short-lived, however. She unconsciously reached for her side. Her fractured ribs, although healed enough for normal activity, were not strong enough for the blows they were receiving.

His next move came so quickly, Samantha almost missed it. She jumped, but not soon enough as his foot crashed into the side of hers. She knew how to counter that move, but she was reluctant to put pressure on her ribs. She stumbled and lashed out with her knife, cutting through Ethan's frock coat and shirt before he painfully wrenched the knife out of her grasp. The knife went skirting across the floor to land out of reach. They wrestled on the floor until, at last, he managed to twist both of her arms behind her, effectively subduing her.

"Damn you!" she spat out at him.

Ethan stood, pulling Samantha up with him. In one swift movement, he sat on the edge of the bed and thrust Samantha across him, still holding her wrists behind her with one of his hands.

She heard the loud slapping noise before she felt the sting and realized what was happening. Again his hand came down on the seat of her pants. Samantha hurled abuse at Ethan using every form of profanity she had ever learned.

"And that's for the profanity!" Ethan said when the last slap of his hand finally came down. "I told you before that if you were going to act like a schoolboy, you would be treated like one." He released her, and Samantha scrambled away, rage boiling up inside. Ethan looked at Samantha's tear-streaked face and swore. "Why the hell did I have to get saddled with a virginal woman who likes to pretend she's a man? Shit!" He took one last look at her and angrily crossed to the door and opened it.

As Ethan emerged into the hallway, he almost crashed into Avery and Caroline. By the look on their faces, Ethan knew they heard the commotion in Sam's room. He closed Sam's bedroom door behind him and turned to face the two.

"Sir," Avery began, when the sound of wood splintering behind Ethan caused him to jump. Ethan whirled around to see the blade of Samantha's knife protruding through the closed door. In a furor, he jerked Samantha's door open again. She was standing across the room, her eyes blazing. Ethan turned. There, buried in the door, was the knife. With a violent jerk, he pulled the knife out of the door. Then, with an explosive curse, he strode out of the room, taking the knife with him, and slammed the door closed behind him.

Caroline's eyes were wide in shock as she clung to Avery's arm. Without a word to either of them, Ethan crossed the hall and entered his room. Caroline scurried around him and lit the lamps in the room. When she turned around, her face paled. "Ethan, you're bleeding!" she exclaimed.

Ethan looked down at his arm. "Shit!" he swore as he jerked his frock coat and bloody shirt off. There was a three-inch gash on his upper right arm where Samantha had cut him.

"Mrs. Cooper, do you have some bandages?" Lieutenant Scott asked.

"What? Oh, Ethan, are you all right?" Caroline cried.

"Mrs. Cooper, please, the bandages?" Lieutenant Scott intervened.

Caroline turned to Avery. "Bandages. Yes, of course. I'll get them."

As soon as Caroline was out of the room, Avery turned back to examine Ethan's arm. "It doesn't look deep," Avery said, "but we should probably have Dr. Cartier look. . . ." He stopped abruptly.

"My being anywhere near Sam right now would not be advised," Ethan replied through clenched teeth.

Avery glanced at Samantha's closed bedroom door and back to Ethan. "Sam—Dr. Cartier—he's a Yankee who attacked a Confederate officer. What do you want me to do, sir?"

"Nothing," Ethan ground out as Caroline returned with

the supplies.

After Lieutenant Scott bandaged his arm, Ethan suggested that they all retire for the night. Caroline slipped quietly into his room some time later, but Ethan politely sent her away. He could hardly be a lover to Caroline when all he could think about was Sam. He never should have touched her like that. She was a young woman. And not long ago, Sam had been gravely wounded. He'd almost lost her, a thought that still caused him such grief that the pain was almost physical.

On the other hand, she drew a knife on him and actually cut him. She could have killed him twice, as she said, but she didn't. Where had she learned to fight like that? He knew she could shoot, but expertly wield a knife, too? She was more of a mystery now, as Samantha, than she had ever been as Sam.

These past three years of war had been nothing but heartache and hell—all of it—except for Sam, that amazing and exasperating Yankee boy who had gotten under his skin, the boy he had come to love like a brother. Ethan looked at the bandage on his arm. "Damn it, Sam," he sighed sadly.

The next morning, when Samantha came down for breakfast, Ethan, Caroline, and Avery were already seated in the dining room. Samantha entered, her face rigid.

"Sam, good morning, dear." Caroline smiled. "I hope you have a good appetite this morning. When Bessie heard that you were here, she had the kitchen prepare everything we had in storage."

For once, Samantha appreciated Caroline's grace and secretly thanked the woman for her kindness. "I thought I would stop by and see how Chloe and the baby are doing, if you don't mind," Samantha said.

"I would be most appreciative," Caroline said.

"And," Samantha continued as she accepted the food offered her, "I'd like to visit the camp today to check on the hospital."

"I think that can be arranged," Ethan said. "Lieutenant, you will accompany Dr. Cartier to the camp when he's ready to leave, and then see that you are both back this evening for Mrs. Cooper's dinner party."

"Yes, sir," Avery Scott answered.

"I mean no offense, Mrs. Cooper," Samantha interrupted, "but I'll probably need to stay at the camp hospital until late tonight. I couldn't possibly make it back in time for your party. I'm certain you understand."

Ethan lowered his glass. "Of course she understands," he said in a level voice, "but there's no need to concern yourself, Sam. Thanks to you, the camp hospital is running efficiently, and conditions have markedly improved in the camp itself. I can't see what would keep you so late." He turned to Lieutenant Scott. "Lieutenant, see that you bring Sam back here in time."

Samantha pushed her chair back from the table and stood. At the risk of incurring Ethan's anger again, she looked over at him. "Perhaps you cannot see what would keep me so late because you're not a doctor. I am, Major."

"Caroline, Lieutenant, if you will excuse us, please." Ethan abruptly rose from the table, his face dark as he walked toward the door of the dining room. "I would like a word with you, Doctor Cartier," he said when he reached the door.

It took all the self-control Samantha could manage to walk over to the door. Once outside in the hall, Ethan took her arm and directed her into a vacant sitting room. He closed the door behind them and turned.

"It's not safe! Have you forgotten that we were attacked

after dark on that same road?" he demanded. "You're making it very hard for me to remember that you're a young woman and not a recalcitrant boy. Well, you're the one who started this charade, Sam, and we'll continue it until I can arrange for your transport north, which, God knows, couldn't be soon enough for either of us. You'll come to Caroline's party tonight where you'll be safe. Furthermore, you'll conduct yourself in a proper manner. I expect you to be charming and gracious to Caroline and her guests. Is that understood?"

Samantha was trembling. She hadn't forgotten the sting and humiliation of his hand last night, but still, she raised her chin defiantly. "Go to hell, Major." She turned to reach for the door, but Ethan caught her and spun her around. Just then, there was a knock on the door and Lieutenant Scott entered.

"Major, the doctor and I had better leave now. Don't worry, sir, I'll have Dr. Cartier back in time for Mrs. Cooper's party," Avery said.

Ethan released Samantha's arm and took a step back. "Lieutenant, if Dr. Cartier is anything less than cooperative, arrest him and bring him back in irons, if necessary."

Samantha was unusually quiet as Lieutenant Scott rode beside her to the Confederate camp outside of Charleston. When they reached the camp, he reminded her he'd meet her at the hospital tent at five o'clock. Samantha nodded mutely.

Belle greeted Samantha warmly when she arrived at the tent and then eagerly walked with her up and down the rows of cots and then across the camp. Belle was so proud of all that she and her girls had accomplished. However, each time she asked Samantha about herself, Samantha changed the subject. Finally, Belle refused to be distracted anymore and demanded to know what was wrong.

"Are you saying that Ethan struck you?" Belle demanded after Samantha had recounted the events of the previous evening.

"I wouldn't say that, but he. . . . When I couldn't get the door open, he opened it, grabbed me, and pulled me out of his room and into mine."

"Well, I'm not surprised at that," Belle said. "I would have done the same had you walked in on me with a man, honey. What happened next?"

"I was angry." Samantha hesitated.

"Yes. Did you say anything?"

"I did more than that." Samantha looked away from Belle. "I pulled my knife out."

"You what?"

"I took my knife out and told him never to touch me again."

"You threatened him with a knife?" Belle exclaimed.

"Yes, and we struggled. I cut his coat with my knife."

Belle's hand flew up to her mouth. "And then?"

"He forced the knife from my hand and proceeded to—"

"To what?" Belle asked, horrified by what she had heard.

"He threw me over his knee!" Samantha unconsciously rubbed the seat of her pants.

"He laid a hand to your backside, did he?" Belle said with relief. "What a mess you've gotten yourself into."

"I can take care of myself, but he insists that I return to that woman's house tonight. After what he did to me! He says I must be there and that I conduct myself in a manner that is charming and gracious. Those were his words," Samantha ground out. "Virginal woman, indeed," she muttered to herself.

Belle frowned. "What are you talking about?"

"It's what he said as he left my room, something about

being saddled with a virginal woman who liked pretending she was a man. That's not fair, Belle," Samantha pleaded. "I don't like pretending to be a man. I never have, but it's what I must do."

Belle put her arms around Samantha. "The first time I met you in that hotel room, I told you I was proud to know you. Now I'm proud to call you my friend. You're an amazing woman, young Sam," she said with a smile.

Samantha separated from Belle. "Thank you, but not so amazing. Lieutenant Scott is coming to the hospital tent at five o'clock. Is there anything that you'd like me to do for you before I leave?" Samantha asked.

A smile slowly began to form on Belle's face. "As a matter of fact, there is. First, we need to find Lieutenant Scott and see if he'll pick you up at my place at five o'clock."

"Why?"

"You'll see," Belle said with a grin. "And I need to talk with my girls. Let's go. We only have a few hours."

"A few hours for what?" Samantha asked as she walked beside her.

When they reached the tent, Belle spoke to one of the orderlies. "Josiah, would you find Lieutenant Avery Scott. He's probably with Major Clark. Tell him that Dr. Cartier and I need to talk with him."

The orderly rushed off as they entered the large hospital tent.

"You wait here. I need to find my girls," Belle said.

Belle returned a few minutes later. "We're all set. Now all we need is Lieutenant Scott."

"Doctor, did you send for me?" Avery Scott entered the tent, a look of concern on his face.

"I did, Lieutenant," Belle said.

Lieutenant Scott looked from Samantha to Belle. Samantha introduced them.

"Miss Belle, we've never met, but most certainly I have heard of you and all that you and your ladies have done here." He stumbled briefly over the word *ladies*. He obviously knew of Belle by her other reputation as well. He smoothly brought her hand to his lips. "It's a pleasure, ma'am."

"Lieutenant Scott, one of my girls is sick, and I'm concerned about her. Dr. Cartier has graciously agreed to see her. I'd like to leave now and go back into town. I understand that you two gentlemen have an engagement this evening. This shouldn't take more than a few hours. Perhaps you'd like to meet Dr. Cartier at my place and go on to the Cooper Plantation from there?"

"I'm under orders to stay with the doctor, ma'am. I don't think I can allow him to leave," Lieutenant Scott said.

"I can't believe that Major Winters-Hunt would prevent my girl from receiving a doctor's care. You're most welcome to accompany us if you wish, but I need Dr. Cartier to come with me. I'm sure we can make you comfortable while you wait, and I promise you'll make it to the party on time."

In her usual manner, Belle started moving the small group to the entrance of the tent. She caught Samantha's eye, signaling her to be quiet.

"Doctor?" Lieutenant Scott asked.

"After everything Miss Belle and these women have done here, I'm certain Major Winters-Hunt would want me to help," Samantha replied. "We can stop at Belle's and still get to the Cooper Plantation in time."

"I see no harm in that," Lieutenant Scott conceded. "Very well, Doctor. I'll accompany you to Miss Belle's."

When they arrived at Belle's, their hostess seated Lieutenant Scott in the parlor. Then she whisked Samantha upstairs. As soon as the door was closed in the upstairs bedroom, Samantha whirled around.

"All right, Belle, what's this about?" Samantha asked.

Just then the door opened, and Jessie and two women entered, pulling a large copper tub with them. Behind them were several more women with buckets of hot water. They were all giggling as they came in.

"Shhh," Belle cautioned them. "We don't want Lieutenant Scott to get suspicious. One of you is supposed to be sick, remember?" She closed the door behind the women as they began pouring the water into the tub. "All right, let's have them," Belle said, turning back to Samantha. Samantha frowned. "Your clothes; take them off," Belle said.

"Belle." Samantha looked quickly at the women in the room.

"They know, honey."

"Oh, Belle," Samantha groaned with disappointment.

"Will you just trust old Belle on this?" Belle asked.

"Lieutenant Scott is waiting, and my disguise has been revealed." Samantha looked at the three women who were staring at her. "I know none of you would say anything deliberately, but mistakes can be made."

"Must you argue?" Belle interrupted. She sighed. "I'm beginning to see what you put Ethan through."

"Belle!"

The door opened, and another young woman entered, carrying a gown over her arm. She walked over to Samantha and held it up against her.

"What do you think, Belle?" the young woman asked.

Belle pulled at the dress, pressing it against Samantha. "We'll know more when she tries it on. Sam is smaller in the bust and hips than you, Suzie. Can you alter it in time?"

"Of course."

"What do you say about going to Mrs. Cooper's party tonight as Miss Samantha Carter?" Belle said to a bewildered

Samantha.

"You can't be serious. Someone may recognize me!"

Belle burst out laughing. "Take a look at yourself!" She pulled Samantha over to a mirror. "You've done far too good a job, my dear. I've seen you with all that concoction off your face; no one else has. And I know what you'll look like in this dress."

"Lieutenant Scott. What will we tell him?"

"The truth," Belle said. "Ethan has trusted him with your life. I believe he can be trusted with this secret as well. Besides, he won't say anything until he talks with Ethan."

"You'll look lovely," one of the women said.

"Major Winters-Hunt will know," Samantha said.

"Indeed he will," Belle said with a wicked grin.

Samantha turned back to the mirror. Slowly, a smile appeared on her face. She reached down, letting her fingers glide across the rich silk. "This is beautiful," she said in awe. "This is a Worth gown!" She turned to Belle. "Where ever did you get this?"

"It's Suzie's," Belle said.

"Oh, Suzie, I can't wear this. Your alterations may ruin it."

"I want you to take it," the young woman said. "It was a gift from a gentleman friend from New Orleans. He likes to pretend that I am a lady of the gentry, and he brings me these fabulous gowns to wear for him." She turned to her friends. "Then he likes me to do things for him that a lady of the gentry would not do."

The women all laughed. Samantha wrinkled her brow, not understanding.

"One thing at a time, Suzie," Belle said, laughing. She turned to Samantha. "Let's get these clothes off of you, and let Suzie fit the dress so that she can work on it while you bathe."

The whole room took on an excited atmosphere. Shareen entered the room, carrying feminine undergarments for Samantha to try. Samantha removed her clothing and began to unwind the gauze. One of the women slipped a hooped petticoat over her head. "Suzie may need to adjust the length," the woman said in explanation. Samantha took a deep breath when the last of the gauze was removed. Suzie was there to slip the dress over her head.

"Good Lord! What's this?" Belle asked.

Samantha self-consciously reached to cover the area on her right side.

"Let me see!" Belle demanded. "You didn't have this scar when you were last in Charleston."

Reluctantly, Samantha removed her hand, avoiding the gazes of the women. On the right side of her chest, a few inches below her breast, was a jagged, red scar, five inches long. On each side of it were the puncture spots where the crude suture material had held the torn skin together. Because the entering lead ball had shred the skin, the scar was an elongated Z shape with multiple small scar lines projecting off both sides of it.

"What happened?" Belle whispered in the now silent room.

Samantha hesitated. "We were attacked by Union troops. I was shot. Here," she said, touching her chest, "and here," she said, parting her hair to reveal the scar on her scalp. "I was unconscious when Major Winters-Hunt found me. He took me back to the camp to Dr. Beauregard. That's when Dr. Beauregard and the major discovered I was a woman."

None of the women spoke. Belle reached up and took Samantha's face in her hands. She kissed her on the forehead and then held her while Samantha rested her head on Belle's shoulder. When Samantha finally raised her head, she was once again in control of herself.

"We'd better get started before Lieutenant Scott comes up to see what I'm doing," Samantha said.

Belle clapped her hands. "All right, girls, back to work."

The dress was fitted, and then Samantha lowered herself into the steaming tub. She would like to have stayed in there for hours, but after shampooing her hair, they wrapped her in a large towel.

"Your dress isn't done yet, Miss Samantha, so you just rest while I brush and dry your hair," Shareen said as Samantha lay on her side on the bed. Samantha wasn't even aware that she had drifted off to sleep until she heard Belle call her name softly.

"Sam?"

Samantha sat up. "I'm sorry. I didn't mean to fall asleep. Is it late?"

"No, honey, but your dress is ready. First, Shareen will style your hair. Come sit over here."

Samantha let herself be led to a small dressing table. "But my hair is so short," she said, "and I have this scar on my scalp."

"Shareen is an expert in the art of illusion. You watch," Belle said.

Shareen artfully pulled Samantha's hair up onto the top of her head, securing it with a few pins. She left it full and soft, with a few curls falling down the back, instead of binding it tightly in braids, as was the fashion. "Men are drawn to a woman's hair," she explained.

Then Samantha stood while Belle's girls presented undergarments. Samantha refused the corset offered. "I bound my chest for the past two and a half years. I'm not wearing it," she said. She did slip into the silk pantaloons and hoop undergarment. The dress and matching slippers were next. The dress was a dark emerald green that drew attention to Samantha's own vivid green eyes. It was cut low in the front, allowing a generous view of the tops of Samantha's breasts. It was tight in the waist and then flowed out over the hoop to the floor. The short, puffed sleeves of the gown were set off at the shoulder, leaving Samantha's shoulders bare. Her pale skin and rich chestnut hair perfectly complemented the luxurious green silk of the dress.

"Now, one final touch," Belle said. She reached behind her and picked up a small box covered in black velvet. Inside was an emerald-and-diamond pendant that hung on a black velvet ribbon.

"Belle! Where did you get this?" Samantha asked.

"I told you. I chose my men carefully through the years, and I always took care of myself. It was a gift from a generous gentleman," Belle said as she tied it around Samantha's neck.

"You're beautiful," one of the young women said appreciatively.

"I can't believe it. You're lovely. You can't be the same Doctor Sam," another said.

"Well, what do you think?" Belle asked as she turned Samantha around to the mirror.

Samantha stared at the elegant woman looking back in the mirror. "I look like my mother," she said softly.

Suzie handed her a matching silk purse and a fan. Samantha turned, hugged each woman, and then returned to Belle. "I think it's time to meet Lieutenant Scott," she said.

Samantha lifted her skirt as she descended the steps to where she found Lieutenant Scott, pacing in the parlor. His back was to Samantha as she entered. Belle and Shareen stood back in the hallway, watching as Samantha approached Avery Scott.

"Lieutenant Scott?" Samantha inquired in a silken, Southern voice.

Avery turned around.

"You are Lieutenant Scott?"

"Yes, ma'am."

"I'm Samantha Seymour, Lieutenant. Dr. Cartier will be joining you shortly."

"Miss Seymour, I'm pleased to meet you," Avery said, inclining his head.

Samantha walked over to him. "Please be seated, Lieutenant. Could I perhaps offer you some refreshments?"

Avery frowned. "Begging your pardon, Miss Seymour, but are you—that is—do you work here?" Avery's face reddened, and he coughed to cover his embarrassment.

"No, I'm a friend of Dr. Cartier's, Lieutenant," Samantha said, smiling. "Would you care for a cool glass of lemonade, Lieutenant Scott, or perhaps a brandy?"

Lieutenant Scott took a moment to recover. "I assure you I meant no offense, Miss Seymour. If you don't mind, ma'am, I would like a brandy," Avery answered.

Samantha turned to Belle and Shareen, who were standing by the door.

"The little imp is good at this," Belle whispered to Shareen.

"That one was pretending when dressed in man's clothes. I don't think she's pretending now. She has worn the gowns from Paris before. She knows what to say and do," Shareen said in a knowing way.

Samantha arched her eyebrow slightly at the women's whispered words. "Miss Belle, a brandy for the lieutenant, please." She returned to where Lieutenant Scott was standing, his confusion obvious. Samantha gracefully indicated the chair behind him. "Please sit, Lieutenant," she said as she chose a chair near him.

"Thank you," he said as he sat down.

Belle appeared with a glass of brandy. Samantha immediately rose and took it from her hand. She nodded her head slightly, dismissing Belle. She smiled to herself as she caught Belle rolling her eyes at her. Samantha handed Lieutenant Scott the drink and sat down near him.

"Lieutenant, I understand from Dr. Cartier that you are under the command of Major Winters-Hunt."

The lieutenant seemed surprised at her statement. "Yes, ma'am, I am. Do you know the major?"

Samantha smiled. "Yes, we are acquainted. I look forward to seeing him tonight at Mrs. Cooper's dinner."

"You'll be going to Mrs. Cooper's?" Before she could answer, the lieutenant's face reddened. "I intended no disrespect, Miss Seymour, when I asked you if you worked here. I . . . I can see you are a lady."

"I've been supporting Miss Belle's work at the Confederate base hospital," Samantha said. She understood the source of Avery's awkwardness. A lady would never enter a known house of pleasures. She watched him take a drink of the brandy and then she continued. "Lieutenant Scott, is it true that Major Winters-Hunt trusts you implicitly?"

"Ma'am?"

"Does the major trust you to keep, shall we say, sensitive information in confidence?"

"I'm not certain I understand you, Miss Seymour," the lieutenant answered with caution.

Samantha laughed softly. "Relax, Lieutenant. It's me he will be angry with, not you."

Lieutenant Scott stood up. "Beggin' your pardon, ma'am, but do you think Dr. Cartier will be much longer?"

"No. I'm ready. We should leave now" Samantha said. Lieutenant Scott frowned. "Lieutenant, it's me, Sam," she said.

"What's going on here?" Lieutenant Scott said roughly.

"I'm sorry to have to tell you in this way. My real name is

Samantha Carter, Lieutenant. We traveled together from Atlanta to Charleston, only you knew me as Sam Cartier."

Avery Scott stared at Samantha, a look of shock upon his face. "Jesus!" he swore.

"And Lieutenant, it's my professional opinion that you should sit down," Samantha said, seeing how pale the lieutenant's face had become. "If it's proof that you require, I can tell you the details of our traveling together, or you may ask me anything you would like."

When he didn't answer, Samantha continued. "I don't know how much Major Winters-Hunt told you about me. I'm from the North, as you surmised. I had disguised myself as a man, hoping to get an appointment to the Union Army Medical Corps, but the major captured me and brought me to the Confederacy."

"I'll be damned," Avery Scott whispered. "The major knows you're . . . you're a woman?"

"He knows now," Samantha said. "As you know, I was wounded. That's when he discovered that I was a woman. He and Dr. Beauregard thought it best that my identity be kept secret and that I continue my disguise as the boy, Sam."

"Your eyes! That's the only thing that's the same. The color is unique. When you first came into the room, I was trying to recall if we had met before. But I certainly would not have forgotten meeting such a beautiful woman."

"Considering the surprise I just gave you, you're very kind," Samantha said graciously.

"I still can't believe it." Suddenly, Lieutenant Scott's expression changed. "We traveled together without a chaperone. We slept next to each other!"

"You followed orders and escorted the boy, Sam Cartier, to the Cooper Plantation, Lieutenant," Samantha said to ease his embarrassment.

"No, this can't be true. You say the major knows who

you are. But last night at Mrs. Cooper's, I heard him wail the daylights out of you. He would never touch a lady in such a manner," Lieutenant Scott declared.

"He would if the lady pulled a knife on him and threatened to kill him," Belle said, entering the room.

"Belle," Samantha said, a warning in her voice.

"It's true, Samantha. You threatened Ethan with a knife. When he tried to take it from you, you said you fought and you actually cut his coat. He's killed men for less."

"Then I guess I should be eternally grateful to him for his kindness," Samantha said sarcastically.

"You didn't just cut his clothing—you cut him," Lieutenant Scott said incredulously. "There was a three-inch wound on his arm. I bandaged it."

"I didn't intend to wound him. Why didn't you send for me?" Samantha asked.

"The major thought it best to keep his distance from you," Lieutenant Scott answered.

"Indeed," Samantha replied and began to pace the room.

Lieutenant Scott shook his head. "Now I recognize the walk of the boy, Sam, but when you first entered the room, if you don't mind my saying, you moved like a lady. I can't believe the two are one. Does the major know that you're coming tonight like this?" he asked.

Samantha stopped pacing. In her softest voice, she answered, "The major said I was making it difficult for him to remember that I was a woman and not a boy." She walked over to him, positioning herself so that he had ample view of her low-cut bodice. "Do you think he'll still have that difficulty?" she asked in mock innocence.

The color rose in Lieutenant Scott's face as he tried to avert his gaze from the top of her dress.

"I think you'd best be on your way, or Ethan will come looking for you," Belle said, cutting in as she took

Samantha's arm, leading her away. "Here are your saddlebag and medical bag, just in case you aren't able to return tonight." She bent close to Samantha and whispered, "Listen here, you saucy little thing. What are you doing?"

Samantha looked back slyly. "Why, what-ever do you mean, Belle?"

"You try those little seductive games on a man like Ethan, and you'll find you have more than you can handle. Do you hear me? You may know a lot about men when a man yourself, but you don't know much about them as a woman."

Samantha glanced away. Belle's criticism was true. Samantha knew how to move in a man's world, but a ladies' world? Ladies like Caroline Cooper?

"Listen, honey." Belle's voice softened. "You're beautiful, but more than that, you have an alluring quality, a spark about you that men are going to be attracted to. They'll be more than just attracted. Gentlemen, like Lieutenant Scott, will contain themselves. But there are others who will not. Honey, you've been a man for so long, I don't think you realize the effect you're going to have tonight."

"That's exactly what I'm counting on," Samantha said.

Belle took Samantha's arm and guided her farther out into the hall. "What's going on in that head of yours?" Belle demanded.

"Belle, we really must be going," Samantha answered.

Belle's eyes widened as she held fast to Samantha. "Ethan! It's Ethan," Belle said, trying to keep her voice down so Lieutenant Scott wouldn't hear them. "You plan on getting even with him tonight. Oh, no, me and my foolish ideas. You're not ready for him, Sam. You're innocent in such matters. A man like Ethan is far too experienced for someone like you."

Just then, Belle's stableman entered the hall. "Miss Belle,

I've brought the carriage around. The doctor and lieutenant's horses are tied to the back."

"Then I guess we're ready to go," Samantha said, breaking free of Belle. "Lieutenant, shall we go?" she called to the other room.

Avery Scott came into the hall. "I still don't like this," he said.

"Lieutenant, your orders are to bring me to Mrs. Cooper's party, are they not?" She turned to Belle. "Thank you, Belle, and please don't worry. I'm in safe hands with Lieutenant Scott." She smiled sweetly at the lieutenant as the stableman opened the door for them.

An hour later, they were nearing the plantation when Lieutenant Scott turned to Samantha. "I don't know what to call you," he said. "I've called you doctor for so long. Do I call you Miss Seymour, Miss Samantha, or Miss Carter?"

"I was afraid if I used my last name, you'd make the connection between Sam Cartier and Samantha Carter. Seymour was my mother's maiden name."

"I see what you mean, although I don't think I would have ever suspected that Sam and Samantha were the same. It was just too improbable."

"Others might, though, especially if both persons are from the North."

"That's true. We don't have many Northerners down here."

They turned onto the lane of the Cooper plantation. It was dusk, and the lights had already been lit, casting a soft, yellow glow out of the windows of the pillared white house in the distance.

When they reached the house, Avery helped Samantha down from the carriage. "You're trembling," he said with concern. "Are you certain you want to do this?"

Samantha looked at him and smiled shyly. "Thank you, Lieutenant. You've been very understanding."

"Let's just hope we both don't live to regret it. Major Winters-Hunt is not someone whom I'd like to cross. I guess you know that as well as I do," he said.

They entered the central hall where Caroline was receiving her guests. The musicians were already playing in the large room off the hall where Samantha could see the swirl of silk, taffetas, and lace as the couples danced.

"Lieutenant Scott, I'm so glad you were able to join us tonight," Caroline said as Avery approached and took her offered hand.

"It was most kind of you to include me, Mrs. Cooper. May I present my cousin, Miss Samantha Seymour? She's recently returned from France and is on her way to New Orleans to join her family. She's had such a dreadful time of traveling that I took the liberty of asking her to accompany me tonight. Cousin Samantha, this is Mrs. Cooper, our hostess."

"Your cousin is lovely, Lieutenant. Miss Seymour, it's a pleasure to meet you," Caroline replied.

"Thank you, Mrs. Cooper. Cousin Avery said you've been most kind to him since he arrived in Charleston," Samantha drawled softly.

"How could I not be, such a handsome Confederate officer," Caroline said. She turned to Samantha. "Have you been away long?"

"I've been visiting family in Paris for the past two years," Samantha answered.

"I'm afraid things have changed in that time. The Yankees are everywhere on our soil," Caroline responded with distress.

"Is Major Winters-Hunt here?" Avery asked.

"Yes, indeed," Caroline said. "Oh, Lieutenant, where's Sam?"

"Sam didn't come," Avery replied.

"Oh, dear." Caroline frowned. "Ethan won't be happy about that."

It was late, and Ethan had been looking for Avery Scott to return with Samantha. What could be keeping them? Just then, he looked across the room and saw Avery talking with Caroline—finally. Sam must be sulking somewhere. He was certain Sam was not pleased about being here, but it was the only way he could keep her safe. Now that he knew she was a woman, he could hardly let her stay alone at the hotel. But Sam was not likely to listen to reason. She probably wandered off to the slave quarters again.

It was then that Ethan noticed the woman talking with Avery. He couldn't see her face; however, she seemed vaguely familiar. Ethan took a few steps toward them when Caroline called to him. Avery turned to look at Ethan, but the woman in the dark-emerald dress did not.

"Major," Avery said, catching sight of Ethan.

Still, the woman didn't turn around. Ethan had a sudden premonition as he moved toward them. He knew that profile, the angle of her jaw, her neck. It couldn't be! She wouldn't dare!

"Ethan, Lieutenant Scott has brought his cousin with him," Caroline said as Ethan came to stand next to her. "Miss Seymour, may I present Major Winters-Hunt? Ethan, this is Miss Samantha Seymour. She's just recently returned from France."

Ethan felt like the floor had just been knocked out from under him. She stood there, calmly looking at him.

"Ethan?" Caroline asked, obviously puzzled by the dark

look on Ethan's face.

"Major," Samantha said in a soft Southern drawl, "if you're trying to recall, we've met before," Samantha said.

Ethan clenched his fists. He wanted to drag her into another room and take her over his knee right now. How pleased she was with herself! He was aware that Caroline was staring at him. Avery averted his gaze.

"Miss Seymour," Ethan said, raising her hand to his lips. *"What the hell do you think you're doing?"* he demanded in French.

"Pardon, monsieur?"

"Don't try that on me, Sam! Just what the hell are you doing?"

"Following orders, you bastard," Samantha said sweetly in French. *"I shall be most gracious, as instructed to be."*

"Where did you get that dress and those emeralds?"

"Ah, you noticed," Samantha said, laughing softly.

"Ethan?" Caroline said as she took his arm. Caroline and Avery had been watching the two of them as they conversed in French, not understanding what was being said.

"Pardon-moi, madam. The major was asking me about Paris," Samantha said to Caroline. "But enough of that. You don't know how much I've been looking forward to going home."

"But my dear, you've heard that New Orleans is under Federal occupation? Surely your family doesn't want you to travel there in these circumstances," Caroline said. Then she turned to Avery. "Lieutenant Scott, you're not going to let her travel there, are you? Better to keep your cousin here in Charleston where it's still safe."

"I would enjoy seeing more of the area," Samantha said graciously and took Avery's arm.

"Cousin Samantha, would you care to dance?" Avery asked, avoiding Ethan's gaze.

"Thank you, Cousin Avery. I'd love to." Samantha

turned to Caroline. "If you'll excuse us, Mrs. Cooper? Major, it was a pleasure seeing you again." She turned gracefully and, taking Avery's arm, allowed him to lead her into the room set aside for dancing.

"Damn!" Ethan swore loudly.

Caroline turned to him, a surprised look on her face. "What is it, Ethan?"

"Sam!" he ground out.

"Lieutenant Scott said Sam didn't come. Really, Ethan, why do you let that boy perturb you so much? It's not like you to let someone get under your skin like that. I'm sure Sam is just fine. Now, are you going to help me greet my guests?"

"I'm sorry, Caroline. Will you excuse me?" Ethan turned and walked into the next room, leaving Caroline standing there with a stunned look on her face.

He spotted them immediately. It wasn't hard to find her. To Ethan, she stood out among all the others. She was smiling as she looked up at Avery, and then she laughed softly as Avery leaned down to say something to her. If she knew that Ethan was watching them, she didn't acknowledge it. As a houseboy walked by with a silver tray, Ethan removed a glass of bourbon from it and downed it in one gulp. He replaced the glass and took another.

For the next hour, he watched as Samantha danced with several of the men present. Avery always stood by, eager to claim her when the men finished their dances. Ethan's anger increased as the evening wore on, such that Caroline gave up trying to charm him and attended to her other guests.

At one point, Ethan overheard a few of the officers talking about Lieutenant Scott's beautiful cousin. He realized with a start that they were talking about Sam. He turned back around to watch as she moved across the floor in Avery's arms. Before he knew what he was doing, he strode across the floor, interrupting their dance.

"You will allow me, Lieutenant?" It was a command, not a request.

Avery hesitated. Ethan didn't give him time to refuse, as he took Samantha in his arms and began to move to the strains of the music.

"Are you finished playing your game for the night?" Ethan asked as he expertly led her around the floor.

"Do I look like I'm finished?" Samantha asked sweetly.

"I think you are," he said as he abruptly stopped dancing and took her arm. He was holding it tightly as he guided her to the main hallway. He turned to a livery boy standing near the door. "Have my horse and Miss Seymour's carriage brought around," he said.

"Ethan?" Caroline called as she hurried toward Ethan and Samantha with Avery following behind her.

"Caroline," Ethan said as he turned and released Samantha's arm. "Miss Seymour is fatigued from her travels. I took the liberty of calling for her carriage."

"I'm sorry you must leave," Caroline said to Samantha. "If you're going to be in Charleston for a few days, please visit again. Lieutenant Scott, perhaps you could bring your cousin back?" Caroline said, turning to Avery, who was standing beside her.

"Thank you for the invitation, Mrs. Cooper. We shall try. For now, I'll take Miss Samantha back to the hotel."

"Hotel? Oh my," Caroline said. "Lieutenant, you're both welcome to stay here for the night. I won't hear of you traveling all the way back into town this time of the night."

Ethan knew this was the last place Samantha wanted to be, so he smiled. "That's very kind of you, Caroline. I'm sure the lieutenant appreciates your offer." He turned to Samantha. "You'll be much more comfortable here than in a hotel in Charleston, Miss Seymour."

"I'm pleased to have you as my guests. If you'll excuse me, I'll have rooms prepared for you," Caroline said and then left the three of them standing in the hall.

"I'm not staying here. Avery, take me back to Belle's," Samantha demanded.

"You're staying here," Ethan said.

"Go to hell, Major," Samantha said sweetly.

"I warned you last night about your profanity."

Samantha's eyes widened at his reference to the previous night, and then they narrowed in fury. "If you think for one moment that I'll let you—"

"Major," Avery stepped in, "perhaps it would be best if I took Miss Samantha back to town."

Ethan released Samantha and turned to his junior officer. "I did not solicit your advice, Lieutenant."

"Ethan," a man called, sighting him in the hallway.

"Damn," Ethan ground under his breath as the man approached. "Edward," he said as he turned to the man and shook the hand offered to him.

Samantha watched Ethan and a few of the guests talking. Now was her chance! She backed away from the crowd until she reached the door. Ethan was looking the other way as Samantha slipped outside. Belle's carriage was there, as Ethan had requested, with Kota and Ethan's horse. Samantha grabbed Kota's reins and untied him. It was difficult with the large hoop under her skirt, but she placed her slippered foot in the stirrup and mounted Kota. She applied pressure to the horse's sides and he burst forward. As she raced away from the house, she glanced back over her shoulder to see Ethan and Avery emerge onto the porch.

Samantha's heart pounded as she urged Kota forward.

She hadn't gone far when she heard the sound of hooves behind her. She didn't have to look back to see who it was. She urged Kota to go faster as she tried to hold down the billowing skirt and worrisome hoop. She exited the lane and was out on the road, grateful that the night sky was clear and the moon bright. She could hear the horse behind her gaining upon her. She made a sharp turn off the road and started across an open meadow. Ahead was a grove of trees. If she could make it to there, she might be able to lose him in there and give herself enough time to escape.

She was fighting to keep her skirt from blowing into her face and obstructing her view as she raced toward the trees, but the skirt and its hoop were slowing her down. Again, she applied pressure to Kota's sides as the horse plunged into the grove of trees. She continued a short distance farther, then halted behind the large trunk of a tree. She could hear Ethan's horse coming through the woods, but the leaves blocked the moon, decreasing her vision. She waited in silence, thinking she had managed to evade him, when suddenly, she was knocked off her horse as Ethan broke through the trees and leaped from his horse onto her.

His arm encircled her waist, and they both hit the ground, rolling. When at last they came to a stop, it took a second for Samantha to regain her breath and orient herself. She scrambled up, tripping over her skirts, and then hit the ground again as Ethan grabbed her, moving on top of her. This time, he didn't waste any time in subduing Samantha, for he knew of her skill. She, in turn, was definitely hampered by the layers of skirt and hoop. She struggled against him, but he effectively pinned her to the ground. "Damn you!" Samantha swore and then ceased struggling, her breathing deep and rapid.

"Sam," he whispered softly, his eyes searching hers.

Ethan's face was very close, and in the moonlight, she no

longer saw anger in his eyes. She could feel his warm breath on her face, the sweet smell of bourbon, his body pressed against hers. When he lowered his lips to hers, she didn't resist. His lips were gentle, and she found the sensation pleasant. The longer his lips lingered on hers, however, the more she began to feel changes in herself. She had never been in such an intimate position with a man, and this was not just any man, this was Ethan, and Ethan was. . . .

Her mind recoiled suddenly, recalling who and what he was, but only for a moment. Somewhere deep inside of her, her heart reached out, trusting. She parted her lips slightly, and then she was surprised to feel Ethan's tongue. It sent waves of pleasure through her, and she found herself seeking him with her own lips. She wasn't even aware that he had released her hands or that she was now holding on to his shoulders. She didn't know how long they lay there, Ethan kissing her. She felt intense waves of pleasure that seemed to be spreading throughout her body, making every part of her come alive with feeling. She was aware of his chest pressing upon hers. She could feel the heat of his thighs through her skirt.

Samantha wanted to cry out in protest when he suddenly removed his lips from hers, but then a new set of sensations began when she felt his lips on her neck and throat. His touch seemed to ignite her, and his lips left a searing heat upon her skin. Each movement he made brought a new wave of pleasure, and when his lips touched the top of her breasts, the outside world ceased to exist for Samantha. An ache began to develop in her breasts, and she pushed up against Ethan's lips, wanting to feel his touch upon them.

She was barely aware of his hand slipping beneath her back and nimbly unfastening the hooks of her gown. The warm night air was suddenly on her breasts as his hand came around again and pushed her gown down to her waist. He kissed her throat again, and then his lips traveled downward. Just when she thought she must be feeling the ultimate pleasure, his lips reached her breasts. Never had she dreamed such feelings existed. As his lips moved from one breast to the other, Samantha thrashed beneath him. The intense feelings confused her—an ache was building up inside of her and a need. A need for what?

"Ethan," she said hoarsely, as she struggled against the heat on her body and the rushing tide overtaking her.

"Oh, God, Sam, tell me to stop," he whispered in her ear, his voice strained.

"Stop? No, don't stop," she pleaded.

Ethan was laying full length on her, and she couldn't seem to press against him enough. Her body demanded more. Then she his felt hand under her skirt and its scorch on her thigh through the thin fabric of her pantalets. He touched her waist where his fingers manipulated the tie; then his hand was inside, rubbing her belly.

Every essence of Samantha's body was alive, and she writhed under his touch, unable to control that odd combination of ache and pleasure. When she thought she could stand it no longer, his hand moved between her legs, his fingers gently touching her. Samantha cried out. Her only thought was of Ethan and his touch. She was rushing somewhere on a tide of indescribable pleasure. But to where? Where was he taking her? She ached inside, acutely aware of a moist throbbing between her legs. As though mentally guiding him, or willing him, she felt the exquisite sensation of his touching her in that most intimate spot and she shuddered. At the same time, she instinctively thrust her hips up to meet his touch and felt his fingers penetrate slightly.

Then, suddenly, he removed his hand and jerked her skirt downward, covering that intimate area on her body where he had just been.

"Pull your gown up," Ethan said urgently.

Samantha didn't respond.

"Major? Miss Samantha? Are you over here?" a male voice called out in the distance.

Samantha was stunned and confused. She struggled but could not focus on anything except the storm of desire pent up inside of her. Suddenly, she was separated from him. He was no longer touching her, pulling both her body and soul into him.

"Sam! Hurry!" he said.

In a daze, Samantha reached for the top of her gown and tried to pull it up, but her fingers were trembling. That movement only made her more aware of the longing that remained inside of her where Ethan's touch had just been. She cried out in frustration.

"Here," Ethan said as he rose up onto one knee. "Let me do it."

Samantha's hands shook as she tried to position the front of her gown while Ethan fastened the back.

"Fix your. . . ." He stopped, glancing down at her skirt, which was still rumpled around her waist. "I'll delay him."

"Major? Miss Samantha?" the voice called again.

Avery Scott rode into the wooded area. Fortunately, the horses and trees blocked his view of Ethan and Samantha on the ground.

Ethan looked back at Samantha. Their eyes locked for a moment, and then he tore his gaze away and walked toward where he heard Lieutenant Scott calling.

"We're over here, Lieutenant," Ethan called.

Numbly, Samantha pulled her pantalets up and tied them. She wasn't even aware of the tears that were falling—tears of desire, frustration, and confusion. She started to stand but felt weak. Just then, both men returned, and Avery slid off his horse and rushed over to her.

"Miss Samantha! The major said that you fell. Good Lord!" Avery said, taking in her disheveled appearance and tear-streaked face. "Can you stand? Should I send for a doctor?"

Samantha shook her head. She took a deep breath to calm the storm still raging inside of her. "I'm . . . I'm not hurt," she finally said, her voice shaking.

"Let me help you," he said, reaching down for her arm.

Ethan placed his hand on her other arm to help. The heat from his touch seared through her, and Samantha jerked away. Avery looked sharply at Ethan, who stepped back and allowed Avery to help Samantha to stand.

"Are you certain you're not hurt?" Avery inquired with concern. "You're trembling."

"I'm a little sore, that's all."

"I left the carriage back at Mrs. Cooper's. Can you ride your horse?" Avery asked.

"Of course," Samantha answered. "I didn't see the low tree branch in the dark. I hit it and was knocked off," she said, trying to satisfy the lieutenant so he wouldn't ask any more questions. She avoided looking at Ethan as Avery helped her to where Kota was standing. She mounted and arranged her skirt as best she could. Kota stepped sideways, sensing the tension in his mistress. He tossed his head as Samantha gripped the reins tightly.

"Are you sure you are able to ride?" Avery asked again.

Samantha nodded and waited while Avery and Ethan mounted their horses.

"We should probably return to Caroline's," Ethan said as they started riding.

"No!" Samantha said as she abruptly stopped Kota. How could he suggest that after what had just happened? How could he even mention that woman's name?

"It's the closest place, Samantha," Avery said. "You need to rest after such a fall. It's the best thing."

Samantha felt as though a knife had been plunged into her heart. "I'll fight you both all the way to that plantation," Samantha threatened, tears appearing again.

Avery sighed and looked to Ethan.

"Belle's place is out of the question," Ethan said.

"I agree. It wouldn't be proper for Samantha to be there," Avery said.

"I would like to be alone at the hotel," Samantha said.

"Samantha, you can't be alone," Avery said.

"I've been alone before," Samantha said quietly.

"Yes, but circumstances are different now," Avery said.

"Yes," Samantha whispered as a new tear moved slowly down her cheek. "Things are different."

"We'll go to Arabella," Ethan said.

"Sir?"

"Sam can rest there for the night, and then we can leave for Washington City in the morning."

"That's another hour's ride," Avery said.

"We'll make it. Lieutenant, you can return the carriage to Belle. Tell her that I'll see that the gown and necklace are returned to her."

Avery hesitated.

"Tell the general's staff that I'll return in a few weeks," Ethan instructed.

"Are you sure you wouldn't like me to come with you to Washington City?" Avery asked.

"That's not necessary, Lieutenant. I'll see Sam safely to Washington City. You should remain here and available to the general."

Avery pulled his horse up next to Samantha. "Will you be all right, Samantha? If you want me to stay," he said quietly to her, "just say so."

Samantha was touched by his offer, for she knew the risk he was taking in defying Ethan's order.

"No, Avery, it's not necessary. I'll be fine." She hesitated. "Thank you for all you've done."

"Maybe after the war is over, you'll come back? My family lives in Arlington. They would welcome you, as would I." He raised her hand to his lips. "It's been an honor, Miss Samantha, truly an honor," he said, and then abruptly turned his horse around and headed toward the Cooper Plantation. He looked back once to wave at her, and then he was gone.

"This way," Ethan said.

"Where are we going?" Samantha managed to ask, feeling her throat constrict again.

"To my home. You can rest there tonight, and then we'll leave for Washington City in the morning."

Samantha held Kota at a stand. Ethan squeezed his eyes shut and lowered his head for a moment. Then he looked at her. "I'm very sorry, Sam," he began. "I have no excuse to offer in the way of an apology for the liberties I took with you. I've never lost control like that. Never. And I've wronged you greatly." When she still didn't look at him, he continued. "I behaved dishonorably, but I want you to know you needn't be afraid of me, Sam," he said softly. "What happened tonight will never happen again. You have my word on it."

Samantha urged Kota into a trot, keeping her tear-filled eyes straight ahead. Ethan moved his horse up next to her. She couldn't look at him. She didn't understand. She was confused. But mostly, she didn't know what to do with the newly discovered desire raging through her.

CHAPTER 8

It was well past midnight when Ethan and Samantha reached Arabella, the plantation that was Ethan's home. It was comprised of several thousand acres of land north of Charleston, bordered on the west by the Cooper River and extending east to the Atlantic Coast, making Ethan one of the largest landowners in South Carolina.

The hour-and-a-half ride had been difficult. Samantha wouldn't speak. She kept her face forward as they rode, but Ethan could see her silent tears. It was all he could do not to reach out and take her in his arms, to hold her, to protect her, to comfort her. He despised himself, for he knew he was the cause of her tears.

What had he done? He never intended to hurt her, and he certainly had not intended what had happened back in the grove of trees. There could never be anything between them. Never! The passion, the desire he'd felt back in those woods, completely surprised him. And it had been intoxicating, irresistible, overwhelming—like nothing he'd ever experienced with another woman.

He tried to apologize to her, to reassure her, but she wouldn't even look at him. Now that they were at Arabella, he'd talk to her and she'd have to listen.

As they drew near to the house, four large hounds emerged from under the cover of trees, barking at the horses. Ethan whistled sharply to them and then spoke. The dogs stopped barking and pranced happily around the horses, managing to stay away from the horses' hooves as they arrived at the house.

The house was a large, red brick structure with white columns rising up from the ground to the roof, forming a portico on the front of the house. Attached to one side was a smaller wing with the same red brick and white columns that rose one story to the lower roof. A light appeared at one of the windows. Then the door opened, and a Negro man and woman stepped out onto the portico.

"Lordy!" the Negro woman exclaimed as Ethan bounded up the steps. He embraced the woman and then the man. "'Bout time you come home," the woman said.

"She worry all the time 'bout you," the man added with a smile.

"Sam?" Ethan said as he turned to look at her. Samantha hesitated and then dismounted.

"Molly, this is Miss Samantha Carter. She'll be staying with us tonight. Sam, this is Molly and Fox Winters," Ethan said, completing the introductions. "Fox, would you take the horses to the stables?"

"I'd rather bed Kota down myself," Samantha said.

Before Ethan could reply, Fox walked over to Kota and rubbed his nose. Then he walked to the side and stroked the horse's neck. "Don't worry, Miss, Old Fox knows how to rub a horse down. Me and horses, we's friends. Don't you worry 'bout nothin'." He reached out and took the reins from Samantha's hand and then those for Ethan's horse. Kota didn't object as Fox led him away.

Ethan walked back down the steps and picked up the saddlebags. "This way," he said, motioning to the house. Molly went ahead of them to light the lamps.

They entered a large open foyer, its ceiling reaching the top of the house. On one side was a staircase that curved upward to the second floor. Ethan dropped the bags onto the polished wood floor as another Negro man appeared. "Frederick!" Ethan exclaimed as the two men embraced.

"I didn't know you were comin' home," Frederick said.

"I didn't either. Frederick, may I present Miss Samantha Carter? Sam, this is my friend, Frederick Winters."

"Pleased to meet you, Miss Carter," Frederick said.

"Frederick is Molly and Fox's son," Ethan said in explanation, and then he turned to Molly. "Molly, we'll be here just for the night, and then we'll be leaving in the morning."

"It'll be mornin' in a few more hours. Look at this girl. Looks like she's all wore out," Molly said as she crossed over to Samantha. "Leave in a couple of hours. Huh! A couple of days would be more like it." She took Samantha's arm. "You must be tired. You come with me, and we'll get you out of that dress and into a nice bed. Then I'll bring something' for you to eat."

Samantha didn't resist as Molly led her up the stairs.

"Molly," Ethan called, "don't put her in—"

"Hush, now," Molly said as she turned to look down at Ethan. "You don't think I can run this house?"

Ethan smiled at the reprimand as Molly continued up the stairs. Then he turned to Frederick. "How about a drink?" They both went into the library, and that's where Molly found them an hour later.

Molly knocked briefly and then, without waiting for a response, entered. Both men were seated, sharing a decanter of brandy. For the past hour, Ethan had avoided any discussion of Sam or himself. Instead, Frederick had updated him on the business of the plantation. When Molly entered, Ethan could tell by the look on her face that he wasn't going to dissuade her from the topic of Sam.

"What's goin' on here, Ethan?" she demanded, planting her feet and resting her hands upon her hips.

"What do you mean?" Ethan asked.

"I mean, Miss Samantha."

"What about her?"

"I got her tucked into bed, but it looks to me like that one has been cryin' her eyes out."

"What did she say?" Ethan asked, staring at his glass.

"Not a thing. She's real nice and polite, and I can tell she's not from around here, but she's not talkin'."

Ethan sighed and stood up. "I'll go talk to her," he said, putting his glass down.

"I put her in Miss Arabella's room," Molly said.

Ethan nodded. "Thanks, Molly."

Ethan took the steps, two at a time, and stopped before the door to the bedroom. He paused a moment, grateful to Molly for her sensitivity. This bedroom had belonged to his mother, although to his knowledge, his mother never slept in this room. She preferred to sleep with her husband in the adjoining room, which was his father's room. She did enjoy reading in the room and would sit for hours sewing in it. When Ethan was born, it had served as a temporary nursery for him until he was old enough to have his own bedroom.

Ethan tapped lightly on the door. "Sam?" he called.

When there was no answer, he opened the door. She was not in the bed, and Ethan could see a tray of uneaten food on the table next to the bed. He stepped inside and found her standing with her back to him, looking out the window. He closed the door and turned to look at Samantha. He immediately recognized the nightgown Molly had given her to wear. Then Samantha turned to look at him, and he forgot about the owner of the nightgown.

"Sam, we need to talk," he said.

"I'd rather not," she replied. She crossed to the door and

opened it. "It's late, and I'd like to get some sleep."

Ethan reached for the door and closed it, remaining inside. He turned to her and put his hands on her shoulders.

"No!" she said as she jerked away.

"I'm sorry. Oh, God, Sam, there's no excuse for what I did tonight. I acted dishonorably. I'm sorry. I never meant to frighten or hurt you, and you can believe me when I say that it won't happen again. You don't have to be afraid of me."

Samantha looked at Ethan. "What am I supposed to do now?" she cried, desperation in her voice. She turned away from him.

"Nothing. Sam, you don't need to do anything. Nothing happened. I didn't take. . . . You're not a compromised woman, you're still a. . . ." Ethan sighed. "You'll forget all about this, believe me. Tomorrow, we'll leave for Washington City. Soon, you'll be home. Your life will return to normal. In time, you'll meet the man who will become your husband. You'll go to your marriage bed innocent and a virgin, just as it should be."

Samantha whirled around, and Ethan was taken aback by the anger that flared in her eyes. "Is that what you think I'm concerned about? You bastard!"

Samantha flew at him. Ethan grabbed her wrists and held her off while Samantha hurled a string of curses at him—curses that he was certain would have brought color to the cheeks of some of his most seasoned sailors. He'd seen her angry before, and certainly they'd argued, but he'd never thought her capable of such vituperation. When she jerked to free herself, he released her. She concluded by calling him every obscene name she knew. If she hadn't been so angry, he would have laughed. Where had she learned those words? How much more was there to this woman that he didn't know? He stopped his thoughts before they went where he couldn't allow them to go. He'd never have the opportunity to answer those questions.

She was pacing the room like a trapped animal. As he watched her, Ethan realized that Samantha was not the least bit afraid of him or hurt. So what was going on in that fascinating head of hers?

Ethan crossed the room and opened the door to the adjoining bedroom. When he returned a moment later, he was carrying a decanter and two glasses. He put them on a table and then turned to Samantha.

"Sit down," he said as he poured two glasses of dark ruby liquid.

"I don't want to sit down," she said angrily.

"We're not going to argue about this, Sam. Sit down."

"Go to hell, Major!"

As they stood there staring at each other, it occurred to Ethan that he was glad she was clad in that thin nightgown and unable to pull her knife on him again, for she looked like she would surely use it. Another thought had gradually been forming in the back of his mind. Was it possible? It would explain her behavior.

"Are you afraid to sit with me?" he asked softly, his eyes challenging her. He saw her eyes widen before she masked her response.

"Of course not."

Ethan indicated one of two stuffed wing chairs. Samantha sat stiffly in one of them. Ethan handed her a glass and then sat in the other, angling it so it faced her. He took a long drink from his glass and then looked back at her.

"Go ahead, try it," he said.

Samantha brought the glass up to her lips and inhaled the aroma. She tipped the glass back and swallowed. Immediately, she started coughing and her eyes watered. When she recovered, Ethan smiled.

"It's not to your liking?" he asked.

"What is it?"

"I would have thought a young man of your age, having spent several years in Paris, would recognize a good French brandy. Would you prefer something else?" he asked.

"No," she said stubbornly. "This is fine." She took another drink, this time a small sip.

"How old are you, Sam? I want the truth."

Samantha hesitated and then answered. "I'm fifteen. My birthday was last month."

Ethan cocked his head. "Last month? I didn't know that. So you were twelve or thirteen when you ran off to Paris?"

"I didn't run off to Paris. My father sent me to live with my aunt while attending a finishing school."

"I see. And you stayed in Paris until returning several months ago?"

"Yes."

"During those two years in Paris, were you always disguised as a man?"

Samantha shifted uneasily under Ethan's gaze. "No," she answered. "I disguised myself during the day when I was at the medical college. I changed clothes at the end of each day before returning to my aunt's home so that she wouldn't know what I was doing. Eventually, she discovered my deception, and my father ordered me to return home immediately."

"So by day, you were a man, and by night, a young woman?"

Samantha wrinkled her brow. "Yes," she answered hesitantly.

Ethan had been watching her carefully, and he was now convinced that he knew why she was so angry. It was a bittersweet revelation. "And in all that time, there was never a man in your life—not until several hours ago."

Samantha's eyes widened. "I'm not the child you think I am," she said. "Of course there have been men. I had many suitors in Paris." She swallowed nervously.

"I don't think so. As a woman and *lady*," he emphasized, "you've never been in the presence of a man without a chaperone. You've never kissed a man before, and you certainly haven't. . . ."

Samantha blushed deeply. "How would you know?" she demanded indignantly. "You don't know anything about me."

Ethan looked directly at her and arched his eyebrows. "On the contrary, I'm probably the only man who possesses intimate knowledge about you. I can attest to your virginity."

If possible, Samantha turned a deeper shade of red.

"Furthermore," Ethan continued, "I'm fairly certain I'm the only man who knows something else about you. My guess is that even you didn't know, until tonight, what your, shall we say, nature is?"

"My . . . my nature?" Samantha stammered.

Her chest was rising and falling rapidly in the thin, delicate fabric of the nightgown she was wearing. Without actually hearing it, Ethan knew her heart was pounding. Just then, there was a knock at the door and Molly entered. She took one look at Ethan and Samantha and marched up to stand before Ethan.

"You ought not to be in here, Ethan, and drinkin' spirits! Now you get out of here and let Miss Samantha get to bed."

"Molly, I'll move about my own house as I please," Ethan said.

"You'll not be movin' into this child's room, not while I'm here. Now you go on!"

Ethan grinned and stood up. "I'm going, Molly, I'm going."

"Huh!" Molly said.

Ethan looked down at Samantha, her eyes still wide and face flushed. "I once told you that I'd be proud to have you as a brother. That was before I knew you were a woman." He smiled slightly and then became serious. "It will be a prouder and more fortunate man than I who will someday call you his wife. It is an honor to know you, Sam. Good night."

Samantha was stunned. She watched Ethan leave her bedroom. She didn't even hear Molly come up behind her.

"Come on, child. You come to bed now. The night is half over," Molly said.

Samantha allowed herself to be led to the bed. Once Molly had Samantha in bed, she put out the lamps and walked to the door. "You sleep as late as you want, child. Ethan won't be takin' you anywhere in the mornin'. You're all done in and need rest. Good night, Miss Samantha."

After Molly left, Samantha lay in the darkened room, her thoughts confusing. She was very much aware of her body, the feel of the nightgown on her skin, the pounding of her heart. Sleep didn't come easily to her that night.

It was almost noon when Samantha awoke the next morning. The first thing she noticed was several dresses laying across a nearby chair. When she went over to examine them, she saw that they were light day dresses, all of them beautifully made and probably costly. On the other chair, where she and Ethan had sat last night, was an assortment of ladies underwear, shoes, and parasols to match. She was studying the garments before her when there was a knock at the door.

"Yes?" Samantha answered.

"Miss Samantha?" Molly opened the door and stepped in. "I see you found the dresses." She elected one. "I took this one in. Let's see how it fits, and then I'll adjust the others."

"They're for me? Why?"

"You didn't bring clothes. I thought you'd need somethin' to wear while you're here."

"Molly, that was very thoughtful of you, but we'll be leaving today."

"Oh, I know all about that, or at least part of it." Molly started laughing. "Menfolk can be such fools. Imagine you dressin' as a boy and them not knowin' you're a woman." Again Molly laughed. "Well, it don't look like Ethan is in any hurry to leave today. It's almost noon. I'm thinkin' you'll be here a few days, so you'll need these."

Samantha was surprised by Molly's gesture and the news that Ethan was delaying their departure. Molly handed Samantha the dress.

"You come downstairs when you're ready, Miss Samantha, and I'll fix somethin' for you to eat."

After Molly left, Samantha slipped into the soft, mint-green dress that had a fitted bodice and full, gathered skirt. She avoided the corset that Molly had provided. Instead, she pulled on a delicate pair of silk drawers. She also left the hoop and petticoat where they lay; she'd had enough of those last night.

As she looked in the mirror, she was pleased with the effect, except that she would have again preferred that the bodice not be so low. She was still disturbed by the conversation she had with Ethan last night in her room. He always seemed to know what she was thinking and feeling. It had been that way since the beginning when he first captured her.

Her mind went back to last night in the grove of trees.

Her chest was flushed, and she could feel her heart beating as she remembered his touch on her skin.

She was still thinking about Ethan when she descended the stairs, not certain where she was to go. The large house was quiet. She hesitantly started walking toward the back of the house, where she found a door that led outside to the kitchen building. Entering it, she found Molly working at a table.

"Miss Samantha! Lordy child, ain't you a pretty one!" Molly walked over to Samantha and reached for the waistline of the dress. "And the dress fits, but I think I'll take the others in a little more. Now, why don't you tell Molly what you would like to eat, and I'll bring it into the house for you."

"If you don't mind, Molly, I'd like to eat here."

Molly smiled broadly. "Then sit down, child."

Molly busied herself preparing a plate of food for Samantha while Samantha looked around the large, airy room. It was clean and neat and surprisingly cool, despite the brick ovens, one of which already contained bread baking.

"Molly, I don't mean to be nosey, but who lives here? This is Ethan's house?"

"Yessum. Ethan's daddy, William Hunt, built it for Ethan's mother, Arabella. The place is named after her. I raised Arabella, I did. Arabella's mother died in birthin', and her daddy, Josiah Winters, gave her to me to nurse. I wasn't much more than a child myself. My Arabella and her William died eight years ago. There's just their Ethan now," Molly concluded.

"This was her dress?" Samantha asked as she looked down at the dress she was wearing. Molly didn't answer but brought the coffeepot over to refill Samantha's cup. Another question occurred to Samantha. "Molly, are you a slave? Does Ethan—"

"Do I what?" a male voice interrupted.

Samantha and Molly turned to see Ethan enter from a back door. He walked over to a bucket and, using a ladle, took a drink of cool water. He was dressed in pants and long boots and was naked from the waist up. His back was to Samantha as he replaced the ladle in the bucket. Samantha had seen Ethan without his shirt before, especially when he thought he was traveling with a boy. Why should she take note of the strength of his back and arms now? His muscles glistened with the moisture of the heat and the work that he'd been about.

He turned around and caught her eyes on him. Samantha looked away quickly, but not before she saw a smile fleetingly pass across Ethan's face. "What is it that you would like to know, Sam?"

Samantha hesitated. She glanced at Molly and then turned to Ethan. "You told me you were opposed to slavery."

Ethan appeared to be considering a response, and then he came to a decision. "Let's go for a walk, Sam." He went over to a wall and retrieved his shirt. He slipped it on but didn't bother buttoning it. Samantha hadn't moved. He came over and gently took her arm, helping her to stand. She allowed herself to be led out of the kitchen.

They walked in silence for a while, past the smokehouse and around to several smaller houses. Samantha scrutinized the plantation and its buildings.

"You won't find any slave quarters on this plantation," he said, reading her thoughts.

"But Molly said—"

"Molly is a free woman, as is her husband, Fox, and their son, Frederick. All the Negroes on this plantation are free people and have been since the day they set foot on it. This way," he said as he placed his arm around her shoulder, just as he had often done when he thought she was a boy, and guided her toward a grove of trees in the distance. "My father's name was William Hunt. His earliest memories were of a small house in the Scottish Highlands with too many children and not enough food. He was about eleven years old when he hired on as a cabin boy for a merchant vessel carrying goods back and forth from the Carolinas to Europe.

"He was fortunate, for the captain of the ship was an honorable man. The work of a cabin boy is hard, and for some, it can be a living hell, depending on the nature of the captain. My father worked hard in exchange for plenty of food, a warm bed, and something he never could have dreamed of back in Scotland: he received an education. The captain was a scholar, of sorts, and in the evenings taught my father how to read, write, and do basic mathematics.

"Over the years, my father worked his way up to first mate under the command of his benefactor, the captain. Eventually, the old captain died, and to my father's surprise, he left his small fleet and shipping enterprise to my father. My father expanded the line and bought coastal property and built docks and warehouses in Charleston. That was the beginning of Hunt Enterprises."

"But your name is Winters-Hunt," Samantha said.

"Yes, my mother's name was Arabella Winters. Her father, my grandfather, owned a large cotton plantation near here. His name was Josiah Winters, and my mother was the last of his line. When my parents married, my father agreed to take my mother's name as well so that the Winters name wouldn't die out. As a wedding gift, my grandfather gave my parents seven hundred acres of prime land that adjoined his own and slaves to work the land."

"Molly was among them?" Samantha asked.

"Yes, but my father was opposed to slavery and freed all the Negroes that his new father-in-law had given him. He then hired most of them back and paid them a decent wage. When my grandfather died, my mother inherited the rest of his lands, joining the properties into one holding as they had originally been. We still plant tobacco, but most of the land is used for the horses. The shipping line was prospering up until the war. Now, of course, the blockade has curtailed the shipping."

"Your ships run the blockade to supply the Confederacy," Samantha said.

Ethan looked at her in surprise. "I didn't know you knew that," he said. "What else do you know?"

Samantha smiled. "I'm learning more all of the time, Rebel." Ethan laughed. Then Samantha became serious again. "But, Ethan, if you're able to maintain your plantation without slave labor, then why can't the rest of the plantations? You once told me that the planters wouldn't be able to survive without slavery. You do."

"No, Sam, not really. I have other resources. If tobacco or cotton was my livelihood, I'd have to plant most of my acreage in it, and then I'd need a hundred slaves to work it. I couldn't afford to pay them all wages. I'd go broke. I'd have to let all the Negroes go, and then who'd work the fields? It takes a lot of people. I'd end up with land that would lie fallow and have no source of income.

"Even here at Arabella, I pay the Negroes who work for me a decent wage, but the tobacco profits alone are not enough to cover their wages. I've been able to keep this place and maintain a certain lifestyle because of other sources of income."

"Your shipping line out of Charleston," Samantha said.

"Among other things," Ethan said.

"So," Samantha said pensively, "even if a planter wanted

to end slavery, he couldn't run his plantation without it."

"So it would seem. It's an old system, Sam. For generations, families have lived with slavery and lived on land that belonged to them long before we became separated from England. Now they must give it up. They see their children's heritage and future being destroyed.

"Many have known for some time that the end was not far away. England, France, and many other countries have outlawed slavery. And if given the time, I'd like to think that we would have done away with it ourselves. But your Mr. Lincoln saw it differently."

"People in the North are clamoring for an end to the war," Samantha said. "Maybe it will end. Both sides will just tire of it and sue for peace."

"No, Sam. A tremendous movement has begun, and it won't stop until its ends are accomplished."

They reached a grassy meadow and sat down under a large tree. They remained there for several hours, agreeing on some subjects and disagreeing on others. Neither was aware of the time, when suddenly a man, running across the grass toward them, interrupted them.

"Mr. Ethan. Molly sent me to fetch you," the Negro said as he approached. "She say to tell you that you have a visitor, a lady."

"Do you know who it is, Clay?" he asked as he stood.

"No, sir, a fancy carriage, though."

"Thank you. Tell Molly we'll be in."

As Clay ran back to the house, Ethan extended his hand to assist Samantha to stand. "I'm not expecting anyone," Ethan said. "No one knew I was coming here, except perhaps. . . ." He didn't finish his sentence. He pulled out his pocket watch and smiled. "Four o'clock. We've been sitting here talking for over three hours. I haven't taken you over my knee once, and you haven't pulled a knife on me or threatened to kill me. I'd say we're making progress."

Samantha could see he was teasing her. She matched the stride of his step as they started walking next to each other. Suddenly, her foot lashed out and, too late, Ethan felt his feet kicked out beneath him. He recovered quickly, but not before he went down on one knee. Samantha gathered her skirt in her hands and started running toward the house, her laugh trailing behind her.

In a matter of seconds, she heard him growl behind her and could hear his footsteps closing in on her. She couldn't outrun him, especially in a dress. His arm was like a vice as it lashed out and wrapped around her waist, lifting her completely off the ground. She wiggled to get free, but he only laughed and slowed his steps to a walk, still carrying her in the crook of his arm.

"Ethan, put me down," Samantha said.

"I should have known you couldn't behave yourself for very long." He smiled and set her down on the ground. "Come on," he said, as he placed his arm casually about her shoulders, as he had so often with the boy, Sam, and turned again toward the house. When they'd almost reached the house, Ethan stopped suddenly. "That's Caroline's carriage. She must have found out that we came here last night." He removed his arm from her shoulders. "I'd better not present myself like this," he said. "We'll go around to the back, and I'll change my clothes."

Samantha spun around. "I would have thought that Mrs. Cooper has seen you in less presentable attire than that," she said, pointing to his open shirt, her meaning clear. "Ah, yes, but she's a lady, the epitome of Southern gentility, correct? You wouldn't have expected her to sit on the grass and talk of war or politics, for it is unbecoming of a lady to do so. And you most certainly wouldn't have handled her as you just did me. Of course not. She deserves your respect, whereas I. . . ." Samantha abruptly turned and started running toward the house.

Ethan watched Samantha run from him. He didn't stop her. Her words stung him because she'd spoken the truth. He wouldn't have treated Caroline that way, but not for the reasons that Samantha thought. He also wouldn't have sat for hours upon the ground, simply enjoying her company—her thoughts—as he had Samantha's. "Damn!" Ethan swore as he entered the kitchen building. "Why did Caroline have to show up now? Molly!" he shouted. "Bring some hot water up to my room. Tell Mrs. Cooper I'll be down shortly."

Ethan entered the great house and used the back stairs. When he reached his room, he saw that the door to Samantha's room was closed. Entering his room, he stripped off his shirt as Clay arrived with a bucket of water.

"Molly said to tell you that you have another visitor, Mr. Ethan, a lieutenant. He just arrived."

Ethan swore again. "Clay, after Lieutenant Scott is settled in the parlor with Mrs. Cooper, ask Molly to come up here, please."

By the time Molly arrived, Ethan was bathed and changed into a waistcoat, sack coat, and pants that matched. He scowled when he opened the door. "Molly, tell Miss Samantha that we have visitors, Lieutenant Scott and Mrs. Cooper, and that she is to join us," Ethan said.

Ethan strode down the hallway and descended the curved steps in the front of the house. He greeted his guests in the parlor and apologized for his delay.

"Ethan, you left in such a hurry last night," Caroline said. "Was something wrong? Lieutenant Scott stopped back at my house for his carriage and told me that you and Miss

Seymour had ridden here last night." Caroline paused, the questions plainly written on her face.

"Yes, Miss Seymour is returning to Virginia tomorrow. She couldn't very well stay with Lieutenant Scott at the camp. I offered my home. She'll be joining us shortly," Ethan said.

"I see," Caroline said, "but why didn't you have her stay with me? I realize you gentlemen don't always think of these things, but it would have been much more appropriate for your cousin to stay at my home," Caroline said to Avery. "Lieutenant Scott, as her cousin, you are responsible for Miss Samantha."

Molly entered just then. "Excuse me, Mr. Ethan, but Miss Samantha sends her apologies. She has a headache and won't be joining you."

"Perhaps I should go see her," Ethan ventured, trying to keep the anger out of his voice.

"Nonsense, Ethan. Lieutenant Scott is her cousin," Caroline reminded Ethan. "But I imagine she would prefer a woman with her. I'll go to her." Caroline stood.

"That's very kind of you, Caroline, but I'm sure it isn't necessary. Molly can care for her, but just in case, Molly," Ethan said as he turned back to Molly, "would you ask Miss Samantha if she would like Mrs. Cooper to visit her?" The last thing Ethan wanted was for Caroline to walk unannounced into Samantha's room. He doubted if Samantha would welcome her warmly.

As Molly started to leave the room, Ethan walked over to her and spoke quietly. "What exactly did Sam say?" he asked.

"Just what have you done to make that child so mad?" Molly accused.

"What did she say?"

"She said she'd ride to hell and back before she'd sit in a

room with you and . . . uh . . . your mistress," Molly said.

"Tell her she joins us down here, or I'll send Mrs. Cooper up to care for her and her headache."

"I'll not bother that child again."

"Molly!"

Molly frowned. "What are you up to, Ethan?"

"I don't have time to discuss this now. Just tell her what I said," Ethan said quietly and returned to Caroline and Avery. "Molly will check on her now and come get you if necessary," he said to Caroline.

Ethan was talking with Avery and Caroline when Molly returned a few minutes later. Ethan looked at Molly's face and frowned. Samantha wasn't with her. He excused himself and walked over to Molly. "Where is she?" he demanded under his breath.

"That one's a stubborn one, I'll say that."

"What did she say?"

Molly frowned. "If I was you, I don't think I'd send Mrs. Cooper up there."

"Why not? What did Sam say?"

"She said to tell you that you could send the whole damn Confederate Army if you wanted. Those were her words. Then she pulled this great big knife out and set it on the table next to the bed."

"When I get my hands on her," Ethan ground out.

"Ethan, will your guests be staying for dinner?" Molly asked, trying to calm him.

"Thanks for reminding me of my manners, Molly," he said quietly and then returned to Caroline and Avery. "Miss Samantha is going to rest until dinner. Molly says it's just the heat. You will, of course, stay for dinner?"

"Ethan, I didn't mean to impose," Caroline said.

"Caroline, you could never impose," Ethan said. "In fact, you should both stay the night. It will be late by the time dinner is over. Molly can show you to your rooms, and you can rest before dinner."

Caroline stood, her eyes radiating an intimacy as she smiled at Ethan. "I think I'd like to rest a few hours. This heat can be oppressive."

Molly was still standing at the door. Ethan turned to her. "Molly, Mrs. Cooper and Lieutenant Scott will be our guests for the night. Would you show Mrs. Cooper to her room? The lieutenant and I have some things to discuss."

As Molly was leading Caroline up the curving staircase in the front of the house, Samantha was quietly leaving the house via the back stairs. She exited the back door and ran across the lawn to the stables. As she stepped inside, she paused a moment, allowing her eyes to adjust to the dim light. The sun was intense outside, but it was cool in the large, airy stable that was shaded by trees. Samantha went to Kota's stall and murmured to the horse.

The time spent pacing in her bedroom hadn't reduced her anger. She felt trapped in the house with Ethan and his lover. So be it. If Ethan wanted to spend his time with Caroline Cooper, then he could. Why should she care what he did?

Samantha led Kota out of the stall to the center of the stables. The floor in the center was made of brick, divided by large, supporting posts that reached up to the arched ceiling. On each side of the brick center were rows of separate horse stalls. A soft breeze blew through the double doors at each end of the building. Samantha brushed Kota, muttering to herself as she recalled Ethan's summons that she join him and Caroline. She put the bridle on and was just tightening the cinch of the saddle when she heard someone come up behind her.

"Miss Samantha?"

Samantha turned to see the Negro whom Ethan had introduced her to when they arrived last night. "Mr. Frederick?"

The man smiled. "Just Frederick, ma'am."

Samantha nodded. "It's just Samantha, then. Hello, Frederick."

The man smiled again as he looked at Samantha. She had changed into her pants, long boots, and a lady's blouse that she had found among the things that Molly had hung in the wardrobe of her room. The blouse was made of sheer white cotton with a high, stand-up collar. Samantha had not bothered to button the collar and had left it open at the neck. It had a tightly fitted bodice that tucked into her pants. She had also rolled the sleeves up above her elbow. She had taken one of the combs that Molly had given her and loosely gathered her hair up on her head. She hadn't thought much about her appearance when she had dressed. She thought only about getting away from Ethan and Caroline, and this was the most practical and coolest thing she had to wear.

"That's quite a horse you have there," Frederick commented.

"He's very special," Samantha said as she rubbed his neck. Kota turned his head to her and whinnied softly.

"So you're a doctor and surgeon," Frederick said casually as he pulled a bench over and sat down by Samantha.

"Ethan told you that?"

Again, the man smiled as he spoke, "Among other things."

"What else did he say?"

Frederick shrugged. "That you ran away from your home, disguised as a boy, and helped the Confederate Army."

"Yes, well, I wasn't given much choice in the last part," Samantha said.

"So I understand. Ethan said that you're a very unusual woman."

"Unusual? Is that what he said? Well, that was polite, at least."

Samantha withdrew a knife from her boot. She took the handle of the knife and began to clean the bottom of Kota's hooves.

"I think my father cleaned his hooves last night," Frederick offered.

Samantha put Kota's foot down and turned. "He did a good job. I can see that now. Your soil has so much clay that I was afraid it might have become packed in last night when we went through the fields. Please thank your father for me. I can see that Kota has been well taken care of."

"My father loves horses; he has a way with them. So does Ethan."

Samantha turned back to her horse. "I thought I'd go for a ride," she said.

Frederick shrugged. "It's awful hot today."

"I know, but I need to get away from here."

"And why is that?" a voice challenged from the stable door.

Samantha stiffened. Ethan and Lieutenant Scott entered the stable. When Samantha didn't answer, Ethan strode purposely over to her.

"You told Molly that you were going to rest. Running away, Sam? How far did you think you'd get?" he demanded.

Ethan grabbed Samantha's arm. Instinctively, she pulled her arm toward his thumb and twisted, easily moving out of his grasp. She knew she was overreacting, but Ethan's obvious relationship with Caroline Cooper and his concern over his appearance in Caroline's presence still hurt her. "I told you, Rebel, never to touch me like that again,"

Samantha threatened.

Ethan looked at the knife in her hand. "And I warned you never to pull a knife on me again," he ground out.

"If I had pulled this out to use on you, it'd be buried in your chest by now," Samantha shouted.

"Ethan, what are you doing?" Frederick asked with concern. "Miss Samantha was just—"

"This isn't your concern, Frederick," Ethan said, his eyes blazing, "or yours either, Lieutenant. I'll handle Sam." He turned back to Samantha, his eyes narrowing. "So it's back to pants and knives again. Where's your beard and mustache, Sam? You've been pretending to be a man for so long that I think you prefer it to being a woman."

Samantha inhaled sharply. His words were like a knife thrust into her. She bit her lip to stop the tears that threatened and turned away, but not before Ethan saw her pain.

"Oh, God, Sam, I'm sorry," Ethan said. He put his hand on Samantha's shoulder. Her reaction was immediate as she recoiled from his touch.

"You bastard!" she spat out. In one swift movement, she whirled around and, with all of her strength, threw the knife through the air. Its tip landed with perfect precision and buried itself into one of the large, wooden center posts of the stable.

"Jesus!" Avery exclaimed.

"Do you think I've enjoyed masquerading as a man these past months, or, for that matter, the previous two years?" Samantha demanded of Ethan, ignoring Avery and Frederick. She was beyond caring what they thought of her. Ethan's words—his disapproval—hurt her more than she realized. "Do you think it was easy to put that vile paste on my face each day? Sometimes my breasts would ache so much from the constriction of the gauze that I couldn't concentrate on my studies. And all the while that I worked and studied, I watched the young men in Paris call upon my cousin and bring her gifts and treat her like she was so special. There were so many times when I almost gave it all up just for a silk dress or for flowers or for a man to ask me to dance. But I didn't. I didn't quit! Then I came home. And what did I find? No one wants a woman doctor. The only way I can be a doctor is to stop being a woman.

"Last night was the first time I had worn a dress in over two years. No man has ever come to call on me. No suitors. How could there be? Men aren't interested in a woman who must scrub blood off her hands several times a day or wade through the stacks of arms and legs she just cut off while men screamed in agony.

"Oh, God!" Samantha cried as her tears fell freely. "I can't bear it—the death, the pain, the mutilation. It's all around me. And I can't stop it! The men . . . the men just keep maiming and killing each other. And they beg me to save their lives. They beg me not to cut off their arms or legs. I don't have the strength for it. I don't! It's ripping my soul apart," she cried, "and there's no one to help me—no one. I'm alone. Damn you, Major! Damn you all to hell!"

Samantha stumbled blindly past Frederick and Avery. Through her blurred vision, she reached the end of the stable where the knife was buried in the wood. She reached out to retrieve her knife, but it wouldn't budge. She placed both hands on the handle of the knife and pulled. Her breath was coming in great sobs as she struggled to free the deeply buried knife.

The three men stared at her in stunned silence, then Ethan walked over to her, followed by Avery and Frederick. "Let me," he said as his hand closed around Samantha's on the hilt of the knife. With one swift pull, he freed the knife from the wood as Samantha slowly slid down to her knees, crying.

"Miss Samantha," Avery said as he reached down for her.

Ethan stopped him. "I'll take care of Sam," he said as he nodded to the stable door, silently dismissing Avery and Frederick.

"Ethan?" Frederick said with doubt.

"It'll be all right," Ethan said reassuringly.

He waited until the two men left the barn, and then he knelt down beside Samantha and pulled her to him. She didn't resist. He held her as the anger, frustration, confusion, and grief of the past several months were finally released. Her shoulders shook as her tears soaked his shirt. When at last she quieted, he pulled away slightly and, with his fingertips, gently brushed the tears off her cheeks. Samantha froze. Then he slowly moved his hands down her neck to her shoulders, all the while not taking his eyes off hers.

Samantha felt such comfort and protection in his arms. She didn't question it; she just accepted it. Her whole body seemed to awaken as his fingers lingered. Her breathing deepened, and she welcomed the feelings overtaking her. He slowly lowered his lips to hers, and Samantha felt another explosion of sensation. She didn't know how long they kissed, but as his kisses deepened, he deftly released the top button of her shirt. It was only a matter of seconds before her shirt was opened, and he lowered his lips to her neck. A myriad of exquisite feelings surfaced, along with a sweet ache deep inside of her. But then, suddenly Ethan pulled away from her and stood, savagely running his hand through his hair.

"Damn!" he exploded as he turned his back to her. "We can't do this, Sam," he said hoarsely.

Samantha was confused. It was as though she had a tremendous thirst and water was in sight, but then abruptly and cruelly, it was taken away. She felt a physical frustration and yearning build up in her that she had only experienced once before—last night when Ethan caught her, when he kissed her.

She was suddenly embarrassed and humiliated to be found undesirable. She pulled her shirt together and tried to button it, but her hands were trembling and clumsy in their attempt. Tears began to fall from her eyes again, and she bit her lip to keep silent as she struggled with the tiny buttons.

"I'll do it," Ethan said softly as he knelt down beside her.

"No!" Samantha cried and turned to hide herself from him.

"Shhh, it's all right," he said gently.

Samantha didn't have the strength to fight him, not when she could feel the warmth of his hands through the soft cotton of her shirt. She chided herself inwardly. What a pathetic creature she must be to find such pleasure in his touch even as he was rejecting her. When he finished, he took both of her hands in his.

"Sam, look at me."

She averted her face. "Ethan, just go. Please. Leave me with some dignity."

"No, I'm not leaving you like this. Look at me." He reached out and touched her jaw, gently turning her face to him. His eyes were warm and intense as he spoke. "Sam," he said huskily, "there's nothing in the world that I'd rather do than make love to you, but it would be wrong. You'd only end up being hurt." He paused. "I can't give you everything that you'd want. I'm not free to do that."

Samantha nodded her head in understanding, turning her head away. "Because you're in love with Mrs. Cooper," she whispered.

"Caroline? No, Sam, look at me."

Samantha reluctantly turned back to him.

"Sam, Caroline has nothing to do with this." Ethan

sighed. "Caroline and I are friends. We grew up together. We have similar backgrounds. I care for her but not in the way you think."

"You're lovers," Samantha said simply.

"It's true," Ethan said gently, "that we've found comfort in each other's arms. We understand each other. But, Sam, that has nothing to do with this." Ethan suddenly grabbed Samantha and held her tightly against him. "Sam, I never want to hurt you. Never!" He held her a moment more and then released her.

"I'm so confused, Ethan. I don't know what's happening. I've never felt this way before," Samantha whispered. She turned her face to him, her eyes moist. "I've always been so sure of everything until you came along, then my whole world turned upside down. Things that I thought were right and wrong are no longer clear to me. I had such glorious ideas about being a doctor, a surgeon, and now I find myself floundering. I'm caring for the enemy, or for what I once thought was the enemy. And then there's you." Samantha looked boldly into Ethan's eyes. "I've spent my entire life surrounded by men, and never have I felt what I feel when I'm near you. I'm a doctor, yet I don't understand what's happening to me when you touch me. I don't know the words to describe the physical sensations I have when I see you, or hear your voice, or touch you. I wish I could stop it—stop what I feel—for now it almost hurts."

"Oh, God, Sam," Ethan said as he crushed her to him. "I'd give almost anything to be the one to. . . ." Ethan released Samantha and stood up abruptly. "I think you'd better go back into the house. I'll take care of Kota."

"But I don't understand."

"Go, Samantha!"

Samantha stood and ran out of the stables.

THE CONFEDERATES' PHYSICIAN

Ethan didn't return Kota to the stall immediately. He stood there, trying to quell the emotions overtaking him. Sam. She stirred deep feelings in him, feelings that he seemed helpless to control. He'd grown to love the Yankee boy, Sam. But Sam was Samantha. He couldn't allow himself to think of her as a woman; he was too drawn to her. He was about to reach for Kota when he heard a sharp whistle. The horse reared up and bolted toward the door.

Ethan ran after the horse. He almost reached him when Samantha appeared and, in one smooth movement, swung her leg up into the saddle. She was barely upright on her horse when Kota shot forward, leaving Ethan standing in a rage. He ran back into the stables and grabbed a bridle as he entered the first stall. Just then, Molly and Frederick came running into the stables, followed by Avery Scott.

"Where is Miss Samantha goin', ridin' out of here like that?" Molly demanded.

"How the hell do I know?" Ethan shouted.

"Well, somethin's wrong. It don't make no sense to take off like that in this heat. What did you do to annoy that poor child?"

"Me?" Ethan swung around to face Molly as he reached for a saddle. "Sam doesn't always need a reason to get annoyed, believe me. She's the most willful, stubborn female God ever created, and when I get my hands on her—"

"Oh, no you won't." Molly grabbed Ethan's arm just as he was about to mount his horse. "You're not goin' after that girl like this."

"Let go of my arm, Molly," Ethan warned.

Molly tightened her grip on Ethan's arm. "I'm not lettin' go. You'll have to knock me down before I'll let go of you," Molly challenged.

"I'd never strike you, Molly," Ethan said with surprise.

"I'll say you won't!" Molly blazed. "I can still take you over my knee and wup your backside if I have to. Don't matter to me how old you are."

Ethan eyed Molly, his anger dissipating. "I believe you would," he said. He took a deep breath. "I can't let Sam wander around alone. She doesn't know the area. She's angry enough that she probably has it in her mind to head north."

"Then Frederick will go after her. He knows this place as well as you. He'll bring her back safely," Molly said.

Frederick stepped forward. "She's right, Ethan. I'll find her and bring her back."

Ethan looked from Molly to Frederick and to Avery. Perhaps they were right.

"All right," he said, handing the reins to Frederick, "but hurry. She has several minutes' lead on you, and her horse is fast."

Frederick mounted the horse. "Do you think she'll head north?" he asked.

"She went east through the field," Avery offered.

"Hell, with Sam's sense of direction, she could be anywhere. She wouldn't know which way was north," Ethan said.

"Perhaps I should go also," Avery said.

"Fine, now you come with me. We need to have us a talk," Molly said to Ethan as she grabbed his arm.

Samantha pushed Kota as hard as she could until she noticed the white lather forming on his sides. She gradually brought him down to a slower pace and then eventually to a walk. He pranced in the heat as though he sensed her mood and was willing to run with her again. She guided him between tobacco fields until she came to a grove of trees.

She found a stream and dismounted. She and Kota drank deeply of the cool water, and then she splashed the cold water on her face and neck.

"I guess we'll have to go back," she said aloud to Kota, "but we can rest in the shade for a while."

She walked over to the base of a large tree and sat down, leaning against it. There were some rocks in the stream that caused a tinkling sound as the water flowed over it. It was a peaceful area and reminded Samantha of the forested areas north of her home. She was sitting there, her knees drawn up, her eyes closed, when Frederick and Avery found her. Kota had whinnied a warning several minutes before the men emerged into the grove of trees.

"Samantha!" Avery said with alarm as he dismounted and came running over to her. "Did you fall? Are you hurt?"

"What are you talking about, Avery? I'm fine."

Frederick joined them, standing as Avery knelt beside Samantha.

"You're not hurt?" Avery asked.

"Of course not. I'm hot, that's all."

"You could have been killed riding off like that. You should never ride like that again," Avery admonished.

Samantha looked up at Avery. She saw the concern in his eyes. "Avery," she said patiently, "we traveled over two hundred miles together. Did I ever give you the impression that I couldn't stay on my horse?"

"But that was . . . I mean . . . you were. . . ." He stopped, a look of confusion on his face.

"That was before you knew that I was a woman," Samantha said. "That was Sam traveling with you. Avery, I am Sam."

"I'm sorry," Avery said. "I've never met a woman like you, Miss Samantha. I mean no disrespect, but it's difficult to know how to treat you."

"Yes," Samantha said sarcastically, "I do seem to be having that effect on people lately. Maybe Ethan was right. In some ways, it was easier being the boy, Sam."

"I don't know about that, Miss Samantha," Frederick interjected. "I can't imagine you as a boy." He smiled pleasantly.

Samantha looked up at the kind face above her. She laughed at herself. "That's because we've only just met." She started to stand, and Avery hastily reached out to help her up. She could see the uncertainty on his face. "Thank you, Avery," she said as she accepted his assistance. "So he sent you two to bring me back?"

"Not exactly," Frederick answered. "My mother sent us."

"Molly?"

"Yes. Ethan started to come, but she wanted to have a few words with him." He smiled to himself.

"Oh?"

"My parents are probably the only two people on Earth whom Ethan cannot easily bend to his will."

"I'm glad to know there are some," Samantha said.

"The major is accustomed to giving orders," Avery said, "but he's an honorable man, Miss Samantha. I've been with him for almost two years now. It's true that he can be ruthless with his enemies, but he's a fair man and a brave one. These are difficult times, and the position that he's taken hasn't been an easy one."

Samantha was quiet for a moment. The loyalty of these two was clear. "I guess we'd better head back then." She walked to Kota and picked up his reins. "I wasn't going anywhere in particular, you know. I just needed to be by myself for a while. Where am I?" she asked as she mounted her horse.

Frederick laughed. "You're still on Arabella, a little less than three miles east of the house." He laughed again.

"What's so funny?" Samantha asked as he mounted his horse.

"Ethan said you weren't very good at directions, and that even if you were trying to head north, you wouldn't know which way to go." He continued to smile.

Samantha noticed for the first time how beautiful his black face was, with dark eyes and a large, full mouth that shone with white teeth. His hair was also black, cut short with tight curls. His smile was so warm that Samantha laughed, too.

"Did he tell you how I got lost going around the edge of Arlington? It doesn't matter if it's day or night, I just can't seem to get the hang of navigating by the sun or stars. He and Lieutenant Quicken's men found me lost in the woods outside of Arlington. I was looking for the Union Medical Command."

As they rode back at a leisurely pace, Samantha recounted the story of her capture by Ethan and the Confederate soldiers and of her subsequent work with Dr. Beauregard and the Confederate Medical Corps. When they arrived back at the house, they went directly into the stable. Samantha dismounted and was greeted by Frederick's father, Fox.

"There's my big boy," he said affectionately to Kota as he walked up to the horse and stroked his neck. "Would you like me to rub him down for you, Miss Samantha?" he asked.

Samantha dismounted. "That's very kind of you, but I can do it," she replied as she started to unfasten the saddle.

"Did you have a nice ride?" a voice asked from the door.

Samantha recognized Ethan's voice immediately and turned as he walked up behind her. His face was impassive and his eyes revealed little.

"Yes," she replied evenly, watching him carefully.

"And do you plan on joining us for dinner, Miss Samantha?" he asked.

Samantha faltered a moment. She'd lost track of the time. Ethan deliberately let his gaze go from her hair down her body to her boots, and then he returned his stare to her face, again showing no emotion. Samantha was aware of the curious looks coming from the other three men present.

"Do I have a choice?" she asked. When Ethan didn't answer, Samantha turned to Fox. "I guess I would like some help with Kota. Thank you," she said, handing the old man the reins. She turned back to Ethan. "It won't take me long to get ready." She nodded briefly to Frederick and Avery and turned to leave.

"I suggest you go up the back stairs so that Mrs. Cooper won't see you. She's probably awake now and getting ready to come downstairs."

Samantha stopped abruptly at the mention of Caroline's name. She turned and walked to the post where her knife had been stuck. The knife was laying on the floor of the stables where Ethan had dropped it when he held her. Samantha bent down and picked it up, appearing to study it as she deliberately walked back to within a few feet of where Ethan, Frederick, and Avery were standing together. In one quick movement, she flipped the knife high up near the rafters of the stable. As it fell back toward the floor, the knife swiftly rotated end over end so that hilt and blade blurred together as the knife gathered deadly speed. Frederick and Avery jumped back just as, in an equally quick movement, Samantha's hand lashed out and caught the spinning knife. Casually, she leaned over and inserted the knife into her boot. She slowly stood up, facing the men. When she spoke, she looked directly at Ethan and smiled.

"But of course, Major. I'll make certain that Mrs. Cooper doesn't see me like this. We certainly wouldn't want to offend the sensibilities of a fine lady like Mrs. Cooper, now would we?"

Avery's jaw dropped open and Frederick's eyes widened, for Samantha had spoken in a perfect imitation of a slow Southern drawl. Only Ethan's face remained like granite.

"Gentlemen, you all will excuse me?" Samantha purred lazily, casting one last, slow smile in Ethan's direction before she turned. She took her time walking out of the stable, letting her hips sway slightly as she had seen Belle's girls do. She smiled to herself when she heard a low whistle coming from the stables.

"That one is goin' to be a handful. Yes, sir, that's quite a woman," Frederick said.

Samantha heard Ethan swear.

"Whoeeeee," Frederick continued. "She's got all that schoolin', handles a horse and a knife like a man, but has the face and body of an angel."

"That's enough, Frederick!" Ethan swore.

Samantha smiled again and continued to walk to the house. She made her way up to her room and closed the door. There was a light tap at the door, and then she heard Molly's voice. "Miss Samantha?"

Samantha opened the door to see Molly standing there with two young Negro boys, each carrying buckets of water. "The water is ready for your bath, and I've laid clothes out on the bed for you," Molly said.

Samantha hadn't noticed the dress and ladies' underwear laying on the bed. The boys walked through the bedroom to an adjoining small room that held a large copper tub. After emptying their buckets, Molly hurried them out of the room.

"I'll return in a little while to help you dress and do your hair," Molly said.

"Thank you, Molly, but I can manage."

"Just the same, I'll come back," Molly said and closed the

door behind her.

Samantha stripped off her clothes and lowered herself into the water. She felt hot and sticky after her ride, and the water was not only cleansing but soothing as well. She shampooed her hair and then gathered it up onto the top of her head with a comb that Molly had given her. Then she slid down into the warm water and leaned her head back on the edge of the tub. She had been resting with her eyes closed for several minutes when she heard footsteps in the bedroom.

"Molly," Samantha said as she opened her eyes and sat forward. "I didn't realize I'd been in here for so long." Samantha gasped when she saw Ethan leaning against the doorframe that joined the bedroom with the dressing room. "What are you doing here?" she demanded as she slid back down into the water.

"Just what was that little performance out there in the stable?" he demanded.

"Ethan, get out of here!" Samantha slid down farther in the water, covering her breasts with her hands.

"Don't tell me you are going to be modest now. You forget that I'm quite familiar with your body," he said.

Samantha felt herself blush.

"Perhaps you should have displayed a little of that modesty in front of Frederick and Avery in the barn, instead of using your wiles like an expensive whore."

Samantha clenched her jaw in anger. She sat forward and leaned against the inside of the tub, concealing herself from his eyes. "A whore, Major? I know I'm inexperienced in some things, but how is it possible to be both a whore and a virgin at the same time?" she taunted him.

It took two steps for Ethan to cross to the tub and lean down to her. He reached out and took her by the shoulders. "Don't tempt me, Sam," he said, his eyes only inches from hers. "That dilemma could be rectified very quickly."

The force of his lips upon hers was assaulting at first, and she recoiled against them. Ethan held her tightly, and before Samantha realized what happened, her own lips parted. Ethan's tongue flickered lightly across her lips, and his force was replaced by a sweet demand. Samantha brought her hands up to his back as his kisses deepened. His lips on hers felt exquisite, and she eagerly returned his kisses.

When his lips moved to her ear, she arched her neck as a rush of feelings flowed through her. She could feel the warmth of his breath upon her ear, causing waves of excitement that seemed to ripple through her body. His voice was soft and low when he spoke.

"Rectified very quickly and easily, I believe," he whispered in her ear. Then suddenly, he was standing up beside the tub, a smug look of satisfaction on his face.

Samantha felt as though a bucket of cold water had just been thrown on her. She screamed with a rage and grabbed the nearest object. The delicate bottle of scented water sailed out of the dressing room, just missing Ethan, who managed to duck before it hit the floor and shattered.

"Now that temper of yours may take a little longer to correct," he said as he turned to go.

"Damn you, Ethan!" Samantha launched into a string of vulgarities and stopped only when she heard another voice from the bedroom.

"What's going on here?" Molly demanded as she entered the dressing room and stopped short, seeing Samantha in the tub.

Samantha blushed deeply and slid back down into the water.

"I warned her before that I would take her over my knee again if she continued with the profanities," Ethan said.

Molly turned on him. "You get out of here! Right now!

Just what do you think you're doin' in here? I'll not have it, you hear me?" Molly scolded as she grabbed his shirtsleeve and started pulling him across the bedroom to the door.

"I just stopped in for a visit, Molly. She's got a terrible temper, too," he said, pointing to the shattered glass on the floor.

"Get on out of here! Now! Or I wup the daylights out of you," Molly threatened as she slammed the door behind Ethan. She turned around to see Samantha standing at the doorway of the dressing room, a towel wrapped around her.

"I'm sorry about the glass, Molly," Samantha said.

"Are you all right, child?" Molly asked.

Samantha didn't answer.

"You wait there 'til I sweep this up."

Molly returned a few minutes later to remove the broken glass. Samantha hadn't moved.

"Now," Molly said gently, "why don't you come over here." She took Samantha's hand and led her to the edge of the bed. "You sit down."

But Samantha couldn't sit still. She jumped up and began pacing the room as Molly tried to dress her. "Child, I can't dress you if you keep movin' 'bout. Stand still. My old fingers ain't as nimble as they used to be."

Molly had chosen a dress made of soft yellow silk and white lace. The bodice was yellow, low-cut, and tightly fitted. At the waist, the dress fell over wide hoops, with alternating panels of yellow silk and white lace. The back of the dress had a row of tiny buttons that Molly struggled to button.

"Did you alter this dress, too, Molly?" Samantha asked.

"Yes, and I knew you didn't want no corset, so I changed the bodice."

Samantha laughed. "You're right about that. I've been binding my chest for years. I don't want anything constricting."

Molly patted her shoulders. "You don't need no corset anyway. Now you sit down and let me do your hair."

"It's not necessary, Molly. I can do it."

Molly stopped and put her hands on her hips. "Ethan is right about one thing: you do argue a lot, Miss Samantha. Now sit down, like I told you," Molly said.

Samantha did as she was told and let Molly style her hair. When she'd finished, Molly led her over to a large oval mirror in the corner of the room. Molly had kept her hair simple, gathering it loosely up on the top of her head, letting a few strands of hair escape down the back.

"I didn't use no nets or braids. You've been wearin' your hair like a boy and hidin' it under a hat. This is much prettier, Miss Samantha. Now best be hurryin' downstairs, child," Molly said.

"I don't suppose you could make my excuses again? Tell them my headache has returned?" Samantha asked.

Molly looked surprised.

"No, I thought not," Samantha said. "Damn him!" Samantha walked to the door, muttering to herself. She reached the door and turned to Molly.

"Thank you, Molly. I don't mean to appear ungrateful."

"I know, child."

Samantha smiled at the older woman and then left the room. She descended the circular staircase in the front of the house. When she reached the bottom, she could hear voices coming from a nearby room. Hesitantly, she walked toward the laughter. Caroline Cooper was the first to see Samantha standing at the entrance to the room.

"Samantha, dear," Caroline said as she and Avery crossed the room to greet her.

"Cousin Avery," Samantha said as she smiled at him and then turned to Caroline. "It's nice to see you again, Mrs. Cooper."

"Oh, please, dear, call me Caroline. Are you feeling better now? Ethan said you had a headache."

Ethan was walking toward them, holding two glasses in his hands. Samantha looked up at him and then turned back to Caroline. "I was feeling better until about an hour ago. Then I was suddenly visited by such an annoyance again." Samantha delicately touched the side of her head as she surreptitiously glanced at Ethan. By the humor in his eyes, she could tell he understood her meaning.

"Perhaps a glass of wine will help," Ethan said as he held the glass out to Samantha. As Samantha reached for the glass, Ethan spoke again, this time in French. *"The crystal was my mother's. I trust you can control your temper tonight and not throw it across the room?"*

Samantha smiled sweetly and replied, also in French. *"I would like to shatter it and use it to carve you up into little pieces. If your mother knew how you had treated me, she probably would agree with me."*

A smile played at the corner of Ethan's lips. "She just might at that," he mused.

"Ethan?" Caroline asked, taking his arm.

"I'm sorry, Caroline. I was asking Miss Samantha if she felt like traveling tomorrow."

"Of course she can't start on her journey home tomorrow. The child has been in her bed all day. Why, her face is still flushed. What-ever can you be thinking? Traveling tomorrow?" Caroline said to Ethan and then smiled at Samantha. "Sometimes I think these men forget that we are not of the same constitution as they are. Imagine thinking that you could ride in a carriage all day tomorrow."

"If Miss Samantha rode a horse," Ethan said, "we would reach Washington City faster."

"A horse? All the way to Washington City?" Caroline replied. "And would you have her ride astride as well?

Really, Ethan, sometimes I don't understand you," Caroline chided gently. "Stop teasing Miss Samantha like that."

"I'm not offended by the major's teasing, Mrs. Cooper," Samantha said pleasantly, "although I do fear that actually riding a horse would be too much for me. I never learned to ride."

Avery suddenly coughed, choking on his drink.

"Cousin Avery, are you all right?" Samantha asked.

"Samantha, please," Avery muttered under his breath as she leaned near him.

"You didn't perhaps poison his drink, did you?" Ethan asked in French.

"Not his, my bastard major, but you would do well to guard your own," Samantha replied in French, still leaning over Avery, who coughed again.

Ethan laughed softly. Caroline looked at him with a puzzled expression and then addressed Avery. "Lieutenant, you should delay your departure another day or so. Samantha is your cousin. You are responsible for her," Caroline said.

Just then, Molly entered to announce that dinner was ready. Caroline took Ethan's arm in a possessive manner and then stopped.

"Excuse me, dear, I forgot my wine," Caroline said as she turned to a table behind her.

"Shall we go into the dining room?" Ethan asked Samantha and Avery.

"I'd rather be walking into a camp full of dysentery," Samantha said under her breath, but loud enough so that both Avery and Ethan heard her. Avery cast a nervous glance at Ethan. Ethan couldn't help himself. He burst out laughing as Caroline approached. She had a questioning look on her face, but Ethan only smiled and took her arm as they crossed the hall into the dining room.

Once seated, Ethan poured the wine and Molly served dinner. The conversation was light and pleasant, carried mostly by Caroline and Ethan. At one point, Caroline suddenly turned to Ethan.

"Ethan, where's Sam? I thought he'd be staying here with you."

Avery was quiet and glanced up at Ethan. Samantha sat back and looked up with interest.

"Oh, Sam doesn't care much for Southern hospitality," Ethan said evenly. "He'd prefer a camp full of dysentery to this."

"Ethan!" Caroline exclaimed.

Avery coughed again.

"Who's Sam?" Samantha asked, looking directly at Ethan.

"He's a boy whom Ethan has been taking care of," Caroline volunteered. "He's a doctor, although you wouldn't guess it by his appearance. He can't be more than eleven or twelve years old. The most amazing thing is that he's from the North." Caroline turned to Ethan. "You never did tell me how he came to be down here in the South."

"He was on his way to the Federal Army Medical Corps in Arlington. He was captured by a Confederate patrol. That's when I met him. He was trying to escape."

"He wasn't here of his own free will?" Caroline asked with surprise. "I assumed he was a Southern sympathizer."

"Sam? I should say not," Ethan answered. "He almost got us killed once when he wouldn't keep quiet about the evils of slavery and the wrongfulness of secession. We'd stopped in a hotel in North Carolina for a meal."

"Well, that explains some of his reluctance to socialize while at my plantation," Caroline said. "But Ethan, I'm surprised that you trusted him to treat our boys. He was a Yankee, and now you tell me that he was captured by the Confederacy and forced to treat our men? As a surgeon, he could have killed our soldiers and none would be the wiser. And a few nights ago, he attacked you with his knife. He cut your arm. How could you trust him?"

Samantha stiffened at Caroline's criticism. "Yes, Major. How could you trust this Sam?" she challenged.

Ethan stared at his glass of wine, as though considering an answer, before he spoke. "I trusted Sam with our soldiers then," he said, "and I trust him now. At the camp in Charleston and on countless battlefields, he's saved hundreds of Confederate soldiers. And yes, he cut my arm. I was trying to take his knife from him, and we fought. His intent was not to harm me. Had he wished to harm me, I fear my wound would have been much more serious. He's very skilled at fighting with a knife and rifle," Ethan added. "Still, I would trust him with my life."

Ethan paused a moment and then continued. "I know Sam is young, and he can be very stubborn, impulsive, and willful. I ought to know. I've taken him over my knee twice. But he's very courageous. His care of our soldiers on the battlefield almost cost him his own life. He was shot twice; Dr. Beauregard didn't think he'd live. I cared for him for five days while he writhed in pain and fever. I've met few men, on either side, with as much courage, honor, and integrity."

Silence filled the room, and then Caroline spoke.

"That poor boy. I'm sorry. I didn't know how seriously he was wounded. We are, indeed, indebted to him," Caroline said graciously. "And you've been very kind to him, Ethan. I know the boy has been exasperating."

Ethan laughed. "Exasperating? Impossible is more like it. There's nothing ordinary about Sam, that's for sure." He paused then, but when he continued, he looked directly into Samantha's eyes. His gaze didn't waver as he spoke. "I can honestly say, though, that I've met few people whose company I've enjoyed more than his. In some ways, he's made the past three months of hell bearable."

"Why, Ethan, I believe you've grown attached to that boy," Caroline said. "You're quite fond of him. I didn't realize you had such fatherly feelings in you."

Samantha tried not to look at Ethan as she struggled to control the emotions and physical feelings growing within her. She was deeply moved by his words. She reached for her glass of wine. At the same time, Ethan picked up the bottle of wine in one hand and Samantha's glass with the other. As he did, his fingers brushed hers, sending ripples of pleasure through her body. How well she remembered his touch on her skin last night in the meadow. She immediately withdrew her hand and folded her hands on her lap.

"More wine?" Ethan asked, his voice deep and steady. Samantha hesitantly accepted the glass.

"Why, Samantha, you're trembling, and your face is flushed. Are you ill?" Caroline asked with concern.

Samantha looked at Ethan. His gaze remained steady, although instinct told her that he knew exactly what was happening to her.

"I think perhaps I have had too much wine," Samantha said haltingly. "I certainly don't want to spoil the evening, but Major, Mrs. Cooper, if you will excuse me, I think I'd like to retire for the evening. Thank you for the lovely dinner."

When Samantha stood, both men rose from their seats.

"Of course, dear," Caroline said.

"Cousin Samantha, with your permission, I'll see you to your room," Avery said, taking Samantha's elbow.

"It's getting rather late. Perhaps we all should say good night," Ethan said.

Caroline stood as Ethan pulled her chair back for her. "Ethan, perhaps you should send Molly to Miss Samantha,"

Caroline suggested.

"Thank you for your concern, Mrs. Cooper, but I just need to rest. I don't need Molly."

"As you wish," Ethan said, bowing slightly.

Samantha turned and Avery took her arm. She didn't look back at Ethan or Caroline. When they reached the door to Samantha's room, Samantha turned to Avery. "I'm sorry if I made things difficult for you this evening, Lieutenant."

Avery laughed. "I'm beginning to see what the past months have been like for the major. And as we are family, I believe you should address me by my given name."

Samantha smiled. "Good night, Avery. Thank you."

Avery raised Samantha's hand to his lips. "Good night, Cousin Samantha," he said.

Samantha entered her room and closed the door. Someone lit the lamps and laid a nightgown on the bed—Molly, no doubt. She sat down on the bed and frowned as she raised her hand as if to examine it. Avery's touch had been appropriate and kind, nothing more. But Ethan's? His touch left such feelings in her. When his fingertips brushed hers at dinner, she was both amazed and confused by the response of her body. She couldn't forget the feeling of his hands on her last night in the grove and again today in the stables. His touch, his kiss—it was wonderful! It didn't matter if he should have done it or not. She didn't care if it was wrong. She enjoyed it. Even now, she felt a rush of indescribable sensations as she thought about him.

Samantha jumped up. What was she thinking! Ethan was a Confederate major who had captured her. He was not some suitor. And she was in the middle of a war, not in her parents' parlor. What was wrong with her? She picked up the nightgown on the bed and placed it over her arm as she reached for the tiny buttons on the back of her dress. She grew more frustrated by the minute as the buttons refused to yield. "Damn!" she cursed after having gotten only one undone. She threw the nightgown back onto the bed. "Why the hell are the buttons on the back of the dress? They should be on the front," she said in frustration as she wrestled with the buttons. "Damn it!"

"I warned you about the profanity," a deep, masculine voice said.

Samantha spun around to see Ethan leaning in the doorway that connected the two bedrooms. There was the hint of a smile on his face.

"It's . . . it's these buttons," Samantha faltered. "I can't get my dress off."

Ethan arched his eyebrows. "Perhaps I can be of assistance," he said smoothly. "Come here." He turned and walked back into his room.

Samantha felt her heart beating wildly as she followed him. He lit one lamp and then a second, filling the room with a soft glow. She looked around. The room was located on a corner of the house so that two of the walls had generous windows. Against one of the walls was a large brass bed, its golden tones shining in the lamplight. There was another door that opened into what Samantha assumed was a dressing room.

Samantha froze as Ethan approached and moved behind her.

"You needed some assistance, I believe?" he asked smoothly.

She felt his fingers on her neck as he deftly released the first button and moved down to the next. He continued until he freed the last button at her waistline.

"Damn, Sam. Don't you wear undergarments?" he asked as the back of her dress opened.

Samantha had refused a corset or camisole and wore only the thin pantalets and the hoop that held her skirt.

"After the constriction of the gauze these past few months, I'd go about naked if I could," she said halfheartedly, trying to conceal her nervousness.

"I believe you would," Ethan replied softly.

Samantha felt the back of his fingers brush lightly up and down her back. She shivered from the sensations that spread through her. He reached up and slid her dress down off one shoulder. When his lips touched her neck and shoulder, she leaned back against him, paralyzed to move. She was completely absorbed in what she was feeling. She felt his hand glide down her back and rest on her waist for a moment. Then his fingers slipped inside of her dress along the top of her pantalets until his hand rested on her abdomen, only the thin cotton separating him from where Samantha wanted him to be.

Involuntarily, a moan escaped from her lips and Ethan turned her slightly, his lips covering hers. His hand slid up as the dress slipped down off one shoulder. Ethan expertly repositioned his hand, first touching the top of Samantha's breast and then cupping the bottom of it.

"Sam, tell me to stop," he said hoarsely, burying his face in her neck. Then he brushed his fingers, lightly at first, across her breast. Samantha was astounded at the explosion of feelings.

"Sam...."

"No," Samantha said. "Ethan, don't stop. Please."

Ethan took Samantha's hand and led her to his bed. She'd never seen Ethan look so intense before. She hesitated. She wasn't afraid of the physical act she was about to commit—her body was craving that. It was the intimacy that frightened her. Who was this man? How was it that he could have such power over her?

Samantha closed her eyes. There was no fear here, only the pleasant sensations she'd experienced before in his presence. This close to him, she inhaled his scent and found it intoxicating. As he continued to kiss her, he again moved his hands down her shoulders, pushing her dress away. When he reached her waist, he pulled back a moment. Samantha couldn't help it. It both excited and embarrassed her to have him so boldly look at her breasts. Her breathing deepened and she looked away. His gaze alone had the power to send ripples of pleasure throughout her body.

Ethan reached for the drawstring that held her hoops. The hoops, along with the dress, fell to the floor around Samantha's feet. Then he eased her down upon the bed and lie down beside her.

It was all starting again, the wave of feelings that she couldn't explain. Such wonderful feelings! She hadn't known that such pleasure existed. Everywhere he touched her, he left an exquisite heat. He shifted his weight so that he was on top of her, and she felt a hardness pressing against the thin fabric of her pantalets.

"Sam, you must stop me now, or there'll be no turning back. We cannot, in the morning, undo what is done tonight," Ethan said clearly, using all of his restraint. "Do you understand?"

"I understand that I've never felt this way before," Samantha said softly between deep breaths. "It's wonderful and painful at the same time. I'm rushing toward something, and I don't even know what. Please, Ethan, don't leave me like this."

"Sam, listen to me." Ethan's voice became rough. "I cannot offer you a future. God, if only I could. But I cannot." His voice softened. "All I can give you is my love tonight."

Samantha stared into his eyes, and for the briefest moment, words formed in her mind. *"There is one; that is why he was sent to you."* She had no idea of their source. She wasn't even certain of their meaning, but if she had any doubt or question about what she was about to do, it vanished. This was where she belonged.

"I'm not making demands," she replied, "and I don't expect promises. I only know that to leave your arms now would be like dying—worse. Please, I'm begging you."

He shifted his weight off her, moving to her side. Samantha was disappointed for she had been unconsciously pushing up against his hardness. Ethan saw the expression in her eyes and chuckled deeply.

"All in good time, my love, be patient."

He continued to kiss her and touch her until Samantha thought she could stand it no longer. Then his hands were on her belly, untying her pantalets, slowly slipping them off. As she kicked them away from her feet, Ethan's hand glided up between her legs, his touch featherlight.

Samantha experienced such a sweet ache deep inside of her, she found herself unconsciously moving her hips as he continued to kiss and touch her. Just when she thought there could be no other feeling better than what she was experiencing, he inserted his fingers gently between her moist folds. She gasped. She was riding a tumultuous wave, and the rest of the world faded away.

She didn't know when Ethan had loosened his own clothing, but her eyes opened wide when she felt his firmness on her thigh. "Now, my love, my Sam," he said deeply and repositioned himself. As he entered her, he encountered resistance. With a quick thrust, he pushed past and into her.

Samantha cried out. The sharp pain brought her out of her world of pleasure. Ethan pushed deeper, and she recoiled at the pain for a second time. She panicked as he started to withdraw, touching the newly torn tissue, sending another stab of pain through her. Then he withdrew, and she felt his hardness gently moving against the outside of her, against her most sensitive spot. The effect was immediate, and once again, there was an exquisite and mysterious clenching deep within her.

Ethan again shifted his position, slowly pushing back inside of her. She welcomed his fullness and the feelings it created. As he began to move rhythmically, her world closed in and only she and Ethan existed. It was back and rushing faster than before, pulling her toward it. She was consumed by the sweet ache and pushed up against him, taking him deeper into her, to the center of her feeling. It was pulling her closer and closer, and suddenly, she stiffened and arched her body up against his, holding it there as the most exquisite sensation in the world exploded throughout her. Ethan covered her mouth with his, and Samantha hungrily kissed him in return. He pushed a final time, deeply into her, and shuddered as she clung to him.

She wasn't certain how long she lay there beneath him, her eyes closed, feeling his chest rise and fall against hers. She just knew that she wanted time to stop—to stay with him forever. At last, though, she felt him shift his weight to the side and prop himself up on his elbow.

"In all of the days I've known you, this is the quietest and most agreeable you've ever been. I wish I'd known sooner that this was all it took to stop you from arguing."

Samantha opened her eyes. Ethan smiled warmly and leaned over to kiss her again.

"Well? Nothing to say?" he whispered gently.

"Never did I imagine it would be like this," Samantha replied, searching Ethan's eyes. She turned on her side to face him and winced at feeling a vague discomfort and dampness.

"Did I hurt you?" Ethan asked.

Samantha saw concern and gentleness in Ethan's eyes. It

stirred emotions that ran even deeper than the passion she'd just experienced. She also knew what Ethan was referring to, and as the realization of what had just transpired between them dawned on her, she glanced down where she had been lying. If she needed evidence to bring her back to reality, it was there on the bed linen. She was suddenly embarrassed and reached for something to cover herself.

"I need to. . . ." She looked away, unable to make eye contact with him. "The linens—they're. . . ."

"Don't concern yourself," Ethan whispered. "Molly will take care of it."

Samantha jerked her head back to face him. "Molly! Oh, no, she'll know!"

"This is my house, Sam. No one will judge you or question you. You may say or do whatever you would like while here. You're an incredible woman, Samantha Carter," he said softly. "Not many women experience such passion their first time, if ever. Stay here."

Ethan rolled away from her and stood up. He walked across the room into the dressing area. Samantha took the opportunity to cover herself and then looked back to where she could see him moving around in the small room. She couldn't help it. She found herself looking at his naked form. When he turned around and crossed the room to the bed, she glanced away.

Ethan's eyes twinkled as he sat down on the bed next to her. "Why, Dr. Cartier, I believe you're blushing. Surely this is not the first time you've seen a man's body."

"No, but I've never looked at a man as. . . ."

"As a woman might?" Ethan said softly. "As a boy at the medical college, did you ever hear men talking about their exploits with women?"

Samantha frowned. "No. I kept to myself. I was a lot younger than the other students and an American," she added. "But there wasn't much camaraderie among the students. They were very serious, and the professors were demanding."

Ethan smiled and pulled a small table next to the bed. Samantha looked up when she felt his hand reach under the linen and touch her calf.

"What are you doing?" she asked as he pulled the covering off her and leaned down. He kissed her lower leg and then her thigh. His kiss was soft as his hand lightly stroked her thigh.

"Ethan?" she whispered. She was both excited by his touch and shy about this new gesture.

"Relax," he whispered, his lips still on her skin. Then he raised his head up and reached to the table next to him. Samantha watched in confusion as he placed a cloth in a bowl of water and then wrung it out. He turned back to her and kissed her belly, his lips lingering. When he delicately separated her thighs, she was helpless to stop him.

The coolness of the cloth against her most sensitive area surprised her, and when she realized what he was doing, she blushed deeply. It was only his persistence and gentleness that helped her to overcome her embarrassment, for this act seemed more intimate than what had transpired between them moments earlier.

Samantha was afraid to look at him as he used the cloth to tenderly cleanse away the stains of her virginity. She felt vulnerable and desperately wanted to be reassured, to have her feelings returned. That, she realized, was the source of her fear. She was helplessly lost and overwhelmed by her feelings for this man, but she knew she could not expect the same from him.

When he finished, Ethan pushed the table away from the bed and lie down next to her. It was as though he read her thoughts. "Sam, it is as I told you. I can offer you nothing. I can promise you nothing. But I want you to know that I meant what I said at dinner this evening. I've met few men with as much courage and integrity as you have. I can think of no one in whose company I've found greater pleasure, even when you're being argumentative and impossible." He smiled warmly and then grew serious. "Fate is a curious and sometimes cruel thing," he continued. "I will always curse fate for not allowing me to have met you years ago, before it was too late. I cannot make you my wife, although God knows I would if I could," he said fervently. "And I don't think you are suited to the role of mistress. You must return to your home before you are irreparably harmed. I'll take you to Washington City tomorrow."

"No. Ethan, I'm not asking for promises, commitments, or words of love," she said quietly, "and I'm not going to Washington City tomorrow."

"Sam, you don't understand. You'll only end up being hurt. I'm taking you back tomorrow."

"No, you're not. You can't force me, Major. I'm neither slave nor soldier, so I'll move about as I please."

"You're a Yankee in enemy territory. Just where do you think you'll go?" Ethan asked.

"To Clement Beauregard; he'll gladly welcome me back. And if he won't, I'll find the next surgical tent and offer my services. Your Confederacy is desperate and won't refuse me."

"Damn it, Samantha, will you listen to me for once? I'm taking you back, even if I have to bind and gag you all the way there."

"Try it, Rebel, and I'll carve you to pieces."

"Will you now?" Ethan rolled on top of her, pinning her down on the bed. "Where's your knife now?" he asked, grinning. "Forgive me, my disagreeable Yankee, but you're hardly in a position to defend yourself."

"Bastard Rebel," she whispered.

"Profanity, again?" he said, and then his lips were covering hers. She could feel the length of his body against her and his hardness pressing against her thigh. The effect was instantaneous, and once again, the world no longer existed for her. There was only his voice, his touch, his being.

Sometime later in the night, Samantha stirred in her sleep. The mists were forming, and she could smell the stench of blood and rotting limbs. Then she heard the cries of the wounded soldiers.

"No," she murmured, knowing what was to come, that the familiar nightmare was upon her, that pain and death were coming to her. Just as the mangled bodies were taking form, she heard an ancient voice cut through the exploding cannons and musket fire.

"There is one who has the strength. That is why he was sent to you, Little One."

Just as quickly, the ancient and familiar voice was gone, leaving Samantha alone with the cries of the wounded. She shivered as the grotesque images appeared.

"Sam, it's all right. I'm here," Ethan said as he drew her closer to him.

Samantha didn't wake up, but she felt the strength of his arms as they encircled her. The bloody images were replaced with feelings of safety and love.

Ethan lay awake long after Samantha fell asleep in his arms. He knew he should feel guilt and remorse over what he'd done. He'd taken a young lady's virginity and was not in a position to do the honorable thing to right the situation. He'd committed a grievous act against Samantha. Yet, as he looked at her, he felt only tenderness and happiness.

He smiled to himself as he recalled first seeing her with

the blade of that damned knife of hers pressed against the Confederate soldier's neck. She was hell-bent on protecting her horse, even though she was outnumbered three-to-one. He supposed that's when it started between them. Sam had the power to stir feelings in him that he didn't know he possessed. And now he loved her, but at what cost?

CHAPTER 9

The elegant oak trees that shaded the house and the surrounding portico filtered the light that streamed through the lace curtains. Samantha turned over in the bed, again hearing the voices that drifted through the open windows. It had been near dawn when she had finally fallen asleep in Ethan's arms. She smiled to herself, remembering the night of lovemaking and then endless talking. It was Ethan who had finally insisted that she sleep. She settled into his arms, feeling safe and content.

"I'm not leaving in the morning," she had murmured as sleep began to descend upon her.

"I know," he had whispered back.

Samantha hugged herself as she recalled Ethan's touch. Then she heard the voices again. They sounded like they were coming from the front of the house. She walked over to the open window and parted the lace curtain. Below, she could see Caroline and Avery standing beside the carriage, talking with Ethan. Then Ethan kissed Caroline on the cheek, and she and Avery departed.

As Ethan turned around, he glanced up to the bedroom window and smiled. "I'm going to ride over the property before it gets too hot. I'd be honored if you would accompany me, Miss Samantha," he shouted up to her.

"I'm not dressed."

"This is my home. You can come just as you are," he teased.

"Ethan!"

"I dare you."

"I'll meet you at the stable."

Samantha didn't think she could contain her happiness. She laughed as she walked into the adjoining bedroom. There, laying on the bed, was the nightgown she hadn't worn last night. It was a sleeveless shift made of soft, white cotton. Its low-cut bodice was trimmed with white lace, as was the hem at the bottom. The front of the gown was open from the low neckline to the waist and could be closed by a white satin ribbon that laced the front up and tied in a bow.

Samantha slipped the gown on. It was very sheer. As she stood in front of the mirror, she started to lace up the front bodice and then stopped. She left the ribbon loosely crisscrossed through the bodice, leaving it daringly open. "I'll take that dare, Rebel," she said. She turned away before she lost her courage, hurried to the door, and peered out into the empty hall. Her bare feet were silent as she ran to the stairs and cautiously descended the wide, curving steps to the foyer. She dashed out the front door and darted across the lawn to the stables, heedless of her bare feet or unconventional attire.

She found Ethan with the horses in the paddock area next to the stable. Kota had alerted him to her approach by whinnying. Ethan turned around just in time to catch Samantha as she hurled herself into his arms, laughing. She threw her arms around his neck and kissed him.

"Is this good enough to win the dare?" she asked impishly. "If not. . . ." She reached down to pull the shift off over her head.

Ethan threw his head back, laughing deeply. "I should know better than to dare an obstinate Yankee anything. You win," he said, catching her up into his arms again. "We never discussed the wager, though. What do you claim as your wage?"

"My equality and independence to decide when and where I shall go."

"Ah," he said, releasing her, "that's another matter. Last night, I only agreed to delay your departure. I still intend to take you to Washington City in a day or two."

Samantha stepped back from him, her hands upon her hips. She smiled secretly. "Tell me, Rebel, just how fast are these horses of yours?"

"What are you doing, Sam?" he asked suspiciously.

"I've heard you say that there are no faster horses in the South. Can they beat a Yankee horse?"

"Kota, for example?"

Samantha didn't answer, but stood there, a smug smile on her face.

"Kota is fast, but not fast enough. Outer Banks was bred for speed. He'd beat Kota."

"Are you willing to make a wager on that?"

"Sam, you're returning to Washington City. I won't change my mind."

"But will you stand behind your Confederate bragging, or are you all talk, just more Rebel wind, as it were?"

"Say what you want to say, Sam."

"Very well. A race. I'll even let you pick the course and distance. The wager is as I said before: my independence to decide if and when I will leave."

"No, I'll not—"

"I knew it. Confederate honor; it's all talk and no substance. That's the problem with you Rebels," she said, deliberately baiting him.

"All right, challenge accepted, Yankee."

"You agree to the wager, then?"

"Yes, if you agree to abide by my decision when I win."

"*If* you win, Rebel."

"Sam, I told you. Kota is fast and strong, but my horses have been specifically bred for speed, especially at shorter distances."

"That may be, Rebel, but Kota was bred for survival. Pick the distance and the course."

A glint came to Ethan's eye. "All right. Remember the creek and grove of trees we went to yesterday? It's about a mile," he said, pointing across the field. "The first person to cross the creek is the winner."

"Done," Samantha said, offering her hand.

The gesture made Ethan laugh, but he shook her hand just the same. "When?" he asked.

"What's wrong with now?"

Ethan laughed again. "All right, Yankee, I'll wait."

"For what?"

"For you to get dressed and saddle your horse," he said as he looked at her, standing there in her nightgown.

Samantha pursed her lips. "That's very considerate of you. We are agreed then—a race to the creek, beginning as soon as I am mounted on my horse."

"Agreed."

A slow smile began to form on Samantha's lips. She and Ethan were standing outside of the paddock. She turned and walked about ten feet away from Ethan. She was sure Ethan thought she was going back to the house to dress. Instead, she spun around. She placed her fingers on her lips and made a peculiar, shrill sound, similar to an eagle's call.

Kota's ears pricked up at Samantha's whistle. The horse stamped his feet, whinnying as he caught sight of her. He broke into a gallop, heading toward the fence. Ethan watched as the horse's front hooves left the ground within several feet of the fence as he sailed over it and galloped to Samantha. He hadn't even come to a complete stop beside her when she grabbed his mane and threw her leg over his back. Horse and rider turned and trotted to where Ethan stood. He stared, mesmerized, as if by magic, Kota trotted a small circle around him. Samantha had neither saddle nor bridle on the horse.

"A mile that way, correct?" Samantha asked, smiling smugly. "I'm mounted. What are you waiting for? Survival, Rebel, remember? It's more important than speed."

The horse stopped next to Ethan by some invisible command she gave it. She leaned down to Ethan and kissed him fully on his lips, and then she was gone, the horse tearing out across the field.

Samantha felt free as she urged Kota on. She could feel his powerful muscles beneath her, only the thin fabric of the nightgown separating her from him. She closed her eyes, her hands resting lightly in front of her on Kota's mane. It had been years since she had sought to free her spirit. Not since she'd been a child under Charrah's instruction had she reached out beyond her physical existence to the spiritual elements surrounding her. She did so now as the horse raced across the field. It wasn't her imagination. She could feel it. Kota felt it, too. His mistress was placing herself in his care as her spirit joined with his, with the wind that blew through her and the sun that shone down upon her face. Horse and woman merged with the life forces flowing around them, both experiencing the pure joy of existing.

The change was subtle, and if Samantha hadn't been so totally joined to Kota, she might not have noticed the slight slowing of his pace. She opened her eyes. Kota was rapidly approaching a grove of trees and was waiting for directions. She signaled the horse with a subtle shift in her weight, and Kota slowed to a walk as they wound their way through the trees to a creek.

When Ethan arrived several minutes later, he found Samantha sitting on the soft grass, leaning back against a tree, a smile on her face. He dismounted quickly and strode over to her, a dark scowl on his face. "How did you do that?" he demanded.

"Why, Major, where-ever are your manners?"

"Don't play games with me, Sam. I want to know how you did that."

"Did what?" she asked innocently.

Just as he was about to reach down for her, she swept his feet and he hit the ground. He glanced up in time to see Samantha laugh and scramble to her feet.

A low growl emitted from Ethan as he lunged and caught her ankle, bringing her down upon the grass. If Ethan had thought he had discovered all of Samantha's secrets last night, the next few minutes proved him wrong.

Samantha had never felt so alive. This was Ethan, the man who had shown her such pleasure through the night and such love. She had nothing to fear from him. She wrestled him with skill and cunning. Each time he thought he'd subdued her, she would break his hold or reverse her position with him. In the end, Ethan's superior strength prevailed, and at last he pinned her under him in a position from which she could not escape.

"Damn little Yankee witch," he muttered close to her face.

"I won the wager!"

"You cheated."

"No, I didn't. You stated the terms."

Ethan loosened his grip on her. Her chest was rapidly rising up and down from the exertion of the wrestling. With one hand, he unlaced the remaining satin on the front of her shift, letting it fall open to her waist.

Samantha grew still. Just feeling his body this close to her—his weight upon her— conjured up visions of the night before. She felt the desire begin to build in her, making her tremble inside. This time, though, she knew what the end would be.

"Make love to me," she whispered. "Please."

"With pleasure." He chuckled deeply as he reached down to unbutton his own breeches and discard his waistcoat and shirt. He pushed her nightgown out of his way and moved his hand to her thigh. She opened her legs for him, and he slid his fingers into her delicate, moist flesh. Samantha writhed beneath him, moans of pleasure escaping from her. There was no need for Ethan to wait any longer, and Samantha cried out as he entered her, taking him deeper and deeper into her until both of them shuddered in the sweet release of each other's arms.

Samantha was aware of her own heart quieting at last. She also could feel Ethan's steady breathing as he lay upon her. He hadn't spoken but had buried his face in her hair. It occurred to Samantha that the emotional feelings she had after making love were as powerful as the physical ones before. Ethan could drive her into a frenzy, where nothing else mattered to her but the passion he created in her and its climax. But afterward, lying close to him. . . .

Her thoughts were interrupted as Ethan separated himself from her to lie beside her. She wanted to hold on to him, to cling to him, but resisted the impulse.

"Where did you learn that?" he asked.

Samantha's eyes flew open in surprise as she looked at him. Ethan started laughing.

"Not that," he said, realizing her misunderstanding. "I'm referring to your fighting abilities."

Samantha felt herself blush. "Oh. I told you I grew up on a frontier ranch with three brothers."

"Your brothers taught you to fight like that?" Ethan asked.

"Not exactly. They just provided me with ample opportunity to practice," Samantha said, giggling. "My cousin taught me when I was a girl. His name is Many Horses. He's a Lakota Indian warrior."

"Your cousin?" Ethan said with surprise.

Samantha stopped smiling. "Yes," she said steadily. "Many Horses is my cousin. We share the same grandfather. My father and his father are brothers."

Samantha watched for the reaction that she'd seen before when she told white persons of her relationship to the Indians. She'd seen the veil that came over their faces as they separated themselves from her, as though she had some disease. She didn't wait for it to appear on Ethan's face. She pushed against him and struggled to get free, but he pulled her to him.

"Let go of me! You needn't worry. You haven't bedded an Indian. I have only white blood in my veins. My uncle and father are half brothers."

"Sam, calm down." He held her still until she quit trying to break free of his grasp.

"I know what you're thinking," Samantha said.

"You don't. You've judged me since the moment we met, and often unfairly. My God," he said, laughing harshly. "I just made love to the most beautiful woman on the earth, and suddenly she turns into the impulsive schoolboy again. Damned if I shouldn't take you over my knee."

"Me? You're the one who—"

"Who did what?" Ethan challenged.

Samantha stopped. It didn't take her long to realize that she'd overreacted. She saw no distaste, hatred, or suspicion on Ethan's face.

"I'm sorry," she said. "Restraint. Many Horses always said I needed to learn restraint."

Ethan smiled. "I think I would like to meet this cousin of

yours."

Samantha grinned. "I guess he was right."

Ethan waited a moment and then released her. He leaned back on one elbow. "Tell me about him."

Samantha sighed and settled herself down beside him. "I was telling the truth when I told you that my grandfather was a French Canadian fur trapper. His first wife was a Lakota Indian woman. She died shortly after giving birth to a son. My grandfather couldn't take care of his son and hunt fur, so he left him with his wife's people, the Lakota Indians. After a few years, my grandfather married again—this time a Canadian woman, a white woman. They had a son, my father, and started a ranch near the Lakota lands. Eventually, my grandmother died. My grandfather was getting old, and he went to live with the Lakota. He gave the ranch to my mother and father."

"And your mother was from Boston?" Ethan asked.

"Yes," Samantha answered. "Her father was a banker. She and my father met when he'd gone to Boston on business." Samantha smiled. "If you think this story is hard to comprehend, can you imagine my mother's reaction? She'd lived in Boston all of her life, the daughter of a banker. What a shock it must have been for her to find herself on the Western Frontier with Indians for relatives." Samantha chuckled again.

"Was it difficult for her to adjust?" Ethan asked.

"Yes, in many ways it was hard for her. When we were children, my brothers and I visited my grandfather often, and the Lakota people accepted us as family. My brothers were treated as brothers of Many Horses. The Indians don't really have a word for cousin, as we do," Samantha added.

"I was treated differently, though," Samantha said with emphasis. "The roles of Indian women and men are clearly defined, just as they are in the white man's society. Women don't hunt or fight. Lakota women rarely ride horses. They walk most places they go. Although they carry knives, they're for utilitarian purposes, not for fighting. Do you remember me telling you about Charrah?"

"The old medicine man who trained you?"

"Yes. He taught me to be a medicine woman when I was just a child, and he also instructed the people that I was to be allowed to move freely about the camp. I started riding and shooting with the Lakota boys. I was terrible at first; I couldn't hit anything. The warriors who were teaching the boys never looked at me or said anything, but they didn't stop me, either," Samantha concluded.

"The day we were attacked by Depardeu," Ethan exclaimed, "I thought you were a boy then, and that was remarkable shooting for one so young. That was some of the best shooting I've ever seen."

Samantha shrugged her shoulders. "I was lucky. We were lucky. It'd been a long time since I'd done anything like that. Kota kept his stride straight and steady so that I could take aim."

"Kota. I have a feeling that horse of yours fits into this, too. You speak to him in the Indian language."

Samantha smiled gently. "Yes." She shifted her gaze over to where the horse was eating. "The Lakota do not break their horses the way the white man does with spurs and force. I trained him the way my uncle, Many Wolves, taught me. Troy helped me." Samantha thought a moment. "Although Charles and Robert also visited the Lakota, they didn't seem to enjoy it like Troy and I did. They were also older, so they stayed to help my father on the ranch. That was one thing that concerned my mother. She thought Troy and I were becoming wild." Samantha smiled.

"I told you Kota was bred for survival," Samantha continued. "That means he must respond quickly. There isn't always time for saddling a horse, or it may be inconvenient to tie him up. There's no mystery, really. I was directing him just like you do your horse, only using a different method. He responds to slight shifts of body weight or position of the leg. This leaves the hands completely free, allowing the warrior to aim his bow or gun and guide his horse at the same time. When I'm not riding him, he can follow commands given in Lakota sign language. I must say, though, at times I think Kota reads my mind. Come," she said, "I'll show you."

She started to pull Ethan up, but he resisted and pulled her back down to the ground. Samantha was surprised when she found herself once again positioned under him, his face near hers. The look in his eyes caused her to lie still.

"Who are you?" he whispered.

His face was serious as he stared at her. One of his hands held hers at her side, while the other he brought up and laced through her hair. Samantha swallowed. She felt overpowered by his closeness and the intensity in his eyes.

"Who are you?" he asked again. "Sam Cartier—willful, impulsive, opinionated, stubborn boy? Dr. Cartier—brave surgeon who has saved the lives of hundreds of soldiers at great risk to himself? Samantha Seymour—lovely young woman schooled in the social graces? Samantha Carter—warm, wild, freely passionate in her lovemaking? Or are you the cousin of Many Horses—trained as a fierce Lakota warrior and medicine woman?"

Samantha trembled inside. She didn't know what he was thinking. She only knew that even now, she wanted to lose herself in him, and she was afraid of the day when he would no longer be there.

"Who do you want me to be?" she whispered.

"I want to know the real Samantha or Sam. No more pretense! I won't be played the fool," he said forcefully.

Samantha calmed herself and looked directly at him. "I am what you see," she said evenly. "I'm all of those people. They make up who I am, Samantha Carter, and . . . I love you."

Ethan's face registered surprise, and then for a moment, Samantha thought she saw pain in his eyes. He squeezed his eyes shut and buried his face in her neck.

He made love to her with a frenzy that she hadn't experienced previously, as though he was driven by some unknown force. Although still considerate, Samantha was aware that he seemed to be more lost within himself, and when at last she felt him shudder and then relax, she noted that he had said that he needed her, but not that he loved her.

For the next four days, Samantha and Ethan stayed at Arabella. The days were filled with laughter and endless talking. Ethan explained the workings of the tobacco plantation, the process of firing the clay that was made into bricks on the plantation, and the selection and care of the horses he raised. He carefully avoided discussion of the war or the future. The nights were filled with passion and tenderness they found in each other's arms.

On the morning of the fifth day, Samantha awoke to find Ethan fully dressed and sitting in a chair next to the bed. He smiled as she stretched lazily and opened her eyes.

"You're already dressed," Samantha commented.

"I must leave immediately. I was only waiting for you to wake up so I could say goodbye."

Samantha couldn't believe she had heard him correctly. She sat up in bed. "Leaving?"

"Lieutenant Scott arrived early this morning. I must go back immediately."

"Go back? Go back where?"

"The general wants to see me," he said simply.

Samantha looked at him. "General Lee?" she asked. When Ethan didn't answer, she continued. "What is it that you do for him?"

"The less you know about what I do, the better. It's safer this way. You can't be implicated in anything you don't know about."

Samantha wanted to ask other questions, but she could see that Ethan would say no more. "Well," she said, "I'm going, too."

"No, Sam, you can't come with me. I want you to stay here. You'll be safe here, and Molly and Fox will take care of anything that you need."

"I can't stay here."

"Of course you can."

"No, I won't." Samantha swung her legs around the side of the bed to stand.

"Sam, please, I didn't wait here to argue with you."

Samantha saw the strain on Ethan's face. "I know," she said, "and I don't mean to be disagreeable." Ethan stood as Samantha stepped to him. His arms felt comforting as he held her. "I understand I can't go with you, but I can return to the medical corps. Where's Clement Beauregard?"

Ethan pulled back from her. "Sam, no! You were almost killed before."

"I can't remain here when I'm needed on the battlefield."

"I don't care. I'd rather die than see any harm come to you."

"But it's not your choice," Samantha said, "nor is it mine," she added softly. "This is the path set for me."

She watched in silence as Ethan raged for the next few minutes. He finally stopped when she told him the only way he could keep her here would be as a prisoner, for eventually, she would leave, whether it was today, tomorrow, or the next day. He finally gave in, agreeing to see her safely to Dr. Beauregard and then to continue to General Lee's command.

"I'll go tell Avery that you're coming with us and that it will be a few more minutes," Ethan said.

When he returned a few minutes later, he stopped upon entering the room. Samantha was standing there in boots and pants and had just picked up the long gauze. He closed the door behind him. Samantha looked up, her feelings a mixture of sadness and resignation. She shrugged her shoulders. "It's the only way," she said.

"Do you mind?" Ethan asked as he crossed the room and sat down in the chair to watch her.

Samantha smiled and then, swallowing, began the process of winding the gauze tightly around her breasts. Ethan frowned as he watched the transformation take place. By the time she put her shirt and waistcoat on, her figure was concealed. Next, she pulled out a jar and walked over to the mirror. She was unable to hide her disgust as she dipped her fingers into the mixture of pitch, sand, and very fine hair stubbles. As she smoothed the mixture onto her face and chin, her eyes began to water.

"It burns my face when I put it on," she explained as she squeezed her eyes shut. In a few minutes, the mixture dried and closely resembled the stubble expected in a young man who was just beginning to develop a beard. As a final touch, Samantha withdrew a light mustache and placed it above her lip. Surveying herself in the mirror, she frowned sadly.

"I think I'll have to cut my hair again. It's grown too much in the last four months."

"No," Ethan said. "It's not necessary."

Samantha turned back to the mirror and pulled her hair back, tying it with a strip of rawhide. Then she reached for her hat, looked in the mirror to make a final inspection, and then turned back to Ethan. "I'm ready," she said.

Ethan crossed the room and stopped in front of her. His eyes were dark and intense. Samantha wanted to cry out, to ask for reassurances, promises that she knew she couldn't ask of him. Despite what she'd told Ethan that first night, she did want to hear words of love, and she desperately wanted to hear promises of a future. Her eyes grew moist, and she felt her chin quiver.

Ethan put his arms around her. "Sam, I don't know what's going to happen. I don't know how long I'll be gone or . . . or if we'll ever see each other again. But don't worry. I'll always know where you are, and if I'm able, I'll come to you."

Samantha mutely nodded her head against his chest as she squeezed her eyes shut to stop the tears.

"Sam?" he said as he pulled back and raised her face to him. He sighed. "It would have been easier if we'd never loved," he said softly.

Samantha swallowed. "Easier, yes, but Ethan, I have no regrets. None."

He crushed her to him and then kissed her forehead. Finally, he separated. "We'd better leave."

Samantha wiped her eyes and walked ahead of him as he opened the door.

Molly, Fox, Frederick, and Avery Scott were waiting for them. Only Avery didn't register shock at Samantha's appearance. "It seems we are to travel together again, Avery," Samantha said.

Lieutenant Scott smiled softly and then raised Samantha's hand to his lips. "I'm honored, Cousin Samantha," he said with a wink.

It took them a week to reach the medical corps and Dr.

Clement Beauregard. Ethan had cautioned her before they left that Avery must never know of their intimate relationship. No one could know. The three of them camped together as they traveled and slept on the ground near the fire at night. Both men allowed Samantha her needed moments of privacy, which was something that had been hard for her to obtain when they thought she was a boy.

When they finally arrived at the surgical tent, Clement Beauregard was shocked to see Samantha again. He and Ethan went into Dr. Beauregard's tent, and by the raised voices, Samantha knew the discussion was not agreeable. Finally, Clement emerged, an angry scowl on his face.

"Ethan wants to see you before he leaves. He's in my tent. I'll see to it that a separate tent is put up for you. You might as well know that I'm against this. God knows I need your help, but it's too dangerous, Sam." Clement stalked away from her.

Samantha's last few minutes with Ethan were cut short by rumble of cannon fire close by, followed shortly by musket fire and cries of men's voices as North and South once again came together in the deadly conflict that was becoming a daily affair. Abruptly, Samantha was once again thrown back into her living nightmare.

In the weeks that followed, the patterns of battle repeated themselves time and again for Samantha. Sometimes the battles were skirmishes, and the wounded were quickly brought back to the surgical tent. Other times, the battles raged for days before one side would withdraw or a temporary truce would be called so that the wounded could be collected and the dead buried.

Samantha no longer noticed the pile of amputated limbs in the corner of the tent, nor did the stench of bowel or putrefied wounds bother her. There were nights when she would return to her own tent completely exhausted but unable to sleep.

The days passed. The heat was intense in August, and most of the food given to the soldiers was rotten. The first of September, the camp was abruptly moved. News spread that the Federal troops, under General Sherman, had succeeded in taking Atlanta, driving out Confederate General Hood's troops that had resisted against overwhelming odds for so long.

It had been six weeks since Samantha had seen Ethan. One day, in mid-September, he rode into the camp. He found her in the surgical tent—her clothing, face, and hair stained with blood that had been there for days. They had only a few minutes together when Samantha went to her tent to rest.

"When did you last eat?" he demanded as he surveyed her thin frame, "or sleep?" he asked as he traced the dark circles under her eyes. Ethan sat beside her and held her while she wept.

That evening, Samantha retired to her empty tent to find several large packages and a note from Ethan. Inside, she found dried beef, salt, beans, fruit, vegetables, and other well-preserved foods. The note was short and to the point: she would gain nothing for herself or the men she cared for if she were to fall ill. The survival of many depended upon her taking care of herself. The food was for her. Little would be gained by sharing it with others. He would come back soon as possible.

October arrived and with it came more disaster for the Confederacy as the Federal troops began their destruction of the Shenandoah Valley. Nothing remained in the wake of the Federal troops. Under the orders of Union General

Philip Sheridan, fields were trampled under and then set afire, destroying the once-fertile land. All livestock was either stolen or killed. Sheridan himself recorded the deliberate massacre of thousands of cows and sheep, even down to the smallest chicken, their bodies left to rot under the sun. The immorality of the senseless slaughter of animals, when the Confederate people were starving, made Samantha ashamed. Not only could the valley not feed its Confederate sons who were fighting in the war, it also couldn't feed or shelter the countless Confederate women and children who had once called the Shenandoah Valley home.

In November, the temperatures cooled and brought some relief, but it was ill timed, for Samantha noted the inadequate clothing that the wounded wore. Many of them had no soles left in their boots or marched barefoot, and the once-proud Confederate uniforms were now in tatters. The men were thin and their skin pale from poor nutrition. They were falling prey to dysentery and typhoid fever, making survival from their battle wounds all but impossible.

The reelection of Abraham Lincoln in November caused a cloud to descend over the Confederate troops, and the hope of an end to the war disappeared. Even Samantha, who greatly admired Lincoln, found herself wishing that McClelland would have won, for then, maybe, the Union would have sued for peace. She still believed fervently in preservation of the Union and the abolition of slavery, but she was sick of the bloody battlefields, the pain, mutilation, disease, starvation, and death. The price being paid was far too high for both sides.

The following week, Samantha found herself on the move again. News reached the medical corps of General Sherman's vow to march to the sea. Confederate troops were desperately repositioned, and Samantha found the surgical tents moved every few days to accommodate the moving battlefield. The battle lines were no longer clearly delineated as countless clashes occurred between smaller units.

It was late in the afternoon one November day when Samantha emerged from the surgical tent. The casualties had been light that day, it being largely a Confederate victory. She was making her way back to her tent when she saw a straggling line of captive Union soldiers being marched into the camp. It was the first time that Samantha had come face-to-face with Union troops since the day she had been shot almost five months previously. At first, she used to walk the battlefields, searching among the dead for any sign of her brothers. After a while, the unit moved too quickly for her to conduct her search, and she gave up the macabre ritual.

Now, as she watched the defeated men walking along, a chill ran through her. Many of them were bleeding from their wounds. Her heart cried out to her countrymen, and she stepped forward.

"Private," she addressed a nearby Confederate soldier, "what's happening?"

"Prisoners, Doc, from today."

"What will happen to them?"

"As soon as the sergeant gets his orders, he'll take them to one of the prison camps."

"But they're wounded."

"They're Yankees," the soldier answered and walked away.

Samantha watched as the Union soldiers sat on the ground in a group, their guards watching them carefully. She ran back into the surgical tent.

"Clement," she said, "there are Union soldiers outside. Some of them are wounded. We must do something for them."

Clement Beauregard looked sadly at Samantha. "Sam, God knows I wish I could, but we don't have enough supplies to care for our own. We can't do anything for them. They'll be treated when they reach the prison camp. I'm sorry."

Samantha couldn't believe what she was hearing. "You would let those men suffer or bleed to death? What kind of a doctor are you?"

"A Confederate doctor," came the reply, not from Clement, but from a voice behind her. Samantha turned to see Dr. Schafley entering the tent. "He's a loyal Confederate just as I am, and those men are the enemy."

Samantha turned back to Clement. "They're not my enemies." She reached for her medical bag and grabbed a stack of dressings. She started to exit the tent when Dr. Schafley stepped in front of her, blocking her way.

"Just where do you think you're going?" he demanded with a sneer on his face.

"Outside, to care for those men."

"You don't have the authority to do that, and I can't allow it."

"You can't stop me," Samantha argued.

"Oh, yes I can. I'm a captain in the Confederate Medical Corps. I can order you placed under guard."

"Try it, Schafley, and I'll—"

"Sam, please," Clement interrupted, walking over to the two. "I know how you feel, but Dr. Schafley is right."

"You don't know how I feel," Samantha shouted as she whirled around to face Clement. "And what about you? Your rank is major. You're head of this medical corps. Would you allow him to do as he says?"

"Of course not, Sam. No one is going to put you under guard."

"But, as a Confederate officer, I can prevent a civilian

from interfering in military business. You couldn't counter that, Dr. Beauregard," Dr. Schafley said with a snarl. "And Dr. Cartier is a civilian."

A thought came to Samantha. When Dr. Beauregard had discovered her identity, he'd offered her a commission with the Confederate Army Medical Corps. Samantha had recoiled in horror. To accept such would be treason. He'd explained to her that it would give her some protection while in the South. Still, Samantha had refused. She turned to Clement.

"You once offered me the rank of captain in the Confederacy, did you not? I accept," she said, not waiting for his answer.

Dr. Schafley's cruel laugh cut through the air. "And do you swear allegiance to the Confederate States of America?"

Samantha swallowed. She had no choice. "Mister Sam Cartier, French Canadian surgeon, does so swear," she said evenly, her eyes holding Clement's.

The old man sighed. "Very well," he said. "It's within my authority to confer rank upon those members of my medical corps."

"No!" Dr. Schafley shouted.

"There's no legal reason not to. Surgeons with battlefield experience hold the rank of captain," Dr. Beauregard said.

Dr. Schafley's face reddened. He moved to block Samantha's exit. "If you think I'm going to let you treat those stinkin' Yankees, you're wrong."

Samantha saw the blow coming. Schafley's small eyes widened and he snorted through his long, pointed nose as he doubled his fist and swung his arm to strike her in the chin. Even though he was twice Samantha's size, she grabbed his arm, pivoted, and used the force of his body to throw the larger man over her back. Dr. Schafley landed on the hard dirt of the tent and looked up in shock to see Sam above him, her knee pressed into his chest and a vicious-looking knife poised in her hand. Samantha watched the fear spread across Schafley's face. With deathly calm, she placed the knife against the frightened man's neck.

"We're of equal rank now, Schafley. That means this is between you and me. Do you want to settle it now?" Samantha could feel Schafley's fear as he lay beneath her, paralyzed to move. "Dr. Beauregard!" she shouted as she kept her eyes locked with Schafley's. "Does the Confederacy have a policy against the humane treatment or medical care of its prisoners?"

"Sam! What are you doing?" Clement stammered as he stood helplessly by. He stared wide-eyed at the knife.

"Answer my question!" Samantha demanded.

"Sam, please stop," Clement pleaded. "Please! We're not men without honor. Of course the Confederacy treats its prisoners humanely."

"Then there will be no objection to my treating the Union soldiers," Samantha said. She stood slowly, withdrawing the deadly knife. Her eyes bore into Schafley's as she placed the knife back in her boot. Schafley didn't move. Samantha reached into her pocket and removed a gold coin. She tossed it down, letting it land on Schafley's chest. "That should more than cover the expense of the supplies I use."

As she turned around, she saw one of the orderlies standing just inside the tent. By the look on his face, Samantha knew he must have heard the shouting and saw most of what had just happened. She knew the young man, for he had assisted her many times.

"Private Salem," Samantha said, "bring clean bandages, soap, and water, and follow me." She looked back at Schafley, who hadn't moved. "You try to stop me again, Schafley, I'll kill you." Samantha picked up her bag and walked outside of the tent. It didn't take Private Salem long to gather the supplies and catch up with her.

"Doc?" the private said as he hastened up next to her. "Or, I guess I should call you captain," he said.

"Doc is fine, Private."

"Well, I just wanted to tell you it was 'bout time someone put that man in his place."

Samantha stopped and turned.

"I just mean, well, all the men know that Doc Schafley doesn't care a damn about enlisted men. He'd just as soon cut off a leg as look at it." He paused. "And, sir, the men consider themselves real lucky if it's you who cuts on them, even if you have to take a leg or arm off. They know they got a better chance of keeping their arms and legs if it's you they get, and more of them live who go under your knife than any of the other surgeons.

"We know you're not from around here," the private continued. "You're not a Southern boy, Doc, you're a Yankee. We all know that. But you care, and that's good enough for us."

Samantha took a deep breath, overcome with emotion. "I wish I could do more."

Private Salem looked back at the surgical tent. "Doubt that son-of-a-bitch Schafley ever seen his own blood." He turned back to Samantha. "We remember, Doc, you was wounded real bad. You know what it's like."

Samantha didn't know what to say. She shivered as she recalled that fateful day she almost died. She thought it was all behind her. She had physically recovered, and then spent the week with Ethan at Arabella where she was at peace. But when she returned to the battlefield, the nightmares also returned, but now it was not just the mutilation and death of the soldiers she saw in her dreams, she relived her own as well.

Samantha silently nodded to Private Salem. He didn't seem to expect her to say anything else, so she turned and walked over to where the Union soldiers were sitting in a group. Kneeling down, she reached out to a man whose arm was roughly wrapped up in bloody bandages.

"I'm a doctor. I'd like to help you," she said.

The Union soldier looked up with surprise as he heard her clear Northern voice.

"Private Salem, pour some water into a bowl for me," she said as she removed the bandage.

"Hey you! Get away from him," a deep voice shouted. The Confederate sergeant, who had brought the prisoners, walked over to Samantha. "What do you think you're doin', boy?" he said as he reached down and grabbed Samantha's arm, pulling her to a standing position.

Samantha jerked her arm free and glared at the sergeant. "These men are wounded. I'm a doctor," she answered.

"These men are Yankee prisoners," he said.

"I'm aware of that, Sergeant, and they need medical attention."

A suspicious look came upon the sergeant's face. "You don't look like no doctor to me."

"Private Salem, am I what I say I am?"

"Yes sir, Doc. Sergeant, the doc here is the best surgeon we got."

The sergeant frowned. "That may be, but he ain't touchin' none of these prisoners." He reached for Samantha's arm again.

Samantha froze and turned an icy glare on the large man. "I don't need your permission, Sergeant, and if you don't remove your hand immediately, I'll have you brought up on charges of insulting an officer."

The sergeant hesitated, but still held on to Samantha's arm.

"Private Salem, if the sergeant doesn't remove his hand immediately, I order you to arrest him, at gunpoint if necessary."

"Yes, Captain," the private replied as he raised his gun.

"That won't be necessary, Private," a voice cut in from behind them. "If the sergeant doesn't release the doctor, I'll shoot him myself."

There was the cold, clear sound of a revolver being cocked. All faces turned to see Major Winters-Hunt, still mounted on his horse and pointing his sidearm at the sergeant. The sergeant paled as he released Samantha and took a step back. Ethan cocked his eyebrow, waiting.

"My apologies, sir," the sergeant said hastily to Samantha.

"I suggest you return to your duties, Sergeant, and let the doctor do the same," Ethan said.

"Yes, sir," the sergeant replied.

Ethan dismounted and gave his horse to an attendant. He leaned close to Samantha. "As soon as I heard the commotion, I knew it had to be you," he whispered. "Can't you stay out of trouble?"

Samantha's heart leaped. She was overjoyed to see him. It had been two months since he had come to the camp for those few brief hours. "I was only doing what I had to do," she replied.

"Why doesn't that surprise me?" Ethan said, a hint of humor in his eyes. "Well? What are you waiting for? I have matters to attend to. I'll see you later, Sam," he said as Private Salem approached.

Samantha tried to calm herself. She was certain that everyone could hear the wild beating of her heart. She turned back to the soldier on the ground and took a deep breath to calm the trembling that she felt inside.

For the next half hour, she moved among the Union soldiers. At one point, she looked up to see Clement

Beauregard approach with an armful of supplies. She smiled in gratitude as she saw the older surgeon kneel down to tend to the wound of another Union soldier.

None of the wounds were life-threatening. When Samantha commented to one of the Union soldiers about how lucky they all were not to have been wounded more seriously, she was informed that those with more serious wounds or who couldn't walk had been left behind to die on the field.

"Rebel Sergeant don't want no dead Yankee bodies to haul around," the soldier explained.

Clement Beauregard was close enough to overhear the conversation. "We can't save them all, Sam," he whispered. "Do what you can do for these men."

Forcing herself to concentrate on the torn tissue before her, she returned to her work. After another twenty minutes, she and Dr. Beauregard were almost finished. She moved toward the back of the group of men. Suddenly, she froze. A man, a Union captain, was sitting on the ground, staring at her. His face was covered with dirt and blood, and he had a ragged, soiled bandage tied around his head. His eyes, however, were clear, and they were a vivid shade of green, the same as Samantha's. Despite the dirt and haggard appearance, Samantha would have recognized that face anywhere. She had searched among the dead and wounded for months, praying that she would not come across it. Now, it was all she could do to walk calmly toward the man. She was aware of those around her as she knelt down in front of him.

"Captain, you're injured," she said quietly.

The man's hand lashed out, catching hers. He squinted hard into Samantha's eyes.

"Let me help you, Captain," she said.

The man just stared, his grip becoming painful to

Samantha, and then he spoke. "My eyes must be playing tricks on me, boy. You remind me of someone, but that can't be."

"Then close your eyes and see with your spirit, brother, but keep silent for both our sakes."

The man's green eyes widened in disbelief as Samantha spoke to him in the Lakota Indian language.

"Sam, is it really you?" he asked in Lakota.

Samantha pulled away abruptly. "Private Salem."

The orderly came hurrying over to Samantha. "Yes, Doc?"

"I can't treat this man out here," she said. "He has a serious head injury. Help me take him into the surgical tent."

"Are you sure, Doc?" he asked.

"I'm sure. Don't worry. He isn't armed. Get some men to help you if you wish. I'll bring the supplies."

Samantha picked up her bag and bandages and walked toward the tent. Private Salem followed with the Union captain. Once inside, Samantha silently removed the bandages on the captain's head. The captain watched in silence as she cleaned the wound and applied a fresh dressing. When she was finished, she positioned herself between the captain and Private Salem, who was waiting by the entrance of the tent. She raised her hands, using the sign language taught to them in their childhood by the Lakota. Then she turned as if to leave. Suddenly, the captain fell forward, his body jerking violently. Samantha reached out to catch him as Private Salem rushed forward.

"Just what I was afraid of—his head injury is worse than it appeared," Samantha said.

When the seizure was over, the Union captain lay still.

"He'll be unconscious for a few hours after that. We'd better not move him," she said.

"Can we leave him here?" Private Salem asked.

"I don't see why not. There's nothing more I can do now. I'm going back to my tent to rest a while. I suggest you do the same."

The private looked doubtful.

"After a seizure like that, he's not likely to regain consciousness for a few hours. Why don't you go over to the campfire and get something to eat. You'll be able to hear him when he awakens."

"If you're sure, Doc."

"I'll come back to check on him," Samantha said as they both walked toward the entrance of the tent. "Oh, and Private, better not let anyone else in until I get back. I wouldn't want something to accidentally happen to the prisoner."

"I understand. I'll stay within eyesight of the tent."

"Thank you," Samantha said.

She tried to affect a calm appearance as she walked toward her tent. Once inside her tent, she tore through her supplies, stuffing food and a small container of water into a bag. Then, as inconspicuously as possible, she walked out of her tent.

It took her a few minutes to reach the horses. She was well known to the men who tended them, as she usually cared for Kota herself. They didn't say anything as she saddled Kota and then did the same to another horse. Quietly, she led both horses away, going around the center area of the camp. When she was certain that she wouldn't be seen, she led the horses to a wooded area behind the surgical tent and tied them up. Then she hurried back to the camp. Calming her steps, she walked around her own tent and over to the surgical tent. Private Salem was seated at a campfire near the entrance to the tent.

"Has Dr. Beauregard finished with the prisoners?" she asked as she approached.

"Yes, sir," Private Salem answered. "He's already gone back to his tent."

"Good. I'll just check on the captain." Private Salem got to his feet. "Stay where you are, Private. If I need you, I'll call. I might as well make an inventory of our supplies while I'm here."

Samantha turned and walked to the tent. She breathed a sigh of relief when she heard the private sit down with his friends. Once inside, she hurried over to the Union captain who was lying still on the table.

"Robert!" she whispered. "Oh, Robert! You're alive!"

Captain Robert Carter stood and threw his arms around his sister.

"Sam! My God, it's really you! What are you doing here?"

"There's no time to explain. Come quickly." Samantha led him to the back of the tent. She removed the knife from her boot and slit the tent from the bottom, opening it enough for the two of them to crawl out. "Follow me," she whispered as she ran toward the stand of trees. When they reached the horses, they both mounted.

"Kota is here, too?" Robert whispered.

"He brought me here," Samantha replied. "Let's go."

For the next ten minutes, they rode in silence as Samantha found her way through the woods. At last, she stopped and dismounted. Robert came up beside her and dismounted.

"We don't have much time. Soon, they'll discover that you're gone," Samantha said. They were on the edge of the woods next to a road. "Follow this road, but stay under cover of the trees. If you continue going west, you're bound to meet up with Union forces by nightfall."

"Me? Aren't you coming with me? What are you doing here? Why are you pretending to be a boy?"

"There isn't time to explain. I just thank God that you're

alive. Go now, quickly!" Samantha said with tears in her eyes.

"I'm not leaving without you."

"Robert, I know this doesn't make sense to you, but I can't go with you. I must stay."

"Are you crazy? Sam! There's a war going on. That was a Confederate camp. How did you get there?"

"You must go. Now! Please, Robert, I love you." Samantha threw herself into her brother's arms just as she heard the voice behind her.

"Now isn't this cozy?"

She didn't have to turn around. She recognized the voice, and even more importantly, she recognized the inimical softness in his voice.

"Ethan," she breathed, and turned around to face him. The anger in his eyes caused her to step back against Robert. Ethan approached them, his revolver drawn.

"Get back, Sam," Robert said as he pushed his sister behind him.

"Once again, it appears I've been fooled by your disguises," Ethan said, his eyes cold. "I could have sworn that there'd been no others before me, but it appears I was wrong. I guess a skilled doctor would know how to feign her own virginity."

Samantha inhaled sharply, Ethan's cruel words cutting her like a knife.

"I'll kill you!" Robert shouted and lunged toward Ethan, oblivious of the gun pointed at his chest.

From the corner of his eye, Ethan saw Samantha rush forward, throwing herself at him. The vision of her filled his head, and he moved his arm to the side, letting the gun discharge harmlessly to the ground. At the sound, the three of them froze.

Samantha looked at Ethan, tears running down her face. Robert jumped forward and pulled Samantha back.

"Robert, let go of me!" Samantha cried. "He won't hurt me," she said as she twisted out of Robert's arms. She turned to Ethan. "Ethan," she said between gasps, "this is my brother."

It took a moment for Samantha's words to register in Ethan's mind. "Your brother?"

"Yes. This is my brother, Robert Carter."

Ethan felt a sudden mixture of relief and fear, realizing what he'd almost done. "Oh, God, Sam!" Samantha ran the few steps into his arms as Ethan crushed her to him. "I'm sorry, Sam," he murmured. He held her for a moment, and then Samantha pulled away.

"Ethan, I'll not let him be sent to a prison camp. I won't. You have to let him go. In a few hours, he can reach the Union lines," she said.

Ethan looked at the Federal captain. He nodded, indicating the horse. "Go ahead, Captain, but don't look back."

Robert Carter reached for his sister's arm. "Let's go, Samantha," he said as he took a step backward, keeping his eyes on Ethan.

"You go, Robert. I'm staying," Samantha said.

"You'll do as I say, Samantha! You're coming with me," Robert ground out.

"Go with him, Sam," Ethan said softly.

"No, Ethan. I won't leave. I'm staying here." Samantha turned to Robert. "Robert, please try to understand. I can't go with you. I'm needed here."

"Here?" Robert accused. "Samantha, I don't know how the hell you got here, but this is the Confederacy."

"I know that, Robert," Samantha said. "They're still men, just like in the North, and they have very few physicians. I can't leave them."

Robert roughly grabbed Samantha's arm. "Those men just slaughtered a fourth of my Iowa Company! Iowa boys, Sam, friends, neighbors, our own people."

"No. Oh, no," Samantha sobbed as she buried her face in her hands.

Robert took her in his arms. "Sam, I don't know what the Rebs did to you down here, but it doesn't matter. It wasn't your fault. Let's go."

Samantha separated herself from her brother. "I can't, Robert," she whispered hoarsely. "I've seen too much to walk away. I can't leave them."

"Them or *him*!" Robert accused. He grabbed Samantha by the shoulders. "Is what he said true? Is it? Did he force himself on you?" His face was an explosion of rage. He crushed Samantha to him. "It doesn't matter, Sam. I'll take you home."

"He's right, Sam. Go with him," Ethan said gently.

"No," Samantha said as she stepped back from Robert. Brother and sister faced each other. "I've done nothing that was not of my own free will, Robert. I'd like to explain. . . ."

Robert violently shoved Samantha from him. She would have fallen from the force if Ethan had not stepped forward and caught her. Robert's face pulled up in an ugly snarl. "Are you married, or are you just his whore?"

Ethan withdrew his sidearm again. "Captain, she's your sister," Ethan said, a warning in his voice, "and were that not so, I would have shot you by now. You speak of her that way again, and I'll kill you."

"Sister!" Robert snarled. "I have no sister. She's dead to me. She's a traitor and a filthy whore." His eyes shot to Samantha. "I hope you burn in hell!"

"Robert!" A strangled cry erupted from Samantha's throat as Robert spun around and ran to the horses. Ethan held her in place as Samantha struggled to run to her brother. They watched as Robert threw his leg up into the saddle and bolted away. He didn't look back to see his sister collapse on the ground, cries of anguish racking her body.

For several minutes, Samantha's cries were the only sound in the forest. Ethan held her, his own despair equal to hers, for he knew in his heart that she stayed because of him. He was responsible for her pain now, and he knew that he'd hurt her again. If only he could undo what had been done. If only he hadn't captured her. If only he hadn't loved her.

At last she quieted, her body exhausted, her spirit crushed. Ethan picked her up and carried her over to his horse. He mounted, still holding her, and rode back to the camp with Kota following. When he arrived, several men rushed forward. By now, the entire camp was aware that one of the prisoners had escaped, taking the young Yankee surgeon with him.

Clement Beauregard was the first to reach them. Alarm showed in his eyes when he spotted Samantha in Ethan's arms. Ethan brushed off the questions and carried Samantha to her tent as Clement followed. Once inside, Ethan closed the tent flap and gently placed Samantha on the cot. She turned on her side and curled up, her eyes closed as the tears flowed quietly down her face.

"My God! What happened? Is she hurt?" Clement asked as he reached for her.

"No," Ethan replied as he stopped Clement. "At least there aren't any physical injuries." Ethan nodded for Clement to step to the other side of the tent with him.

"They said she was abducted by a Federal officer who escaped," Clement said quietly. "But, Ethan, Dr. Schafley has gone to the commanding officer. He's accused Sam of deliberately aiding the prisoner to escape. The rest of the prisoners have been moved out."

"Damn," Ethan swore under his breath.

"What happened, Ethan? This charge is serious. She'll have to face Colonel Olley. The colonel is on his way."

"Noah Olley is a fair man. I'm certain that when he hears of the special circumstances, he'll dismiss the charge," Ethan said quietly.

"What special circumstances, Ethan?"

Ethan sighed. "She did help a prisoner escape, Clement. The Federal officer was her brother."

"Oh, no," Clement said, his face stricken. He glanced over at Samantha and then back to Ethan. "There's more, Ethan," he whispered urgently. "Dr. Schafley has accused Samantha of attempted murder."

"What?" Ethan said with surprise.

"Yes. When the Federal prisoners were first brought into camp, Sam came into the surgical tent to get supplies to treat them. Dr. Schafley tried to stop her. He grabbed her and took a swing at her. I was on the other side of the table, and before I could stop him, she . . . she . . . well, it happened so fast. She threw Dr. Schafley over her shoulder and onto the ground and pulled a knife out of her boot. A knife! She had him pinned down and was pressing it against his neck when I reached them."

Ethan swore again. "Schafley's a fool. He's lucky he's still alive."

"Ethan, he's accusing Sam of trying to kill him. I can barely believe what I saw, but it's true."

"If Sam had wanted to kill him, Schafley would be dead now, and you couldn't have stopped her." Clement frowned in confusion. "Sam grew up on the frontier," Ethan explained. "She may have been the daughter of a wealthy rancher and educated in Paris, but she was also raised by a Lakota Indian tribe. The Indians trained her to be a medicine woman, Clement, and a warrior," he said pointedly. "I've seen firsthand how deadly she is with a knife and rifle. She could have easily killed both of you, if that had been her intent." Ethan saw the shock on Clement Beauregard's face. "I'll explain later. I want to talk to Colonel Olley. You better take Sam over to the surgical tent in case he wants to see her, and then will you stay with her? Her brother said some terrible things to her," Ethan whispered. "He denounced her as his sister and called her a traitor."

"Oh, no." Clement squeezed his eyes shut as he shook his head back and forth. Then he looked at Samantha. She was lying on her side, her knees drawn up as though in pain. She whimpered softly as tears flowed out of her closed eyes. "I'll take care of her, Ethan."

The two men then walked out of the tent just as Colonel Olley rode up on his horse, accompanied by a small contingency of officers. "Dr. Beauregard, what the hell is going on here?" the colonel barked as he dismounted. "I have a regiment to move out. I don't have time for this. Can't you handle your surgeons?" he angrily demanded.

"Sir," Clement Beauregard said.

"Ethan, do you know anything about this?" Noah Olley said, seeing Ethan for the first time. He didn't wait for a reply. "Where's this surgeon of yours, Beauregard?"

Clement Beauregard hesitated. "He's not feeling well, Colonel."

"I don't give a damn how he's feeling. I need some answers. Get him!"

"Noah, if you'll allow me, I would like a word with you first," Ethan said.

"If you can clear this up, Ethan, I'd appreciate it," Colonel Olley said.

"Perhaps Dr. Beauregard can take Dr. Cartier to the

surgical tent while we talk in private?"

Colonel Olley nodded in Clement's direction, dismissing him, and then Ethan guided the colonel away from the curious soldiers who had approached.

Samantha couldn't tell how much time had passed since Clement brought her to the surgical tent while Ethan met with the colonel. Her tears had dried, but Robert's words of hatred remained. They echoed in her mind, in her heart. She was drowning in her pain when Ethan entered.

"Dr. Schafley has dropped the charges," Ethan began.

"And the escaped prisoner?" Clement asked as he glanced at Samantha.

"Colonel Olley knows the truth, or at least part of it. Your disguise is still intact, Sam. You're the Yankee boy surgeon I captured. The prisoner was your brother, and you did help him escape. However, given the service you have rendered to the Confederacy, Colonel Olley has dismissed the matter."

"What happens to me now?" Samantha asked.

"I'll take you to Arabella where you'll be safe. You need to rest, Sam."

Samantha mutely shook her head in disagreement.

"Ethan's right, Samantha," Clement said. "You've hardly eaten or slept these last four months, and the month before that, you were wounded. You can't continue here. You're near exhaustion."

"I don't want to rest," Samantha said. "I . . . I don't want to think about—"

"Sam, he didn't mean it," Ethan said.

"Oh, but he did, and I can't blame him," Samantha whispered.

"Sam, listen to me. Your brother had just come out of a

battle in which he lost over one fourth of the men under his command. He was angry and probably feeling guilty, blaming himself for their deaths. He wasn't thinking clearly, and he used you to vent his anger."

"He said I was a traitor," Samantha said quietly as new tears formed in her eyes. "My brother said I was dead to him."

"Words of anger from a man who was confused and hurt," Ethan said.

Samantha's lip trembled as she looked at Ethan. "Was what I did so wrong?" she whispered.

"No one can answer that question but you, Sam. Your brother can't. I can't. Only you can." He paused. "But I think you know the answer. You knew it as a young girl in that Indian village when the holy man made you a medicine woman—a medicine woman not just for the Indian, but for all men. He was with you then, and he's been with you here." Ethan paused. "You just need some time, Sam."

"There is one who has the strength. That is why he was sent to you."

Where had she heard those words before? Why were they echoing in her mind now? She saw herself in a dark void, and then it was as though the sunlight appeared and burned away the night fog. Ethan was standing there, and Samantha once again found peace in his eyes.

"All right. I'll do whatever you say."

"It'll be dark soon," Ethan said. "We can leave under cover of night. Pack a few supplies. I've a matter to attend to before we leave. Lieutenant Scott will be traveling with us. We'll have one stop to make before we go to Charleston."

Samantha nodded mutely to Ethan. She turned to Clement. When his arms came around her, she held on tightly to the kindly man who had become her friend.

CHAPTER 10

Ethan and Samantha left that evening accompanied by Avery Scott. Samantha preferred to leave quietly with few people knowing of her departure, especially in light of the day's events. Avery was solicitous. Samantha was not sure how much Ethan had told him about her brother's escape and the subsequent charges brought against her, but by his manner, she thought Avery probably knew that she had helped Robert escape and of Robert's denouncement of her as a traitor.

Both men were quiet as they rode with her well into the night. When at last they stopped to sleep, Samantha was given her privacy, and then a place was made for her to sleep near the small campfire. Avery and Ethan took turns keeping watch and sleeping on the other side of the fire.

When morning came, they set off again. They reached the port city of Wilmington in less than a week. It was late in the afternoon when Ethan led the way to the dock area and found a place to stable the horses.

"Where are we going?" Samantha asked once she was assured that Kota was comfortable.

"I must meet with some men. They're waiting now," he said as they walked out of the stable. "This is Wilmington, the last Confederate port still open."

Samantha was walking between Ethan and Avery. She didn't have to be told the importance of keeping this port open. As they neared the docks, she saw bales of cotton waiting to be shipped. Farther out from the shore, Samantha could see Confederate gunboats patrolling the harbor area, which was also guarded by Confederate forces at Fort Fisher.

Ethan led them down to the wharf and over to a plank leading up to a sleek, gray vessel. He stepped aside to let Samantha go first. She stopped. "This is where you are to meet these men?" she asked.

"Yes."

"Perhaps I should wait here," Samantha said, leery of the situation.

"Relax, it's perfectly safe," Ethan said with a smile and started walking up the plank. He turned and extended his hand to her. Still she didn't move.

"Why must you meet these men here? Why not in the city?" she asked.

"That will become clear soon enough."

Still, Samantha hesitated. "Who does this ship belong to?"

"Me," Ethan said simply as he reached down and placed her hand in his.

Samantha reluctantly walked up behind him, followed by Avery Scott. Ethan led the way toward the bow of the boat. They descended down a narrow set of stairs to a hallway dimly lit by lanterns. Ethan walked again to the bow and then knocked on a door. It was immediately opened by a stern-looking man of Ethan's age. He had dark-red hair and a full beard to match. His face was handsome and weathered from the wind and sun. When he saw Ethan, he broke into a broad smile.

"Ethan! It's about time you arrived. These Yankees were getting nervous," the man said in a lazy Southern drawl.

Ethan smiled. "And I'm sure you did everything you

could to put them at ease?"

"But of course!"

Ethan and the red-bearded man shook hands, and then the man stepped back to allow Ethan, Samantha, and Avery to enter the cabin. Once inside, he closed the door. Samantha looked around. The cabin was surprisingly roomy. It was paneled in honey-colored wood and held a table, several chairs, a small desk, and a curtained sleeping area.

"Sam, this is George Macon," Ethan said as he turned to the man. "George is the captain of this ship. George, may Miss Carter use your soap and water?"

"Miss?" Macon said with confusion.

Samantha looked to Ethan. He silently nodded his head.

"This way . . . uh . . . ma'am," Captain Macon said hesitantly as he directed her to a small table along the wall of the cabin.

Samantha was aware that Ethan was waiting for her. She washed the disguise off her face and then returned to where he and Avery were standing. Two men were sitting at the table. They stood as Ethan walked over to shake hands with them. Then Ethan turned and motioned for Samantha and Avery to approach.

"Gentlemen, I believe you know Lieutenant Scott, and may I present Miss Samantha Carter? Sam, this is Mr. Gerald Taper, my solicitor, and this man," Ethan hesitated, "why don't we just call him Yankee. No offense?" Ethan said to the other man.

"None taken, Mr. Hunt. Ma'am," the man said, inclining his head to Samantha.

"Miss Carter," Gerald Taper said in greeting.

Samantha could see surprise and uncertainty on the faces of the two men as they looked at her.

"I would like Miss Carter to remain," Ethan said, seeing the questioning looks on the two men's faces. "Shall we get down to business?" He turned to George Macon. "George, if you would make Miss Carter comfortable?"

The two men sat down at the table as Ethan joined them. The table was too small to accommodate five people, so Captain Macon placed two chairs against the wall for Avery and Samantha.

"Did you have any difficulties getting here?" Ethan asked the man he'd called Yankee.

"No. We set sail from Boston on one of your Federal freighters and then, once in open sea, transferred to this ship. I fear it won't be so easy on the return, though. Federal warships are headed this way."

"Captain Macon will set sail as soon as we have completed our business. Shall we begin?" Ethan asked. He removed papers from his coat. "All assets of Winters-Hunt Enterprises of Charleston are to be merged with those of Rhodes and Hunt of Boston. Stephen Roland, my solicitor in Charleston, is aware of these changes. All assets are to be listed under the ownership of Ethan Hunt and Nathaniel Rhodes, both of Boston. This includes all assets and properties now owned by Ethan Winters-Hunt and registered in the Confederate state of South Carolina."

Samantha frowned and turned to Avery. Before she could ask her question, Ethan continued.

"The laws of the State of Massachusetts, a Federal state, will now govern the disposition of all my property. As Ethan Hunt, I'm a well-established businessman of Boston and will be protected by Massachusetts' law. Winters-Hunt Enterprises of Charleston, a Confederate enterprise, will now be lawfully owned by a citizen of Massachusetts and, as such, cannot be confiscated as spoils of war by a victorious Federal soldier or any other legal maneuver. The ownership of the plantation Arabella is also to be transferred to Ethan Hunt of Boston. I'll need a copy of the immediate transfer of ownership before you leave. I will have it delivered to Arabella. That should protect the plantation should the Yankees ever reach that far."

Both of the men seated at the table looked up briefly. The utter destruction being leveled upon the South was well known.

"To the second order of business," Ethan continued. "My shares in the Bank of Boston, numbering fifty-two percent, are to be transferred immediately to Miss Samantha Carter to her sole ownership."

It was a moment before Samantha's mind registered what Ethan said. "You!" she said as she jumped up from her chair. "That's my grandfather's bank!" She advanced to the table. "When my grandfather died, he left the stock to his two daughters—my mother and aunt. My silly aunt married a Frenchman who promptly sold her interests. To you, Mr. Hunt?" Samantha asked, emphasizing the name.

"Not to me, but to my partner in Boston, Nathaniel Rhodes," Ethan answered.

"You lied to me! When I asked you to deliver a letter to that bank to be forwarded on to my father, you didn't say a word. You knew who I was," Samantha accused.

"I never lied to you, Sam. You took me by surprise when you gave me that letter. I saw no purpose in discussing business at that time. If you'll recall, you'd just been gravely wounded, and I'd just discovered that you were not the boy, Sam Cartier, but instead a young woman named Samantha Carter. I did not know of your family's connection to the bank."

"It was deceptive!"

"And your disguising yourself as a boy was not?" Ethan countered.

Ethan turned back to the men at the table, who stared at him with puzzlement. Samantha was still trying to grasp all that she had just learned when Ethan continued.

"There's one more document that needs your signature," Ethan said to his solicitor. "It relates to the matter of one Miss Samantha Carter, physician and surgeon. The letter details an account of the capture of Miss Carter, who was then disguised as a boy and using the name of Sam Cartier, outside of Arlington, Virginia on May 1, 1864. Dr. Carter was taken against her will behind Confederate lines and forced to serve as a surgeon in the Confederate Army. In the capacity of surgeon, she treated both Confederate and Federal soldiers. She attempted to escape on numerous occasions, but was returned to the Confederate Medical Corps.

"I have signed the document, as have Dr. Clement Beauregard and Lieutenant Avery Scott, both officers of the Army of Northern Virginia under the command of General Robert E. Lee. Should there ever be any question of Miss Carter's loyalty to the North, you are retained as council to represent her and to present this letter in her defense," Ethan concluded.

Samantha stared at Ethan. Everything was happening too fast. She was both confused and deeply moved by his gesture. Once again, he was protecting her. Before she could say anything, Ethan continued.

"That concludes my personal business. Now, do you have information for me?" Ethan asked of the man he called Yankee.

Samantha watched as the man withdrew papers from his coat and spread them out on the table. Avery stood and walked over to the table, leaving Samantha by herself.

"This is an analysis from the War Department in Washington. It details the position and strength of all the Union forces." The man placed another paper on top of it. "This is a summary of the latest communications from

General Grant. You can see he plans to move these regiments," the man said as he pointed to the paper.

Samantha listened in shock as the man continued to discuss the positions and strength of various Federal forces, as well as the North's military plans. Ethan studied the numbers before him.

"The North hasn't employed half of its men of fighting age, whereas we have used virtually all of ours," Ethan said. "We've no reserve. The North hasn't even brought all their resources to play," he said grimly as he surveyed the numbers.

"There's more," the Yankee man continued. "Five more ships will be leaving soon, heading for here. It won't be long, Mr. Hunt, before Wilmington is barricaded."

"And then we are strangled," Ethan said, "cut off from the rest of the world. Even using all my resources, I couldn't possibly ship enough food, clothing, or armaments overland to supply the Confederate Army."

"Grant's moving two additional divisions to close the lines to Petersburg, too," the Yankee man continued. "It's only a matter of time. Once Petersburg falls, there's nothing to stop him from marching on to Richmond, which, by all reports, will be his next move."

Ethan sighed. "I had discerned as much. Lee's forces have been defending Petersburg against Grant's larger forces for almost six months now. If General Lee retreats to Richmond, it'll be over." Ethan looked at the Yankee man. "Your reports are very thorough. In your opinion, what's the final estimate?"

"The Confederacy can't last more than a year, Mr. Hunt. It will probably be over in six months."

"And if General Lee surrenders?"

"General Grant will demand nothing less than an unconditional surrender. But Grant is a professional, Mr.

Hunt. He admires General Lee's skill and genius. He knows that Lee has outmaneuvered him countless times. If the Confederacy had the resources the North had, it would be Grant who'd be surrendering. I believe it will be done with honor."

The room was still. Ethan nodded. His shoulders slumped as he hung his head down.

"I'm sorry, Mr. Hunt," the Yankee man said. "You're a man with allegiance to two countries—two countries that are at war with each other. Both could not win."

"I know," Ethan said and leaned back in his chair. "Fate is a strange thing. Who would have guessed that all those years ago in London when I came upon thugs attacking a young man from Boston, by saving him, I would find myself in the position that I am in today? I saved his life and he became my best friend, only to die a few years later of some damn disease. His father, Nathaniel, became like a father to me, making me his heir in the place of his dead son.

"I wanted my business arrangements in the North with Nathaniel to be separate from my father's business in the South, Winters-Hunt Enterprises. I used my father's family name, Hunt, for my Northern business. I legalized the name Ethan Hunt and established my residence with Nathaniel in Boston for several months out of the year. Nathanial generously changed the name of his business to Rhodes and Hunt. I never dreamed that I would be at war with myself one day."

The room was quiet. Samantha was astounded. Finally, the pieces were fitting together. Ethan had always been so evasive about his position in the army. Samantha was shocked as the realization struck her. Ethan was a spy! He used his identity and contacts in the North to supply information to the South.

The spell was broken by Ethan. "Captain Macon, prepare

to set sail." Ethan stood and extended his hand to the men at the table. "Gentlemen," he said as they shook hands, "thank you. You'll depart as soon as Gerald has completed the papers transferring ownership of my properties. I won't contact you again until it's over. Safe journey."

"God speed, Mr. Hunt," the Yankee man responded.

"Lieutenant Scott, a word please," Ethan said as he walked over to where Avery and Samantha were standing. "You can leave immediately. Deliver these papers personally to General Lee. I'll take Sam to Arabella. That's the safest place for her until I can arrange for her transport north. General Lee will have new orders for me, although God only knows what else I can do," Ethan said sadly.

"Yes, sir."

The next few minutes passed in a flurry of activity as Lieutenant Scott departed, Captain Macon prepared to set sail, and Ethan and his solicitor signed documents. And then Ethan and Samantha were mounted on their horses, heading to Charleston. There was so much she wanted to say to him, but she could see he was lost in his own thoughts. So they rode in silence until sunset, when Ethan indicated they would make camp.

Samantha placed their blankets by the fire and sat down, but Ethan didn't join her. He remained standing, staring at the fire.

"Ethan?"

It was a moment before he answered her, and then his words surprised her.

"I don't know how to keep you safe," he said suddenly. "It had been my intent to send you back on my ship. You could have transferred to one of my Northern vessels while at sea, and then Gerald would have arranged for your return home. But with Federal warships heading toward

Wilmington, it was no longer safe. There was the chance they would fire on the Confederate vessel before you could transfer."

"I see," Samantha replied.

"No, Sam, I don't think you do. Arabella is safe for the time being, but once Sherman reaches Charleston, my maneuver back on the ship is no guarantee that the Yankees won't set fire to Arabella and shoot anyone trying to escape."

"Ethan!"

"It's happened, Sam. I've seen it happen." He ran his hand through his hair in exasperation.

Samantha jumped up and threw her arms around him. He crushed her to him. When he kissed her, she felt as though her body was awakening from a long, deep sleep. It'd been four months since she'd spent the week with Ethan at Arabella, and he had aroused desires in her that she hadn't known existed. Since that time, she'd seen him once, and it had been brief. That was when he'd left the food for her. She'd been too exhausted and grieved by the continuous casualties of the war to draw more from him than just a few hours' shelter.

Last week, when Ethan returned, she was plummeted into the events of her brother's escape. She'd been deeply wounded by her brother's words of hatred, and again she turned to Ethan for strength and shelter and found it with him.

Now, however, her body was remembering his touch, his caress, and the feel of him inside of her. She recalled the joy of being in his arms while at Arabella, and a wave of desire passed through her. She loved him, and time had not changed that.

They held each other closely through the night, giving free run to their passion and then resting in each other's arms. The pattern was repeated as they traveled south, riding during the day, avoiding the towns and farms in their path, and holding each other through the night, oblivious to the cold and rain.

They arrived at Arabella at the end of the first week of December. Arabella was just as beautiful as Samantha remembered. Even in the winter, the land was still green and the air sparkled in the cool temperatures. As they rode up the lane, the hounds ran to meet them as they had that first night Ethan had brought Samantha to Arabella. Molly and Fox were at the door as they stopped their horses.

"Ethan! We was wonderin' if you would be home for Christmas," Molly said, "and you brought Miss Samantha with you."

"And my old friend, Kota," Fox said as he stepped forward to the horses.

"My goodness, child! Just look at you!" Molly exclaimed, surveying Samantha's appearance. "You're skin and bones! You look like you haven't eaten in months. And you still ain't got proper clothin'. Runnin' all 'round the country in men's pants. It ain't fittin'. I'll get to makin' some more alterations while you eat some of Molly's cookin'," she said.

Molly was true to her word, for over the next several days, she appeared with a complete array of women's clothing that she adjusted to Samantha's slim form. There were day dresses, evening gowns, riding habits, as well as lingerie and complete accessories. At one point, Samantha inquired about the source of all of the gowns. Who did they belong to?

"They's yours now," Molly said with a smile.

Ethan's response to her question was even more perplexing. He had come into her room moments later. For an instant, Samantha saw a dark shadow come over his face, but he didn't immediately answer her.

"They're of the finest workmanship and design," Samantha continued, "made by the leading couturiers of Europe. Most of them look as though they've never been worn."

"I don't believe they ever were," he said stiffly, "but I really wouldn't know." He turned abruptly and walked to the door.

"Ethan?"

He looked back and smiled, the expression of a moment ago gone. "I'll saddle the horses and wait for you outside. Put something on, or if you wish, you may come like that," he said, letting his gaze roam over her half-clad form.

"You go on and get out of here! Don't go talkin' to Miss Samantha like that, not when I'm around," Molly said as she pushed Ethan out the door.

Samantha laughed, for Molly, Fox, and Frederick were obviously aware of her relationship with Ethan. Ethan moved about his plantation with ease and was openly affectionate with her, as though it was perfectly natural for her to be sharing his bed at night as well as his companionship throughout the days.

During the first week at Arabella, Samantha's days were filled with love and laughter as Ethan rarely left her side for long. Her nights were consumed with passion as she eagerly returned Ethan's lovemaking. She felt contented, something she had never known outside of Ethan's arms. He, alone, seemed to be able to soothe the tide that had always raced within her, giving her peace.

At the end of the first week, Ethan, Samantha, and Frederick were eating dinner together when their conversation was interrupted by the sounds of the hounds barking. Ethan frowned as he and Frederick both stood.

Molly entered the dining room, looking worried.

"Stay here," Ethan said to Samantha as he and Frederick left.

"Who could it be, Molly?" Samantha asked.

"Don't know this time of night. These days, things is real jumpy 'round here."

Samantha was surprised when, a few minutes later, Ethan and Frederick returned with Avery Scott.

"Molly, another place for the lieutenant," Ethan said.

Avery walked over to Samantha. "Cousin Samantha," he said with a smile as he raised her hand to his lips.

"Avery, it's good to see you," Samantha said sincerely.

Avery turned back to Ethan and took the seat next to him. He handed a paper to Ethan. Samantha watched as Ethan unfolded the paper and read it. She noticed the slight pallor that came to his face, but then it was gone. His face was rigid as he held the paper over the candle on the table. As the paper curled up, its brown remains fell in ashes onto the white linen tablecloth.

"There's more," Avery said. "Fort McAllister has fallen."

Ethan sighed and closed his eyes briefly. "Savannah?" he asked quietly.

Avery shrugged. "No news yet."

"Once Sherman captures Savannah, he'll turn north. God help us when he reaches Charleston," Ethan said.

Both men were silent, each contemplating the terrible reality to come. Ethan broke the silence.

"Did you read General Lee's orders?" Ethan asked his lieutenant as he stared at the charred remains laying on the table.

"Yes, sir," Avery responded.

"We'll go see Major Clark tomorrow. I'm not certain I can be of much use to General Lee from this point on. He'll see for himself what Grant and Sherman's plans are. We all will," Ethan said softly.

Samantha listened a few minutes more as Avery and Ethan talked, and then she excused herself and left the room. Even though Ethan had predicted that it would come to this, Samantha could tell that the inevitable march against South Carolina and Charleston had affected him deeply. She was thinking about him as she walked out onto the front porch. What if Arabella was destroyed?

It was a cloudless night and the stars were bright. She was staring at the sky when her eyes were drawn to the moon. It would be full tomorrow night. She suddenly gasped. Full tomorrow night! She did some rapid calculations in her mind. Her monthly courses were several days late. She'd never been late! Never! She'd learned to count the days carefully the past two and a half years, while masquerading as a boy, so that she was prepared.

"No, it can't be," she whispered to herself. "A few days' delay doesn't mean a thing."

But what if it was true? Why hadn't she thought of that possibility before? She had been foolish. Again! How would she tell Ethan? She recalled the number of times he had told her that they could have no future together. He never spoke of one. In fact, he'd made it clear to her that there could be no promises made between them, no words of love exchanged.

Samantha sat down on the steps. Did he love her? Certainly they had a passionate physical relationship. And he had protected and cared for her. He had provided for her financial security. She thought of all the hours they had spent together. Suddenly, the image of Caroline Cooper intruded upon her mind. Previously, he had a relationship with Caroline. Was it different from what he shared with her?

With a cold shock, Samantha realized just how precarious

her relationship was with Ethan. In the year she had known him, they had only spent three weeks as lovers—the past two weeks and one week after she had been wounded and he brought her here. Despite the hours of lovemaking and companionship, there was nothing conventional about their relationship. So why was she thinking that Ethan might behave conventionally if he knew that she was pregnant? She felt a sense of panic begin within her. She couldn't possibly tell Ethan—not yet. It might not even be true.

She waited outside a few more minutes, taking deep breaths to calm herself. When she finally entered the house, she found Ethan and Avery still in the dining room. Frederick and Molly were also there. Samantha hesitated at the door until Ethan beckoned her in.

For the first time in weeks, she felt like an outsider. Ethan and Frederick were discussing Arabella and the means of protecting it when the Yankees came. Arabella would be too much of a temptation for the Yankees, with its rich fields, ample supply of food, and, of course, the horses. Even with the documents of ownership, the plantation was vulnerable.

They discussed the destruction caused by Sherman's advance and the inevitable capture of Savannah next. As Samantha listened to these people talk about defending their home from the invasion of the enemy, she realized that she was the enemy. The defensive actions that Ethan and Avery discussed were against her people, her country.

"The area planters are meeting tomorrow night at the Cooper Plantation," Ethan said. "They've asked Major Clark to address their concerns."

"Do you want me to come with you?" Avery asked.

"That's not necessary. You've more important matters to attend to," Ethan said.

Avery nodded his head in understanding. After a while,

Samantha excused herself on the pretext of being tired; however, she lay awake a long time, confused by her own thoughts. It was in this very bed that it all had started. No, that wasn't true. She realized now that Ethan had the power to affect her even when she'd been disguised as a boy. She just hadn't recognized the emotions for what they were—she'd fallen in love with him. Sometime in the months between his capture of her and before she'd been wounded, her feelings for Ethan had gone from fear to trust and finally to love.

She thought about the past two weeks with him and that other week so long ago. She laughed, despite herself, when she recalled the time she had pulled the knife on him and of all the battles they'd had when he thought she was a boy. She was suddenly overcome with the feeling that it was all coming to an end. He'd tried to tell her that, hadn't he? Just what had she expected?

It was during the early hours of the morning when Samantha finally fell asleep. Ethan still had not joined her.

CHAPTER 11

Samantha awoke the next morning to muted footsteps in the bedroom. She opened her eyes to see Ethan buttoning his shirt as he finished dressing. Sensing her movement, he turned and smiled.

Samantha wrinkled her brow. "I didn't hear you come to bed last night."

"I didn't," Ethan said simply.

She sat up in the bed. As she did, she pulled the linens over herself to cover her nakedness. Ethan saw the gesture and smiled. "How is it that you can make love with complete abandon one moment and be modest the next?" he asked. He bent over and kissed her deeply on her lips. "I have business in Charleston. Would you like to go with me? You would need to disguise yourself, of course."

Ten minutes later, Samantha was mounted on Kota, and they were riding away from Arabella. Suddenly, Ethan started laughing. She turned to him. "Why are you laughing?" she asked.

"Sam, I don't think you realize how effective your disguise is. It's not just your attire and facial hair; it's also your actions, the way you move. I look at you riding your horse, and I can't believe you're the same woman who shares my bed. You sit a horse better than any cavalry man I've ever seen."

"I grew up roping and herding cattle, and the Lakota warriors were exceptional horsemen."

He shook his head and smiled at her. "I think I'll conclude my business quickly so that we can return to Arabella and spend the afternoon together. What do you say?"

"I say the sooner we get to Charleston, the sooner we get back to Arabella." She had barely finished speaking when Kota shot forward, his powerful legs leaving Ethan behind.

Eventually, Samantha slowed Kota so Ethan could catch up with her. When they arrived in Charleston, they went to the docks first. Samantha remembered the first time she had come here with Ethan. The cannon fire from the Union Ironsides pounding away at the Battery and Forts Sumter and Moultrie had frightened her. The thundering of the cannons continued this day, but Samantha no longer flinched at the sound.

They left the docks and rode to Ethan's offices. At his suggestion, Samantha waited outside while Ethan went inside. An hour later he emerged, a grim expression on his face. She watched him place a piece of paper in his coat pocket. "Let's go," he said.

She wanted to ask what was troubling him, but decided against it. They rode in silence, Ethan deep in thought, until they reached Arabella. As they entered the lane leading to the house, Ethan turned to her. "My apologies, Sam. This wasn't how I thought the afternoon would be. Avery will be arriving shortly. He and I must talk privately."

"I understand. Is there anything I can do?"

For the first time since leaving Charleston, he smiled at her. "You can wash that silly beard off your face and accompany me to the Cooper Plantation tonight."

"The meeting you mentioned last night?"

"Yes. The planters will be there with their wives. Caroline will serve dinner before the men retire to discuss matters."

Samantha spent the afternoon alone. After a leisurely bath, she selected one of the gowns Molly had adjusted for her. It was not as fancy as the one she had worn to the last dinner party Caroline Cooper had given. This gown was much simpler and yet elegant in its simplicity. The bodice, although deeply cut like all of the gowns Molly altered for her, was made of soft, cream-colored lace over silk. The skirt was a deep chestnut brown, full over Samantha's hoops. It was trimmed in a lace that matched the bodice. The contrast of the light bodice and dark skirt, and Samantha's own dark hair nearly matching the color of the skirt, was striking.

When she emerged from the bedroom, Ethan and Fox were waiting on the portico. Fox smiled at her. "Ain't never seen no boy lookin' so lovely, Miss Samantha," he said.

"Thank you, Fox, but the credit goes to Molly. My hair, the gown—all Molly's magic touch," Samantha said, smiling. Ethan started to help her into the carriage, but Samantha stopped. "Ethan, I can't forget my medical bag."

"Sam, you won't need that tonight."

"You're probably right, but do you mind?"

"And how do we explain that, Miss Seymour?"

"We'll leave it in the carriage. No one need know."

When they arrived at Caroline Cooper's plantation, the other guests were discussing the events at hand. Caroline welcomed them warmly and then moved on to oversee the preparations for dinner. As Ethan and Samantha greeted the other guests, Samantha noticed the splendid attire of most of the dozen women present. She leaned over to Ethan and whispered, "It doesn't look as though the war has touched these people at all."

Ethan understood the meaning of her comment. "They have, through generations of training, learned to ignore what is ugly around them."

Samantha was nervous as Major Clark came over to speak to them. As the minutes went by, she relaxed, seeing that he did not suspect her identity.

At another point, Samantha felt Ethan tense. She looked up to see Gerald Depardeu across the room. Depardeu didn't attempt to hide his animosity as he nodded to Ethan. He then turned his eyes to Samantha. Although he smiled and bowed slightly from the waist, Samantha shivered. She recalled the night that they had been attacked on the road. Ethan was certain that Gerald Depardeu and Franklin Montgomery had been responsible for the attempted murder. When Samantha had questioned Ethan about his suspicions, he'd refused to discuss the matter further.

To Samantha's further dismay, when it came time for dinner, she found that she had been placed next to Gerald Depardeu. Caroline seated her two-dozen guests at the elegant, long table with husbands and wives separate, thus distributing the unequal number of men and women present. Samantha noted that Ethan had been placed at the other end of the table on Caroline's right side.

Samantha did her best to talk with the middle-aged planter on the other side of her and the young woman across from her. She spoke to Gerald Depardeu only when he addressed her directly, and then she kept her responses brief. She was relieved when the meal was over, and Caroline invited the ladies to join her in the parlor. She tried hard not to look at Ethan, but just as she was exiting the room, she glanced back in his direction. Immediate warmth spread through her body, and she felt her pulse quicken. She smiled to herself as she averted her gaze and followed the women out of the room.

Ethan had surreptitiously watched as Samantha left the

room and hadn't missed her glance at him. He still couldn't believe she'd been able to fool him all those months. How could he have believed she was a boy? He could read her so well now. Even across the crowded room, he'd seen the desire that had filled her eyes. He smiled to himself, and then turned to focus on Major Clark's words.

"We'll extend the earthwork fortifications," Major Clark was explaining to one of the planters when there was a commotion outside the window. He stopped talking and walked over to the window. Several men rose from their seats to join him.

"What's happening out there?" a man asked.

"Several Negroes are looking at something on the ground," another responded.

Ethan walked into the hallway just as Caroline emerged from the ladies' parlor with one of her Negroes. She closed the door and turned to Ethan.

"What is it, Caroline?" Ethan asked.

"He says there's been an accident and one of my people is hurt." She turned to the Negro. "Where is he?"

"Right outside the door, Miz Cooper."

The rest of the planters came out into the hall and followed Caroline and Ethan out to the front of the house.

"Get a lantern," Caroline said as they stepped down from the portico.

The slave Job was lying on the ground with several other slaves crowded around him. As the lantern was brought forward, he could be seen writhing on the ground, his cries of pain muffled by his clenched jaw. Caroline jumped back when she saw the mangled flesh of his thigh, the blood already staining the dirt in front of the porch. One of the planters took Caroline's arm to support her. Another knelt down by the slave.

"The bone is sticking out through the skin. He's a

gonner, poor buzzard," the planter said.

"Oh, Job," Caroline said.

"What happened?" another asked.

"The horse spooked and knocked Job down, then done run over him," one of the Negroes said while he held the horse and carriage at bay.

"That's my horse," one of the planters said. "I'm awfully sorry, Mrs. Cooper."

"What a mess," another planter said. "He'll not live."

"Get Sam!" Ethan shouted as he knelt down by the injured slave. "Hurry!" No one moved. Ethan turned to see a confused look on Caroline's face. He turned to the Negro standing next to him. "You. Go into the house and bring Miss Seymour. She's with the ladies."

Samantha and the women were sitting in the parlor, wondering what the excitement was all about, when a Negro knocked on the door and entered. "Miss Seymour?" he said as he looked expectantly at each woman.

"I'm Miss Seymour," Samantha said.

"Mr. Winters-Hunt is askin' for ya, ma'am. They's all outside."

Samantha excused herself and followed the man out onto the porch of the house. "Ethan?" she called, unable to see past the crowd of men.

"Sam, over here!"

The men moved aside as Samantha lifted her skirts and hurried down the steps. She rushed over to where Job lie on the ground and knelt down, heedless of the blood soaking through her skirt. "Hold his leg," she said to Ethan as she began to tear away the remaining shreds of the man's pants. "He'll bleed to death if we don't stop this."

Ethan gently lifted the leg as she placed the strips of torn cloth around Job's thigh. "I need my bag, and we must move him someplace where I can work."

Ethan looked up to another one of the slaves standing back. "My carriage is over there. Do you know which one it is?"

"I knows, sir," another slave answered.

"Get Dr. Cartier's medical bag. It's on the seat of my carriage." He stood and looked to the other Negroes. "You men help me carry him to the kitchen."

"You can't do nothin' for the poor buck, Miss Seymour," one of the planters said. "Just let him go."

"I'm sorry, Mrs. Cooper," another man spoke. "My horse did it. I'll pay for it. Just tell me what he was worth to you."

"Don't count your money yet, Mrs. Cooper. He may just live. Of course, his value may be less, now," Samantha ground out, the pretense of a Southern accent gone.

Caroline didn't answer, for she was staring wide-eyed at Samantha. Samantha ignored the shocked look on Caroline's face as a Negro approached with her medical bag. She grabbed it and followed as Ethan and the other Negroes carried Job through the long hall of the house and out the back door to the kitchen building.

As Ethan and the slaves carried Job into the kitchen, Bessie turned. "Oh, Lordy! Job! What happened?"

Samantha rushed ahead of the men and cleared the table.

"It's you!" Bessie exclaimed as she recognized Samantha. "Dr. Sam!"

Samantha paused for a moment. "Bessie, right? Bessie, I need clean cloths, water, and soap."

"Yessum."

Samantha loosened the cloth on Job's leg. The blood immediately began to soak the table. She pushed her sleeves up and removed needle, thread, vascular clamps, and a scalpel from her bag.

"Ethan, can you help me?" she asked without looking up.

From that point on, Samantha focused all her attention on the man lying on the table before her. "Job," Samantha said, leaning over the man. "I'm going to try to set this bone in your leg and sew you back together. It's going to hurt, though. You've got to stay as still as you can."

Ethan motioned for the remaining slaves to hold Job. As Samantha began to dissect away skin and muscle, searching for the bleeding vessels, Job shrieked and jerked.

"Let me die! Let me die!" he screamed as he tried to twist from under the grasp of the men.

"You listen to me, Job!" a voice cut in. Bessie pushed between the two men who were holding Job down on the table. "I done watched Chloe's belly bein' cut wide open with a knife to bring that boy of yours into this world, and she barely made a sound. Because of Doc Sam, here, you still have a wife and a fine baby. Now you hold still like she tell you! You hear me, boy?"

Someone placed a wooden spoon in Job's mouth, and he bit down on it as Samantha resumed working. When at last she had located and tied all the torn blood vessels, she turned to Ethan. "Once the bone is set, I'm going to need something to splint the leg."

Ethan nodded and returned a few minutes later with wooden poles. Bessie tore strips of cloth. "All right, Ethan," Samantha said, "when I tell you, pull his lower leg this way, and I'll set the bone back in place." As Ethan complied, Job let out a final scream and sank into unconsciousness.

Samantha secured the leg and then sutured the muscle and skin back in place. Finally, she wrapped the wound securely in clean bandages and fixed the poles as splints to immobilize the bone.

"Bessie, I don't know if he'll keep the leg," she said when she finished. "He's young and strong but he bled a lot; breaks like that don't always heal." She wiped her hand across her forehead, unaware that she had smeared blood on her face. Her bodice of once cream-colored lace was now crimson with blood. "He's not going to be able to move for some time. He must remain in bed with the splints in place. It's very important—assuming he doesn't develop a fever and die in the next few days—that he doesn't move his leg. I'll show you how to roll him on his side to take care of him. With luck, in eight to ten weeks, he'll be walking again, with a limp, of course."

Ethan procured a flat board to place Job on. Samantha showed Bessie and the others how to roll him, keeping the leg straight. She also instructed Bessie how to change the bandage without disturbing the splint.

"We'll take him to his cabin now," Bessie said. "Chloe don't know yet."

Samantha smiled briefly. "Chloe, how's young Sam doing?"

"The fattest baby you ever done see."

"Thanks, Bessie," Samantha said as she placed her arm around the large black woman's shoulders. "That leg is going to hurt like hell when he wakes up, and I don't have any medicine to give him for the pain. You better have a few men there to make sure he doesn't thrash around until he understands."

"I'll see to it. Now why don't you sit down over here?" Bessie said as she pulled a chair out near a smaller table. "Darcy," Bessie called. A young Negro woman appeared. "Get some soap and water so that Miss Sam can clean up, and then get some hot coffee for her. Have one of the other girls scrub this up," she said, indicating the blood-drenched table and floor. Then she followed Ethan and the men out of the kitchen.

Darcy, her dark face paler as she looked around, hesitantly approached with a bucket of water, soap, and linens. Samantha smiled at the young Negro. "Thank you," Samantha said. Darcy waited until Samantha had washed the blood from her hands and arms and then removed the soiled water and linen. As Darcy reached for the coffeepot, a feminine voice cut in. "I'll do that. You see that this is cleaned up, like Bessie told you."

Samantha looked up to see Caroline Cooper take the coffeepot from the stove. Her hands shook as she poured two cups of coffee and brought them to the small table where Samantha was seated. Caroline was very pale as she sat down, placing a cup in front of Samantha. Her face was rigid, although Samantha noted that she winced as she looked at her blood-soaked gown.

"So," she began in a restrained tone, "it appears that I am beholden to you twice now, Dr. Sam Cartier, or is it Samantha Seymour?"

"Both, I guess. Samantha Carter is my name."

"I see. And what else was the truth and what was deception?"

Samantha was quiet a moment. "Sam's story was the nearest to the truth. I am from the North. I did study medicine in Paris, but I'm not French."

"And Lieutenant Scott?"

"We're not related."

"And does he know who you are?"

"Yes, he does."

Caroline pinched her lips together. "And was Ethan a part of this all along?"

"No," Samantha said evenly, "he thought I was a boy. He only discovered I was a woman in early July."

"Oh, yes," Caroline said, restraining her anger. "That was when Lieutenant Scott brought Miss Seymour to my party instead of Sam. Ethan knew then."

"Yes."

"You must have had a good time, Miss Carter, foolin' we poor, stupid Confederates," Caroline said with anger. "I welcomed you into my home, and you made a mockery of that hospitality!"

This was the first time that Samantha had seen Caroline without her air of gentility. She couldn't help but feel sorry for her. "No," Samantha said softly, "I never mocked you, although it's true that I was never comfortable here."

"Oh, yes, that's right! According to you Yankees, we are cruel, immoral people, whippin' our slaves, chaining them up like dogs." Caroline leveled her gaze upon Samantha. "Well, tell me, Miss Carter, or whoever you are, have you seen anything like that here?"

Samantha looked over at the two young Negro girls scrubbing the table and floor. She turned back to Caroline. "No," she said simply, "but you tell me, Mrs. Cooper, how much money would you have demanded from that planter to replace your damaged property?"

"You don't understand," Caroline said fervently. "I take my responsibilities and obligations seriously, and that includes caring for my people. I take care of my people!

"We have an ordered way of life here. Everything is in its place, and there is peace, not like up north where people are always rushin' around, fightin', and have the manners of bullfrogs. And you call us uncivilized!"

Samantha blinked. "Bullfrogs?" She couldn't help it. After all that had happened that evening, Caroline's criticism struck her as funny. She tried to cover her mouth, but a smile crept out. "Actually, that's not a bad description. I've met a few men like that."

Caroline seemed momentarily confused by Samantha's smile. Then she sighed, the anger of a minute ago dissipating. "We've got men like that down here, too," Caroline confessed, the two women sharing common ground for the moment. "Several of them thought they should marry me when I became a widow. They didn't think a woman could possibly run this plantation alone."

Samantha nodded her head in understanding. She took a sip of her coffee, pondering what to say next to Caroline Cooper. "I've been in the South for almost a year now," Samantha began, "and one thing I've learned is that things are not as simple as I once tried to make them. While cruelty exists, it exists on both sides, as does goodness."

Caroline glanced at the Negro woman scrubbing the table. "The Yankees will destroy us, won't they?" She stood up, not waiting for Samantha to answer. She carried both cups over to the stove and refilled them. As she brought them back, she sat down and looked directly at Samantha. "Why are you here in the Confederacy? Was the story about Sam true? Were you forced to care for Confederate soldiers?"

Samantha thought for a moment. "Yes, it's true that a Confederate patrol captured me when I was on my way to the Union Medical Corps. Ethan forced me to come with him, and yes, he literally dragged me into that first Confederate surgical tent, but no one forced me to care for those men. I'm a medicine woman," she said softy. "I'm a doctor, a surgeon."

Samantha looked down, embarrassed by her own emotion, and then continued. "At first, I used to watch for a chance to escape and go back north. Ethan guarded me closely," she said with chagrin, "and when he wasn't there, I was so busy with the wounded that escape wasn't even a consideration.

"After a while, I couldn't leave," Samantha said. "I still believe the Confederacy is wrong. But," she continued, "I've learned that it's not an even fight. You're outnumbered. You have inferior weapons. You lack sufficient food, clothing, and medical supplies. It's only been the genius of General Lee and a few others that have kept you going this long. This is where I'm needed the most." Samantha looked directly into Caroline's eyes. "I believe that the day will come when we'll no longer be enemies but one Union again."

Caroline didn't speak immediately. When she did, she watched Samantha closely. "I'm not so certain that many men, on either side, would be as compassionate to the enemy. Is that the only reason why you've stayed?"

Samantha didn't answer, but looked away.

"And does your family approve of this?" Caroline asked.

"They don't know," Samantha said quietly.

"They don't know where you are? Do they think you're with the Federal Army?"

"No." Samantha turned back to Caroline. "It's a long story," she said, shrugging. She briefly recounted her story. "And that's when Lieutenant Quicken and Ethan captured me," she concluded.

"Good Lord!" Caroline exclaimed. "And your father and brothers still don't know where you are?"

"When I was wounded, Ethan discovered I was a woman. He sent a telegram to my father, telling him that I was safe. The telegram didn't say where I was."

"I still can't believe it. It is absolutely unconscionable that Ethan, or anyone on General Lee's staff, would force a woman, even if she is a surgeon, into duty."

"After I was wounded, only Ethan, Lieutenant Scott, and Dr. Clement Beauregard knew I was a woman. Everyone else still thought that I was a boy. When Ethan found out, he did try to send me back, but I refused."

"I believe I understand. You're in love with him," Caroline said evenly.

Samantha looked away and stood up. "I really had better

be going...."

"Samantha, please sit down. I don't mean to pry, and I'm not your enemy. I misjudged you, and for that I apologize. Please, sit. You may not believe this, but I bear you no ill will. I'm grateful to you for what you did for Chloe and Job, and, perhaps more importantly, for what you've done for our Confederate soldiers. I admire you." Caroline smiled briefly. "I actually like you, and I think that perhaps under different circumstances, we could have been friends."

Samantha was uncomfortable, but she sat down.

"Ethan is in love with you," Caroline said. "I've known him many years, and I've never seen him look at another woman the way he looks at you, and it's obvious that you love him. Are you lovers?"

Samantha was shocked at Caroline's blatant question and felt herself blush under Caroline's scrutinizing gaze.

"I thought so," Caroline continued. "You must forgive my impropriety. That's not something a lady would ask another, but these aren't conventional times, are they? How much do you know about Ethan?"

Samantha frowned. "What do you mean?"

"Nothing," Caroline said. "You should go back home, Samantha."

Samantha stiffened at Caroline's words.

"Despite what you must think of me," Caroline said, "I'm thinking of your welfare. Things can never be the way you'd like them to be."

The two women stared at each other.

"I should go check on Job," Samantha said as she stood up suddenly, ending the conversation. She walked as far as the door when Caroline spoke again.

"Samantha, if you should ever need anything...."

Samantha didn't turn around, but she paused at the door before hastening outside. She stepped out into the night, the ground lit by the lights of the great house. She started walking in the direction of the slave cabins when a voice called to her.

"Miss Carter?"

Samantha turned around to see Major Clark walking toward her. "Major, you startled me," she said.

"My apologies, ma'am. Major Winters-Hunt is in the house with the other planters. He asked me to escort you there when you're ready to leave," Major Clark said.

"I need to see Job before I go."

"I'll accompany you, with your permission, of course," he said.

"Of course." Samantha looked up at the man standing before her. "Are you angry with me, Major?"

"Ma'am?"

"For deceiving you by presenting myself as a boy," Samantha said.

"You saved the lives of hundreds of men under my command. I'm forever in your debt." Major Clark bowed slightly, offering his arm. Samantha started to take it and then stepped back. She looked down at the bodice and sleeves of her dress that were still covered in blood.

"Your uniform, it would be ruined," Samantha said in apology as she disengaged herself.

Major Clark reached out and took Samantha's hand, placing it through his arm, ignoring the dampness still on her dress. They walked in silence to the slave quarters, and then Major Clark waited outside the cabin while Samantha examined Job. Satisfied, Samantha and Major Clark returned to the house. As they approached the front door, Samantha hesitated.

"Major, I'd prefer not to go into the house like this," she said, indicating her gown. "Would you please ask Major Winters-Hunt if it's possible to leave now?"

"Of course," Major Clark said, raising Samantha's hand to his lips. Then he turned and entered the house. Samantha walked over to one of the large, white columns and leaned against it. Altogether, it had been a strange night.

When she heard footsteps behind her, she thought that perhaps Ethan was outside. She turned, expecting to see him, but was surprised to see Gerald Depardeu walk up to her.

"An abolitionist!" he hissed. "I should have guessed." His face was close to hers, his breath foul. "Abolitionist trash! That's nigger blood on you, girl. How does it feel?"

In that instant, Depardeu was spun around as Ethan's fist slammed into his jaw. A crack pierced the air as fist connected with bone. Blood spurted from Depardeu's mouth. As he reached for his chin, Ethan sank his other fist into Depardeu's midsection, knocking the wind out of the man, causing him to double over. As he started to sink to the ground, Ethan's knee came up to meet Depardeu's face, breaking his nose.

"Ethan!"

Ethan let Depardeu crumble on the ground before him. He turned to Samantha. "Are you all right?"

"Yes," she said.

Gerald Depardeu was moaning on the ground. Major Clark came out to the porch as another man helped Depardeu to stand.

"Did you see it? Did you see what he did? I want him arrested!" Depardeu screamed.

"I'm sorry, Mr. Depardeu, I saw nothing," Major Clark said.

"My nose is broken, my jaw, too!" Depardeu screamed in pain.

"If you two gentlemen have a dispute, perhaps you should settle it as gentlemen," Major Clark suggested.

"Should you wish to challenge Mr. Winters-Hunt to a duel, I will see that it is fairly executed."

"Careful, Mr. Depardeu," a nearby planter cautioned. "Mr. Winters-Hunt is known to be one of the best marksmen in South Carolina."

"Get my horse," Depardeu yelled.

One of the Negroes appeared almost immediately with Depardeu's horse. Depardeu jerked the reins out of his hand and climbed clumsily into the saddle. He looked back only briefly, turning a murderous look upon Ethan, and then he delivered a vicious kick to his horse and left.

"I've thanked Caroline for her hospitality and told her that we're leaving. I think we've had enough excitement for the night, don't you?" Ethan asked as he took Samantha's arm.

It was not until the carriage was well away from Caroline's plantation that Samantha spoke. "Ethan," she began hesitantly, "what do we do now? Everyone knows who I am, and that man, Depardeu. . . ." She shuddered.

Ethan pulled her close to him. "I'll take care of Depardeu in good time," he said. "For tonight, I just want to be with you. I have to leave in the morning."

"Leave? Where are you going?"

"No questions, Sam."

"But Ethan—"

"Please, Sam," he said quietly.

Samantha didn't press Ethan for any more answers. She'd seen Major Clark give him a letter earlier in the evening and watched as Ethan read it, his face a mixture of sadness and resignation. They rode home in silence, the questions remaining in Samantha's mind.

CHAPTER 12

Samantha dressed carefully as Molly prepared breakfast for her. Surely Ethan would be back today; it was December 24, the day before Christmas. It'd been a week since Caroline Cooper's dinner. When Ethan and Samantha had gone to their room after returning to Arabella, he'd made love to her during the night, holding her closely afterward. He was unusually quiet that night. Once or twice, in the moonlight, when he thought she was asleep, Samantha caught him staring intently at her.

"What is it?" she'd asked. His answer had completely confused her, given the passion they'd just shared.

"I fear the day will come when I will cause you great pain," he had said.

"Ethan, how can you say such a thing?" Samantha had replied, reaching out to him.

"Will you be able to return to the North, Samantha, and forget about me? You must go on with your life. Go back to your family and forget it all—the war, the killing, your own wounds and pain, and me."

Tears formed in Samantha's eyes.

"Sam, remember this always: there won't be a day in my life that I won't long to have you by my side, to see your face, to hear your voice, nor a night when I won't reach for you. But, for your sake, I should never have loved you. You must forget me."

He'd seen how distressed she'd become and pulled her

closer to him, refusing to discuss the topic anymore. Then, in the morning, he'd told her that he'd have to leave for several days.

That was one week ago. How she'd missed him! As she put the finishing touches on her hair, she came to a decision. She was certain she was one month pregnant. She would tell Ethan when he returned. No matter what their differences, surely they could overcome them. This war was not going to last much longer. Even Ethan said that. Samantha was still thinking of this when she heard sounds coming from outside. Perhaps Ethan was back!

She ran to the window and pushed the lace curtain aside. A carriage pulled up, one that Samantha didn't recognize. She watched as a portly man disembarked and then turned, offering his hand to a woman. Samantha jumped back, recognizing the man. It was the same man who'd been with Gerald Depardeu last summer. The men had met Ethan and Samantha in the stable behind the hotel in Charleston. Shortly after that, several men had ambushed Ethan and Samantha on the road. Ethan had been certain that Gerald Depardeu and this man had been responsible.

Samantha stepped back to the window. Molly came out of the house. Samantha watched as a woman stepped out of the carriage. The woman looked briefly up at Molly and then turned to the man beside her. Caroline Cooper! What was she doing with that man, and why had they come to Arabella? Samantha was even more surprised when several Negroes started unloading trunks from the back of the carriage. When they were all on the ground, the man turned back to Caroline and kissed her on the cheek. Samantha watched as he got back into the carriage and departed.

Samantha heard the door open and voices in the large hall below. She turned, checked her appearance in the mirror once more, and walked to the door of the bedroom. The fact that Caroline might decide to come to visit was not such a strange thing, but it looked as though she was moving in. Samantha hurried to the front steps.

"Molly," Samantha began as she descended the stairs. She stopped as the woman with Molly turned her attention toward Samantha's voice. It was not Caroline at all! Samantha didn't move as the woman looked up at her. The resemblance was there, but on closer inspection, Samantha could see differences. Both women had blonde hair and fair complexions and were about the same height. But where Caroline Cooper was very pretty, this woman was perhaps one of the most beautiful women Samantha had ever seen. Her face was perfect, as though made of fine porcelain, and her eyes were a deep-blue color. She arched an eyebrow as she took in Samantha's presence and then slowly removed her hat and handed it to Molly.

"Do we have a guest, Molly?" the woman asked.

A peculiar sensation came over Samantha as she watched the women below. Molly's face was stricken as she glanced up at Samantha and back to the woman before her.

"Molly! I asked you a question!" The softness left the woman's voice, and Molly shifted uncomfortably.

"Miss Samantha is a houseguest, Miss Juliet," Molly answered.

"Of course," the woman answered, "a guest of Mr. Ethan's, if I'm not mistaken." The woman turned back to Samantha. "Well, perhaps we should become acquainted, Miss. . . ."

A sick feeling came over Samantha as she walked down the steps. "Carter, Samantha Carter."

The woman nodded. "Miss Carter." She turned to Molly. "Molly, bring some refreshments to the parlor. I should like to talk with Miss Carter."

"Miss Juliet," Molly began, "don't—"

"Molly, has your hearing gone bad on you? I said to bring refreshments. Mr. Ethan may allow you certain liberties, but I will not. Now go at once!" She dismissed Molly and crossed the hall to an open door. She glanced back at Samantha. "Miss Carter, would you care to join me?" She didn't wait for an answer but walked into the room.

Samantha swallowed, for the nausea she was feeling at the moment was very real.

Molly looked up briefly as Samantha descended the remaining steps. Her face held both pity and sorrow in it. When Samantha paused at the bottom of the steps to speak, Molly turned toward the back of the house. Samantha walked to the door of the parlor.

"Ah, Miss Carter, won't you come in?" the woman said. She was standing in the room, and Samantha could not help but notice her regal bearing. "It's not often that I meet one of Ethan's. . . ." The woman paused. "What shall we call you, Miss Carter?"

"I beg your pardon?" Samantha said as she walked into the room.

"You're not from around here, are you?" the woman drawled. "No, I don't believe you are. If I'm not mistaken, you're a Yankee." The woman's eyes had grown cold despite the smile upon her face.

"Yes, I'm from the North," Samantha answered, the sickening feeling in her stomach becoming greater.

"Tell me, Miss Carter, did he tell you that you could keep the gown?" the woman asked, glancing momentarily at the dress Samantha was wearing. "Was that part of your price?" The beautiful woman turned and sat down on a nearby chair. "Times must be harder on poor Ethan than I thought if he must now turn to Yankee whores. And he brought you to Arabella? He's never done that before."

Samantha was trembling. If it weren't for the sickening

feeling, she could at least say something.

"Well, I really don't mind. I never wore any of those gowns anyway. They were Ethan's choices, not mine. Take whatever he promised you and get out." The woman dismissed her.

Molly entered just then.

"Ah, Molly, put the tea over here. Miss Carter won't be joining me after all." The woman looked back at Samantha. "Well, what is it? Don't tell me he owes you money as well?"

"Miss Samantha, child," Molly began.

"Molly, what time is my husband expected back?" the woman asked imperiously.

Molly turned to her. "Sometime today, Miss Juliet."

"See that a room is prepared for my father, also. He'll be staying with us."

"I don't understand," Samantha said. "Your husband? Molly, who is this woman?"

The woman laughed. "Go ahead, Molly, tell her who I am. Ethan has obviously forgotten to tell this one. How pathetic!"

"Please, Miss Juliet," Molly said.

"Oh really, Molly, she's no different from any other whore, except that I think my husband has sunken to the lowest depth possible by bedding a Yankee whore."

"Husband? What's she talking about, Molly? Who is she?" Samantha demanded.

The woman laughed again. "You poor, stupid thing! At least he was honest with the others. I'm Juliet Montgomery Winters-Hunt. I'm Ethan's wife."

The words hit Samantha like a knife thrust into her chest. She couldn't get her breath as the words echoed in her head. The room started to spin, and she reached for a nearby table.

"And if you think that you can persuade my husband to

continue to let you stay here, you're wrong. What-ever was he thinking bringing you to Arabella?"

"You're lying," Samantha choked, the words barely audible.

"Oh really, Miss Carter. Don't try to tell me you didn't know that Ethan was married. The role of the little innocent won't work with me. You see, I know all about my husband's appetites, and I certainly was not about to accommodate his baser nature myself. No *lady* would. I tried to supply him with Nigra bed wenches when we were first married. That was the civilized thing to do. But he always preferred to find his own, like that Cooper woman," she said with disgust. She looked back at Samantha. "You're just one of many and have served your purpose. Now leave before I have you thrown out."

"Miss Juliet! You got no call to talk to Miss Samantha like that," Molly said boldly.

Juliet stood. "I warned you, Molly. I am mistress of this house, and if you cannot do your work, I'll replace you. My husband may have freed you, but I will run this house."

"You're an evil woman, Miss Juliet. Evil! And your threats don't scare me none. You're the one who should be scared when Mr. Ethan hears what you said to Miss Samantha."

Juliet laughed. "You stupid nigger. What's he going to do? I'm his wife!"

Samantha couldn't listen anymore. She felt as though she was going to be violently ill. She ran blindly out of the room and up the steps. She didn't even hear Molly call her name. Somehow, she made it to the bedroom before she started retching. Molly appeared from behind her and held her shoulders as Samantha's stomach emptied its contents. Samantha sank slowly down to the floor, her hooped skirts billowing out around her.

"It's not true! It's not true! He wouldn't have lied to me." She was rocking back and forth, clutching herself as she trembled.

Molly knelt beside her. "Hush, child," she said, wrapping her big arms around Samantha. Samantha grabbed wildly at Molly.

"Tell me it's not true, Molly. Tell me that woman is not Ethan's wife," Samantha pleaded.

Molly's own grief was evident. Samantha could see the truth on Molly's face. "Samantha, child, I'm sorry."

"No!"

"Ethan's married. He's been married for seven years. I thought surely you must know that. . . ."

Suddenly, Samantha pushed Molly from her and stood up. "And these are her clothes? He gave me her clothes to wear?"

Samantha brutally tore at the gown she was wearing, ripping it until she finally had loosened it enough to pull it off. All the while, her sobs filled the room. She dropped the shredded grown onto the floor and ran blindly into the adjoining bedroom, the one she had first occupied before going to Ethan's bed. She went to the large armoire and pulled out her bag. Molly followed her into the room and watched while Samantha took out a pair of pants, socks, and boots. Her movements were wild and frantic. She grabbed a clean shirt and put it on, covering her nakedness. Her hands trembled as she tried to button the small buttons through her tears.

When she finished dressing, she threw her coat over the bed and placed her saddlebag, the small blanket that she used when she traveled, and her medical bag beside the coat. She reached in the bag, removed her knife, and inserted the knife into her right boot. She was like a wild animal, in shock and trapped. Samantha returned to the armoire one more time. Her hands shook as she reached inside and felt the cold steel of her Henry rifle.

Just then the door opened and Juliet entered. "Still here?" Juliet asked. She took in Samantha's appearance, dressed in pants, boots, and shirt. "Well," she said with disdain, "I can see why he gave you my gowns to wear."

Samantha closed her fingers around the rifle. She spun around, cocking its lever as she did so, and aimed the rifle at Juliet.

"No, Miss Samantha!" Molly exclaimed.

Juliet paled and backed up against the wall of the room, all of her superiority and assurance now replaced with fear.

"Molly, do something!" Juliet cried.

"Get out of my way, both of you!" Samantha shouted.

Both women backed away from the door. Samantha kept the rifle aimed at the women as she picked up her rolled blanket, saddlebag, and medical bag. Then she backed out of the room, the rifle still aimed at both women. Once in the hallway, she ran down the back steps and pushed the rear door open. She hadn't seen Frederick coming and collided with him, almost falling over. Her bags fell to the ground.

"Whoa, there, Miss Samantha, what's your hurry?" he asked as he bent down to pick up her bags. Then he saw her face. "What's wrong? Are you all right?" he asked with concern.

Molly burst through the back door. "Samantha, child, where are you goin'?"

"What's goin' on here?" Frederick demanded of his mother as he stood up.

"Miss Juliet arrived," Molly said quietly.

Frederick closed his eyes briefly as he looked down at the ground. Then he focused on Samantha. "What are you goin' to do?" he asked gently.

"Your concern is most touching, both of you," Samantha

said with sarcasm.

"Samantha," Frederick said as he reached out to her arm.

Samantha jerked her arm away. "Yes, I must say your kindness is overwhelming. It's too bad that neither of you thought enough of me these past months to tell me the truth," she shouted through new tears.

Frederick looked over to his mother. "Does Ethan know Juliet is here?"

"I'm sure he don't," Molly answered.

"Get out of my way, Frederick!" Samantha said as she brushed past him.

"Frederick, you can't let her leave on her own," Molly said.

Frederick caught up with Samantha as she neared the stables. "Where are you goin'?" he asked, matching her quick stride.

"I'm leaving!"

"But where are you goin'? You can't just take off across the country. It's not safe."

Samantha stopped. He was right. Where could she go? She had no one here—no one except Ethan. Her heart twisted with pain, and her eyes filled with tears. She didn't even have him. She never did.

"Is there someone you can stay with?" Frederick asked gently.

"Belle. Belle will help me." Samantha stopped as the realization came to her. "Belle knew, too. Everyone knew but me. You all lied to me!" Samantha cried and blindly started running to the stable.

Frederick caught up. "I'll take you to Miss Belle's," he said.

"I don't want your help!" Samantha shouted.

"You shouldn't travel alone, Miss Samantha."

Kota pranced nervously, sensing his mistress's distress as

she put the saddle on him and tied her supplies to the saddle.

"I'll see you to Miss Belle's," Frederick replied as he saddled his horse.

"I don't want your help. Stay away from me!" Samantha shouted as she swung her leg up into the saddle and raced out of the stables. By the time she reached the end of the lane and turned onto the road, she already had a substantial lead on Frederick.

Samantha rode blindly, urging Kota on. She would need money, and Belle was the only one she could go to. She didn't know how long she had been riding when she rounded a curve and recognized the entrance to Caroline Cooper's plantation. More lies! More deceit! A carriage accompanied by several riders was coming out of the lane on the Cooper plantation.

"Hold up there!" one of the riders shouted as Samantha approached. The carriage came to a stop as the riders spread out across the road.

Samantha brought Kota down to a trot as she approached the riders. They withdrew their guns and pointed them at her. There was no way she could outrun the guns nor could she reach her own rifle without provoking the armed men. From behind her, she heard the distant sound of hooves. She twisted around to see Frederick racing toward her.

"Stop!" one of the men said as he leveled his gun on Samantha.

She obediently halted Kota several feet away from the carriage. Her eyes widened in surprise when she recognized the man giving the orders.

Gerald Depardeu smiled slowly. "Well, if it isn't Miss Carter, the abolitionist." He took in her appearance. Her hair had come down and was streaming wildly about her shoulders. Despite the chill in the air, Samantha had not put her coat on. He let his eyes move slowly down her chest to her pants and her stride position on the horse.

Samantha looked nervously about her. Two other men on horseback circled around her.

"Miss Samantha, are you all right?" Frederick called as he slowed his horse and drew up to the men.

"I'm fine, Frederick," Samantha said. "I was just paying my respects to Mr. Depardeu." She turned to Gerald Depardeu. "I really must be on my way. If you'll excuse me." She started to walk Kota forward, but Depardeu put his horse in front of her.

"Not so fast, Miss Carter. I'd like to have a word with you."

Samantha looked back at Frederick. Just then, the door to the carriage opened and a man stepped out. Samantha tensed, recognizing the man who had been in the carriage with Juliet this morning.

"What have we here, Gerald? Looks like a wild one," the man said with a malicious laugh.

"Oh, that she is. I'm sure your son-in-law can attest to that," Depardeu replied.

"Oh?" the man said, looking at Samantha with interest.

"This here's Miss Samantha Carter. She's a Yankee and been keeping Ethan company at his place."

"Has she now," the man said, his gaze boldly taking in Samantha. "Well, I can't fault my son-in-law's tastes in wenches. She does indeed appear to be a wild one," he laughed.

"Miss Samantha is leaving, Mr. Montgomery," Frederick said.

"You talking to me, boy?" Franklin Montgomery said as he turned a vile look upon Frederick.

"Winters-Hunt's niggers always have been uppity,"

Gerald Depardeu said.

Samantha was frightened. One of the men was holding his gun aimed at Frederick, and the other still had his aimed at her. She couldn't risk reaching for her rifle.

"I heard tell that there was a problem with niggers spying for the North," Franklin Montgomery said. "Looks to me like we caught us one."

The men laughed.

"Frederick is no spy," Samantha said indignantly.

"Yes siree, and traveling with his Northern accomplice," Montgomery said, eyeing Samantha. "Too bad. I wouldn't have minded finding out what my son-in-law found so appealing in this one, but I haven't the time." He turned to Gerald Depardeu. "Take care of them. I'll meet you later." He turned and stepped back into the carriage.

As the carriage pulled away, Samantha heard Frederick shout to her. "Go, Samantha!"

She whirled around just as one of the men swung the butt of his rifle, crashing it into Frederick's head. Samantha screamed as Frederick fell off his horse. She reached for her own rifle but stopped as she heard the cold sound of a revolver being cocked.

"Step down, nice and easy, Miss Carter," a man said as he pointed the revolver at her head.

Samantha was paralyzed with fear. She dismounted and looked at Frederick, who was unconscious on the ground. Kota stamped his feet nervously.

A slow, evil smile grew on Gerald Depardeu's face. "The penalty for spying is hanging. Josh," he said to the man standing over Frederick, "you got a rope on you?"

"Sure do."

"Over there," he said, motioning with his head to the trees along the road. "I'm sure a fine lady like Miz Cooper wouldn't mind if we borrow one of her trees."

"No!" Samantha screamed. "You can't do that! Leave him alone!"

"You ought to be more concerned about what we're going to do to you, Miss Carter," Depardeu said. "We don't like Yankees, especially spies. Bring her over, too."

Samantha had never felt such terror in her life. She was clearly outnumbered by Depardeu and his men. One of the men pushed her toward the trees, holding a gun to her back. Gerald Depardeu had also withdrawn his gun as the man called Josh dragged Frederick over to the trees. Samantha watched in horror as he tied a rope around Frederick's neck and then tossed the other end over a low-hanging branch. He then pulled the rope, putting all of his weight on it. It functioned like a pulley, slowly hoisting Frederick up by his neck.

Samantha screamed and started to rush forward when the other man struck her across her face with his gun, knocking her down. A blinding pain shot through her head and her vision darkened. She was on her hands and knees when she looked up to see Frederick dangling from the rope. She was about to reach for her knife when a pair of hands roughly grabbed her, jerked her to a standing position, and then again, a fist smashed into her face. Samantha crumpled under the pain.

Gerald Depardeu laughed as he aimed his gun at Samantha. "I've a keen need to see what's under those pants you wear," he said, still mounted upon his horse.

Josh walked over to Samantha. The man who had struck Samantha grabbed her from behind. Through her pain and grief, Samantha saw Josh reach out and grab the collar of her shirt. The fabric ripped as he tore it open. Samantha screamed, and in that instant, another loud noise pierced the air as Kota whinnied. Suddenly, the large black horse was there. He reared up, his hooves coming down on Josh's back just as Josh reached for Samantha's pants. Josh fell backward and Kota reared up again. This time, there was a sickening crack as the horse's powerful hooves came down on Josh's head, crushing his skull.

The man behind Samantha pointed his gun at Kota. She saw it through her blurred vision and pushed against the man. The revolver discharged, missing Kota. The horse reared again.

"Kota! Go!" Samantha screamed blindly, signaling the horse.

Kota reared and then bolted into the woods.

"You bitch!" the man screamed. He slammed his rife into Samantha's face, snapping her head backward.

"When you're finished with her, kill her!" Depardeu ordered. "Then clean this up," he said, pointing to Josh's body. He spurred his horse around and galloped away.

Samantha felt herself being shoved to the ground, and a heavy weight fell on her. She struggled to keep the blackness away that was threatening to envelop her as the pain spread across her face. The man clawed at her breasts, and then she felt his weight ease off her for a moment as he grabbed the waist of her pants and ripped the fabric. He tore viciously until nothing remained to block his way. She felt him spread her legs and then move on top of her, preparing to enter her. Samantha couldn't see through her swollen eyelids, but she blindly reached down to her boot, and, with the last ounce of strength she possessed, withdrew her knife, plunging it into the man's side.

A strangled cry emitted from the man's throat as he twisted around, trying to get a grip on the knife. Samantha held on and ripped the knife forward between the man's ribs, slicing through lung, blood vessels, and finally around to the heart itself. A merciful blackness overcame her as the man's blood drained out upon her naked body.

She was floating in darkness again. It was a familiar place. She wasn't afraid. She knew he would come to her, and he did.

"Rest. This body will live," the ancient voice said.

"And the one beginning within it?" she asked.

"It, too, will live."

"Stay with me, Charrah."

"No, it is not for me to decide. There are two here who must leave."

"Frederick?"

"No, he is to remain. The other two, they have not learned," the holy man said sadly. "They must return, now."

For a moment, Samantha, too, felt the sadness of the heavens. "But, Charrah, I also have failed. I took the life from one of them."

"It was to be. Rest, Little One."

Ethan and Avery were seated with Caroline Cooper in the parlor of her house when a Negro ran into the room.

"Miz Cooper, Miz Cooper! Come quickly!" the slave said.

"What is it?" Caroline asked.

"Dink, he done heard some shootin' in the front fields. Come quickly. There's some dead!"

"What are you talking about?" Ethan asked, jumping up from his chair.

"Theys hung 'im!"

"What?" Avery Scott said with alarm.

"Jesus!" Ethan swore.

"Bring the horses and my buggy!" Caroline said.

"Buggy's right outside, Miz Cooper. Paci took Mr. Winters-Hunt and Lieutenant Scott's horses out back to water them."

They ran down the front steps to Caroline's buggy. Ethan was the first to get in.

"Maybe you had better stay here, Caroline."

"Oh, no I'm not. These are my people and this is my

land."

Avery helped her into the buggy and jumped up beside her just as Ethan slapped the reins against the horse. It only took a few minutes to reach the end of the lane and round the curve in the road. The first sight they saw was several of Caroline's slaves lowering a body that was dangling from a tree branch. As they drew nearer, Ethan felt like someone had just knocked the breath out of him. A large black horse was nervously pacing around and rearing up, frightening the slaves who were trying to go near something on the ground.

Ethan brought the buggy to a stop and jumped out as Avery helped Caroline step out the other side. Avery and Caroline ran to the man who had been lowered to the ground. Ethan froze, recognizing the horse beyond Caroline and Avery.

"Oh, Jesus," Avery swore. "Ethan! It's Frederick!"

"He's still alive!" Caroline shouted. "Ethan, he's alive."

"God, please, not again!" Ethan pleaded as he ran past them.

"That's Samantha's horse!" Avery shouted as he recognized Kota.

"Stay with Frederick," Caroline said to her slaves as she stood up and ran behind Avery and Ethan.

Ethan reached Kota first. At the approach of the three, Kota whirled around, rearing up. Ethan jumped back, almost knocking Avery down.

"Easy, boy, easy, Kota," Ethan said soothingly. The horse's nostrils flared, but he stood still. Ethan continued to talk to him until at last the horse backed up, allowing the three of them a complete view of the bodies on the ground. Nearest to them was a man, his skull cracked open, his head a mass of hair, bone, and blood. Caroline screamed and reached for Avery's arm.

"Sam!"

This time, the heart-wrenching cry came from Ethan. Avery moved away from Caroline as he, too, saw Samantha lying on the ground.

"Oh, God, no! Please, God," Ethan cried as he reached for Samantha.

Avery knelt beside Ethan as Caroline came around to the other side of Samantha's body. Slowly, Ethan rolled the man off Samantha. Her hand fell away from the knife and dropped limply to her side. The large knife protruded from the man's chest as Ethan let him fall onto his back. His eyes were wide open, a look of horror on his face. Caroline screamed again and looked away.

Samantha's chest, abdomen, and thighs were covered with blood. The brown earth beneath her was also soaked with blood. She lay there, lifeless, her eyes closed.

A strangled cry erupted from Ethan as he knelt in anguish over Samantha's exposed body.

"Ethan, she's still breathing!" Avery said.

Caroline forced herself to turn around and look at Samantha.

Ethan ignored the tears that were blurring his vision. He placed his hand on Samantha's chest and felt her heart beating strongly.

"Caroline, give me a cloth—something I can use to wipe this blood away."

Caroline looked around helplessly for a moment and then raised her skirt. She tore away a large section of her petticoat and handed it to Ethan. She watched as he mopped the blood away from Samantha's chest. He wiped the blood off each breast and her abdomen. His hand trembled as he continued to move the cloth downward to Samantha's thighs. He returned to her chest.

"Help me turn her on her side," he said. Caroline reached out, and they gently rolled Samantha over. Ethan looked closely as he ran his hand over her sides and back, wiping away the blood.

"I'll be damned. It's all his," Ethan said. "She stabbed the bastard, and he bled to death on top of her. I don't see any wounds on her," Ethan said, relief pouring out of him. "She's going to be all right."

"Ethan," Avery said, "maybe not. Looks like he . . . Sam was. . . ." He didn't finish but glanced quickly at Samantha's naked body and then turned away, the implication clear to both men.

"No!" Ethan said. "She wasn't."

"Ethan," Avery began, his own anguish great as he knelt beside Samantha.

"No. She stopped him. I know her. She killed him before he was able to . . . , and he died too fast and too easily," Ethan ground out as he removed his jacket and covered Samantha's naked body. He reached up to her face. A large welt had developed on the left side of her face, and her right eye was blackened and swollen. Her lower lip was bleeding. A moan escaped her lips as Ethan turned her head to the side.

There was a commotion behind them. Ethan and Avery turned to see Frederick struggling to walk over to them. Ethan stood and reached out to his friend. Frederick took his arm and leaned on it. "Miss Samantha!" Frederick cried, looking down at her still form.

"I think she'll be all right. We've got to get you both inside," Ethan said.

"I'm okay, Ethan," Frederick said hoarsely as he rubbed his neck.

"What the hell happened here?" Ethan demanded as he turned back to Samantha.

"It was Depardeu and. . . ." Frederick stopped.

"Who?"

"Franklin Montgomery."

Ethan froze.

"They stopped us on the road. Montgomery accused me of bein' a spy and Samantha of bein' an accomplice. He didn't do nothin' himself. He left Depardeu and two of their men to do their dirty work."

"That's enough. You can tell me the rest when we get Samantha back," Ethan said as he knelt down again. "Caroline, can we take Sam to your house?"

"Of course, Ethan, I'll help you."

Ethan started to pick Samantha up and then stopped. He looked over at the body lying next to Samantha and grabbed the handle of the knife. It had been pushed in all the way to the hilt of the blade. He pulled the bloody blade out, staring at it for a moment.

"She once threatened me with this at your house, Caroline," Ethan said, looking up at Caroline. "Do you remember?" he asked as his eyes filled with tears. "I tried to take this away from her and we fought. That's when she cut my arm. She's very skilled. It took me several minutes before I was able to get it away from her, and then I warmed her backside pretty hard. You should have heard her language," he finished, his voice choking with emotion.

"We did," Avery said gently. "You're lucky you didn't end up like this." He pointed to the dead man on the ground.

"No, she never intended to hurt me."

Ethan stuck the knife under his belt and then bent to pick Samantha up. She moaned as he lifted her.

"It's all right, Sam. You're safe," he murmured to her.

Although Kota was skittish, he allowed Avery to tie him to the back of the carriage. Avery then gave instructions to Caroline's people regarding the two bodies. When that was completed, he climbed into the carriage with Ethan,

Caroline, Frederick, and Samantha.

"I'm sorry, Ethan," Frederick said.

"Not yet," Ethan said tersely. "Once I'm sure Sam is going to be all right, you can tell me. There'll be time then. I know where to find them."

No one said anything as they approached the big house. Bessie and a few others were waiting on the front porch. Caroline disembarked first.

Avery stepped out next and held his arms out. Ethan leaned out and handed Samantha's limp form over while he stepped down. He then took Samantha back in his arms.

"Lordy, it's Miss Sam!" Bessie exclaimed.

Caroline led the men to a bedroom upstairs. As Ethan gently laid Samantha on the bed, she began to mumble.

"What's she saying?" Caroline asked.

Ethan only recognized one word. "She's speaking an Indian language—Lakota. I've heard her speak it before, although I don't know what she's saying." He paused. "Charrah, the name she is saying, is the name of an Indian holy man she knew as a child. According to Sam, he had some magical abilities. He taught her healing arts and made her a medicine woman among his tribe when she was just a girl. The Lakota Indians also trained her to be a warrior."

"A warrior?" Avery said with surprise.

Ethan knelt beside Samantha. "When she was shot during the retreat at Kennesaw, I didn't think she would live. She was unconscious for days. She kept calling his name and talking to him in that Indian language. Later, when I asked her about it, she didn't remember it."

Bessie entered, carrying a pitcher of warm water, linens, and soap.

"Bring them over here," Caroline said. "Ethan, why don't you, Lieutenant Scott, and Frederick wait in the parlor while Bessie and I bathe her?"

"I'm not leaving," Ethan said.

"Ethan, please. It'll be all right."

"I'm staying here."

"We'll wait in the hall," Avery said as he and Frederick left the room.

"Ethan?" Caroline said, expecting him to do the same.

"When she was wounded, she was unconscious for four days. When the fever came, I cared for her and bathed her all through the night for several days until the fever finally broke. I'm not leaving her," Ethan said softly.

Caroline sighed. "All right, Bessie, let's get what remains of these clothes off."

Ethan held Samantha's hand as Caroline gently bathed Samantha, pausing briefly as she passed the cloth over the scar on Samantha's right side. She looked up questionably at Ethan.

"Confederate lead. She was shot in the head, too."

"Oh, Ethan," Caroline said sympathetically. "I remember when Sam was wounded. You said he almost died. That's when I still thought she was a boy."

Bessie and Caroline carefully bathed Samantha and then placed a clean nightgown on her. Bessie made a cool compress of herbs and placed it on Samantha's bruised and swollen face. "I don't understand why she's still unconscious," Ethan said.

"She just need to rest, Master Ethan," Bessie said. "She's a strong girl. She'll be all right."

Ethan lowered his head, running his hand through his hair. "Frederick!" he called.

Frederick entered the bedroom and closed the door, leaving Avery in the hall.

"All right, Frederick, what happened?" Ethan asked.

"Sam had run off. Ma sent me after her. Montgomery, Depardeu, and two men were comin' down the road. They stopped us. They said some awful things to Miss Samantha and accused me of bein' a spy. That's when one of them hit me with a rifle, and I don't remember anythin' else until Mrs. Cooper's people were helpin' me to stand up."

The room was silent. Ethan finally spoke, his voice barely a whisper.

"Why was Sam leaving?"

Frederick hesitated. "Miss Juliet arrived this mornin'."

"Oh, Jesus." Ethan closed his eyes, realizing what must have happened.

"Ethan, how could you!" Caroline exclaimed, turning on Ethan. "You never told her you were married? Samantha was young and innocent. You must have known she was falling in love with you, and you let her!" Caroline angrily accused. "Do you know what you've done? You're despicable!"

Ethan stood. He looked from Caroline to Frederick. The accusations were on both their faces. He turned away and walked over to the window.

"Miss Sam, honey."

They all turned at the sound of Bessie's voice.

"You done give us an awful scare," Bessie said as she leaned over Samantha.

Samantha's eyes were open, and her head was turned toward Bessie. "Bessie, where am I?" Samantha started to raise her head and then fell back on the pillow.

"Samantha, dear, rest. It's all right. You're in my house," Caroline said.

"Caroline?" Samantha said. Then she felt the compress on her face and pushed it aside. She winced as she touched her cheek. She moved her fingers to her eye, which was partially closed from the swelling.

"You're going to be all right," Caroline said gently.

A frown creased Samantha's face. They watched as her

vision slowly cleared.

"Frederick. Oh, Caroline, they killed him," Samantha sobbed and struggled to sit up.

Caroline gently pushed Samantha back down onto the bed. "No, he's alive."

"No, I saw them. They hung him. I tried to stop them, but I couldn't. They held me at gunpoint and kept beating me." Samantha was crying now, her breath coming in irregular gasps. "Kota killed one of them. Kota tried to save me. Then the other one tried to shoot him." Her words were all tumbling out together between her sobs.

"Shhh. It's all right now. You're safe," Caroline said as Samantha continued to cry.

"He beat me and tore my clothes off. He knocked me down on the ground and tried to . . . he tried to . . . I killed him with my knife," she finally whispered. "I had to. They killed Frederick and were going to kill me, too. I killed him just like the Lakota warriors taught me when I was a girl. I pulled the blade all the way around to his heart, just like Many Horses and the Lakota taught me," she said softly.

"Miss Samantha?" Frederick stepped forward and knelt beside the bed.

"Frederick!"

He smiled at Samantha. "They tried to kill me, but failed. Some of Mrs. Cooper's people cut me down."

"Oh, Frederick." Samantha sat forward and threw her arms around the man. He held her as she rested her head on his shoulder. "Frederick," she kept repeating over and over.

"You better lie down," Frederick said as he gently pulled away.

Samantha was facing away from Ethan and had not seen him yet. It was all he could do to restrain himself. When he heard her voice, he wanted to rush to her side, to hold her, to tell her he was sorry, to tell her he loved her. But Bessie,

Frederick, and Caroline were there. He needed to be alone with Samantha. He stepped away from the window and walked to the bed. "Sam?" he said gently.

Samantha turned toward Ethan. "Ethan!" she cried with joy, and then her smile faded. She appeared confused. Then Ethan saw it on her face: the hurt, the pain, and the devastation in her eyes. She turned toward Frederick. "Let me out of here, Frederick," she cried. She pushed him out of her way and stood. As she took a step, she stumbled. Ethan was around the bed instantly and caught her.

"No!" Samantha cried. "No! No!" She beat her fists against Ethan's chest. "I hate you," she screamed, her face streaked with tears as she sobbed and struggled against his grip. He held her tightly as she struck out wildly until at last she slowly collapsed on the floor, crying. Ethan knelt beside her and pulled her against him. Samantha's soft whimpering was more devastating to him than her screaming had been.

"Leave us," he said, his voice strained with emotion.

Bessie, Frederick, and Caroline silently left the room, closing the door behind them.

Samantha was standing on the balcony, looking out over the fields of Caroline's plantation, when Ethan stepped out from the bedroom.

"Sam, you must let me explain. You can't keep walking away from me."

Samantha gripped the railing. She'd lost track of the time since the others had left her with Ethan. She'd cried while Ethan held her, until at last, she'd pushed him away.

"Sam, look at me." Ethan grabbed her arm and turned her shoulders toward him. Samantha grasped the railing tighter and kept her face forward. With a sigh, Ethan released her.

"I met Juliet seven years ago," he began. "I was in Boston when I received word my parents had fallen ill with a fever spreading throughout costal South Carolina. I left immediately, but they died before I reached Arabella. Franklin Montgomery and I had business dealings in the past, and he came to my office in Charleston to offer his condolences. Juliet was with him. I married Juliet at the end of that summer, after having known her for only four weeks.

"She was beautiful, charming, and gay—everything I thought I wanted in a wife. I was a fool!" he said. "My first glimpse of the real Juliet came on our wedding night. I'll spare you the intimate details and just say that Juliet finds the marriage bed to be disgusting and beneath her dignity. Perhaps it was not completely her fault. Juliet had been raised to view the physical aspect of marriage as a vile act that must be endured to produce children. It's not an uncommon view among the Southern aristocracy. I thought that, with time and patience, I could show her. . . . I was wrong," Ethan said.

"The second night was worse than the first. I was not without experience where women were concerned, and I tried everything I could think of to put her at ease. It was no different that night. She hated the act, and she hated me.

"The third night when I came into our room, I found one of Juliet's slaves sitting on my bed. Juliet had found a way to meet her marital obligations. She announced that she would no longer share my bed but would provide me with a bed wench each night. It seems this was a practice of her daddy. She had several slaves sent up from her father's plantation in Savannah for just this purpose.

"When I asked her about her plans for a family, she informed me that she had no intention of ruining her figure by bearing me countless 'brats.' If, by chance, a pregnancy resulted from our two nights together, then she would bear that child, but that would be the last. Needless to say, a child did not result from our brief honeymoon," Ethan said with heavy sarcasm.

"I was appalled by her statements, and the prospect of raping my wife every night did not appeal to me," Ethan said with bitterness. "That was just the beginning. She lived with me for three years. During that time, I found out what a shallow and callous woman she is. She likes being my wife because of the money and position it affords her, or at least she did until I started making my opinions concerning slavery public. She was furious. Several of the larger planters were angry with me, and that affected her social position. I'd also caught her mistreating some of the Negroes working for me.

"In the end, living together became intolerable for both of us. On the pretext of her father's poor health and my absences with the outbreak of the war, Juliet moved back to Savannah to her father's plantation. That was almost four years ago. I supply her with money to maintain her extravagant lifestyle, and she stays away from Arabella. A marriage made in heaven, wouldn't you say?"

Ethan turned to face Samantha. "I never meant to hurt you, Sam. I never intended for any of this to happen. God, I tried to stop it!"

Samantha whirled around. "Did you, Ethan? How? By lying to me?"

"I tried to send you back north. I told you to forget about me. I told you I couldn't offer you a future."

Samantha took a deep breath, shuddering as she inhaled. "Yes, Ethan, you told me," she admitted. "But from the moment I saw you step from the brush with Lieutenant Quicken's men, I felt something stir deep inside of me. I can't explain it. I was so afraid of you that day." She paused. "But it was there inside of me, and it grew stronger each time I was near you. I could no more resist you than I could resist breathing.

"You told me there couldn't be a future, that you couldn't ever marry me. I thought it was because of the war—because I was a Yankee and you a Southerner. I held on to the hope that after the war, there would be peace between our people. That you would...."

"Sam, I tried to tell you," Ethan said gently.

"No. You were not entirely truthful. You never told me you were married. You let me hope. Had I known that you were married, I would have resisted you. I would have found a way to resist you. I never would have gone to your bed knowing you had a wife. But you didn't tell me that. Instead, you let me love you." She stopped as a thought too painful to consider entered her mind. "But you knew that, didn't you, Ethan? You knew I never would have loved you had I known you were married. That's why you never told me." He didn't have to answer. She saw the answer in his eyes. "Oh, God," she cried as the realization hit her.

"Sam, I'm sorry," he said as he reached for her.

Samantha jumped back as though she had been struck. "You used me. I was just a dalliance, a distraction from the war." Her tears burned her battered face and lips. She couldn't breathe. Her hand trembled uncontrollably as she covered her mouth. "My . . . my brother was right! All this time, I was just a Confederate major's whore," she said in a strangled voice.

"Sam!"

Her entire body was trembling now, and she felt disoriented. She looked wildly about the balcony for a means to escape. She gritted her teeth and clenched her fists at her side. "Get away from me, Ethan," she said as she backed toward the bedroom door, "for I swear to God, if I lay eyes on you again, I will kill you!"

Ethan remained on the balcony alone, his vision blurred by his tears. He wanted to go to her. He had to make her understand that he loved her—a love that was only surpassed by the hatred he felt for himself. When he finally went inside the house, he used a different door to avoid seeing Samantha. He found Caroline and Avery sitting in the parlor.

"There are some things I must attend to," he said abruptly.

"Depardeu?" Avery asked.

"Yes."

"I'll go with you," Avery said as he stood.

"No, Avery. You must not be associated with what I'm about to do."

"I care about Samantha, too," Avery said.

"Enough to commit murder?" Ethan challenged.

"I'll do what is necessary," Avery responded evenly.

Ethan sighed. "Thank you, Avery, but Sam is my responsibility. It's my fault this happened. I captured her. I forced her into this situation. I must do this alone."

"What about Montgomery?" Avery asked.

"I'll deal with him in my own time." Ethan turned to Caroline. "Frederick will need to stay here until I've finished what I must do." Ethan walked to the door. "And Caroline, would you take care of Sam? Tell her I'll be back tonight."

Samantha watched from the bedroom window as Ethan rode away. She was dead inside, or at least she wanted to be. The pain in her soul was so great that she would have welcomed death at that moment. But she wasn't alone. There was another to think about. With tears in her eyes, she placed her hand on her abdomen to draw comfort from the child beginning within her.

She couldn't stay here. She couldn't bear to see Ethan again. Despite her threat, she was afraid that, where he was concerned, she had no pride or dignity of her own. She would almost be willing to beg him to let her stay as his mistress. So that was it. That was what she'd become. She could accept that, but she wouldn't bring a child into the world under those conditions. Not her child. Not Ethan's.

She walked to a chair where someone had placed her saddlebag, medical bag, blanket, and rifle. Laying there, on top of everything, was her knife. Samantha trembled as she reached for it. Someone had obviously cleaned it. It would be so easy. She could end the pain—the knife could do that for her.

"Oh, Charrah, what happened?" she whispered. "All of my plans. Nothing has turned out the way I had thought it would. I've killed three times. I've loved, and it has only caused pain. Now one, not yet born, will have to suffer the consequences. I've failed."

Still clutching the knife, she reached for her saddlebag. Her fingers brushed against the familiar buckskin. She pulled the shirt and pants out and inhaled the scent of the buckskin as her tears dropped onto it. "If only I could be that child again, kneeling at your side. There was such magic in your hands, Charrah. I could feel it in mine, too." She looked down at the shirt. "Now there is only death and pain around me. And forgive me, Charrah, but I want to die, too. I want no more of this life," she said as she looked at the knife in her hand. "I want to die," she whispered.

As she slowly sank down to the floor, she brought the tip of the knife toward her chest, aiming for her heart. But, despite her intent, her hand began to tremble so violently that she released the knife and let it fall to the floor. Then she buried her face in the buckskins and cried.

When at last there were no more tears, Samantha stood, removed the nightgown she was wearing, and placed it on the bed. Without thinking, she slipped the buckskin shirt over her head and then pulled on the buckskin pants. The soft buckskin boots were also in her bag, as was a small amount of fur. She inserted the fur into the boots before she slipped her feet into them and put the long underwear into her saddlebag. She would need the added warmth now that winter was here.

When she was dressed, she closed her eyes, the familiar clothing of her childhood soothing her. Suddenly, she could feel it. Strength was flowing into her. It didn't chase her pain away, nothing could do that, but it gave her the courage she needed to do what she had to do—live. She stood there a few minutes longer, opening herself up to that which had come to her.

"The Spirits do not abandon one whom they have chosen. They have chosen you, Little One. You must learn to walk with them and accept that which is given unto you. It will not always be easy. Can you do that, Little One who wishes to be medicine woman?"

Charrah! How long ago had he spoken those words to her? She had been very young then and not yet put to the test.

There was a knock at the door, and Samantha opened her eyes.

"Samantha? May we come in?"

It was Caroline. Samantha took a deep breath. "Come in, Caroline."

As the door opened, Samantha reached for the knife laying on the floor. She heard a gasp behind her and turned around to see Caroline's startled face. Avery was behind her. He, too, had a look of shock on his face. It was a moment before Caroline could speak.

"Samantha, what are you doing?" she exclaimed.

"I'm leaving, Caroline."

"You can't!" Caroline said.

"Samantha, I don't think that's wise," Avery said, stepping forward.

"I must," Samantha replied.

"Like that?" Caroline asked incredulously.

"When is Ethan returning?" Samantha asked.

Caroline frowned. "Sometime tonight."

Samantha nodded. "It's almost two o'clock. I'll have to cover a lot of distance before nightfall. Would you have me wear a silk gown, Caroline? This is practical, and it will keep me warm. I intend to stay under cover as much as possible and ride as fast as I can."

"Samantha, you look so . . . so different, like an. . . ." Caroline didn't finish.

"Indian?" Samantha supplied. She looked down at herself. "I was wearing this when the Confederates captured me outside of Arlington. Of course, they thought I was a boy. I had the paste and mustache on my face and my hair was short." She smoothed her hand over the dark stain on the front of the shirt. "Ethan took me to the Confederate surgical tent. I doubt if the blood stains will ever come out," she said, her voice a hollow whisper. She sat down on the bed. "That was a year ago." She unconsciously turned the knife over in her hands as they began to tremble again, images of the morning's terror coming into her mind.

"Samantha, you need to rest," Avery said.

"No." Samantha stood up abruptly. "I would like to ask a favor of both of you. Caroline, could I ask you for some food to take with me? If possible, I would like several weeks' supply. I want to avoid the towns until I'm in Washington City."

"This is insane. Ethan would never permit it," Caroline said.

"Ethan!" Samantha's eyes blazed. "Ethan has no claim over me, as you well know," Samantha retorted.

"Samantha, you're not thinking clearly," Avery said.

"Oh, but I am, Avery. For the first time in months, I am. Will you help me? I would like to borrow some money. I won't need much, just enough to buy grain for Kota as we get farther north. Once I reach Washington City, I can wire my father for money and repay you."

"Samantha, you cannot travel all that distance alone. You'll get lost. You're also likely to run right into a battle. The whole Confederacy is one battlefield. You can't do it," Avery said.

"Listen to him, Samantha. You can't leave now. You can stay here with me. Please," Caroline said.

"No," Samantha retorted, and then she saw the hurt look on Caroline's face. "I'm sorry, Caroline. You're being kind, and I'm grateful for your kindness, but I must leave." She paused. "May I speak to Avery alone?"

The room was quiet while the three of them looked at each other. "Of course," Caroline said with a worried look on her face. "I'll be out in the kitchen if you need me."

When Caroline closed the door behind her, Samantha began to pace. Avery waited quietly. Finally, Samantha looked up. "This is going to be more difficult than I thought. Could we go for a walk, Avery?"

"Are you sure you feel like it?"

"Yes."

"All right, as long as you promise not to run away while we're walking," Avery said with a grin. "I once had to escort the boy, Sam, to Charleston, remember? I know how clever he can be."

"No tricks, I promise," Samantha said.

The afternoon sun warmed the cool air as they set out across the expanse of cotton fields. They walked along in silence, Avery letting Samantha take her time.

"Avery," she finally said, "I must leave today. I can't stay here or anywhere else where I might see him again."

Avery sighed. "Forgive me, Samantha, I don't mean to intrude. I'm trying to do what is best." He paused. "You're in love with him." It was a statement, not a question.

Samantha struggled to steady her breathing. The pain and the sense of betrayal were still so acute. "Yes," she whispered.

"Until this morning, I wasn't certain. Does he know?"

Samantha looked at him with surprise.

"I assumed, of course, that he was unaware. Are you saying that he actually encouraged your feelings?" Avery asked doubtfully.

Samantha winced. Avery didn't understand. He didn't understand their relationship at all. How was she going to tell him?

"No matter," Avery continued, "you needn't see him. But until arrangements can be made for your safe conduct to Washington City, you can't leave. It also wouldn't be wise for you to present yourself to the Federal Army while here. That might lead to questions regarding what you've been doing in the Confederate states. Give me some time to arrange things."

"I can't," Samantha whispered. She turned to him, her eyes moist. "I'm pregnant, Avery. I'm carrying Ethan's child."

Samantha saw the look of unconcealed shock on Avery's face.

"But how can that be?" Avery blurted out. "Samantha, dear, you're still innocent about such things," he started to explain. "You don't understand. You can't become with child just because you're in love with him or because he may have held you in his arms at some time in order to comfort you."

"Avery! I'm not a mindless twit. I'm a doctor!"

Avery stared at her, the realization and shock plainly evident. When Samantha could bear his scrutiny no longer, she turned abruptly and started to run.

"Samantha, wait!" Avery easily caught up with her. He reached out and turned her toward him. He grimaced as he saw the tears flowing down her swollen and bruised face. "Forgive me," he said. "I had no idea that Ethan. . . . I don't know what to say."

Samantha could see the confusion on Avery's face as he continued.

"Ethan is a gentleman, Samantha. He would never take such liberties. He would never compromise a lady's virtue." Avery paused. "But he has, hasn't he?" he said, his confusion evident. "I don't understand how this could happen." A thought suddenly occurred to him. "Samantha, did he force you? He did, didn't he!"

"No, Avery, I went to him willingly," Samantha said softly through her tears and then turned and started walking slowly. Avery was beside her. "You don't have to say anything, Avery. I know what you must think of me," Samantha said.

"Do you?"

"Yes." Samantha stopped. "I've confessed to being a woman of low moral character, have I not? I've shared a man's bed without the benefit of marriage. The fact that I didn't know that he was married does not change things in the eyes of the world. I believe that there are words for women like me." Samantha started to walk again.

"Does Ethan know?"

"No!" Samantha turned toward Avery. "And he must never know. You must swear to me that you'll never tell him."

"What will you do?"

They began to walk again. "I don't know. I just know that I want to go home. I'll have to tell my father and brothers. They'll be shocked and angry. I don't know if they'll take me back; they may not. They may cast me out. I have a lot to account for. No matter what you may think," Samantha said, indicating her buckskin clothing, "we're not that different on the frontier than you are here. The same rules and conventions apply," she said quietly. "I'm a ruined woman now. And of course, there's the matter of my aiding the Confederacy. A traitor and a whore—that's what my brother called me just before Ethan let him escape. He disowned me; he said I was dead to him." Samantha absently wiped the newly formed tears, wincing again as she touched her battered face. "I . . . I need to go someplace where my child will be safe. If my family won't take me back, I'll go to my cousin's Lakota village. The Lakota Indians will accept me and protect my child."

Avery reached out and gently turned Samantha to face him. "You said you knew what I must think of you. Shall I tell you?" Avery didn't wait for an answer. "I think you're an extraordinary young woman who has great courage."

"You're being kind, Avery, and I'm not feeling so courageous now. God forgive me, but my greatest sin is not in carrying this child." She looked away and then turned her face back to Avery. "It's in wanting him, even now." Samantha brushed the tears away and began to walk. "You see now why I must leave immediately."

"What about the child?" Avery asked softly.

"Would you think me terribly immoral if I told you that the child is the only thing that comforts me now?"

"No, but I'd suggest that perhaps you're not thinking of the child. You're hurting and are thinking of yourself."

"I can hardly go to Ethan. And I can't stay here."

"Where will you go?"

"Home."

"And then what? You said it yourself, Samantha. Even if your family does accept you back, a woman cannot have a child without a husband. Your child will be a bastard. You'll be rejected by society and so will your child. Your family will also be shamed. They can't protect you from that. That's the harsh reality. And raising your child as an Indian?"

"Stop it, Avery! Just stop it!" Samantha screamed and began crying again. Avery drew her to him, holding her as she wept.

"I'm sorry. I don't mean to be cruel. I'm trying to help," Avery said gently.

"Then help me by loaning me some money so I can leave. I have no other choice."

"There's another choice," Avery said softly as he held her.

Samantha stepped back and looked at him, a frown on her face.

"I can give the child a name," Avery said.

Samantha was confused.

"My name," Avery said, "and all rights ascribed to it. He would have my name and not just that. No one need ever know that I'm not the child's natural father. I'm the only son in my family. That means that I'll inherit the family properties. As my firstborn, your child, if it is a boy, will inherit from me. We're an old Virginia family. We may be Confederates, Samantha, but we're also related to Martha Washington, and my father is cousin to Mary Custis, General Lee's wife. My parents are kind people, Samantha, and would welcome you into our family."

"Avery, what are you saying?" Samantha was dumbfounded. "Are you asking me to marry you?"

"Think about it, Samantha. It would be an answer to

your problems. You could go to my family in Arlington as my wife, expecting our first child. You'd be safe there. No one would know that circumstances are any different."

"I would. You would!"

"I'd be a good father to your child, Samantha. I'd consider it my own. And I'd be a good and honorable husband to you."

Samantha's head was reeling. She couldn't believe what she was hearing. "Avery, I can't marry you. I'm carrying another man's child."

Avery's jaw tensed slightly, but he didn't speak. Samantha looked at this man who'd been kind to her this past year, but whom she hardly knew. She realized the enormity of his gesture, and her heart went out to him. "Oh, Avery, you'd do this for me?"

"I would be honored," Avery replied.

When Avery and Samantha returned to the kitchen building, Caroline was waiting.

"Well, Avery, did you convince her to stay?" Caroline asked.

"No, Caroline, we'll be leaving immediately," Avery replied.

"We?" Caroline exclaimed.

"Yes, I'll accompany Samantha as far as Arlington."

"Are you mad, Avery? Have you both lost your minds?" Caroline turned to Samantha. "Samantha, I know Ethan has hurt you. He behaved abominably, but you can't just run off like this. And Avery," Caroline continued as she turned back to him, "you could be court-martialed for leaving now."

"Oh, Avery, is that true? I can't let you come with me," Samantha said.

"Nor can you make the journey alone," Avery answered. "This is what we must do. I can secure supplies for us along the way, but we'll need some food to last us a few days," Avery said as he turned to Caroline. "Will you help us, Caroline?"

"Why? Why must you do this?" Caroline asked.

Samantha watched as Avery took command of the situation. "I understand if you don't want to risk involvement. What you said is true, although it would be up to Ethan, as my immediate superior, to press charges," he said to Caroline.

"And when he hears that you helped Samantha to leave, he will. He'll be furious, Avery."

Samantha swallowed. "You're wrong, Caroline. It was Ethan's plan all along to dispense with me. He was planning to send me north as soon as he could make the arrangements. I've simply relieved him of the burden."

Caroline looked at Samantha. She could see Samantha's jaw quiver and the tears threatening.

"No," Caroline said softly, "you're wrong. Don't misunderstand me. I'm not defending Ethan. No gentleman would have encouraged your feelings as he did. But you should know that Ethan loves you."

"Caroline, please don't."

"No, you listen to me," Caroline continued. "I would know, wouldn't I?" Caroline sighed. "I've known Ethan all of my life, and he's never been in love until now. I'm sorry for you. I'm sorry for Ethan, too, for he loves you. You're the only woman he's ever loved."

The room was quiet, and then Samantha spoke in a whisper. "He has a wife."

"Yes, well, since when has love been important in marriage?" Caroline asked.

Samantha stared at Caroline a moment and then spoke. "If you'll excuse me, I'll get my things."

When Samantha returned, Avery was waiting with the

supplies Caroline had packed for him. Saying goodbye to Caroline was more difficult than Samantha would have imagined. She recalled how she'd disliked Caroline Cooper when she'd first arrived. A lot had happened since then. Thankfully, Avery once again took control of the situation, and in a matter of minutes, Samantha and Avery were riding away from Cooper Plantation, heading north.

It took Samantha and Avery three weeks to reach Arlington. At first, Avery had been concerned with the pace that Samantha had set. She rode as though chased by demons. She looked wild, dressed in buckskins, her hair flying out behind her as her great black horse carried her along. There was an awkward moment when Avery suggested that, in her condition, she shouldn't be riding so hard.

They covered a lot of distance that first day and stopped only when the sun had set. Samantha had been eager to get as far away from Ethan as she could. Avery built a small fire and they huddled close to it, eating in silence. The only other sound was that of not-too-distant cannon fire and a steady, cold rain that had begun to fall.

Avery was unsure of how to conduct himself. By convention, he and Samantha shouldn't even be traveling together. Young ladies were never alone in a man's company. When it came time to sleep, he erected a crude tent for Samantha. He placed his own blanket outside under the protection of some trees. That was the first night that the nightmares returned to Samantha. She screamed, calling to Ethan, but he wasn't there.

"Samantha. Samantha, wake up."

Samantha reached out, and a man's arms came around her. Slowly, the grisly images of the dream faded, and

Samantha felt the cold night air on her tear-streaked face. She looked up in the dim light to see a concerned Avery Scott.

"You were having a dream. Are you all right now?" Avery asked, still holding her in his arms. He didn't ask any more questions, but spent the remainder of the night at her side in the tent. By the end of the first week, he no longer placed his blanket outside of the tent, for almost every night, Samantha would cry out during the night. He never asked her about the dreams, for the terror and pain were evident in her eyes. When she called out for Ethan, he held her until she quieted and slipped back into sleep.

Several times during their travels, they had to hide in the thick woods to avoid encountering Union troops. The sounds of muskets and cannons were everywhere, and sometimes they could actually hear the screams of men falling in battle over the next ridge. The farther north they went, the more they traveled at night. There was less chance of being discovered, even though the bitter night winds were chilling. Fortunately, Avery knew the countryside well, and they were able to make it to Arlington without confronting Union or Confederate soldiers. They arrived in Arlington on January 19, the same day that Union General William Tecumseh Sherman marched into South Carolina.

CHAPTER 13

The sun had just set when Samantha rode up to the large, brick-pillared house of the Scott plantation. She could see light coming from the windows of the massive structure.

Avery and Samantha had actually arrived in Arlington that afternoon. They'd hidden in a grove of trees on the outskirts of the Scott tobacco plantation. Avery had explained that the whole area was under Federal occupation now, and that it wouldn't be safe for him to accompany her to his house. He couldn't risk being seen and captured.

They waited until dusk, and then Avery gave her directions to his home. Before departing, he'd written a letter to his parents. "This is for my parents," he said as he handed her the paper. "Would you like to read it?"

"Avery, I wouldn't read your private letter," Samantha had replied.

"I know that, but I thought you might want to know what I've said about you."

When Samantha didn't open the letter, Avery spoke. "I've asked them to offer their hospitality to you for as long as you desire it. You may stay with my parents as long as you need to, Samantha. I told them something of your circumstances." Samantha frowned. "No, not about that," he said, glancing unconsciously to her abdomen. "I told them about your capture and that you've been held by the Confederacy this past year." He hesitated. "I also told them of my fondness for you. I didn't betray any confidences,

Samantha, and asked them not to question you." He smiled slightly. "They will, of course, inquire as to my well-being."

Samantha took Avery's letter. Then, the two of them sat down to wait. At sunset, Avery hesitantly kissed Samantha's cheek before saying goodbye. Samantha clung to him for a moment and then hastily wiped away her tears as he helped her into the saddle. Samantha turned Kota northward and continued for another thirty minutes, arriving at the Scott plantation just after sunset.

Samantha dismounted now in front of Avery's home. She was exhausted from the long ride from Charleston. It had taken them three weeks, riding twelve hours each day and sleeping very little on the cold ground. She tied Kota to the post and walked up the steps. There was no other choice for her; there was no other place to go.

She approached the massive door and knocked on it. In a matter of minutes, a Negro opened it. "Yes, miss?" he said hesitantly as he took in Samantha's appearance.

"I'd like to speak to Mr. and Mrs. Scott," Samantha replied.

The Negro looked doubtful. "Your name, please?"

"Samantha Carter. Please tell Mr. and Mrs. Scott that I bear news from their son, Avery."

The Negro looked surprised and then recovered. "Won't you come in, Miss Carter? I'll get the master. Please wait here," the man said as he ushered Samantha into the parlor.

It'd been three weeks since Samantha had been inside a building of any kind, let alone a house as fine as this. She was so tired. She longed to sit down on the comfortable settee in front of her, but she hesitated. She glanced down at her travel-worn buckskins. If she had any doubt as to how she must look, it was erased as Jacob and Mary Scott entered the room. They immediately took in her appearance, the look of shock plainly upon their faces. Jacob Scott recovered and stepped forward. He was a handsome man of medium height and weight with slightly graying hair. His wife, Mary, was short and plump, her wide hoopskirt making her look shorter than she was.

"Miss Carter? I'm Jacob Scott and this is my wife, Mary. I understand you have news of our son?"

"Have you seen him? Is Avery all right?" Mary asked apprehensively.

"Yes, Mrs. Scott, he's fine," Samantha replied. "I only left him half an hour ago."

"But how can that be?" Jacob asked.

"I didn't mean to alarm you. He asked that I give this letter to you," Samantha said as she withdrew the folded paper from her pocket. The room seemed very warm. As she stepped toward Mr. and Mrs. Scott, the room grew dark and she couldn't focus her eyes on Mr. Scott. It was difficult for her to maintain her balance. She reached for a nearby table and felt herself sinking downward as the darkness closed in. She would have fallen if Jacob had not rushed forward to catch her.

"Mary, help me," Jacob cried as he caught Samantha in his arms.

Samantha was vaguely aware of hands easing her down onto a chair.

"Ben!" Mary called. "Bring me a glass of water," she said to the Negro man who appeared at the door.

Samantha kept her eyes closed as she waited for the sickening vertigo to pass. She could feel the perspiration on her forehead and the pounding of her heart. Then a glass of water was thrust into her hands.

"Miss Carter, can you drink this?" Mary asked.

Samantha opened her eyes. Her vision was still hazy, punctuated by a sprinkling of tiny lights dancing in front of her, but she could see the gentle face of Avery's mother.

"Are you all right, Miss Carter?" Mary asked with concern. "Drink this."

Mary supported Samantha while she drank the water. Slowly, the little lights dissipated and the dizziness left her.

"Thank you, Mrs. Scott," Samantha said weakly. "Please accept my apology. I don't know what came over me. Here's Avery's letter."

Mary took the paper from Samantha's trembling hand and gave it to her husband.

"Miss Carter, are you well?" Jacob asked kindly.

Samantha's heart was still racing, but her vision was clear. "Yes, Mr. Scott, I'm fine. I didn't mean to intrude. I'll leave you to your letter," she said as she started to stand.

"Nonsense. You sit yourself down, Miss Carter," Mary said as she took Samantha's arm and gently pushed her back onto the chair. "We're so grateful to receive news of our son."

As Samantha obediently sat down, Mary returned to her husband's side as he opened the letter.

"You will excuse us, Miss Carter? We haven't heard from our son in some time," Jacob said as he and his wife began to read the letter.

Samantha glanced away as the older man and woman read Avery's letter. The silence in the room was deafening when, at last, Mr. Scott folded the paper and placed it in his pocket. Samantha looked up to see confusion and surprise on the older Scotts' faces.

Mary turned to her husband. "What does this mean, Jacob? I don't understand."

Jacob patted his wife's hand. "It means that Avery is well. That's all that is important, Mary. We must honor his request."

"But Jacob...."

"Hush, Mary," he said gently and turned to Samantha.

"Miss Carter—is that how you wish to be addressed?"

Samantha didn't understand. "Pardon me?"

Jacob frowned. "Miss Carter, do you know the contents of our son's letter?"

"I know only that he's asked you to allow me to stay here until I've rested. I believe he also mentioned something of my whereabouts this past year."

This was more difficult than Samantha had anticipated. Perhaps it was the strain of the last three weeks' journey under rugged conditions, or because the pain of Ethan's betrayal was still so acute. Her eyes glistened despite her efforts to clamp her jaws together. She looked away as she swallowed hard to loosen the constriction that was tightening in her throat. She suddenly felt trapped before these people who were watching her. She wanted only to escape.

"I think perhaps this was a mistake," Samantha said hesitantly. "I must leave now," she said as she stood and turned toward the door.

"Please, Miss Carter, wait."

Samantha stopped.

"Forgive us. We're being terribly ungracious," Jacob began. "Your coming here has been a surprise to us, but we're grateful for news of our son. Please, you must be our guest. You need rest. If you don't mind, we'd like to talk with you in the morning. But for now, Mary will see that you're made comfortable." Jacob turned to his wife. "Mary?"

"Of course, Miss Carter, please do us the honor of accepting our hospitality," Mary said as she moved to Samantha's side and took her arm. "You must be hungry as well as tired. I'll have a room prepared for you and a meal brought up. You just come with me, my dear." Her voice was warm as she smiled gently at Samantha.

Samantha hesitated. "You're very kind, and yes, I'm tired. I would appreciate the rest, but just for tonight. I'll leave tomorrow."

"Well, we'll talk about it tomorrow after you've had a good night's sleep."

Samantha had insisted on bedding Kota down in the stable herself and then returned to the main house, carrying her bags and rifle. A surprised look crossed Mary's face when she saw the rifle, but she quickly returned to the task of directing that a bath be prepared for Samantha as well as food and drink.

When they were in the bedroom that had been given to Samantha, Mary spoke again. "May I have your clothes unpacked while you bathe, Miss Carter?"

Samantha smiled. "I'm afraid I have no clothes to unpack. I left in a hurry, and this is all I have," she said, indicating her buckskins.

"Well, don't you worry. I can give you one of my nightgowns to wear tonight, and tomorrow we'll see what we can find for you."

The house slaves finished pouring water into the copper tub, and Mary sent them out of the room. She returned a moment later with a nightgown, which she laid across the bed. "Would you like some help?"

"No, thank you. I can manage." Samantha smiled weakly.

"Very well, then. I'll return when you are finished."

Samantha appreciated the privacy Mrs. Scott gave her. When Mrs. Scott returned later with a tray of food, Samantha had bathed and was already asleep.

When Samantha awoke the next morning, it was to sunshine coming through the lace curtains at the window. She opened her eyes to see a Negro woman hanging clothes in the wardrobe.

The woman turned and smiled. "Good morning, Miss Carter. I'm called 'Lacy.' Would you like me to bring your breakfast to you?"

"Oh, no, I should get up."

"These are for you," Lacy said as she finished hanging the garments in the wardrobe. "Miz Scott done sent the master over to their daughter's house early this mornin' to fetch them for you."

Samantha felt as though she'd already imposed upon Avery's parents enough, but she couldn't put her buckskins back on—at least not while she was still in the Scott's house. The buckskin shirt and pants should be brushed down and hung out in the air, and she needed time to consider her options. She could telegraph her father, but she needed to rest before she started the journey home.

Samantha dressed, and then Lacy took her to the dining room. Lacy indicated that Mr. and Mrs. Scott wished to speak to her when she was finished eating.

A half hour later, Lacy escorted Samantha into a small room. Jacob was seated at a desk, making entries into a leather-bound ledger, while Mary sat in a chair near a window, her needlework in her hands.

"Come in, Miss Carter," Jacob said as he stood. "Please, sit down."

Samantha crossed to a chair near the desk and sat.

"Are you feeling better this morning, Miss Carter?" Mary asked.

"Yes, and please thank your daughter for the dress. Matilda? Avery spoke of her."

"Oh, you're quite welcome, my dear. She was pleased to hear of Avery's letter. Matilda lives on the next plantation. She'll probably come for a visit in a day or two. It's not easy for her, with her husband away. Her husband is with General Lee's Army of Northern Virginia," Mary said proudly, and then hesitated. "I'm sorry. You are, of course, a Yankee. I meant no offense, Miss Carter."

"We don't mean to be inhospitable, Miss Carter," Jacob said. "Since the Yankees took over this area, they've freed our slaves and prevented us from engaging in any business enterprises. They've confiscated most of what we own. I was unable to plant last year, as were most of the other planters in this area. If we can't plant, we can't survive." Jacob closed his ledger and walked around the desk. "But that's none of your concern. We'd like to speak to you about our son's letter," he said as he withdrew the paper from his coat. "Frankly, Miss Carter, it's a puzzling letter."

Jacob walked over to stand in front of Samantha. Mary put her sewing down on the table next to her.

"Our son has asked us to respect your privacy, and we certainly don't mean to pry. He's also asked that we extend our hospitality to you for as long as you desire." Jacob paused. "We are pleased, of course, to honor our son's request. You are most welcome, Miss Carter."

Samantha was uncomfortable in the Scotts' presence. She stood. "Mr. Scott, I appreciate the gesture, but I think coming here was a mistake. You and Mrs. Scott are very kind, but I think it would be best if I go to Washington City. I can telegraph my family from there."

"But you can't travel to Washington City alone. Where would you find lodgings? You can't possibly stay in a hotel alone," Mrs. Scott said, her shock apparent.

Samantha looked at the woman seated before her. Had Samantha forgotten? Had she been away from civilization that long? Mary Scott was a lady. Of course she couldn't fathom a woman traveling alone. A lady would always be in the company of her husband or a male relative who was her chaperone and protector.

"Miss Carter? I'd like you to read this," Jacob said. In his hand was Avery's letter. "Perhaps then you'll understand our confusion."

Samantha hesitated and then slowly reached out to take the letter.

January 19, 1865
Arlington, Virginia
Dearest Mother and Father,
I have entrusted this letter to Miss Samantha Carter. As she can attest to, I am fit and well. It grieves me to be so close to home and be unable to see you. I pray that this war will not endure much longer, although I fear for our Confederate States when it's finally ended.
This must be brief, as I cannot linger here long. I humbly ask you to look after Miss Carter and extend your hospitality to her for as long as she desires it. It's not for me to divulge her private affairs, but I will tell you this much: she has been a captive of the Confederacy since May of last year. During that time, she was held against her will. Despite this infringement upon her, many Confederate soldiers owe their lives to her.
You should know that I have come to regard her with great affection. I have offered her my hand in marriage, although she has refused it. It is still my hope that she will reconsider. In the event that she does not, I have offered her the use of my name. Should she wish to return to her home as Mrs. Avery Scott, she has both my permission and blessing.
Time is short and I must leave. I hope to be home soon. May God bless and watch over you both.
I remain your loving son,
Avery

Samantha's hand trembled as she handed the letter back to Jacob. She took a deep breath. "I'm a doctor, Mr. Scott, a surgeon," she began. Samantha saw a frown pass Jacob's face. She would prefer not to have to tell these people of her ordeal, but she could see their confusion and concern for their son. She told the Scotts of her education in Paris and subsequent disobedience of her father. She recounted the morning of her capture by Lieutenant Quicken's men and her service in the Confederate Medical Corps. She was careful to omit any reference to Ethan. Once, Mary, who had a look of horror on her face, interrupted her.

"I don't believe it!" Mary interjected. "The Confederacy would not take a lady captive."

"Ah, but you see, Mrs. Scott, my disguise was very good. They thought I was a Yankee boy," Samantha said as she continued. When she concluded, Mary again spoke.

"Even after you were wounded and they knew you were a woman, they still held you captive?" Mary asked. Jacob had gone over to stand beside his wife, patting her gently on the back. Her distress over Samantha's story was plainly evident.

"Not exactly," Samantha said evasively. "I was assured that when it became possible, I would be returned to the North. Circumstances became such this past month that I had to escape. Your son helped me."

Silence filled the room. Samantha walked over to the window and gazed out across the expanse of winter-bare fields. Finally, Jacob spoke.

"Our son's letter indicates that he holds you in high regard, Miss Carter, and I believe I can see why he does. You refused his offer of marriage, but there is the matter of his name. I don't understand."

"Mrs. Scott," Samantha said as she turned to look at the pale woman seated in the chair. "Would you allow me to speak with your husband alone?"

Mary seemed immobile, still shocked by Samantha's story.

"Mary," Jacob said, "why don't you see what Lacy's up to

in the kitchen. I'll join you in a moment." Jacob escorted his wife to the door, and after she left, turned back to Samantha and waited patiently.

"I'm afraid I've upset your wife," Samantha began. "I can see that she is a kind woman, and she is a lady. I don't think that what I have to say would be appropriate for her to hear. I assume, Mr. Scott, that you are worldlier. That's why I asked to speak with you alone."

Samantha sighed and her lip trembled slightly. She'd hoped to keep her secret until she reached home, but this man deserved an explanation; he deserved to hear the truth. "Avery helped me to leave Charleston at great risk to himself," she began, her voice soft. "It was essential that I leave. You see, Mr. Scott, I am with child." Samantha turned away. "I'm carrying the child of a Confederate officer."

"My son's?" Jacob asked.

Samantha turned back. "No, Mr. Scott, Avery was always kind to me and treated me with respect. He's a gentleman, and he's been a friend to me." Samantha paused. "When he learned of my condition, he offered to help me. He brought me here and, as you read, asked me to marry him. I refused. Mr. Scott, I'm very fond of your son. He's one of the kindest and most honorable men I've met, but I couldn't enter into a marriage with him, not with circumstances as they are. I believe he understood. That's when he offered me the protection of his name.

"I'm returning home soon, and I don't know if my family will accept me. After what I've done, they may cast me out. Some would consider my care of Confederate soldiers an act of treason." Samantha recalled her brother's hateful words to her. His condemnation was another pain she would always carry with her. She swallowed. "But to be unmarried and carrying a Confederate's child? I'm certain I don't need to explain what a disgrace that would be in their eyes.

"I don't know what I'm going to do. Avery was right about one thing, though. I can't afford to make any rash decisions, and I'm very tired, Mr. Scott. Avery and I rode fast and hard the past three weeks, taking very little time to sleep. And the months before that, there was little food and very little rest as I moved from one battlefield to another. My strength is gone. I just need to rest a few days before I try to travel to my home on the Iowa Frontier. But I'm a Northerner, a Yankee, and I'll understand if you'd rather that I not stay here," she finished quietly.

Jacob took a deep breath. "These are not normal times, Miss Carter, they're dreadful times, and one can only guess at what you have endured at the hands of the Confederacy. You must surely hate us all for what was done to you. You didn't have to tell me these things. You showed great courage. I will honor my son's request; it's my privilege. You're welcome to remain with us for as long as you wish. I offer you and your baby my home, the honor of my name, and my protection. No one, Yankee or Confederate, will harm you while you are here."

"Thank you," Samantha said quietly. "Mr. Scott, I bear no ill will toward the Confederacy. My hatred is reserved for but one Confederate officer."

"The child's father?" he asked boldly, his own anger apparent at the affront he believed had been committed.

Samantha didn't answer but turned away, but not before Jacob saw her eyes fill with tears. She knew what Mr. Scott was thinking—that her condition had resulted from force. Let him think that. It didn't really matter anymore.

Samantha didn't know what Jacob said to his wife, but the Scotts were kind. Mary hovered around her but didn't ask any more questions. After a week, Samantha approached Mr. Scott. "I'd like to notify my family that I'm safe. Is it possible to send my father a telegram?"

That afternoon, Jacob took Samantha into Washington City. She didn't have to wait long for a reply. A messenger brought it the next morning. After he left, Samantha opened the telegram and read her father's words:

SAMANTHA STOP PRAISE GOD YOU ARE ALIVE STOP STAY WHERE YOU ARE STOP WE'LL COME TO GET YOU STOP WE LOVE YOU STOP PAPA

Mary found Samantha in the sitting room, the telegram on her lap. For Samantha, the telegram signaled the beginning of the end. Soon she would be home, and all of this would be behind her, all of it—Ethan, too. For not the first time, she wished that she had died on Kennesaw Mountain. The grief that Samantha felt seemed to tear her soul apart. She sat there, silent tears flowing freely, her pain too great for words.

Mary hastily called her husband. Samantha limply handed the telegraph to him.

"But, my dear," Mary said, "this is good news, isn't it?"

"Yes," Samantha finally whispered, "it is."

Later that night, Mary awoke to the familiar sounds coming from Samantha's room. She slipped into Samantha's room, as she had done every night since Samantha arrived, and held her hand until Samantha quieted.

When Mary returned to her own bedroom that night, she eyed her husband accusingly. "Something awful must have happened to that child, Jacob, and I want to know what it was," she demanded.

"Mary—"

"I'll not be put off, Jacob. What did she say to you?"

"I can't betray her confidence, my dear," Jacob said quietly.

"Jacob! Have you heard her when she has those nightmares? She mumbles about blood everywhere, men crying out, dying, and cutting off arms and legs. Tonight, she screamed and grabbed her chest like she was in great pain. Jacob, you've no idea."

"Mary, you see her as a girl, but remember that, as extraordinary as it may seem, she's a trained doctor. She served as a surgeon on the battlefield. She was wounded. Many a soldier has suffered as she does now, the demons of war plaguing them long after the last shot is fired."

Mary thought about what her husband said. "I believe that's part of it, but there's more. There's such pain and hurt that lingers in her eyes long after she wakes up. Something awful happened to her, I know it."

"Does she talk about it during the day?"

"No, she avoids discussing the war. Oh, she's more than willing to talk about Avery when I ask her. I believe she truly does care for him. But that's all. She won't discuss anything else."

"Respect her privacy, Mary. I dare say she's suffered more at the hands of the Confederacy than we have suffered at the hands of the Yankees." He looked at his wife. "You're very good to her, Mary. Avery would be pleased if he were here."

The next several weeks passed quietly for Samantha. She tried to help Mary as much as she could, but there were times when Mary would find her staring, unaware of her surroundings, lost in some painful memory.

This day, Samantha was seated in the dining room with Mary and Jacob as Lacy served the midday meal. They were interrupted by Ben, one of the house slaves who, like Lacy, had elected to remain with the Scotts after the Yankees had come.

"Master, there's a Yankee soldier at the door," Ben said.

Jacob stiffened. "Mary, you ladies stay here, and I'll see what he wants."

"Be careful, Jacob," Mary said, a worried look on her face.

Jacob left the dining room and walked into the main hall of the house. The Federal soldier stood inside the door where Ben had left him. As Jacob approached, he could see that the soldier wore the insignia of a Federal captain on his uniform. He was wearing the formal officer's uniform with a crimson sash around his waist, a sword at his side, as well as his sidearm. His boots were polished, and the brass on his uniform shone. He had removed his hat upon entering the house and was holding it in his right hand. The left sleeve of his coat was pinned to the side of his coat, the sleeve empty. He was tall; his hair and closely cropped beard were dark. He stood there confidently as Jacob approached him.

The Federal captain inclined his head slightly. "Mr. Jacob Scott?"

"Yes."

"Mr. Scott, my name is Charles Carter," he said as he extended his hand to Jacob. Hesitantly, Jacob shook it. "Mr. Scott, I'm looking for Miss Samantha Carter."

"Oh?"

"Yes, sir. I understand that she's staying here, or at least she was three weeks ago. Samantha is my sister."

Samantha and Mary had remained in the dining room, as Jacob instructed. But then Samantha heard Jacob talking. She excused herself from the table and walked toward the voices. "Charles?" she said as she entered the hall. With a cry, she lifted her skirts and ran across the hall.

"Samantha!" Charles Carter stepped past Jacob and caught Samantha as she threw her arms around him. "Samantha, we were afraid you were dead," he said as he hugged her to him. Charles broke the embrace and looked at his sister. "How long has it been? You left for Paris three years ago. That was the last time I saw you. You're all grown up."

"Charles," Samantha said compassionately. She didn't hesitate, but reached out and touched his sleeve, feeling the short stump at his shoulder where once his arm had been. His eyes widened in surprise. His embarrassment was obvious, but Samantha persisted. "Has it healed well? Do you feel any pain?" she asked.

A slight smile passed his lips. "So you really are a doctor."

Samantha didn't smile but looked at him with concern.

"Don't worry," he said. "I'm alive. That's more than I can say for a lot of my friends."

"How did it happen?"

Charles shrugged his shoulders. "Our unit joined Sherman's army. We had just captured Chattanooga and moved into Georgia. I was wounded just before we reached Atlanta. God, what a bloodbath. You can't imagine."

Atlanta. Her head exploding in pain. Her chest on fire. The smell of the Georgia earth as she lay there, feeling her blood draining out of her body. Suddenly, the air in the room was pressing in on her and she couldn't breathe. Samantha swayed. Charles reached out and caught her with his one arm.

"Sam! Are you all right?"

Jacob was just about to leave to allow Samantha and her brother some privacy, but he stepped forward now. "Captain, perhaps you would like to escort your sister to a chair," he said, indicating the adjacent parlor. "This way,"

Jacob said as Mary came up behind him.

Samantha held on tightly to Charles until he and Jacob helped her to sit. Charles sat down next to her, taking her hand in his.

"Forgive me," Samantha said.

"Sam? Are you ill?" Charles asked with concern.

Samantha looked at her brother's worried face. "No, Charles, I'm fine. I just felt suddenly warm," she assured him. She glanced up to see Mary. She was glad for the distraction and introduced her brother to her. Charles stood while being introduced and then sat down again.

"Sam, where have you been? Pa said that you left in April. He found your note and then Many Horses came to tell him that he'd taken you as far as Washington City. Pa contacted every senator and banker in the North. He even wrote to the Union Medical Corps Headquarters in Washington City. He had people looking everywhere for you. You completely disappeared! And then shortly after I was sent home in July, a telegram arrived from Grandpa's bank in Boston saying that you were safe. No one at the bank seemed to know where the telegram came from. Nothing. No name. No mention of where you were. Just a message from you saying that you were safe. Sam, where were you? Why didn't you contact us?"

Samantha impulsively turned to her brother and threw her arms around him again, holding him tightly as she wept. With his one arm, Charles held her.

"Sam? Sam, honey, what is it?" he asked gently.

"I'm just so glad that you're alive," she said roughly, burying her face in his shoulder.

Charles laughed softly. "You have a strange way of showing it. You're crying."

Samantha shook her head. "You don't understand. I used to look for you and Robert. I would walk among the bodies on the battlefield, searching the faces. Sometimes the bodies were so badly mutilated or decomposed that they were beyond recognition, and there were so many bodies—thousands of them. We usually had to move on before I was able to search them all. After a while, I stopped searching. There was never any time. There were too many wounded." Her voice died away.

Charles separated himself from Samantha. "What are you talking about, Sam?"

Trembling, Samantha looked at her brother. She reached out and gently placed her hand along the line of his jaw. "I was in Georgia when Sherman's troops started moving to Atlanta. I was at Kennesaw Mountain, Charles—there, and a hundred other places—Fredericksburg, Chancellorsville, Spotsylvania, Franklin, Chickamauga. I don't remember them all."

"Samantha, how can that be?" Charles asked incredulously.

Samantha swallowed. "When I left last April, I was going to the Union Medical Corps Headquarters. I didn't make it. I was captured by a Confederate patrol on May 1 outside of Arlington. I've been with the Confederacy since then—that is, until four weeks ago when Mr. and Mrs. Scott's son, a lieutenant in the Confederate Army, helped me to leave Charleston and brought me here."

Charles's eyes widened in shock.

"When I was captured, I was disguised as a boy and wearing my buckskins. When the Confederates realized that I was a doctor, they took me with them. I was a Yankee boy with a skill that they desperately needed."

"Good Lord! They kept you a prisoner all this time?"

"It wasn't exactly like that. I worked as a surgeon on the battlefield in the Confederate Medical Corps."

"But how could the Rebels—"

"Charles," Samantha said, placing her fingers upon his lips, "there will be time to talk about this later. Please? I can't talk about this now," she said as new tears formed in her eyes.

The Scotts had graciously invited Charles to rest at their home before he and Samantha left. Samantha knew how difficult that had been for them. Charles's uniform was only a reminder of the danger Avery was still in. Samantha could see that Charles was also uncomfortable staying on a Confederate plantation. In the end, it was Samantha who insisted that they not delay their departure.

Saying goodbye to the Scotts was difficult. In the four weeks that she had been with them, Samantha had grown fond of Avery's parents, and they were the only link she had to the last year of her life—her only link to the Confederacy and to . . . to Ethan. Once she left with Charles, all of it would be gone forever.

Mary and Jacob both held her to them as they said goodbye. "You're always welcome in our home," Jacob whispered as he held her closely, "should you ever need anything."

Samantha brushed a tear aside. How could she ever thank this honorable man for his kindness? She would miss him.

"I will miss you, child. You will write to me?" Mary asked as they said goodbye.

"Yes," Samantha said, and then she made Mary promise to write to her with any news of Avery.

It was midafternoon when Charles and Samantha rode out of Arlington and started the long journey home.

CHAPTER 14

Charles and Samantha boarded a train in Washington City on February 17, one day before the Federal Army seized Columbia, South Carolina. Charleston fell to Sherman's troops the same day. Samantha didn't learn of the destruction of the city that had become such a part of her life until two weeks later.

Despite her promise to Charles that there would be time to explain things, she remained withdrawn on the long train ride west. When they stopped in cities, she stayed on the train or walked back to the cattle car where Kota was. She politely avoided conversation with other travelers. Charles tried unsuccessfully to learn what had happened to her during the past year when she had been in the Confederacy. She refused to discuss it.

"Sam?" he said one time. When she didn't answer, he touched her shoulder. "Samantha?"

She was startled by his touch and turned to him.

"My God, Sam, what did those Rebels do to you?" he asked as he searched her face. "It's in your eyes. I saw that look enough in the war to know that something bad happened to you."

"Please, Charles, don't ask me," she whispered.

In the end, he stopped questioning her and quietly reached out and held her hand as the train steadily made its way toward home.

Charles had a wagon waiting at the train station when they arrived in their frontier town. He loaded their bags onto the wagon and tied Kota to the back of it, then they headed out of the town for the hour drive to the Carter ranch.

As the wagon crept along the snow-covered trail, Samantha shivered. She should have changed into her buckskins. Even with the heavy traveling coat, her hoopskirt was impractical now and provided little warmth.

They'd been traveling for fifty minutes when she twisted around to look at Kota. The large horse was prancing and tossing his head in the air, resisting the restraint on him.

"Charles, stop the wagon," Samantha said.

"What? It's freezing, Sam."

"This will just take a minute," she said as she climbed down. They were on Carter land now and would reach the house in another ten minutes. She walked back to Kota and removed the rope and halter from him. She put her face against his muzzle, feeling the warmth of his breath, and then released him. "Kota, go!" she said, signaling the horse. The horse pranced in a circle around her and then suddenly darted forward. The powerful legs, which had lacked exercise on the train, now stretched out, sending snow flying behind him as he galloped across the open range, his black color in contrast to the white expanse before him.

"He'll be waiting at the ranch for us," Samantha said as she climbed back into the wagon.

Charles smiled at his sister and urged the horses into a gallop. As they came over a ridge, Samantha saw Troy, her twin brother, mounted on Kota. Kota was racing toward the wagon, Troy waving his hand in greeting, a big smile on his face. As he came to the wagon, he spun Kota around so that he was running beside the wagon. Charles grinned at his younger brother and urged the horses and wagon on faster.

"Hi, little sister!" Troy yelled as Kota propelled him forward, racing the wagon. He grinned broadly. "I wasn't sure he was going to let me ride him." Kota had neither saddle nor bridle on. Troy was guiding the horse using only his legs, as Samantha did. "Come on!" Troy shouted, motioning for Samantha to join him.

"I can't!" Samantha shouted back.

"You never could keep up with me," Troy taunted.

Samantha saw the familiar challenge in Troy's eyes. "We'll see about that!" she shouted.

"Samantha, what are you doing?" Charles asked as Samantha removed her heavy traveling coat. She then reached up under her skirt and loosened the hoop frame, letting it fall down around her ankles as the wagon sped forward. She stood up, gathered her skirt with one hand, and tied it into a knot.

"Just keep the horses going at this pace," she shouted to Charles as the wind whipped against her face.

"What!" Charles exclaimed, a look of horror upon his face.

"Ready?" Troy shouted.

"Ready!" Samantha yelled.

Troy reached out with one arm as Samantha suddenly jumped from the speeding wagon, grabbing his arm and swinging her leg over Kota's back as the horse sped on. Her hat flew off, and her skirt billowed out behind her.

"Not bad, little sister!" Troy shouted over his shoulder as Samantha's arms came around his waist. She hugged herself close to his back, blocking the wind from her face as Kota surged forward, leaving the wagon behind.

When Charles finally arrived with the wagon at the front of the house, Samantha and Troy were still seated on Kota, laughing together.

"What kind of a stunt was that?" Charles angrily

demanded as he climbed down from the wagon.

"Child's play, big brother, child's play," Troy answered as he threw his leg over Kota's neck and dismounted. He winked at Samantha. "Sam used to be able to do it from a fifteen-foot cliff." He turned back to Samantha and reached up to her. As Samantha jumped down, Troy's arms came around her. "I've missed you, Sam. Thank God you're alive!"

Seth Carter had been in the barn when his grandson came rushing up to him. "Grandpa, Ma said to fetch you! Papa, Uncle Troy, and Aunt Samantha are home," the boy cried. Seth grabbed his grandson's hand and started running with him back to the house. He found them gathered in the parlor—Samantha, Troy, Charles and his wife, Jeanie, with their young daughter, and Lilly, Samantha's former governess. The next few minutes passed amid cries of joy, tears, and hugs as the family welcomed Samantha home. Seth held his daughter to him, reluctant to release her. "I thought I'd lost you, Samantha. First your mother, and then you," he said.

"I'm sorry, Papa. I never meant to cause you pain," Samantha said.

"You're home now; that's all that matters," Seth replied. "Let me look at you."

Samantha stepped back.

"You forgot something," Charles said good-naturedly as he placed Samantha's saddlebag on the floor and held up her hooped petticoat.

"Charles!" Jeanie said, her face coloring.

"It's all right, Jeanie. Pa and Troy have seen a woman's undergarments before," Charles said.

"I took it off so I could ride Kota. I didn't mean to embarrass you, Jeanie. I'm sorry," Samantha said.

"Not as sorry as you're going to be, young lady," Seth interrupted. "I ought to take you over my knee right here, running off like that. Not a word in a year. Where in the hell have you been?" Seth roared.

Seth was not really angry. He was so grateful to have Samantha home at last. But the change in Samantha was instantaneous. Her smiled vanished. When she looked back at her father, he was shocked by what he saw. The haunted face of a woman he didn't know replaced his daughter's laughter and smiles.

"Mr. Carter," Lilly interrupted, "poor Samantha hasn't even had a chance to change out of her traveling clothes. She must be tired. Why don't I take her upstairs and she can freshen up—maybe rest before dinner."

Lilly didn't wait for a response but linked her arm through Samantha's and started walking toward the stairs. "I have my own questions," Lilly said, smiling, "like why you ran off and left me to face the wrath of your father. If it hadn't been for Charles and Jeanie's young ones, he surely would have dismissed me."

Seth watched Lilly continue to prattle as she and Samantha ascended the steps and disappeared into Samantha's bedroom. He turned to his eldest son. "What the hell was that about? You would have thought I beat her the way she looked at me. Is she all right?"

"I wish I knew, Pa," Charles said and then turned to his children. "You children go outside," he instructed. Once the children were out of the room, he turned back to his father. "Every time I tried to ask her where she's been or what had happened to her, she refused to answer," Charles said. "And the place where I found her in Arlington? It was a plantation owned by some Confederates. Scott was their name. This much Samantha told me: when she left here last April, she tried to reach the Union Medical Corps in Washington City.

She got lost and was captured outside of Arlington by a Confederate patrol. They took her south with them."

"What?" Charles's wife, Jeanie, exclaimed.

"Yes. She was disguised as a boy. Somehow they learned that she was a surgeon, and they took her south. As near as I can gather, they forced her to work as a surgeon for them. Pa, it sounded like she was in some awful places. They kept her on the battlefield with them! Apparently, the Scotts' son is a Confederate officer, and he helped her to escape and brought her to his parents' home in Arlington."

"God damn!" Seth swore.

"There's one more thing though: she saw Robert."

"Robert!"

"Yes. He was being transported with some prisoners, and she said he escaped. She said he was alive when she last saw him."

"Good God!" Seth exclaimed. "Where?"

"She wouldn't say. She didn't want to talk about it. It really upset her. She wouldn't say anything more."

"What do you mean? She must!"

"I don't think you should force her, Pa," Troy said. "Give her some time."

Seth agreed not to question Samantha further, but for the next six days, he watched his daughter carefully. She answered politely when her family spoke to her and smiled as she watched Jeanie's children play, but always behind her smile was a haunted look. Lilly reported to Seth that she often found Samantha alone and crying in her room. Troy said he also came upon her in Kota's stall, crying. Seth was worried about his daughter.

"This isn't like Samantha," he complained to his sons. "She was always so full of life. Hell, she was a handful to raise! I'd give anything to have that headstrong, disobedient girl back again. What, in the name of God, did the Confederates do to her?" Seth demanded at the end of Samantha's first week home.

Seth and the rest of Samantha's family found the answer to Seth's question that very night. Her scream pierced the quiet sleep of her family members. Seth bolted out of bed and collided with his eldest son in the hallway. Jeanie was holding a lamp, illuminating a look of fear on all their faces. Seth was the first to reach Samantha's room.

"Samantha!"

All three of them stopped at the foot of the bed. Samantha was crying, tossing wildly about in the bed, her eyes closed. Jeanie was lighting more lamps in the bedroom when Troy burst into the room. Seth, Charles, and Jeanie turned and gasped.

"You got to wake her, Pa. Now!" Troy's face was deathly white, streaked by his own tears. "I saw it, Pa! I saw it all!"

The three looked at Troy, stunned. Troy raced around the side of the bed and leaned over Samantha. He shook her shoulders. "Sam, Sam! It's me, Troy. You got to wake up, honey. It's over. You're safe. You're home, Sam!"

Seth felt helpless as he watched the communication between his two youngest children. Samantha opened her eyes to see a grief-stricken Troy leaning over her. Then Seth saw it: Samantha's nightmare was reflected in her twin brother's eyes. She started to cry. Troy sat beside her and rocked her in his arms as Seth, Charles, and Jeanie crowded near.

Seth didn't know how long his family stood around Samantha. Finally, her words came tumbling out, words that he couldn't believe. Jeanie looked like she was going to be sick and finally ran from the room. Seth, in all his years, had never witnessed the horror Samantha described. Even Charles, himself wounded in the same war that Samantha described, grew pale. Finally, exhausted and freed of the images for the time being, Samantha laid back on her pillow. It was like a vigil: none of the men wanted to leave the room until they were certain that Samantha was resting peacefully. Jeanie returned finally as Samantha was drifting off to sleep. She sent the men out, stating that she would stay the rest of the night with Samantha. Reluctantly, Seth led the way. The men didn't return to their bedrooms, but went down to the kitchen.

They sat in silence around the table, each still recoiling from what they had heard, each deeply troubled for Samantha. Charles spoke first. "I dream sometimes," he said, "not like that, though. I hear the muskets and cannons, smell the gunpowder, and I get real scared. I even see the faces of some of the men I fought. I remember being shot and being carried into the surgical tent. Pa, that tent was nothing like the surgical tent Sam described. They gave me chloroform during the surgery and then something for the pain afterward. Oh, it was bad, and I'll never forget it, but it was nothing like where Samantha was.

"She's right about something else, too," Charles continued. "The Rebels that we captured were a sorry lot—ragged clothes, worn-out shoes or barefoot, most of them hadn't had a decent meal in a long time, some of them just kids, too. Don't misunderstand me. I'm proud of what I did. Those people were trying to tear this Union apart. But, Pa, I was a soldier. It was my job to fight and to kill as many of them as possible. The Rebels were doing the same to us. But Samantha! Jesus!"

"Sam wanted to save them all," Troy said quietly. "That's all she ever wanted to do." He looked at his father. "I think she died a little with each one of them she couldn't save."

Samantha awoke as the light filtered into her room. She'd been dreaming of Ethan, and her body ached with need. She could almost feel his touch on her skin; she could remember the feel of him inside her. Samantha hurled her pillow across the room. It landed on a small table, sending the table's contents crashing to the floor. She would prefer the nightmare to this. "Damn him! Damn Ethan Winters-Hunt to hell!" she screamed.

The door opened, and a startled Jeanie stepped inside. "Samantha, what's wrong?"

"Nothing, Jeanie. I just knocked something over," Samantha said as she stood up.

"You're crying. Oh, Samantha," Jeanie said sympathetically.

"I'm all right. I just need to go," Samantha said as she reached for her clothes.

"Go? Go where?"

"To see Many Horses."

"Samantha, wait. I'll get your father," Jeanie said as she hasted out of the room.

When Jeanie returned a few minutes later, she had Seth, Troy, and Charles at her side. The men stopped and stared as they entered the room. Samantha was dressed in her buckskins and held her rifle in her hand.

"Samantha, where are you going?" Seth asked with surprise.

"I need to see Many Horses," she said.

"They're gone, honey," Seth said gently. "He took his tribe north to Canada. They left last August."

Samantha stood there, staring at her father and brothers. She felt trapped. Trapped in the hurt, betrayal, and pain that Ethan had left in her. Trapped in her inability to control the burning passion and desire she still felt for him. Trapped in the love she still felt for him. Trapped in a body that survived death. Trapped in a life she did not want. She pushed past her family and broke into a run down the hallway and stairs. She didn't stop when she heard her father call to her, but ran to the barn.

Kota stomped his hooves as she hastily grabbed a bridle. He seemed to sense her desperation, for as soon as she placed the bridle on him, he took a step forward. She grabbed a handful of mane and swung her leg over his bare back. Responding to his mistress's urging, Kota shot out of the barn, barely missing Troy, Seth, and Charles, who had followed Samantha outside.

Samantha urged Kota on, oblivious to the frigid wind that cut at her face. The horse sped across the plains, following the light touch of Samantha's calves. She didn't slow him until she came to a wooded area, the branches bare in the winter. She wound through the trees and crossed a small stream, its water frozen. Finally, she came to rest in the place where, when she was a child, the Lakota tribe had made their camp.

Samantha didn't dismount but stayed on Kota, welcoming the warmth that his body provided. The wind moaned sorrowfully as it blew through the cold, deserted camp. There was nothing left now—only memories of a joyful time in her life that had also been cruelly ripped from her.

She lost track of time in the depth of her grief, but after a while, she began to shiver. Her tears stung her face in the cold, freezing on her eyelashes. Still, she didn't move. She needed to talk with Many Horses. He would understand. She needed answers.

"But the answers are within you, Little One. Why do you seek them elsewhere? When will you learn to accept what The Spirits have given you?"

Charrah! Samantha jerked her head around. The only

sound was the wind whistling through the trees. Even Kota stood quietly, instead of stomping his feet or tossing his head. Samantha sat there, the words echoing through her mind as her tears flowed down her face, burning as they froze in the winter wind.

"But how do I stop the pain?" she whispered aloud as she searched the gray winter sky above her. "I love him, but I can't live with the pain he left in me. I find no joy in life. I'm consumed by the hurt he caused, and yet I yearn for him. I ache with longing for him, day and night. I'd welcome death, Charrah. Why didn't you just let me die when I was shot? I wish I had died! I want to die!" she cried to the heavens.

"Foolish child!" came the retort.

She wrapped her arms about herself, overcome with anguish. "Then teach me, please, I beg you. Teach me as you did when I was a child. Teach me how to live with the loss, the longing, the pain," she cried desperately.

"Accept what you cannot change. Accept what is—the joy and the pain. You must accept all that The Spirits have given you, Little One, in order to walk with Them. You are not abandoned, my child. Walk with Them."

Through her tears, Samantha looked at her hands, gloved against the cold. There was skill and healing in her hands, and there was wisdom and power in the spirit that had been placed within her when she was just a small child. But she was not God. She was not of The Spirits. She could only do that which was given to her. It was as Charrah said: she must accept it all—the gift and the pain.

There was a sudden change in the wind. The bitter wind was stilled, replaced by a breeze that was warm and soft, with a sweet fragrance that gently touched her face. Samantha bowed her head in respect and reverence.

Sometime later, Samantha was riding Kota back toward the ranch at a calm, walking pace, despite the cold, when Troy galloped up to her. "You all right, Little Sister?" he asked as he turned his horse around to walk beside her.

Samantha smiled at his insistent use of that name. "I'm fine, Little Brother. I hope I didn't scare anyone back at the house."

"Oh, we Carters don't scare that easily, except for Jeanie, maybe." He smiled, then cocked his head. "Sam, who's Ethan?" Troy asked.

Samantha startled. She looked at her brother as they rode their horses next to each other. "Where did you hear that name?" she asked steadily.

"You kept repeating it during your nightmare."

Samantha took a deep breath, her face forward. "He's the father of the child I'm carrying."

Samantha's family was seated in the parlor while a fire blazed, warming the room. Samantha had insisted that Lilly also be present, since what she had to say would affect her as well. She'd waited until the evening, after Jeanie's children were in bed.

"There's something that I must tell you," she began, "and I can't delay any longer. You know a little of my life this past year, but there's more. I told you I was disguised as a boy when captured by the Confederates. I worked as a battlefield surgeon for them. But eventually, the officer who captured me, Major Ethan Winters-Hunt, discovered I was a woman. I was wounded during a battle at Kennesaw Mountain. I was shot twice: in the head and in the chest." Samantha grimaced. "The pain was unbearable. I remember thinking that I would probably bleed to death there, and then I lost consciousness."

Jeanie's eyes filled with tears. Seth inhaled sharply. Troy

swore.

"Major Winters-Hunt—Ethan—found me and took me back to the chief surgeon. That's when Ethan and Dr. Beauregard discovered that I was a woman." Samantha shrugged. "They didn't think I would live. I was unconscious for several days with a high fever and had lost a lot of blood. With battle wounds like that, I don't know how I survived, either. I should have died." Samantha hesitated and then spoke softly. "Ethan took care of me during that time."

When she continued, her voice was strong again. "When I recovered, Ethan was furious. I guess he could justify forcing a boy into service for the Confederacy but not a woman.

On several occasions, he tried to send me back, but I refused to go. I stayed with the Confederate Surgical Corps."

"Why, Samantha?" her father asked incredulously.

"I don't know if you'll understand. Robert didn't," she added softly. "He called me a traitor, Pa, and denounced me as his sister. He said I was dead to him."

"Robert!"

"He was brought in as a prisoner. He escaped, but not before he called me. . . ." Samantha stopped to regain her composure. Robert's words still were like a knife twisting in her heart. "He was well the last time I saw him," she whispered. "Ethan let him escape, and I stayed with the Confederacy until December. But then, circumstances changed." She paused to gather courage. "In December," she said, "I learned that Major Winters-Hunt had a wife in Savannah. By then, I had fallen in love with him and was carrying his child."

Jeanie swayed in her chair. Charles automatically reached for his wife, his arm coming around her. He looked at Samantha, his eyes wide in shock, his face rigid. Troy swore under his breath.

"He forced himself on you!" Seth cried in a strangled voice.

Samantha looked at her father. "No, Papa," she said evenly. "He did not. I went to him freely." She paused. "I loved him."

"I'll kill him!" Seth ground out, his fury barely controlled.

"The man is without honor. You're a lady! He was a married man, and he took you without any regard for your innocence!" Charles blurted out.

"I made my own choices," Samantha retorted. "I chose to stay and help the Confederacy. Ethan didn't force himself upon me. I chose to share his bed."

"You don't know what you are saying," Charles shouted. "You couldn't!" Charles jumped up from his chair. "Sam, you were innocent. You didn't understand what would happen when you went to . . . to his bed. You couldn't know."

"Do you think I'm a mindless twit, Charles? I'm a doctor! I chose to share his bed."

"You wouldn't do that!" Charles shouted back. "You're not a. . . ."

The silence hung in the air.

"A whore?" Samantha said. "Go ahead, say it, Charles," she challenged. "That's what Robert said. He said I was a traitor and a Confederate major's whore. And if that's what I am because I chose—"

"That's enough! I won't hear another word!" Seth roared at his daughter. He was suddenly upon her. He grabbed her and slapped her violently across her face, causing her head to jerk to the side as she stumbled backward and almost fell from the force of the blow.

"Pa!" Troy screamed as he caught Samantha in his arms.

"No! Pa, stop!" Charles shouted at the same time as he

jumped between Samantha and her father.

Samantha reeled from the shock of her father's strike, her face burning. Her father had never struck her before. Never! Not when she was a child, not even last year when he'd summoned her home from Paris after discovering she had disobeyed him. Her face was red-hot from where he'd hit her, and she could taste blood inside of her mouth. She jerked free from Troy's arms and pushed Charles aside so she could face her father.

"Go ahead, Pa, hit me again," she challenged as she wiped the blood from her mouth with the back of her hand. "It won't be the first time I've been beaten," she said. "Two confederates beat me until I was unconscious, and you might as well add murderer to traitor and whore. I killed three men, Pa." Undaunted, Samantha recounted the ambush on the road and attempted rape. When she finished, the room was deathly quiet, except for Jeanie. She was sobbing openly now, her face hidden in her hands where she sat. Charles was still standing, gaping at his sister. Seth turned his back to Samantha, his fists clenched.

"Ethan doesn't know about my pregnancy. I told his aide, Lieutenant Avery Scott, and Avery helped me to escape. He took me to his parents' plantation in Arlington."

Samantha advanced on Charles. "Confederates, Charles. The enemy! Mr. Scott had only known me three weeks, and Avery less than a year. And yet, Avery and his father offered my child and me the protection of their home, their family name, and family honor."

Samantha grabbed her father's arm and jerked him around to face her. "Now I need to know something from you, Pa! From all of you! No matter what you think of me and the man who started this child growing within me, this child is a Carter. He or she carries your blood, and Mama's, and Grandpa's, too. Can you be a grandfather to my child?"

She whirled upon Charles. "Can you be an uncle, Charles, or will you see the bastard child of a Confederate major and his whore? And what about you, Troy?" she ground out. She turned back to all of them. "If you can't accept me and this child, then tell me now. I will not have my child treated like a bastard by my own family."

No one spoke, the anger and shock of the last several minutes still frozen on their faces. The silence hung in the air interminably. Even Jeanie's sobbing subsided. Just when Samantha thought she could stand among them no longer, they were all startled to hear a chuckle.

"You never were one to mince words, Little Sister."

They all turned to Troy, who had spoken.

"How can you laugh?" Seth roared. "Have you heard what your sister said?"

"Yes, Pa, I heard every word, and that's exactly why I can laugh. She's alive, Pa! She's alive!" Troy put his arm around Samantha's shoulder and pulled her to him. "Those three men you killed, well, I'm proud of you, Sam. They got what they deserved. And as for the other?" Troy boldly looked at Samantha's abdomen. "Shit, Sam, you've been wild since you were a child. There's a spirit inside of you. Charrah saw it. Hell, I don't know, maybe that old holy man gave it to you.

"That spirit guides you, Sam, it guides you. But it can't be tamed—not by the Confederates, not by Pa, not even by you. It's strong. It's where you get your strength, and it protects you. It kept you alive." Troy smiled at his sister. "You never did anything the conventional way in your life. Why would I expect you to make me an uncle in the conventional fashion?" Again he smiled. "But just don't have a girl, Sam. One of you is enough for any family." Troy kissed Samantha on the cheek and then folded both his arms around her.

"Thank you," Samantha whispered as he held her tightly. "Thank you."

After a moment, Troy turned to his father. "Well, Pa? Last night you said you'd give anything to get Sam back. I'd say that she's back—back from hell! Did you hear what the Rebs did to her? She was at war, Pa. She was a surgeon on the battlefield. Do you know what that means?"

Troy deliberately pointed to Charles's empty sleeve. "That's what she had to do! Her hands were soaked in blood, day after day, for almost a year. They shot her in the head and chest. She almost died! She was beaten and almost raped. She had to kill three men to stay alive. None of us, including Charles, has had to endure what she did this past year. I don't know of any woman who could have survived all that she did. She's alive, Pa. She and the baby she carries are alive. That's all that matters, Pa. That's all that matters!"

Seth stared at Samantha and Troy, his anger burning. The silence weighed heavily in the room. Finally Seth spoke. "I will kill him if I ever get the chance," Seth said coldly. "I will kill that Rebel with my bare hands."

Samantha buried her head in Troy's shoulder, the silence pressing in on her.

"If Pa doesn't kill him, I will," Charles finally said, breaking the silence, "but I will care for your child as though it were my own. Jeanie and I both will."

All faces turned toward Seth expectantly. Seth lowered his head and then looked back into his daughter's eyes. He reached out to Samantha. Hesitantly, she came into his open arms.

"I will kill him," Seth Carter repeated quietly, his own eyes filled with tears. "But I love you, Samantha, you and my grandchild that you carry. I'm sorry. I'm sorry I hit you." He crushed Samantha to him and wept, something he hadn't done since Samantha's mother died.

Later, the family went into the kitchen, and as they sat around the table, Samantha told them of her plan for hiding the circumstances of her pregnancy. She told them about Avery Scott's offer of marriage. She also told them of her refusal of marriage but her plan to use his name.

In the weeks that followed, it didn't take long for the townsfolk and people on the surrounding ranches to learn of the tragic death of Samantha Carter's husband, a Union lieutenant from somewhere out East. So many people had lost sons, fathers, and husbands that no one questioned one more loss among themselves. What made it particularly sad was that the young widow was expecting her first child.

While Samantha was working to build her new world in preparation for her child, Ethan's world was collapsing in the South. He was sitting in his tent, examining documents and maps, when a private informed him that Lieutenant Scott had arrived.

It had been two months since Ethan had returned to Caroline's to find that Avery and Samantha had left. He'd been furious and started to go after them, when Caroline intervened. "Ethan," she had said, "you broke Samantha's heart. If you truly love her—and I believe you do—you'll let her go. Seeing you again will only cause her more pain. Let her go. Lieutenant Scott will see her safely to her people."

Two months. Ethan was still haunted by the memory of Samantha's tear-streaked face. Not a day passed that he didn't consider deserting, leaving his precious South, to go find her. But Caroline was right. Finding Sam would only cause her more pain. For that reason, he hadn't searched for her, nor had he reported Avery's absence. He never doubted that Avery would return, and now he had. Avery entered the tent and immediately stood at attention.

Ethan looked at his junior officer. "There's no need for formality, Lieutenant," he said.

Avery relaxed but avoided looking at Ethan. The silence hung in the air.

"Where is she?" Ethan finally asked.

"I took her north, across the lines. She's safe, sir," Avery responded.

Ethan wanted to ask more, but other than Caroline, Frederick, Fox, and Molly, no one knew of his relationship with Samantha. He wasn't certain what Sam told Avery to persuade him to help her escape, but Ethan couldn't imagine that she would have told him of their intimate relationship. She wouldn't reveal that. For now, he would have to be content with Avery's response.

"Columbia's destroyed," Ethan said as he stood. "General Sheridan's moving troops toward Petersburg. We need to get these reports to Petersburg. If we leave now, we might make it."

"It's going to be difficult," Avery said as they exited the tent. "I barely made it back. Sherman has over one hundred thousand men closing in on us."

Avery and Ethan left immediately. They spurred their horses northward, trying to go around the two armies as they clashed. They'd been riding an hour when, suddenly, muzzle fire exploded around them. Avery slumped forward in his saddle. Several more shots rang out, just missing Ethan.

"Can you get to those trees?" Ethan shouted to Avery.

They raced for some protection as the Federal troops continued to fire. Ethan dismounted and pulled Avery off his horse and behind the thick brush. Cannons were exploding behind them, and all around was a sea of blue uniforms.

"Is it bad?" Ethan asked as he pushed Avery's blood-drenched coat aside. Ethan winced upon seeing the extent of the wound.

"I can't make it," Avery said. "It's no use. You go while you can."

"I'm not leaving you here."

"It doesn't matter," Avery said, his breath coming in irregular gasps. "My arm's gone. I'm bleeding too much. I'll not last much longer."

"I'll get you to the surgeons."

"Huh. They'd as likely kill me. Ah," Avery cried in pain as he clutched his shattered arm. "Bad luck. All the time Samantha was here, I never got a single scratch. Now, when I need her, she's far away."

"I'm not a surgeon, but I learned a thing or two from her," Ethan said as he removed the sash around his waist. He placed it around Avery's arm and pulled it tightly across the wound to compress the torn blood vessels. Avery cried out in pain as Ethan applied more pressure. "I'll have to tie you onto your saddle, but we're getting out of here."

Ethan brought the horses over and knelt down to pick up Avery. Avery grabbed Ethan's arm.

"There's something I must tell you. It's about Samantha," Avery said.

"It can wait," Ethan said. "We've got to get you to a doctor."

"No, I must tell you now. I may not be able to later."

Avery was beginning to shiver from the loss of blood. His face was pale as he looked at Ethan. "Samantha asked me to help her to leave. I did. I also asked her to marry me."

Ethan was stunned.

"I took her to my parents' home in Arlington. Ethan, you took a young woman's virginity," Avery whispered weakly.

Ethan looked at Avery sharply. He couldn't believe Samantha would have revealed their intimate relationship to anyone.

"I never thought you to be a dishonorable man," Avery said.

"I'm afraid where Samantha was concerned, my honor was not important to me," Ethan finally said.

"But to seduce an innocent young woman," Avery countered, gritting his teeth as a wave of pain passed over him.

"It was wrong," Ethan said quietly.

Avery was watching Ethan intently. "Do you love her?" Avery asked.

"It doesn't matter now."

"It matters to me. I need to know, Ethan."

"Yes," Ethan said quietly, "I love her. Without her, nothing in this life has meaning to me. Nothing. Do you know how many times I considered deliberately putting myself in harm's way? Just one more Confederate casualty of the war. I wish to God that lead you carry had hit me," Ethan said emotionally as his eyes filled with tears. Then he stood, once again in control. "We've got to get you out of here," he said sternly. He reached for Avery.

"Wait," Avery said. "Ethan, she refused my proposal of marriage, but I think she's taken my name."

Ethan did not understand. "What are you talking about?"

"I offered her my hand in marriage and my name for the child she's carrying—your child," Avery said softly as he struggled to remain conscious. "I thought you should know in case she or the child should ever need. . . ."

Avery slumped in Ethan's arms.

CHAPTER 15

Ethan sighed and lowered his head, the strain of the last four years taking its toll on him. The end had come at last, just as he knew it would. General Lee's line had been stretched to over fifty miles. Thirty-five thousand starved Confederates tried to hold out against Grant's one hundred fifty thousand. The line finally broke on April 2; Petersburg fell, followed by Lee's retreat and surrender on April 9. Three days after that, the last Confederate forces, under the leadership of General John B. Gordon, formally surrendered. The war was over. Ethan wondered, was it worth it? Did any good come out of the four years of slaughter? Had he done the right thing?

He leaned against the fence and gazed out over the empty green pastures. They were all gone now—the horses that he'd loved. The only horse left was the one that he had ridden in the war. The rest, he supposed, were dead, their bones scattered across the Confederacy. He could start over, but did he have the heart for it?

He'd been fortunate. Arabella was one of the few plantations to survive Sherman's march into the Carolinas. The homes of his neighbors had all been burned to the ground. In his sadness, he smiled to himself. It was too bad that General Lee hadn't had Molly in his army. Ethan could picture Molly confronting the young Federal lieutenant whose intent it had been to set fire to Arabella. Apparently, Molly had marched out onto the front portico with legal documents in one hand and a loaded gun in the other. In the end, the raiding party left, and Molly returned to the house where a cowardly Franklin Montgomery and Juliet had hidden.

Juliet. Ethan recalled the look on her face when he'd returned after Lee's surrender. It was obvious that she and her father had hoped him dead. He might as well be, for that's how he felt. Even his beloved Arabella could not replace the emptiness he felt inside.

A carriage pulled up to the house. Ethan watched Stephen Roland, his friend and solicitor, and Judge Martin Mills climb down from the carriage. No one knew how legislative matters would be handled in the recently defeated South, but the judge had assured Ethan that in civil matters, his authority remained. Ethan walked toward the carriage. It was time.

It was an unseasonably warm April in the Iowa Frontier. Samantha sat outside on the porch steps, letting the sun's rays flow over her. She could hear her family celebrating inside the house. Her father had gotten the whiskey out of the cupboard, and her brothers were toasting the end of the war. The war—it was finally over, but at what cost? So many dead.

No one had heard from Robert since the day Ethan let him escape—the day he had cursed Samantha and denounced her as his sister. The Carter family still held hope that he was alive—that he would find his way home now that the war was over.

Samantha's thoughts were interrupted by the sound of the front door opening. She turned to see Troy emerge from the house. He was carrying two glasses of whiskey. As he sat down on the steps next to her, he handed a glass to her.

"I think you need this more than we do," he said. "You sure as hell deserve it more than we do. You earned it, Sam."

She stared at the golden-brown liquid in the glass. "No, not me. All those men who died, it's for them," she said as she tipped her head back and tossed the fiery liquid down her throat in one gulp.

Troy looked at her, a question on his face. "I assumed this would be the first time you tasted whiskey. Where did you learn to drink like that? Paris?" he asked.

Samantha stared at the empty glass. "No, not Paris."

"Oh. The Confederacy," he said with an edge.

"Yes, the Confederacy. Thank God the killing has finally stopped," she said quietly.

"Yes. Maybe now your nightmares will stop."

Troy's statement surprised Samantha. "How'd you know I was still having them? Do you . . . do you still *see* them?"

"No," Troy said, "not since that one time when you first came home. It's more like I feel them. I'm sorry, Sam. I'm sorry I can't do something to help."

"Does Pa know?"

Troy nodded his head. "Yes. We stopped coming into your room. I told Pa that seeing us around your bed seemed to upset you even more. I hope I did the right thing."

"You did." She stared at her empty whiskey glass. "He was able to stop them—the nightmares." She didn't have to tell Troy who she was referring to, for she felt her brother tense next to her.

"Shit! Sam, I've got to ask you something."

"I know." She turned to him. "You want to know why."

"Yes, I want to know why you did it. Helping the wounded Confederates—Charles doesn't understand that, but I do. You're a medicine woman. But the other . . . to become the Rebel's. . . ." He paused.

"Whore?" Samantha supplied.

"I was going to say 'lover,' " Troy corrected. "Jeanie convinced Pa and Charles that you were out of your mind at the time. What woman wouldn't go crazy in those circumstances? But I don't believe that. You're strong, Sam. You didn't go crazy, and you're certainly no man's fool. So why? Why that Rebel?"

Samantha sighed deeply. "I've asked myself the same question. Why did I fall in love with him? Why do I still love him in spite of the pain, the hurt he's caused? It makes no sense. But from the moment I saw him, I felt something stir deep within me, which was strange because I was so afraid of him when he captured me." She paused and looked at her brother. "Loving him . . . I can't imagine any other path for me—then or now.

"I could tell you he's a good man, and that's true. He loves this country, North and South. He opposed slavery and secession, but when Federal troops attacked, he fought to defend his land, his people. He's intelligent, brave, and a fierce opponent. He can also be gentle, understanding, and compassionate. He protected me. He cared for me. He's a man of character. Under different circumstances, you would like him."

"A man of character does not take an innocent woman to his bed, Sam," Troy said sharply.

"No, a man of character does not, no more than a woman of character, raised on the frontier by a good family, goes willingly to his bed," Samantha replied.

Troy stared at Samantha a long time, his anger barely concealed. Then he put his arm around her and pulled her to him. Samantha rested her head on his shoulder.

It was midday when Ethan dismounted and walked up

the steps of the porch. He turned around, surveying the property. It was a large ranch with two barns, various cattle pens scattered about, and several outbuildings. It had taken him a month to reach the Iowa Frontier, and now he was here at last. The next few minutes would be the most important of his life. He turned back to the door, knocked, and waited.

"Hello, stranger," a man said as he opened the door. "Can I help you?"

For a moment, Ethan didn't speak. He stared at the man standing in the threshold of the door. Ethan remembered allowing one of Samantha's brothers to escape during the war. That brother, Robert, had harshly judged Samantha and had caused her great pain. Ethan could see the family resemblance in this man standing before him. Samantha had said her brother Charles was a captain in the Federal Army. That would explain why the man had only one arm.

"Good morning, sir. I have come to see Miss Samantha Carter," Ethan said. "My name is—"

"I know who you are," Charles ground out just as his fist flew toward Ethan's face.

Ethan ducked as Charles's knuckles glanced off his chin.

"I'll kill you where you stand," Charles shouted, lunging forward.

Ethan jumped to the side and sprang forward into the hallway of the house. He spun around to face his adversary. "I'll not fight a one-armed man," Ethan said.

"Perhaps this will even the odds," Charles said as a knife appeared in his hand.

Seeing Samantha's brother crouched, holding a knife, reminded Ethan of Sam the first time she had threatened him with her knife. His heart softened at the memory. "Shit," he said with exasperation. "Do all you Carters carry knives?"

"Charles?" a masculine voice called.

Ethan glanced to his side while keeping his eyes on the knife held by Samantha's brother. A young man entered the hall, and for a moment, Ethan held his breath. The man had Samantha's eyes, skin tone, and rich chestnut hair color. He looked very much like Sam had when he first saw her, disguised as a boy. The young man had a surprised look on his face as he surveyed the scene before him.

"It's him!" Charles shouted. "The Rebel!"

Troy's eyes flashed, just as Ethan remembered Samantha's doing when she became angry, and then Troy smiled. Ethan couldn't believe it. It was Samantha's smile! So this was her twin brother, Troy, the one she had been so close to.

The young man continued to smile as he withdrew a knife from his boot. "You ready to die, Reb?"

"I'll not fight you, sir."

Troy shrugged his shoulders. "Doesn't matter to me—I'm going to kill you, one way or the other."

Troy's speed surprised Ethan, and Ethan barely moved in time as Troy's knife cut through his sleeve. Ethan swore.

"You little whelp! Give me that before you hurt one of us," Ethan shouted.

Troy lunged again. This time, Ethan caught his hand, and the two of them fell to the floor, rolling together into the adjacent parlor. Ethan got one hand free and smashed his fist into Troy's nose. Troy fell back as the blood poured from his face. His grip tightened on the knife. As Ethan attempted to stand, Troy's foot lashed out, causing Ethan to lose his balance. As he fell forward, Troy struck out again with the knife.

Once again, Ethan managed to barely avoid the blade as it thrust toward his midsection and sliced through his coat. Troy recovered, and the two were locked in a deadly struggle. Ethan's mind was reeling. He was at a distinct disadvantage. Troy was bent upon killing him, but he couldn't kill Samantha's brother! Troy sensed the hesitancy in Ethan and made one final move. Ethan's reluctance to hurt Troy gave Troy the edge he needed. He freed his hand and thrust the knife upward as they rolled. Ethan felt a sharp sensation on his neck. Troy was suddenly above him, pressing the blade downward into Ethan's neck. Ethan wrapped his hands around Troy's. It was a battle of strength, with Troy having the advantage of being on top. The blade pierced Ethan's skin, and he felt the warmth of blood run down his neck.

Troy could taste righteous vengeance as he struggled with his opponent. The Rebel was strong, but not strong enough. Troy pressed the blade and got the satisfaction of seeing the first blood appear. He tightened his grip, preparing to push the deadly blade into the Reb's artery and then pull it across, slicing his windpipe. This Rebel had been the source of his sister's pain. He was going to kill the Reb. Now!

He shifted his focus from the Rebel's neck to his eyes, and suddenly, Troy froze. He watched as the Rebel's blue eyes turned almost black, and in the blackness, an image formed—an ancient face from Troy's childhood. The old holy man spoke to him in the Lakota language. *"Do not attempt to destroy the one who has been chosen for her, my son, for it is to be."*

Ethan saw the sudden change in his opponent. The color seemed to drain from Troy's face, and his grip lessened. Ethan didn't know what caused Troy to hesitate, but Ethan had enough. He was going to put a stop to this before the boy got lucky and sunk the blade into him.

Ethan shifted his weight slightly and drove his knee up

into Troy. As Troy fell to the side, Ethan rolled with him. He released one hand and smashed it into Troy's face. The knife slid across the floor. Ethan stood up, pulling Troy with him. As they came to a standing position, Ethan buried his fist in Troy's midsection, causing the young man to double over. He sensed a movement behind him and spun around, withdrawing his revolver. He cocked the hammer and placed the end of the barrel against Troy's head as the young man slumped in front of him, desperately trying to inhale a breath of air.

"Drop your gun," Ethan ordered as Charles pointed a gun in his direction.

"What the hell is going on here?" Seth Carter thundered as he entered the parlor.

"I said, 'Put the gun down!' " Ethan commanded.

"Do as he says!" Troy rasped, still gasping for breath.

"Who the hell are you? What do you want?" Seth demanded.

Ethan looked over at the older man and realized he must be Seth Carter, the patriarch of the family. "I've come for Samantha, sir," Ethan said.

"It's him, Pa," Charles said accusingly, "the Rebel!"

"You!" Seth exploded. He started forward but stopped as Ethan raised the gun again.

"Your gun, sir," Ethan said to Charles.

Charles looked helplessly to Seth. Seth nodded, and Charles placed the gun on the floor.

"Where's Samantha?" Seth asked.

"She's still out on Kota," Troy said with a grimace as he clutched his midsection.

"Sit down," Ethan commanded as he nodded to the chairs. "We'll wait for Samantha."

Seth and Charles reluctantly sat down, keeping their eyes on Ethan. Troy started to move, but Ethan tightened his grip on his arm and pushed his revolver into Troy's side.

"Not you," Ethan said. Although it wasn't serious, Ethan could feel the blood on his collar from where Troy had nicked his skin with the knife. "The last time someone bested me in a fight, it was your sister. She left a three-inch scar on my arm where she cut me. I think I'll keep this gun on you."

Troy laughed. "That's Sam, all right."

Ethan cocked his head and looked at the young man in his grip. Troy had been intent on killing him a few minutes ago, but now, Ethan sensed no animosity in him. Troy was relaxed, the fight in him gone. Ethan was puzzling over this when he heard the door open and footsteps in the hall.

Samantha was late returning from her ride. By now, her family would be seated in the dining room for the midday meal. They were probably worried. Samantha was in her seventh month of pregnancy, and her father, especially, didn't think she should still be riding astride on Kota. She was proceeding to the dining room when she heard voices in the parlor.

"Papa?" Samantha called. She stepped into the parlor and froze. He was standing there, just as she remembered him. She'd been dreaming of him for so long, the dreams a mix of joy and pain, and they always ended the same—she could never have him, leaving her feeling wounded and broken. She inhaled deeply, trying to calm her racing heart. So many powerful emotions flooded her mind.

"Oh, hi, Sam," Troy said casually, breaking the silence in the room.

Samantha pulled her eyes away from Ethan to Troy.

"Uh . . . Sam, do you think you could ask the Rebel to get his gun out of my gut?" Troy asked calmly.

Samantha looked back at Ethan—his blue eyes, dark hair,

strong jawline. She yearned to touch him, to run to him, to feel the reassurance of his arms around her.

"Sam? The gun?" Troy repeated.

Samantha blinked. "Ethan," she said, her throat constricting.

Then he smiled at her, his eyes flicking to her enlarged abdomen. "You're beautiful," he said softly.

Unconsciously, Samantha placed her hand on her abdomen.

"Avery told me everything," Ethan explained. "He didn't intentionally betray your confidence, Sam. Sherman's forces overran us, and he was wounded. That's when he told me."

"Avery? Is he . . . ?"

"He survived. He lost an arm, though. I stopped in Arlington before coming here. He's doing well." Ethan paused. "He said to tell you his offer of marriage still stands."

As though suddenly remembering Troy, Ethan holstered his sidearm and released Troy. Troy stepped away just as Seth jumped up and charged toward Ethan. Ethan spun around, withdrawing his revolver again.

"Ethan, no!" Samantha shouted.

Seth stopped a few feet away from Ethan when he saw the gun aimed at his chest.

"Papa!" Samantha said as she rushed forward and stepped in front of her father.

"I told you I would kill him!" Seth shouted. "He took you against your will! He forced you—"

"No," Samantha cried. "I told you it wasn't like that. I went to him freely."

Charles sprang forward to stand beside his father. "He ruined you, Sam," Charles cried. He grabbed Samantha by the arm. "Go upstairs and we'll handle this," he ordered.

"Ruined me?" Samantha stammered.

Charles's slur was like a knife thrust into her. She reeled away from him and felt strong arms come around her. Then, just as quickly, Ethan released her and stepped in front of her. He hit Charles in the face with a force that knocked him down onto the floor.

"You're a fool, Captain," Ethan spat out. "Do you have any idea how extraordinary your sister is? Do you know anything about this woman?

"Yes, I captured her, forced her into the service of the Confederacy, and forced her to stay with me. The child she carries is mine. But if you malign her again, brother or not, I will kill you."

Charles and Seth stared at Ethan, the threat clear. Once again, Troy broke the silence.

"I won't kill you, brother," Troy said, "but I sure as hell will beat the shit out of you if you speak about my sister like that again."

"How can you take his side?" Seth blazed.

"I'm not taking the Rebel's side; I'm taking Sam's side."

"That's enough!"

The men all turned to the feminine voice. Samantha advanced on them, her fury barely controlled. She stopped in front of Charles. "I don't need your pity, Charles. I'm neither helpless nor ruined!" She turned to Troy, "And I can stand up for myself."

"Sam," her father began.

Samantha looked to her father. "And you! If you truly care about me, you'll stop making threats!"

"He hurt you, Sam," her father said with anguish.

Samantha took a deep breath. "I know, Papa," she said softly. "I love you for wanting to protect me. I'll do the same for my child. But," she said as tears formed in her eyes, "he still holds my heart. You can't change that. Please."

Seth's jaw tightened, but he silently nodded and stepped

back from her.

"I would like to speak to Ethan alone," Samantha said. She looked from her father to Charles and Troy. "Leave us, please."

The men didn't move until, once again, Troy came to his sister's aid. "Pa? Charles?" he said. "Let's go. We can wait for Sam in the kitchen."

Reluctantly, Seth and Charles followed Troy out of the room. Samantha watched them leave and then turned to face Ethan.

"Why are you here, Ethan?"

"I've divorced Juliet. She and her father are in Texas, where they will remain until their deaths."

"What? Divorced! I don't believe it!"

"It's true. That's why I'm here."

Samantha was confused. That meant he was free, but instead of joy, she felt an unexplained anger. "Do you think that makes everything right? Did you think that if you got rid of Juliet, I'd just fall back into your arms? After you deceived me all that time?" Samantha's emotions were whirling out of control. She launched into a stream of profanity. When she paused to take a breath and sort through the confusing thoughts in her head, she saw a twinkle in Ethan's eyes.

"I see your language hasn't improved, Sam. I warned you about the profanity. Have you forgotten what happened the last time?" he asked.

The memory of Ethan taking her over his knee flashed in her mind. "You wouldn't dare," she said, taking a step backward.

Ethan grabbed her shoulders. "One way or another, Sam."

Just as she was about to protest, Ethan's lips came down on hers. She was so shocked that it was a second before she could respond. By then, her body had begun to respond on its own. Even if she could ignore the desire that flowed through her body, she couldn't quiet the yearning of her soul. When he released her, she looked up into his eyes.

"You're a bastard, Rebel," she whispered softly as the tears escaped down her face.

Ethan smiled gently. "And you're a stubborn, willful Yankee."

"You took my love when you had no right to," she said.

"There are some who would say you wantonly offered your love when you had no right to."

Samantha smiled slightly, her lips trembling. She lifted her chin defiantly. "They would be wrong. It was my right."

"Yes," he said, his eyes burning into her, "as it was mine."

Samantha's throat constricted. "What is it you want of me?"

"I want you to share my life and allow me to share yours. I want you to be my wife and let me be your husband and the father of your children. I want you to let me love you. Nothing in this world means anything to me without you. I love you, Sam."

Samantha was losing herself in Ethan's eyes—eyes that she knew so well. "I would not have survived were it not for you. You protected me," she said softly. "You cared for me. You gave me your strength when I thought I could endure no longer." Ethan gently wiped a tear away from her face. "You gave me peace," she said, "when I was surrounded by pain and war. You gave me joy and made me laugh," Samantha said, recalling their long days spent at Arabella. "You gave me your love," Samantha said, a joy spreading throughout her.

"It was all that I was free to give you," Ethan said softly.

Samantha hesitated a moment. "I want to practice as a

doctor."

A smile played at the corner of Ethan's lips. "That's why I abducted you in the first place, remember?"

"You captured a boy. I'm a woman."

"I am, my love, aware of that. Every curve and every hollow of your body is burned into my memory, although there are some changes," he said, looking warmly at her pregnant form.

Samantha blushed.

Ethan suddenly changed the subject. "Arabella was spared," he said. "Most of the other planters' homes were burnt, their buildings and fields destroyed. Charleston was demolished. I want to see South Carolina rebuilt. I want a hand in its rebuilding." Ethan hesitated. "The war made me a very rich man, or it made Ethan Hunt of Boston very rich. I plan on using that money to rebuild. I'll start with my shipping line. The entire wharf must be reconstructed before we can even begin bringing in badly needed goods. That will employ many." He looked directly at Samantha. "I can afford to live anywhere in the world, but I want to live at Arabella. Could you live there, Sam? It wouldn't be easy. It's chaos, now. There's an intense bitterness toward the North. Not everyone in Charleston knows what you did for the Confederate soldiers. There are some who will see you only as a Yankee, the cause of the destruction of their homes and lives."

Samantha looked into the depth of Ethan's eyes. Ever since she could remember, she'd been driven by unseen forces—the spirit inside of her, as Troy and Many Horses said. Under Charrah's guidance, she learned to walk with Them. As she searched Ethan's eyes, she now wondered if that spirit had led her to the war, not to the Union, as she had planned, but to the Confederacy. There she'd met Ethan, and from the very beginning, he'd unleashed within her a passion that was just as fierce as the spirit that had flowed in her as a child. She was driven to Ethan just as she had been driven to the ancient arts of healing and modern medicine. The words rang out in her mind, in her soul.

"There is one. That is why he was sent to you."

"I lost my heart to a Confederate major at Arabella," Samantha said as she smiled through her tears. "I will live with you there or anywhere you choose."

Ethan crushed her to him, holding her as though he would never let her go. "I love you, Sam," he whispered in her ear. "I love you. There's nothing in this life that means more to me than you and this child. I know what I did was wrong, but God forgive me, I would do it again," he said fervently.

"I know, my love," Samantha murmured in his arms, "as would I."

Special Letter to Readers

Thank you for reading *The Confederates' Physician*. Studying the US Civil War and visiting the battlefields have always been profoundly moving experiences for me. Then one night, while sleeping, I had a dream that gave rise to Samantha's story in *The Confederates' Physician*, which continues in the sequel, *Diary of the Confederates' Physician: Samantha's Legacy* (published April 2022).

I'm always interested in readers' thoughts and would love to hear from you! What did you like, love, or dislike in *The Confederates' Physician?* What questions do you have? You can write to me at alisonlasdellnovels@gmail.com or contact me via my website https://alisonblasdell.com.

Finally, reviews are vital to an author. If you enjoyed *The Confederates' Physician*, would you please leave a review on Amazon?

Thank you, again, for spending time in Samantha's world and mine! I hope the hours you spent reading provided an enjoyable escape from your day-to-day responsibilities.

Best wishes,
Alison Blasdell

ACKNOWLEDGMENT

I would like to express my appreciation to several people who contributed to the publication of this book:

Joyce Mochrie, certified copy editor/proofreader, for her meticulous attention to detail and extraordinary kindness.

Amanda Gardner, for using her exceptional skill as a graphic artist to create the beautiful cover design.

Raleigh Blasdell, for her management of my social and print media venues with proficiency and humor.

Judy Smith for her selfless assistance in marketing events.

My First Readers for their very helpful and insightful comments: Sandy Brewer, Vallie Gould, Judy Smith, Ed Smith, Grant Blasdell, Melanie Green, Malinda Church, and Wayne Wright.

AUTHOR'S NOTE

This is a work of fiction, but I have tried to remain historically accurate when presenting the details of the US Civil War from 1864-1865. The locations of battles, commanding officers, and losses suffered by Confederate and Union (Federal) forces are as precise as possible, given that data from that time period can be contradicting. So, also, are the descriptions of the inadequate food, clothing, and supplies of the Confederate forces during the last year of the war.

Medical education in the US in the mid-1800s most often took the form of learning from a practicing physician in lieu of attending medical school. Furthermore, US medical schools were of a poor quality and rarely offered surgical training. Many graduates had never seen an amputation, and yet, the surgeons of the war are estimated to have performed seventy to one hundred thousand amputations.

Disease accounted for approximately two-thirds of the deaths sustained by Confederate and Union forces. While Semmelweis, in 1847, did reduce maternal deaths following delivery by insisting medical students wash their hands, the notion that wound putrefaction (infection) or diseases resulted from microbial organisms was not advanced until

Pasteur performed his first test of pasteurization and published his germ theory in 1864.

The role of women in the 1860s was prescribed. Very few women attended medical school in the 1860s; those who did were probably disguised as men. Several noteworthy female physicians (Blackwell, Crumpler, Hawks, Walker) did not disguise their gender. For the most part, these women fought against the prevailing biases of the time. Women were also banned from the military. Interestingly, we now know of several hundred women who disguised themselves as men and fought alongside their husbands and sons.

President Abraham Lincoln did suspend habeas corpus, in effect allowing the incarceration—without cause or benefit of the court—of anyone who was critical of the Union war effort. Furthermore, ordinary Union citizens criticizing Lincoln's war were subject to military courts instead of civil. The unconstitutionality of such action has long interested legal scholars, as has the questionable constitutionality of forcing states to remain in the Union.

Finally, The Confederates' Physician is a love story placed in the middle of the bloodiest time in American history. It is impossible to romanticize the loss of lives. Over 750,000 American men died in that war; they died from battle wounds, disease, and abject starvation. Another 750,000 survived but were wounded. One-fourth to one-third of all men who fought in that war never returned home.

In my story, three Carter siblings went to war: Charles, Robert, and Samantha. Charles lived, but suffered the loss of an arm. Robert never returned home; his remains were presumably buried in an unmarked grave. Samantha was mortally wounded, but, aided by powerful spirits and the strength of Ethan's love, survived.

Alison Blasdell

TOUCH THE SKY
A NOVEL BY ALISON BLASDELL
AVAILABLE ON AMAZON

Can the Power of Love Survive Three Thousand Years?

What if you could see into the past and uncover a mysterious secret deliberately erased from history—an ancient ability so threatening that it was obliterated from human consciousness and buried deep in the unexpressed DNA of the descendants of a select group of Bronze Age people?

Jennifer Bracken is visiting the British Museum in London when she falls, hitting her head. While unconscious, she sees life through the eyes of a young priestess from a long-ago Bronze Age civilization. Assuming the experience was the result of striking her head, she discounts the episode and goes to visit her best friend in Scotland. There, at the foothills of The Highlands, the visions return, both frightening and compelling. Each time they occur, Jennifer is drawn deeper into the young priestess Cela's life.

Driven to discover if such a Bronze Age society ever existed, she enlists the help of noted archaeologist, Derek Rannoch.

Derek is astonished by Jennifer's detailed descriptions of that era. He demands to see the source of her information in exchange for his assistance. Jennifer refuses, but she needs his archaeological expertise. She must find a way to convince him to help her, for an uneasy feeling begins to overtake her. As Derek and Jennifer's turbulent—and often antagonistic—relationship develops, Jennifer is inexplicably drawn to him, feeling safe in his presence, but safe from what?

Touch the Sky takes the reader on a mesmerizing trip back and forth between the Bronze Age and contemporary times—a trip that will challenge our notion of science and reality and affirm our belief in the immortality of love.

Alison Blasdell

Made in the USA
Las Vegas, NV
08 February 2023